RED

HEARTS

All my Best

J. M. Barlog

J M Barlog

BAK
BOOKS

CHICAGO, ILLINOIS

RED HEARTS

Published by BAK Books

Library of Congress Catalog Card Number: 99-094726

ISBN 0-9654716-2-4

BAK Books are published by BAK Books, a division of BAK Entertainment, Inc. Its trademark, consisting of the words "BAK Books" is Registered in U.S. Patent and Trademark Office.

BAK Books
333 N Michigan Ave Suite 932
Chicago, Illinois 60601

Printed in the United States of America
OPM 0 9 8 7 6 5 4 3 2 1

Other novels by J. M. Barlog

Windows To The Soul

Necessary Measures

Dark Side

To my son Cory,
who has the courage to listen
to his inner spirit.

Now you will feel no rain,
for each of you will be shelter to the other.

Now you will feel no cold,
for each of you will be warmth to the other.

Now there is no loneliness for you,
for each of you will be companion to the other.

Now you are two persons,
but there is one life before you.

Go now to your dwelling place,
to enter into the days of your togetherness.

And may your days be good and long upon this earth.

Apache Wedding Blessing

They sat huddled in abject silence, framed by tarnished aluminum double-door casings and behind glass as if the subjects of some macabre photograph. Shackled, gagged and assembled as human shields, four men and two women prayed for one of God's miracles. Eyes white with terror stared blankly into the still night. The gunmen believed they held absolute control, having barricaded the only entrances with innocent human flesh. Police would never be crazy enough to attempt a straight-on assault with hostages posed in their line of fire. Amid the eerie buzz of parking lot halogen lights, nothing moved beyond the plate glass doors of Jerry's Super Sound Warehouse on Pleasant Hill Drive in Albuquerque.

Beyond sight of the gunmen inside the building, the rear doors to a black Special Operations truck banged open. Lieutenant Dakota Blackwood strapped a Kevlar vest tight across his lean six-foot quarterback frame and took up his M-16 as beads of icy sweat trickled off his granite chin. He secured a pair of flashbangs to his belt then handed two more to the man beside him. Breathing became forced as he contemplated the odds against them. They were undermanned and ill-equipped to bring the crisis under control.

"Mike check," Dakota said, after fitting his microphone to his lips and earpiece snugly into his left ear.

"Red 1 set," came from the officer closest to him.

"Red 2 set," came from the next officer.

"Red 3 set."

Time had become their worst enemy. Dakota led his team to a secure observation post where they could monitor the doors without revealing themselves to those inside. Dakota's Apache heart hammered inside his chest. He looked over the callow officers beside him, clad in black jumpsuits and sucking cigarette smoke deep into their lungs. They held it there a long time before letting it slip away into the night.

No one spoke while a thousand concerns raced through Dakota's mind—all of them somehow tied to death. They could only guess at how many hostages were inside. Intel had been scarce. The siege came completely by surprise. Someone reported witnessing four masked men burst into the store three hours earlier. Were there only four? Or had sleepers infiltrated the establishment in advance of the main assault? How sophisticated was this group? Did they have a tactical strategy in place to defend their position? The exact number of guns inside had yet to be determined. These answers were vital intelligence Dakota needed. He knew they would likely have to go in without them.

This was not an exercise—the hostages inside were real—not cardboard training placards. Regardless of training, no one can ever really know for certain the right way to handle a hostage crisis such that life can be preserved.

Thursday nights were usually a bargain hunter's delight for stereo gear and computers at Jerry's Sound Warehouse. As if being situated a distance from the Coronado and Winrock shopping centers weren't bad enough for business, once the Cottonwood Mall opened, Jerry's had to ruthlessly slash prices to keep traffic flowing into his establishment rather than the new megamall. So, he enticed browsers with what he called his 'Thursday Night Madness.'

Only this Thursday night the madness became literal.

A slight-framed but formidably-armed gunman, shouldering a defiance that often comes at the price of innocent lives, crossed the glass doors undaunted. Ski masks made them faceless; Uzis made them heartless.

Eighteen helpless uniforms looked on from scattered positions across the deserted parking lot. For three hours, police waited; trying to negotiate a peaceful resolution, but ready to invade at a moment's call. Before long, tension alone held the power to trigger a violent reaction.

Negotiations sputtered at the onset, stalled before they could take root. Anger seethed from the building. Police negotiators sent patience back in. Sporadic gun bursts kept police on the verge of assaulting the building. Yet no bodies had been tossed out and police were hoping they could find a way to save the hostages.

Within the first hour, the situation escalated from unstable to volatile. Three hours deeper into the standoff, the breakdown in communications left police with a single option.

Police Captain Vance Washington refused to yield as long as hostages were involved. The gunmen refused to release even a single body until police delivered a helicopter to the parking lot.

Now at 10:22, negotiations reached critical mass. The men in black promised carnage at the turning of every minute. Demonstrating their resolve, one terrorist yanked a praying hostage to his feet, pushed him before the glass doors as a spectacle, then he fired into the pleading man's thigh. His agonized scream clawed under the skin of every officer being held at bay.

Eighteen police weapons fell into line; each leveled on the hooded demon. It took iron will to stave off a fusillade of bullets.

For all their vain attempts at negotiating, police never uncovered the gunmen's real demands. Everything came out as double talk. Though negotiators patiently probed and pried, nothing it seemed, short of an assault, could end the standoff.

Red 3 lay perched across from the sound warehouse on the roof of an Auto Zone parts store. His finger rested beside the trigger while his cross hairs tracked a hooded target moving past the doors. The sharpshooter eased his lip mike closer.

"Red leader, Red 3, I've got a clear target crossing the doors."

Static funneled into the sharpshooter's ear. His pounding heart marched off the seconds while he waited. For now the man in black had gained a reprieve.

"Red 3, I need an intel update," Dakota's voice broke through the static.

"I've confirmed two targets. One remains near the hostages at the doors. The other appeared briefly then receded back into the interior. I could've taken them both down on your signal."

The gunman continued beyond the rifle's line of sight.

From behind the Operations truck, in the middle of hastily arranged squad cars that formed a command post at their core, a uniform shouldered this way in with a short, overstuffed man in tow.

"Tell the captain what you just told me," the uniform instructed.

"Tell me what?" Washington snarled at the unwanted intrusion. His eyes never left those six ashen faces pleading for life from behind the double glass doors.

"Well goddamnit, keep checking," Washington barked into the radio mike. He shot the man a cold, cursory glance.

"Captain...you need to hear this," the officer started, then yielded to the timid man, whose eyes bounced like rubber from one officer to another.

"What I said was, I'm an HVAC contractor, Gerald Davis, and I worked on the roof air conditioners on that building."

"So?" Washington said, then turned away and keyed his microphone anew.

"What I mean is, there's a roof access door that doesn't lock. The hinge is rusted clean off."

The words stopped Washington mid-sentence.

"Get Dakota over here, right now," Washington ordered.

Dakota checked the magazine for his 9mm Beretta, then pulled a second M16 off a rack in the Operations truck. He slid a fresh magazine into the rifle and clipped two more to his vest. He had been in range of the man's voice. The words seized him.

"Where?" Dakota asked, shouldering his way in. Darkness hid the fire in Dakota's eyes. In preparation for their inevitable assault, he secured his flowing shoulder-length raven's hair at the base of his neck with a tie band. Doing so gave him a fierce renegade warrior appearance, the kind of face that glares out from the pages of history books. In that moment, standing face to face, Dakota detected disdain in Gerald's eyes.

"Southeast corner. I worked up there about two weeks ago. I told the owner about it after I finished up."

Washington turned to a bespectacled Azar Vileandro standing beside him. He owned Jerry's and had been brought to the scene by police shortly after receiving the call that unknown assailants had seized his establishment. Azar had bought the business from a man named Wilfred a decade earlier and like the previous owner, he left the original store name intact. Somehow Azar's Super Sound Warehouse just didn't have the right ring to it.

"That right?"

"Yes, that's right. He said the bracket had rusted off. I didn't do anything about it."

Suddenly a slight smile creased Azar's face. Nothing could undo the damage done this night, but at least police might now have a way of saving the hostages.

"What's the door open up to?"

"A storage room."

Dakota and Washington exchanged a measured glance. Maybe there's a God after all. Like synchronized minds, each knew exactly the other's thoughts. Each could witness the mechanization of the other's mind at work behind their eyes.

"Risky," Washington muttered, thanking the man and motioning for the officer to lead Gerald away.

"It's our only shot," Dakota offered, already reaching for the grappling hooks in the van. He passed them on without comment to the men beside him. It would be hours before an FBI SWAT team would arrive. Washington feared they had but minutes before bloody bodies began being tossed out.

"Red 3, we've got a way in. You make certain the doorman can't cause any grief," Dakota relayed into his mike. He offered a thumbs-up to Red 1 and Red 2 standing beside him. They responded in kind, though neither could hide the apprehension in their eyes.

"We can't wait any longer. You better make a decision," burst in Cal Sturges, a weasel-eyed, scrawny sycophant from the mayor's office. He combed his fingers through curly straw-colored hair. Cal liked pushing around the power he thought he commanded; though few acknowledged it.

"You've got the go-ahead, what the hell are you waiting for?" he persisted annoyed at Washington's seemingly obvious hesitation.

"Fuck...patch me to the mayor again," Washington barked into his mike like an angry pit bull. He muttered something about the fucking FBI while he waited.

A harried Lisa Roberts grabbed her microphone and fired animated instructions to Maury Templeton, her gangly, just-out-of-college-can't-do-anything-right cameraman.

"No, no," she snarled, pushing him to the right, "keep the doors over my left shoulder."

Templeton shifted the cumbersome camera on his shoulder as if it were a boulder and hastily set the lens, praying he got it right.

"You got it yet, Jimmy Olson?" Lisa badgered, glancing over her shoulder, angry they might miss the opportunity of a lifetime. This could be one of those rare life-changing situations that would catapult her out of this stinking town and into a major market.

"Not yet," the callow Templeton replied.

"Damn you, Zack Krieger, calling in sick today of all days."

"I got it...let's kick some cinematic ass," Templeton said, feigning a seasoning he only wished he had. He borrowed Krieger's words, which Krieger had coined to indicate when he was good to go.

KGGM's top cameraman, Zack Krieger, was the man to have slinging a lens in a crisis. Zack never screwed up an opportunity. Lisa liked working with Zack—she owed a fair amount of her own success to his instincts and professionalism. Though she promised she would take him with her when she moved up, his drinking problem had kept her uncertain as to the wisdom of such a decision.

Roberts, on the other hand, hated Templeton, the candy-ass wuss. Even after three months at the station, he still couldn't get anything right. The harder he tried, the more he screwed up.

Lisa fluffed her blonde, withered hair, stopping when the harsh camera light washed her face in a pale, surreal glow.

"There seems to be movement near the front doors. Police have yet to release any details except to say that the gunmen are demanding a helicopter. Negotiators are still pressing for the release of a pregnant woman said to be in some distress. No word yet as to why the men have taken over the store."

The camera eye eased over Lisa's shoulder to catch a gunman as he slammed the butt of his Uzi into the base of a male hostage's skull. Templeton sucked in a breath as his eye captured the shattering scene. It came purely by accident while fumbling to locate the iris adjustment.

Then the masked face turned into the camera. Mashing down the wrong button, Templeton zoomed in until the white hatred in those eyes became the focus of the screen. That few seconds burned an indelible image of hate into the hearts and minds of every viewer in Albuquerque.

"Cut," Lisa snapped impatiently, already moving on for her next shot. "Now, can you follow me without getting lost?" she demanded.

Few could endure her grinding, caustic personality for very long. Zack Krieger proved out as one of the few. Maybe that's why he leaned on the bottle for support.

Templeton struggled with his camera while trying to hold the gap between them to within a few paces. His flaming red hair set him apart in the midst of the throng of reporters and other cameramen. In his haste to pursue that next Kodak moment, he had to swallow the momentary bliss the last shot had brought him.

Lisa threaded her way through a wall of black and whites arranged to shield onlookers; chasing that one shot that would vault her to the top of the nightly news.

"Maury, over here. Something's happening. Keep rolling and stay locked on the hostages. Something's going down."

Lisa's instincts had set the hair on her neck on edge. She felt an explosion imminent. Her reporter's sixth sense was taking over control and directing her.

Crack!

A rifle's report erupted out of the tense still air.

All eyes went to the rooftop across the street. Maury, however, trained his camera on the front of the warehouse. The double front doors shattered and glass fell like a wall of water.

A startled gunman dove to clear the line of fire as another barrage of gunfire poured into the building. A blinding flash of white light erupted, riding the resounding boom that shuddered out of the building. Hostages scrambled from the building through the portal where once the glass doors had been. A staccato melee of high-powered gun blasts erupted from deep inside the bowels of the Sound Mart. Acrid bluish-gray smoke churned out the doors, clinging to the unmoving air.

A desperate faceless gunman darted across the opening, shooting wildly at the hostages as he went. A second later, the rooftop shooter dropped the gunman in full view of onrushing uniforms and cameras.

Twelve seconds after it had begun, the gunfire ceased, leaving behind the screams and cries for help that took over the night. Beneath the curling smoke, a wounded man crawled to freedom, dragging a shrieking woman over the shattered glass.

Dakota emerged first from the smoking edifice, waving his rifle in an 'all clear.' The gunmen had been neutralized—the threat removed. Now they had the dire task of tallying up the cost in human lives. In total, nineteen people were free. Two, however, would not walk out of that building. All the gunmen were dead. Lisa and Maury worked against the current of men and women rushing toward the paramedics. She wanted to reach the men now dragging the dead bodies over the shards of glass. They were the heroes of the moment. They had risked their lives to save the innocent. The accolades would be theirs.

Grace Blackwood stared at the television screen from her bed; her head propped against a wall of marshmallow pillows. Without warning, a 'stinger' ripped through her insides like a bolt of lightning. Every muscle contracted in response. She fought the fired pain with locked jaw and clenched fists.

Huddled beside her, eleven-year-old Lauryn, watched Grace's fingers constrict involuntarily around the comforter. She couldn't bear to look back into her mother's eyes. She couldn't bear to see the torment her mother had to endure. The pain would hurt so badly that it would leave her mother mute for minutes. Lauryn bit at her lip to hold back the rush of tears pushing to get out. She had to be strong. She reached out, clutching her mother's forearm. That gentle touch made Grace's pain just a bit more bearable.

Seven-year-old Heather, nestled inside Grace's other arm, refused to look back at her mother's contorted face. It was far too difficult for her to endure, let alone understand.

Please make it go away, Heather thought, her elfin face, which usually wore an impish smile, turning into a rare frown. *Please make my mommy better.*

Moving flashes of television light from the bureau danced across their faces. Grace's once vibrant strawberry-blonde hair was no longer her own, and her skin had taken on an almost parchment-like pallor. Still, she was a fighter and mustered the obscure outline of a smile to allay the mounting concern in Lauryn's innocent blue eyes. Simply taking Lauryn's hand into her own let Lauryn know she would come through all right. Her pain had diminished and would soon be gone. But both knew it would not stay gone forever.

Lauryn, the worrier, always sensed the pain of others and always rushed in to help in any way she could.

Despite an arsenal of potent drugs, the demon continued to grow wild inside Grace's body; a demon taking perverse pleasure in clawing her insides with razor-like talons. However, no drugs existed that could neutralize the fear swelling inside her heart. Some days she felt she was winning; some days the demon won. But winning a battle is one thing, and winning the war is something else. Grace might lose some battles against this monster, but she was determined to win the war.

When the pain at last fell back into the sea and tranquillity again reigned, Grace leaned over to kiss Heather on the top of her head. Her smile tried to hide her suffering. Then she bestowed the same upon Lauryn. Lauryn, in turn, clutched her mother's hand so tightly that Grace's knuckles again grew pale. But Grace would do nothing to stop it. These simple gestures fueled the courage inside her to keep fighting. And she sensed that their contact fueled Lauryn's tenuous courage. Lauryn gazed up with watery eyes and tried to muster a smile on her expressive face. She had always been such a happy child, Grace thought, gazing into those innocent eyes. But not lately.

"It's gone," Grace whispered.

This vicious demon sought to destroy more than just Grace's life. It wanted her children's lives as well. Lauryn, eleven-going-on-nineteen, listened well and learned about cancer, and despite her tender age, she understood. Grace could see it in those eyes. Lauryn gave of her herself, but in the end, both she and Heather were being cheated out of their mother and their childhood innocence.

Assured that her mother's pain had truly dissipated, Lauryn returned to the intrigue of Humphrey Bogart and 'The Maltese Falcon.' Movies helped Grace forget, even if only for a little while, of the strife now playing out in their lives. Grace loved the old classics; when words and emotion swept you away rather than violent explosions and casual sex. Lauryn was quickly becoming a fan of actors and actresses long since gone from this world.

Both Grace and Lauryn knew there would be no sleep until they knew. Watching television served merely as a distraction. While Lauryn and Heather focused on the movie, Grace stared vacantly at the screen...waiting for something else.

"Do you think he did it, Mommy?" Lauryn asked.

At any moment, the plot would unravel and their questions would be answered. Anything to occupy the mind and force worry to arm's length.

The series of sudden beeps and the SPECIAL BULLETIN overlay along the bottom of the screen stopped Grace's heart. She drew air deep into her lungs.

Please...don't let it be....

"We interrupt this program for a special news bulletin," the droning male voice announced. Then the screen bloomed on the blaring neon of Jerry's Sound Mart.

Both girls moaned.

Grace tightened her arms around them, hugging them with all the strength she could muster. That was Dakota's earlier emergency telephone call. The call that drove him suddenly from the house when he promised he would be here with her. The kind of call every policeman's wife dreads.

A worn and wilted Lisa Roberts filled the screen, her ashen face dulled by the blaring lights. She forced an expressionless visage upon her face, though inside raging excitement coursed through her veins.

"This was the scene shortly after eleven this evening when police brought the hostage standoff at this electronics outlet store to an abrupt end."

Behind Lisa, a grim Dakota, shouldering his M16, crossed the camera's eye, jerking open his vest.

"There's Daddy!" Heather chimed. She understood very little of what they said. All she understood was that her father was on television. And that made him special.

Grace gasped.

Lauryn grabbed her mother's hand as they exchanged a glance of dread. Though Lauryn said nothing, those searching eyes conveyed the fear consuming her heart.

"It's okay. He's okay," Lauryn offered in her mix of budding adolescent and reluctant adult voice.

"Lieutenant Dakota Blackwood of the Albuquerque PD led a team of three crack policemen in through the Sound Mart roof, where they then killed four gunmen before...."

"Daddy's okay, girls. It's all over now. Thank God he's all right," Grace whispered, finding the strength to squeeze the girls closer to her. They shared each other's warmth beneath the down comforter while they watched the changing scenes on the screen. Heather couldn't have understood and Lauryn could only guess what the story really meant.

Grace's prayers had been answered. So many of her prayers in the past had been ignored. Dakota was safe. In a few hours, he would be home. She would remain awake to be there for him when he arrived. They would need each other to get through the night. Their lives, it seemed, were filled with demons.

Angela Walker leveled the remote to switch on a nine-inch black and white television she kept on a small cart in her bedroom. It kept her company during lonely nights. Tonight, however, she was not alone. Velvety black, shoulder-length hair still wet from a shower framed a face that took on a satisfied glow as she paused before the blossoming screen.

Wearing only lacy, high-cut panties that concealed little, Angie watched Lisa Roberts fill the screen. For a long moment, silence, confusion, and the hiss of an open microphone came through. Police scurried about behind her. The Sound Mart sign served as the lead-in for the story.

"God..." Angie said, just above a whisper.

A camera light swept over Lisa as she turned to profile and moved closer to interview her subject.

"Lieutenant Blackwood, how many hostages were injured? Were any killed? How many gunmen were there?"

Dakota crossed the screen momentarily, his Apache face grim and somber. But instead of responding, he continued through the camera's vision and disappeared.

Lisa reacted with her usual professional improvisation and turned back to the eyes of everyone viewing at home. Despite the police attitude, she refused to squander this precious air time.

"Police expect to make a statement in the next few minutes," she said without missing a beat.

The camera shifted to the building's shattered doors. An eerie light played off thin streams of lingering smoke. Viewers just tuning in might think they were seeing some war-torn city half a world away.

"In case you've just joined us, the hostage drama at the Sound Mart on Pleasant Hill is finally over..."

"Frankie, come here," Angie called, folding her arms over her breasts in response to the sudden emergence of goose flesh, which had also caused her coffee-colored aureoles to harden involuntarily.

"They freed some hos..."

A thin silver picture wire snapped tight around Angie's waiting neck. Her hand jerked up—but too late. Inky blood splattered the television screen as Lisa returned.

Angie gasped, clawing helplessly at her throat. Blood chortled in drowning gasps from her lips and nose. She dug her fingers into her own flesh, fighting for a chance at one more breath. Clinging to the edge of her life, Angie sucked in with a whoosh, hoping for a single second more.

But she would be denied. Her bulging eyes rolled back until only the bloodied whites remained. No sounds left her severed throat. Her body quaked violently as she released her arms, and her soul, to death.

"We've just learned that four hostages were injured in the exchange. All are at this moment being rushed to Lovelace Medical Center. As far as we could tell from our vantage point, none of the gunmen have survived the assault."

Lisa paused on the screen. At the same time, Angie's body thumped to the floor with a horrible looseness.

Lisa Roberts continued her report.

2

Monday morning and the Oncology waiting room at St. Joseph's Medical Center resembled the quiet of a chapel. Windowless walls washed in soothing earth tones with only a smattering of pictures enveloped the dozen people that scattered themselves about the room as if seeking to be alone in a crowd. If they spoke at all, they spoke in hushed whispers. The few thumbing through magazines and newspapers gave the place an almost monastic or library-like air.

Those waiting used the time to prepare for what awaited them beyond an eight-foot unmarked oaken door. Some would escape unscathed the dreadful aftermath of their treatment. Others might endure mild bouts of indigestion and heartburn. A few would curse God for having ever come to this place.

No words had yet been crafted that could diffuse the gloom smothering those now sitting in the leather chairs. The wall clock ticked off its constant reminder of just how precious time can be. But then everyone waiting here had already learned that lesson.

This Monday morning was no different than a thousand other Monday mornings. Faces change but the routine remains the same. This demon does not discriminate: Hispanic, Indian, Anglo, African-American, and a few Asians, all in varying stages of their treatment. Cancer—the equal opportunity destroyer.

First-timers were easy to spot. They emit telltale signs in the waiting room: overt tremors and crudely phrased questions seeking to discover what awaits them beyond that oaken door. A fear of the unknown flowed out of their eyes. A fear they would come to understand. But one thing remained present in all their eyes—hope. Always hope. No drugs, no radiation, no pain can ever destroy the hope that lies within the human spirit.

Grace had sat here so many times before that she felt like it had become a part of her. She had endured the lengthy and caustic torment of a treatment for a disease without a cure. Two years ago, they claimed her cancer had gone into remission. They said the demon was gone.

They lied.

As she stared at nothing, her mind traveled back to a time and place that now seemed to exist only in another world. Now thirty-five, her life at sixteen seemed more like an old movie playing across the scratched screen of her mind. Five weeks before her seventeenth birthday, she fled her rural Wisconsin home with two hundred dollars and a determination that would never abate.

Seeking to evade a troubled childhood, a father's violent temper and a mother's indifference, she had escaped one horror only to endure the pangs of another—the loneliness that accompanies homelessness. She ended up in Albuquerque not by design, but when, as the bus bound for Los Angeles pulled into the Albuquerque station, she spied a HELP WANTED SIGN in a Raley's department store window across from the station. Fate had always guided her. She decided she would trust it then. That sign she believed had been placed there for her and she had to trust in it. She took the chance, and despite trembling hands and uncertain answers in the interview, the personnel director offered her the job. She accepted and began the arduous struggle of living on her own. The woman that hired her, Marjorie, a Navajo, saw something in those lapis-colored eyes that even Grace never realized she had.

After Grace's first week of work, Marjorie provided Grace with temporary shelter to get her off the streets until she could find a place to live within her budget. One lonely woman helping another. At the time, Indians were not accepted in the city, but Marjorie refused to let prejudice and hatred keep her from living her life. She had found a friend in Grace, as Grace had found a friend in her. Two months later, while working two jobs—days at the department store and nights at a cafe down the street—Grace earned enough to leave Marjorie's couch and move into a studio apartment of her own. Someone had trusted her, no questions asked, and Grace owed her a debt of deepest gratitude.

By nineteen, she had pulled her life together, lived on her own by sharing expenses with a friend she met five months after arriving in Albuquerque; a friend who, in time, became her sister-in-law. A year later, still working at the cafe, fate had intervened once more when the most godlike man she had ever seen walked through the door. She met Dakota and her whole life changed. Bronzed skin, slicked-back raven's black hair and eyes so deep and entrancing they captured the soul. An Apache raised in a white man's house, he shattered her myths of the Indian people. Dakota was hard working, ambitious, disciplined and caring. Yet for all his gorgeous looks and gracious charm, he seemed unable or unwilling to fit into either of his worlds. A University of New Mexico sophomore when they met, he consumed her life so completely right from the beginning that she knew in her heart their love could never be broken.

The oaken door opened with an ominous creak, snapping Grace back to the present. A young Hispanic man in white lab coat exited. He crossed the waiting room, careful to avoid eye contact with any of those staring up at him in anticipation, then he disappeared into the corridor.

A reprieve.

Grace glanced up at the clock. Dakota paced before the chestnut leather sofa where Grace sat. He hated hospitals. Hated to have to be there even for routine homicide investigations. Only death and suffering inhabited this place. No joy was ever found here.

He found it impossible to sit beside Grace. His interest and concentration evaporated within the first paragraph of any magazine article he attempted. Pacing helped. Pacing forced him to think about something other than why he was here.

Dakota's turn to glance up at the clock. Time the trickster. It loved to play upon the hopes and fears of its servants. It speeds up when it wants or slows to a crawl to lengthen suffering. The clock always chose to be an adversary; never an ally.

Grace hated the waiting. Another of a bagful of traits she shared with Dakota. Neither could stand by patiently and wait. For a moment, Grace sought the comforts of a prayer. But she abandoned it before the end. Even talking to God failed to quiet the pounding inside her chest.

Damn this disease for stealing her vitality and fading her beauty. At thirty-five, she looked fifty. She deserved more than fate had dealt her. She had so much still to give Dakota and the girls. *Damn this fucking disease.* A tear slipped out the corner of her eye.

Dakota saw it, sat down beside her and covered her hand with his.

Neither talked. Words were meaningless now. Grace never doubted Dakota's love—knew he would be there to help her through this once more. And once more she would beat the odds; she would beat this damn disease.

The great oaken door opened again with its wretched creak. This time the dungeonmaster filled the frame, one hand resting on her hip while the other moved the clipboard closer to her glasses, so she could read off the name of her next victim.

"Grace Blackwood," the frumpy black nurse announced, "we're ready for you."

Grace smoothed her synthetic red hair; it would have to hide the truth for a while yet.

Dakota helped her up and kissed her gently on the cheek as if she were leaving him forever.

"I love you," he whispered so that only she would hear. The words fueled her courage and gave her a new strength with which to pass through the great oaken door.

Grace squeezed his hand, then wiped away the tears brimming in her eyes.

It was time.

Dakota cared little that others stared at a swarthy-skinned Apache and a snow-white Anglo woman. He packed up his courage and his anger and retreated to the hall. Grace must face this alone.

"How are you feeling today?" the nurse asked.

Grace nodded an answer; inside, she cursed God for what she was about to endure.

Dakota's unwavering commitment to his community and his family earned the Blackwoods a comfortable split-level home in a lushly landscaped and quiet old country club neighborhood in Albuquerque. His position also ensured that the neighborhood saw frequent patrol cruisers along their street. Most of the neighbors were friendly; a few avoided the Black-woods, either because they disliked cops or hated Indians. And one family—a trailer-trash, redneck family of six—seemed incapable of overlooking the color differences in Dakota and Grace's marriage and told them such at a neighborhood association gathering a few years earlier. They never spoke again.

With some slick financial wizardry, thanks to a bank vice-president brother, that same lieutenant's salary would afford the luxury of braces in a few years, a once-in-a-lifetime dream vacation to Tahiti the Blackwoods indulged in after Grace beat cancer the last time, and the chance to keep their daughters' dreams alive as they grow up. But all the money in the world can't force some wishes to come true.

Grace broke from Dakota's arm the moment he opened the front door. She dashed for the nearest bathroom to keep from vomiting on the floor. Time would slow to a crawl over the next forty-eight hours as Grace endured the vicious side effects of her treatment.

Cole and Laurianne Blackwood stood helpless in the foyer as Grace whizzed past with hands clamped over her mouth.

"Come on, Heather, we'll go outside for a while," Lauryn said, always ready to shoulder the responsibility for her little sister.

Laurianne turned away to hide tears. She had been forced to watch Grace deteriorate over the past three years; leaving only the withered shell of what was once a beautiful, vibrant woman.

"I'll make sure she's all right," Dakota said, as he left them standing in the hall.

Later, after Grace had been made comfortable in her bed, Dakota entered the den, where Cole and Laurianne waited, each staring in their own direction. The faint sounds of the girls outside at play permeated the glass panes.

"I'll make dinner before I go. Green Chile okay?" Laurianne said.

"Sure," Dakota answered, hiding behind a vacant stare.

"That would be great," Cole said. He left his chair to stand at the window. As he stared off, Heather dashed past, pausing momentarily to pull her lips open wide with both index fingers and stick her tongue out at him. He responded in kind, something he wished at times he could do to some of his persnickety customers at the bank.

"The girls okay while we were gone?" Dakota asked without looking at either his brother or Laurianne.

"Wonderful. Lauryn insists on doing everything for herself. Says it's cinchy. Everything's cinchy. Guess that's her new word. She won't let me lift a finger," Laurianne said.

"I know...at times I worry she's taking on too much with this. She's no longer a happy little girl."

"How long will Grace be this way?" Laurianne asked. The words were like rocks in her mouth that she had to spit out.

"Few days. She should be better by Thursday."

"Want me to stay? I'll stay. Cole can rough it without me until Thursday."

"No problem," Cole offered.

"No. I'm on a departmental leave of absence. I can handle things for now."

"Just say the word, Dakota, and we'll stay," Cole insisted. He never could read his brother's face. Yet Dakota read him like a book. It had to be an Indian thing.

An Apache and an Irish-German growing up sharing the same bedroom—who would have thought it possible? Back in 1969, when Emil and Rosemary Blackwood believed they would never be blessed with children of their own, they went against the community grain at the time and adopted Dakota, an orphaned Apache whose parents had died in an automobile crash.

The young Dakota had been the unintended product of a turbulent, short-lived marriage between a spirited Jicarilla Apache woman and a fiery Mescalero Apache man. The locals blamed the accident on the man, who had been drinking the night of their deaths. No one bothered to investigate beyond the obvious. After the accident, the respective Indian councils turned their back on the orphan. Rosemary, who for years had volunteered her teaching skills in Dulce at the Jicarilla Apache reservation, learned of the tragedy and immediately fixed in her mind that her solution would serve all concerned best.

Scaling a mountain of bureaucracy and mindless paperwork, Emil and Rosemary persisted until the adoption finally went through and two-year-old Dakota became a legal Blackwood. Albuquerque, at the time, scorned the arrangement, but the Blackwoods always chose to live their lives against the grain and, as such, ignored the other white families. Right was right. And adopting Dakota seemed right. Though Apache, Dakota became a Blackwood, and thereby entitled to all the rights and privileges that accompanied the name.

Three years later, Rosemary surprised Emil—she became pregnant. Cole became the second and final child of the Blackwoods of Albuquerque.

Cole grew up knowing Dakota as nothing other than his bigger brother; the one who doled out answers when Cole became confused; the one who stood beside him—whether right or wrong—when he got into trouble. Dakota, as a child, knew only that he was different and as a result didn't quite fit into the world around him. Together, they opposed the white man's discrimination and endured the years when Emil chose a bottle of tequila over his wife and family. Regardless of what happened in their lives, no matter whose womb they had each descended from, they would always be brothers. In the truest spirit of brotherhood, if not in heritage, they were brothers of the heart.

Cole's awkward sidelong glance conveyed a hidden signal, because Laurianne abruptly rose from the sofa and excused herself to check on the girls.

"I'll start dinner in about twenty minutes," she said as she left.

Dakota looked up, returning from a faraway place when Laurianne closed the door behind her.

Cole returned to his chair rubbing his hands together in a nervous way. Then he sat facing Dakota, gazing at him for a long moment through green, envious eyes. Envious that Dakota maintained a full head of hair, while his own had grown sparse on top. Jealous that Dakota had a cop's lean frame, while his spread to that of an overstuffed banker. Jealous that Dakota had two daughters, while he consoled a fallow Laurianne. Jealous that Dakota was the older brother, and he was relegated to being the younger. Yet he never in his life desired to be an only child, which would have been his fate had his parents not adopted Dakota.

"How you doing? You all right? I mean, you need anything?" Cole started. The edge in his voice snared Dakota's attention.

"I'm okay. We'll deal with this thing one day at a time. We've been down this road before. Grace's going to lick this thing."

A strained pause slipped into the room while Cole assembled in his mind what he wished to say. He had rehearsed it a hundred times in his head and now he had to deliver. He rose and stopped at the fireplace.

"I saw what you did Thursday night. At that appliance store with the gunmen."

"We did what we had to do. The situation went critical real fast."

"Ah come on, Dakota, that's not what I mean, and you know it." A rush of pent-up anger escaped through Cole's voice.

Dakota detected an edge of fear in each of Cole's words. Cole always had trouble speaking his mind to Dakota. He needed time to work up to those issues that impassioned him.

"You can't do that anymore. What's the matter with you?"

"That's my job. I'm not a big shot bank vice-president. I'm a cop. That's what I do. And I do it the best I can."

"Bullshit. Most of the people in that place would have spit in your face just as soon as look at you. Besides, there were fifty other cops who could have done what you did." Cole unleashed his fettered emotions. It had to be said. He had kept silent on this far too long. He knew most of what he had just said was bullshit. Nobody could have gone in there the way Dakota did. Not one of those other fifty cops could have pulled that rescue off without losing hostages. Dakota had a way with controlling danger and Cole knew it.

Dakota left the chair. He crossed the den, coming face to face with his brother.

"You don't know what went on inside that building, Cole. You don't know what we faced. We were running out of time. I had to go in there, goddamnit! I had to save those people."

Cole breathed in deeply. He felt his heart pounding out of control. His hands and voice trembled. He wanted to reach out to his brother, but instead he stopped himself.

"Why does it have to be you? Why can't you let someone else do it? Sit behind a desk, so you can be here when Grace and the girls need you."

"Because...it's my job. That's why. If I hadn't gone in there, they might have all died."

"And what about Grace? She needs you. The girls need you more than ever. You can't risk your life anymore. Can't you understand that? Fuck those people! They hated us. You need to be here. Why can't you understand that."

Dakota said nothing.

"You've got to be here for them..."

Cole stopped, placing his words and his feelings in check. He turned away when he noticed Lauryn standing at the window, now privy to their exchange, observing without understanding the fear and anger in both their eyes.

"Who wants to go get ice cream for tonight's dessert?" Cole yelled through the glass as Heather flattened her nose against the pane. The girls bounced up and down in affirmation. Cole's conversation with Dakota had ended.

In the late eighties, visionary real estate developers gobbled up huge chunks of land skirting the city on the west and began putting together Albuquerque's future. Although they completed the seventh and final building of the hugely popular and ultramodern Silver Springs apartment complex five years ago, they still fell well short of accommodating the immense influx of young professionals flooding into Albuquerque. High-tech business meant high-tech people with high salaries. Jobs sprouted up faster than cacti in the desert. But rapid growth brought with it ever more complex social problems, such as increased crime against property, an emerging drug infrastructure, and one other which Albuquerque had failed to resolve.

The complex offered roomy apartments with access to a sparkling well-maintained pool and a running path just across from the three northern most buildings. Silver Springs developers had dipped into the well of newfound prosperity and had come up brimming with full occupancy for three years running. The waiting list never dried up.

Set on the prestigious side of the city, Silver Springs even seemed capable of avoiding the social ills permeating the core of every other urban center.

But that was about to change.

The patrolman rapped patiently on the door to apartment 204 for the third time. Another nuisance call, he thought, expecting to complete a five-minute report, close the call and move on.

"Can't you break it open?" Jessica Collins asked, standing beside the officer.

The officer merely smiled.

"This isn't the movies. Let's wait for the manager."

"Angie wouldn't have missed work again today without calling in. I know her well enough to know that. She just wouldn't do it."

"Did you notice her car in the lot?"

"The white Jetta. It's parked in her spot."

"How long have you known this Angie?" the officer inquired, more chitchat than official. He glanced at his watch, realizing he would be the last one back in for shift change.

"Two years."

"Maybe she took off for the weekend with a friend."

"She still would have called in."

"Yeah sure. Is Angie any chance one of those live-in-the-moment road trip types?" the officer asked with doubt in his voice. "The Sandias are great in the fall."

Jessica's glare delivered more answer than he required.

"How old is Angie?"

"Twenty-four. And she's very responsible. She missed work on Friday and she didn't show today."

The officer refrained from further knocking, satisfied that Angie was either out of the apartment or she had gone deaf over the weekend. Tilting his head slightly to reach the radio mike clipped to his shoulder, the patrolman updated dispatch as to his status. Then he casually crossed his arms and leaned against the railing to wait for the manager.

Jessica backed away in search of the still-absent complex manager.

Two minutes later, a hunched-over Filipino man climbed the stairs with some difficulty and a key ring jingling at his belt. The metallic rattle offered an air of importance and authority.

"Angie Walker, she good lady, you disturb," he said, reluctant to even remove his keys.

"It's just a well-being check. We want to make sure everything is okay," the officer said, indicating he wished the door opened without further question.

"She good lady, no trouble."

"She missed work Friday and today. She didn't call in. I'm worried about her," Jessica said.

"Okay, I open. She good lady. Angela always pay on time. No trouble."

"I'll bet if the rent were late, you'd be first in line to get inside," Jessica mumbled under her breath.

Having said his fill, the manager removed his key ring, selected the appropriate key (each key having a number taped on them) and unlocked the bottom lock. He tried the door but the dead bolt had also been engaged. Selecting another key, this one appearing barely used and having a number on it that neither matched the apartment door nor the key he had selected previously, he unlocked the dead bolt and pushed the door open with a toothy perfunctory smile. Afterward, he stepped out of the way as if his involvement had been completed.

The uniform, however, stopped before entering. A stench assaulted his nose. The acrid air of death escaped the moment he broke the door seal. Inside, dusty light pouring through the door settled on an otherwise orderly apartment.

The living room showed no signs of disturbance, along with the small kitchenette to the side that appeared neat and orderly.

The officer paused just inside the apartment. He stared at the half-open bedroom door twelve feet before him. Motioning Jessica back, he indicated that both she and the manager were to remain outside.

"I'd better handle this," he said, his eyes scanning the expanse.

With revolver out and nightstick in the lead, the officer approached the bedroom door, careful to keep the room as undisturbed as possible. Using the baton, he eased the bedroom door completely open.

Every window in the apartment had been tightly closed. Drawn curtains kept the overcast sky from peering into the room. The only light now spilled in through the open front door and most of that never reached the bedroom. But the officer needed little light to discern exactly what inhabited the room. Long before the officer entered the bedroom, he knew what he would find.

But still the officer froze at the open door. He withdrew at a run, retching over the railing while Jessica and the manager looked on. When he finished, the officer barked commands into his radio. He moved both the woman and the apartment manager away from the apartment door.

Jessica trembled, clamping her hands over her mouth. Tears stole away her sight. She didn't need to see to know what had happened to her co-worker.

"Get downstairs and direct the other officers to this apartment."

Jessica's cries opened doors in the two adjacent Silver Springs buildings.

3

Detective Sergeant Adrian Broncowski, Bronc to those who knew him well, started his Monday P.M. shift thinking more about his off-duty days of Tuesday and Wednesday than his pending caseload. He had two ringers still open on the board and neither had any fresh leads to pursue. Ringers were those homicides destined to remain unsolved forever. Black marks on a detective's record. And though the cases may never officially close, they just cease to receive police attention. Most of the time soured drug deals and homeless deaths quickly turned into ringers.

Carrying a bull's mean frame and a neck almost as thick as his head, Bronc had no reason to feel ashamed of his given name. No one dared poke fun at Adrian, even as a child. He just liked Bronc better.

Coming off a slow weekend shift, he looked forward to the next two days off. Maybe he'd drive up to the Sandias. Maybe do some fishing. Then he remembered a postponed promise to paint the living room for his wife.

Things had slowed in Homicide. And that was fine with Bronc. The last thing he wanted to do was to bust his butt on some unsolvable drug slaying.

After a lackluster shift briefing, Bronc checked the duty board. His smile withered; his whistle fell silent. His turn to man the phones. He hoped that meant an evening staring at the television set sitting on a file cabinet in the corner of the squad room.

Not a chance.

At 5:32 Bronc's first call of the shift came in: a stiff at the Silver Springs apartments. The location induced a puzzled scratch at his peppered hair. The action reminded him he needed a haircut. A stiff in Yuppieville, he thought quizzically. Bronc's intuition flashed drug overdose. Happy, successful yuppie gets too much of a good thing.

However, when Bronc arrived, he realized just how far out in left field his intuition had been. The moment Bronc entered that apartment and began assessing the crime scene, he became the primary detective for the investigation. An investigation destined to flip his life upside down and inside out. Within a minute, Bronc knew exactly what he had drawn. His probing hazel eyes, framed by bushy brows, soaked in the entire grotesque scene. What he saw convulsed his stomach, paled his face, and sent sweat rolling down his doughy cheeks.

The Boulder Hill killer.

Two hours into the investigation and Bronc still had yet to approach Angela's mutilated body. The tedium of collecting details from the crime scene consumed all his concentration. The body remained untouched.

The uniform who discovered the body lingered, albeit unwillingly, outside the apartment. His shift ended hours ago; he was hungry and his feet ached, but he wouldn't be going home for awhile yet. Bronc insisted that he remain on the scene until the detective himself had a chance to talk with him. And before he talked with him, Bronc wanted to collect as much information as he could from the bedroom.

Standing motionless at the door, Bronc catalogued every detail in the bedroom. He spoke to no one. He wrote down everything, trusting nothing to memory. No clue, no scrap of evidence however slight, could be neglected. Bronc's seasoned eyes missed nothing. Uncover the physical evidence before disturbing the scene, he cautioned himself. Above all else, do not in any way contaminate the crime scene. Police screw-ups all too often let killers walk. He knew exactly what this murder meant.

In a homicide investigation, only the primary detective issues orders relevant to the analysis in progress. And every uniform and detective present complies without question. One man takes full responsibility for beginning and then monitoring the vital chain of custody for evidence processing. So far Bronc had issued only one order: get a situation report to Captain Washington and request his presence at the crime scene.

An evidence technician, new to the department and anxious to get in and get out so he could get home, requested permission to enter the bedroom.

Bronc barked an angry refusal. Not yet. There were too many things to see. Still too many questions in his mind. He wrote with fervor and encrypted phrases to save time.

Captain Washington arrived as the last rays of the crimson sun dipped beneath the horizon. With the captain at his side, Bronc approached the brutally lacerated body of Angela Janine Walker.

Washington's face went slack. His worst nightmare had returned. The three-by-five inch note scribbled in crude writing and pinned to Angela's panties as she lay face up on the bed insinuated one thing—a serial murder. That note, an unreleased element of a complex signature pattern, meant the Boulder Hill killer had returned. A signature of terror delivered to the people of Albuquerque—a serial killer's undeniable calling card.

"Merry Christmas, Ellie," Washington read the note aloud.

"October's a little early for the holidays," the callow evidence technician said. He regretted the words when he caught the glares from Bronc and Washington.

The words on the note sent icy shivers through everyone in the room. Disbelief glazed Washington's pale brown eyes. Albuquerque's worst nightmare had come back to haunt them.

Bronc had the forethought to order the uniforms at the scene to isolate the media a safe distance away. Right now only a chosen few knew what Angie's death meant—the five men inside that room: Washington, Broncowski, two evidence processing technicians and a photographer.

"The sonofabitch is back," Bronc said ominously, feeling a knot squeeze his stomach until he tasted bile in the back of his throat.

"Keep the press as far away from this as possible for now," Washington ordered.

He and Bronc retreated to the living room while the technicians collected and cataloged every physical item in the bedroom. Standing in the center of the room, but not far enough away to escape the stench, Bronc and Washington listened as the uniform recounted the discovery.

"You're certain both locks were engaged?" Washington pressed.

"The manager unlocked the bottom lock first, tried the door, then unlocked the dead bolt above it," the uniform replied.

Bronc took notes but said nothing.

Another uniform appeared in the apartment doorway.

"Media's getting real antsy, Sarge. They want to know how much longer before they're going to get something?" the uniform said.

"They'll never let me get away without giving them something," Bronc said.

"Just the essentials. We need time to get organized before the press gets this. How long before you remove the body?"

"Maybe an hour. Cap, you going to turn this over?"

"I don't know what I'm going to do."

For two years the killer had been silent. Now, for reasons known only in his sick and twisted mind, he decided to be silent no more.

Washington's normally stoic countenance paled.

Death comes in threes.

Returning to the bedroom, Washington stared at the carnage that had become the Boulder Hill killer's trademark. The pretty young woman on the bed unknowingly became identified victim number four. Four that they knew of.

"Time of death?" Washington asked Bronc.

The detective wrote feverishly into his notebook.

"A co-worker, Jessica Collins, said Miss Walker missed work on Friday. Miss Collins called police when Angie failed to show up for work again today. In the past two years, it seems Angie Walker never once had an unexcused absence from her job. Until now."

"So we back into Thursday."

"Collins said Walker left work at her normal time, but said nothing about any plans for the evening."

"Neighbors?"

"Nothing yet. I've got two detectives interviewing neighbors now. I'll review the statements before I leave the scene."

"Family?"

Bronc leveled his pen toward a pair of framed pictures on the bureau. One portrayed Angie with a man and woman—her parents, Bronc surmised, judging by the subjects' age and the stilted pose against a blue dappled background. The second picture, a black and white glossy of a dark-haired teen leaning with pride against the door of a shabby pickup, proved more intriguing. The youth appeared fifteen, maybe sixteen; too young to be Angela's intimate friend, but Bronc had to withhold judgment until he knew more.

"Any pictures of a boyfriend or lover?"

"None. I spotted a stack of family pictures in the closet."

"Next of kin been notified?"

"Not yet. No personal directory."

Washington raised a quizzical brow.

Bronc shrugged.

"Checked all the obvious places: purse, night table, drawers in the bedroom and kitchen. No personal telephone directory in the apartment."

"You think?"

"Could be Angie knew her killer. That implied the killer maintained enough composure after the crime to methodically go through the place and remove evidence that might connect him to her."

"Forced entry?"

"None."

"Anyone find her keys?"

No one present offered an answer.

"Either of you pick up anything so far?" Washington asked the evidence technicians while the photographer snapped away.

"No sir."

Washington backed out of the bedroom. He had been away from this for fifteen years. The foul stench had crawled under his skin.

"Prints?" Bronc asked hopefully when he noticed a technician packing up his case.

"Eight total, two latents, but I think we're going to find they're the victim's. Just a guess."

"I shot everything you asked for, Bronc," the photographer said, his camera hanging off his arm as if it were a lead weight. "Any new requests?"

"You get the bathroom?"

"Got a couple of the blood splatters on the toilet bowl."

"Listen, Bronc, I need to get out of here. I can't handle the smell any longer," the captain said.

Washington withdrew to the balcony and sucked the cool night air deep into his lungs. It would take more than the air to purge himself of the smell. His uniform would have to go to a professional cleaner to rid it of the remnants of death.

Bronc remained behind in the bedroom, staring for a while at the clothes hanging in the closet. He trained himself to see everything as evidence. Don't feel and don't see the person as once being alive.

Nothing expensive on the clothes rack: a lot of mix-and-match, working-girl budget items. Angela appeared to be a woman of moderate means and the necessary discipline to live within those means. A half dozen pairs of shoes lined the closet floor; most of them with worn soles.

A few minutes later, Bronc stepped onto the balcony and lit a cigarette. The smoke did little to soothe his rumbling stomach.

Washington gave him a look.

"I thought you quit?" the captain asked.

"Almost," Bronc answered, staring at a black sky wild with stars.

"Almost? You either did or you didn't."

"Fine. I didn't."

Washington hated cigarettes. His wrinkled nose let Bronc know. Bronc laughed. Cigarette smoke was fragrant in comparison to what emanated from that room.

For the amount of time it takes to smoke a cigarette, they watched the lights of Albuquerque stretching into the surrounding desert. They both knew more death clung just beyond that horizon. The last time the Boulder Hill killer murdered three people before he fell silent.

Now they had to try to stop him from killing again.

"You know what you have to do, Cap."

"I know. Dakota worked the Boulder Hill murders two years ago."

"I don't have a problem with you assigning this to Blackwood. By all rights, it's his case."

"It's not that simple. He's on a leave of absence. His wife..."

Bronc took one last deep drag, then tossed the filter over the railing.

"The clock's started. We don't have much time to think about this," Bronc said.

"Can you keep the bloodsuckers away?"

"I'll try. We've kept the press out so far. But I think they already suspect something. I know we've successfully blacked out the nightly news, but I can't say what's going to hit the papers tomorrow."

"It's your crime scene, Bronc. You work it and don't miss a thing. For right now, you're primary."

Bronc returned to the bedroom with the weight of Albuquerque crushing his shoulders. The weight of a half million people, or more aptly, potential victims of a vicious serial killer. Angie's cloudy eyes stared at the ceiling. Bronc thought he could see the pain the girl must have suffered before dying. He wished there were some way to avoid what he had just been dealt. He would gladly relinquish the responsibility and the pressure. He didn't want the burden of more deaths if he failed here. By all rights, this belonged to Dakota Blackwood.

Two years ago, Dakota unraveled the complex signature pattern of the Boulder Hill killer. He successfully linked three disparate victims to a single, cunning, psychopathic killer.

Give it to Dakota, Bronc told himself, he's the best. He'll find the killer. Now Washington expected Bronc to succeed where the best had failed.

"Okay, let's turn the body," Bronc said to a technician.

The signs of rigor mortis had disappeared from the body, Bronc noted, indicating that Angie had been dead more than twenty-four hours. He suspected Angie had been dead about four days. Bronc wouldn't make it home tonight; nor would he have the next two days off. He would also be giving up such luxuries as sleep and regular meals over the next month.

Death comes in threes, he thought as he stared at the once attractive but now mutilated girl, who once smiled and dreamt of a future.

4

Dakota slipped out of bed, careful to avoid disturbing Grace. He had refined the action to an art form as a result of the many late-night calls. Most junior grade detectives sought Dakota's input while a crime scene remained fresh. In the dim morning's glow, he fumbled into department sweats, then left Grace with a kiss on the forehead; a kiss no more than a gentle brush of his lips.

Her skin radiated warmth—bordering on feverishness. Her night had been difficult and for the moment she had found the meager comforts of sleep. Dakota sought to allow her the tenuous peace while he got the girls off to school.

One day at a time, he told himself. You beat this thing one day at a time.

He stumbled into the kitchen to find Lauryn already at the counter wrapping sandwiches, while Heather sloshed milk around trying to hit her cereal bowl.

"Let me help," Dakota said softly, relieving Heather of the cumbersome carton and finishing the job. He spared enough in the process to fill her Flintstones cup; a cup whose paint had worn off ages ago.

"You could have stayed in bed, Daddy," Lauryn offered, tucking Heather's peanut butter and jelly sandwich into her lunch box. Heather refused to eat anything but non-meat sandwiches which left only peanut butter and jelly, or cheese and mayonnaise; both of which Lauryn found disgusting.

"You don't want my help?" Dakota said, feigning disappointment.

"This is cinchy. I took care of everything," Lauryn said as she whisked around the island like a pint-sized efficiency expert maximizing her efforts.

"There's coffee in the pot for you."

"Get out of here!"

"Really. Auntie Laurianne taught me how to make it. I put it on ten minutes ago. I didn't think you'd be up. We really can get ourselves off to school."

"You girls are truly amazing."

Dakota kissed Lauryn on her forehead, much to her dismay. That was for little ones, she thought. He filled his lungs with the rising coffee aroma as he reached to remove a mug from of the cupboard.

Lauryn handed him one from the dishwasher strainer.

"Reusing cups and silverware means less clean up and makes our job easier."

"I see. I thought maybe I'd walk my girls to the bus stop this morning."

The words froze Lauryn with lunch bag in hand. She turned back to her father, her face aghast. How could he even consider such a thing?

"Don't you think we're a little old for that? Mom *never* walks us to the bus stop."

"Well, your mom gets to spend a lot of time with you. I don't. I just thought it would give us a chance to spend time together. You can tell me what's going on at school."

"Dad, I have friends. I don't think it's a good idea for you to walk us. You know what I mean?"

"Sorry. You're right. What could I have been thinking?"

"How long will you be staying home from work?"

"Just for a while...until your mother's better and can take care of things again."

Lauryn switched to her patented 'what-exactly-do-you-mean' look suggesting that she had serious reservations concerning the very core of whatever had just been said.

"I can take care of things for Mom while you're at work."

"It won't be for very long."

"Let's move it, Heather, we've got three minutes to get to the bus stop," Lauryn said, assisting a lethargic Heather out of her chair and filling her hand with her lunch box.

"I'm not done yet. Let me finish..."

"You're done. We have to go."

Leaving behind a trail of milk and cereal droppings on the table, Heather abandoned what remained of her breakfast and clung to her lunch box.

"I'm still hungry," Heather whined.

"Then learn to eat faster," Lauryn insisted.

Dakota could only offer Heather a look of sympathy. He stopped the girls at the front door, where he knelt down to button Heather's pink knit sweater and hug her before letting her pass out the door.

How can anyone still provide these two a blissful childhood when something so horrible surrounded their lives? Dakota realized he had to try harder to make them feel happy about their everyday living. He couldn't let the black cloud of Grace's disease take away the excitement they deserved with each new day. A happy childhood leads to content adulthood; you can never go back to recapture what is lost in youth. Children need to feel safe and nurtured in their homes. Dakota felt he was letting them down.

"How do I look, Lieutenant?" Lauryn said, pausing at attention and saluting like a callow officer under Dakota's command. Her dimpled Shirley Temple smile wormed right into his heart.

"Perfect. Now give the lieutenant a hug," Dakota said, with his arms out and waiting.

"Dad."

Dakota stole one anyway, along with a kiss on Lauryn's forehead. His hug lasted a long moment, saying nothing. Heather paused halfway down the stairs, waiting for Dakota to release Lauryn. But Lauryn wasn't quick to pull away from him, either. It seemed to Lauryn like a moment they could share just between the two of them. Something she relished but seldom received.

"Mom's going to be all right, isn't she?" she asked in a whisper as if she expected his response to come in kind.

"Sure. Now go take care of your sister."

From the stairs, Lauryn glanced back, but only for a second, searching for something more than just Dakota's words. Was there something in his eyes? Something that had shaken the conviction of his own words.

Then Lauryn caught up to Heather, took her hand and they hurried off.

"What do you want me to make for dinner?" he called.

"Pizza, carry out!" Lauryn shot back.

Dakota watched until they reached the end of the block. He would make more time for them over the next few days; find out what they liked and do it with them. A ringing telephone brought Dakota back into the house sooner than he wished. Lauryn was growing up too fast. A minute ago, she was in first grade. Now she's a developing take-charge young lady. The next time Dakota looked, she'd be a high school senior.

He stretched to snatch the phone before it woke Grace. In the process, he reminded himself to turn off the ringer on the bedroom phone the next time he went up there.

"Lieutenant Blackwood?" the caller asked in a firm yet feminine voice that emptied out of the phone weighted with determination.

"Yes?"

"Lisa Roberts, KGGM news. I've just learned the Boulder Hill Killer has claimed another victim..."

"What?"

"Will you be heading up the investigation? When will the task force be reactivated? Why are police keeping the media in the dark?"

Dakota said nothing. When Lisa persisted, firing off her questions in a tone evident that she expected answers, Dakota hung up.

Within seconds, the phone rang again. This time Dakota turned the caller over to the answering machine. Lisa had no intention of giving up without a statement for her broadcast.

"Lieutenant Blackwood," the machine spit out, "you investigated the Boulder Hill serial killings two years ago. Are you going to be in charge of the Angela Walker murder? I just want a statement...I know you're there."

Dakota's stomach convulsed. An acrid fluid backed up into his throat. Two-year-old images flashed across his mind as if he had just witnessed them yesterday. Gruesome carnage he had buried away a long time ago, but had never been able to forget. What is seen can never be unseen. He relived those images of death and hatred zipping from one corner to the next in the darkest recesses of his mind.

Sweat dappled his forehead.

Dakota focused the whole of his life around one objective: winning. Winning drove the inner spirit. Winning drove Dakota each day. That same spirit kept Grace fighting the odds. She must succeed. Winning now meant everything.

He had to succeed. He had to solve the crime. He had to get the bad guy at any cost. Now the stinging cost of failure rang inside his brain. Two years ago, the Boulder Hill killer escaped. He lost. Now innocent people would pay the price of his failure. It was personal.

The Boulder Hill killer had claimed three victims, eluded him, and then quietly disappeared. The cases—his cases—a string of macabre murders, remained unsolved. Winning is not everything in his line of work. Winning is the only thing. Winning saves lives. Winning clears the scum off the streets.

When the leads dried up, as well as the victims, Dakota concluded that maybe the killer had met the same fate as those he stalked or maybe he'd been arrested and was sitting in a prison cell somewhere where he couldn't kill again. Bad assumption.

Now he was back. Or was he?

Dakota cast worried eyes toward the stairs. Grace. The most important thing in his life right now. Grace and the girls. They needed him more. He had just begun his leave of absence to be here for Grace. With the aggressive radiation and chemo, she needed him now more than ever. She couldn't win alone. He had to be here fighting alongside her.

Together they could beat anything. He couldn't...

But those relentless demons in his mind had been awakened—replaying the horrors he had buried two years ago. It all came flooding back. His turn to man the phones. A young girl, Sheila Davis, found murdered in her apartment. The severed neck, the blood, the ritual execution. Sheila was the first. But the killer didn't stop there. Less than two months later, Janet Hegler died next; she was mutilated so badly that it took dental records to positively identify the body. Dakota had bore witness to the tempest of rage that consumed the killer's being.

Dakota suspected the victims were linked. While two pairs of detectives investigated the murders separately, Dakota commingled the investigative reports and through that grim union, he gradually deciphered a complex signature.

One man had killed both victims.

The manner in which the killer displayed the bodies convinced Dakota. In each case, the hands had been positioned in a certain fashion and the legs splayed in an identical fashion. Regardless of what he tried, Dakota never could come up with a way for the appendages to end up that way naturally. The killer had intentionally positioned the bodies in a way that meant something to only him.

In time, Dakota had released his information regarding the deciphered signature and the press as a result labeled the fiend responsible the Boulder Hill killer. Even though the two women died by two different weapons, police were then confident that the same hand had been used to take both lives.

The morbid news sent Albuquerque into rumbling unrest. Every citizen became alarmed. A monster lived in their midst, stalking them as they went about their daily lives. Before long, a third victim surfaced. Now police and press alike knew they were dealing with a bona fide serial murderer.

But a male became the killer's third victim. And many disputed that Steven Ashecroft, a twenty-four-year-old junior accountant, whose friends said had a timorous demeanor, had fallen victim to the Boulder Hill killer.

It took Dakota five weeks to convince those in authority—his captain, the mayor, and the FBI—that their male victim did indeed connect with the two women. Only after exposing the subtle similarities between the display of the male body and the two female bodies did the authorities agree. The fact that Steven Ashecroft's genitals had been mutilated before death ran counter to all their theories; something undetermined in the earlier ritual killings. The press wanted to link the Ashecroft killing to some kind of satanic ritual, though Dakota believed otherwise.

The result of linking three deaths together legitimized the Boulder Hill killer as a serial murderer. No one could even guess how high the tally might rise if the police failed to track the killer down.

Death comes in threes. Albuquerque waited for the next victim.

But the killing unexpectedly stopped. The Boulder Hill killer disappeared while the city nervously waited for more victims to turn up.

At the time, Dakota knew he was closing in on the killer. He remained one step away from the clue that could put him on the killer's doorstep. If he closed his eyes, he could see its nebulous silhouette floating just beyond reach. Winning is everything.

But even after three victims, the killer's meticulous nature kept police from uncovering his identity. The condition of the crime scenes, sanitized after each murder, clearly indicated their killer removed any evidence linking him to the crime.

Those were the irrefutable actions of a serial killer that had become experienced—these were not his first slayings. It also indicated his crimes were not dictated by intense rage or impulse. He devoted significant time and effort to planning and executing his crime. And that preparatory time period could have been weeks, months or even years before the actual crimes were committed. It also indicated their killer was not merely a killer of opportunity. He seemingly created the opportunities to murder his victims.

Dakota had believed one thing at the time of the original investigation and had never strayed: their best chance of catching the Boulder Hill killer lie in finding that vital link to his first victim. Research derived from interviewing convicted serial murders had shown time after time that a serial murderer's first victim is someone he has most often known casually. His first kill comes from some link to his inner psyche. Dakota had turned his efforts to trying to find the killer's first victim when the killings unexpectedly stopped. Most believed the killer would rack up a dozen bodies before police nailed him.

Dakota had become the primary on all three cases....

"Who was that?" Grace asked, from the bottom stair.

"Grace, you're up," he said, burying what had consumed his mind so much that he failed to notice Grace standing six feet from him.

"Couldn't sleep. Who was on the phone? Don't they know it's seven-thirty in the morning."

"Some bonehead selling roofing. How are you feeling? You want something to eat?"

Dakota pressed the erase button on the answering machine and moved to take Grace into his arms.

A state of nervous agitation consumed the City Hall conference room where reporters and cameraman gathered awaiting a promised press conference. Most shifted about, questioning each other in hopes of uncovering something in advance of the official announcement. The promised four o'clock press conference was already thirty minutes late. The longer they waited, the more supposition and innuendo spread.

A tight-lipped police department only heightened suspense. Something big was up. Everyone knew it. The idle hours waiting for official word spawned speculation, and before long, every reporter present had concocted his or her own version of the announcement from bits and pieces floating around.

Now, instead of information, the mayor's assistant fed reporters excuses for the delay and washed them down with promises that the announcement was just a few moments away.

Lisa rooted herself front and center before the podium, refusing to stray. Her informants had already earned their compensation. She had already written her story for the six o'clock broadcast and now wondered how many of her colleagues even had an inkling of the imminent announcement. She checked her watch frequently. How would it look if her broadcast hit the air waves minutes after the announcement? They'd know she had been tipped off. There was no way she would have had the time to write up the story and get it on the air. There were two ways of getting an exclusive in this town, and Lisa never balked on doling out either.

When a Tribune reporter probed Lisa for information, she offered her traditional poker face and a confused shrug, knowing all the time the announcement would reveal some very difficult truths about the Angela Walker murder.

From the genuine distress in their voices, Lisa surmised the police department had done an admirable job of keeping her cronies in the dark. She could likely be the only one in the room who actually knew what was really going on. Even the police couldn't keep Lisa from unearthing the truth. And they thought they had good detectives.

Lisa learned early in her career that to succeed she had to become an information broker who paid well—both in money and amenities. Where money failed, she offered something few men would easily turn down. Information drove her profession. She made sure the right people in the right places knew it: from police, to hospital staff, to the most powerful in city government.

And Lisa never missed a trick. She cultivated little, inconspicuous friends with attentive ears who had access to places where good ears earned good dollars. And Lisa was a pack rat when it came to information. Anything she gleaned, she tucked away until she was ready to offer it up to the world. Not many had the moxie to scoop Lisa. She could get it and she could keep it from her colleagues.

And Lisa leveled a middle-finger response to those who accused her of banging the right people to get what she wanted. Use it if you got it, she always said. They were all jealous of her success. And she didn't have to screw anybody to become the best.

Finally, after a forty-five minute delay, Captain Washington marched through a door and centered himself behind the podium. Detective Adrian Broncowski followed in his wake along with Cal Sturges, a self-proclaimed up-and-comer in the mayor's office. Pete Rodman, an obscure FBI special agent assigned to the Albuquerque office, entered last. Lisa had instructed her assistant to compile a complete file on him after the Sound Mart incident. Seemed his name surfaced as the one who had dropped the ball when reporting the seriousness of the situation to his superiors. As a result, the FBI never dispatched their SWAT team to assist the local police. Sooner or later, she figured, the Bureau would muscle in on the Boulder Hill killer investigation. Rodman appeared stiff and stilted before the press like the rookie he was. Must be inexperienced at high profile cases, she concluded. But his presence turned out to be the tip-off. Her informants had hit the target right in the bull's-eye.

The conference room fell into eerie silence. The reporters knew the players and sensed the gravity of the situation. The mayor's office and the Bureau were involved. That meant heavy stuff.

Floodlights opened up on the four while cameras clicked away. The cameras honed in on the grave concern writ across Washington's face and in his eyes. The faces of the men delivered the preamble to what would follow. Only a blind reporter would have failed to grasp the depth of the announcement even before Washington uttered that first word.

Washington's starched uniform looked as if he had just put it on. Unfortunately, he had nothing on that would hide the stress.

Lisa smiled inside. She had been right about everything—except...the one man she expected to see was obviously absent. It looked like some quick rewrites would be in order.

"Thank you all for coming on such short notice and for your patience throughout the delays. I'd like to complete my announcement in its entirety before fielding questions. So please, wait until I tell you I'm ready for questions."

Neither Sturges, Rodman, nor Broncowski moved behind the captain. But their wary eyes were telling a story of their own. Something big had developed and the police were about to let it out to the world.

"At approximately six-fourteen P.M. on Monday, September fifteenth, a young woman's body was found at the Silver Springs apartments. Homicide detectives arrived shortly thereafter and initiated their investigation. The twenty-four-year-old woman lived alone. And at this time we are withholding her name pending notification of next of kin."

Washington paused to clear his throat, painfully conscious of how stilted and unfeeling his delivery seemed.

"Evidence at the scene indicates the murder to be the work of the Boulder Hill killer."

Hands shot up and a clamor of voices flooded the room. Every reporter vied to be heard. No one cared to hear the rest of the announcement. The words from two years earlier remained fresh in their minds.

Washington waved off reporters, waiting for the room to return to silence. As much as he wished to keep this news from the press, the fear of leaks had forced the department into going public. No one wanted to have to explain an obvious cold shoulder toward the media later.

"This is all we are certain of at this time. Effective immediately, we are reactivating the Boulder Hill Killer Task Force with Detective Sergeant Adrian Broncowski as task force leader. He is currently the primary detective on this latest homicide case."

Bronc's face offered not the slightest glimmer of recognition.

"I'll take questions now."

"How did the woman die?" a reporter blurted over the voices of six others vying to get their questions in.

"Strangulation."

"How can you be certain it's the Boulder Hill killer? What do you have that ties this killing to the others?" another asked.

"We're certain. The Boulder Hill killer leaves his undeniable mark."

"What is that mark?"

"We're withholding that at the present."

"Will the FBI be brought in?"

"The Federal Bureau of Investigation has offered us the use of their extensive computer facilities, and Special Agent Peter Rodman, behind me, will assist Detective Broncowski. But our own task force detectives will be handling the investigation."

Washington hoped to get through the conference without having to face any difficult questions. The reporters would have little time to come up with them.

"Captain Washington, two years ago the Boulder Hill killer murdered three people in Albuquerque...you're saying that you know for sure the killer has resurfaced?"

"Yes."

"Captain Washington," Lisa blurted out, seizing momentary control of the conference. She paused until those around her grew quiet.

"Two years ago, Detective Dakota Blackwood headed up the investigation. Why isn't he in charge of this case, if you're sure the killer has returned?"

"Detective Broncowski is one of our top detectives. He investigated this latest crime scene after the call came in. He is more than capable of heading up this investigation."

"But two years ago Detective Blackwood had the highest clear rate in the department and he failed to catch the killer," Lisa forced in before having to yield the floor to other reporters surging to be heard.

"What is the department's plan for protecting the public against this crazed lunatic?" a straw-haired, busty female reporter pressed. She was from the University of New Mexico's daily student newspaper and felt stifled by the reporters surrounding her.

"We're doing everything we can. But until we catch this guy, we're stressing that the public take extra precautions. We want all citizens in Albuquerque to be astutely aware of activities in their neighborhoods, and to contact the police should they see anything out of the ordinary. As before, we will thoroughly investigate every call we receive. A special telephone line is being set up just to take calls related to the Boulder Hill killer investigation. Presently, detectives are following up on a number of leads. We're going to get this guy."

"But what are you doing right now to get him...before he kills again?"

The question shot like a dagger through the air. Washington couldn't determine the sender.

"As I said, we're following up on a number of promising leads and we're confident we can make progress in the short term."

"How can you be sure it's the Boulder Hill killer and not just some copycat?"

Washington turned to Bronc to field that question. Sweat trickled down the captain's robust cheeks.

He was relieved to shift the pressure off himself; even if only momentarily.

"The man who killed our latest victim left behind a signature that matches undeniably to the three murders of two years ago."

"Were there signs of forced entry?"

"No."

"Does that mean the victim knew her killer?"

"Not conclusively. We're working that angle right now."

"What leads are you following up on?"

"It would be premature to release that information. However, we will make every attempt to keep the public informed as to the status of this investigation. Right now we need the help and cooperation of the people of Albuquerque."

"Mr. Sturges, what input has the mayor's office given to this?"

Cal stepped forward, quick to snare the podium from Bronc. He scanned the gathering before speaking as if this were a political campaign.

"The mayor is providing every resource available. We will find—and stop—whoever is responsible for the young woman's death."

"What about the FBI? Why aren't they being brought in to handle this investigation since you believe the serial killer has returned?"

"As you all will remember," Captain Washington said, returning to the podium, "the FBI provided us with a very detailed and, we believe, accurate profile of the person we're seeking. We will be providing the information from the crime scene to the Bureau's Psychological Behavior Unit for their confirmation. But as far as we're concerned, the Boulder Hill killer murdered our latest homicide victim."

"You're sure it's not the work of a copycat?"

"We're sure. Thank you for your indulgence. Detective Broncowski will be in charge of the investigation and we will keep the media current in our findings. As soon as the next of kin have been notified, we'll release the victim's name to all of you."

Though a clamor of voices arose, pressing for that one last question, Washington, Broncowski, Rodman and Sturges left the conference room. Nothing could hide the strain on Washington and Broncowski's face as they departed.

5

"You okay, Dakota?" Bronc asked, before breaking the police seal.

Dakota paused before the door to apartment 204. He knew even before entering what he would find—a gruesome reminder of his past failure. Nothing could ease the notion that he could have prevented this. Part of Dakota demanded he enter that apartment; another part warned him to stay out. Once a scene crawls under the skin, you can never be rid of it. It held the power to distort logic and steal sanity. A force beyond the door seized Dakota and he knew he could never turn away.

For an instant, Dakota thought about Grace back at home. He thought about the pain and suffering...thought about death.

"I'm okay."

Passing through the door meant no turning back. No unseeing what the eyes have seen. The imprints of such a crime leave indelible tracks on the mind. Tracks that stay with you every day for the rest of your life; it becomes part of you. A part that drives you until you end it or until you reach the brink of your own sanity.

Dakota grabbed the knob. It wiggled in his hand. He pushed the door in.

"Manager says cheap locks. Most of the apartments are the same. Not enough to justify forced entry."

The darkened rooms stank of death. Sealing the place preserved the scene and entombed the fetid air. Angela's body was long gone, but every other aspect of her heinous murder remained intact for police to examine over and over, hoping that somewhere within these walls they would find that one elusive clue left behind that would ultimately reveal the killer's identity.

Dakota checked his heart and spirit at the door. He switched over to his left brain—the clinically detached self. Become the observer who sees all and inside feels nothing. The left brain shows no emotion...it just analyzes.

This was a crime scene. Uncover that overlooked minuscule trace of evidence that would nail the perpetrator. Nothing more. See no victim...feel no pain and sympathy...see only the killer occupying this place. Never connect with the victim's face. Stand away—gaze on from a distance.

"Semen found?" Dakota asked, as his eyes swept the living room. A clean ashtray on a corner table snared his eyes.

"Angela smoke?"

To answer, Bronc worked down a file he removed from under his arm.

"The killer smoke?"

"No cigarettes found either in the apartment or the victim's purse," Bronc said. He had already worked that angle to a dead end.

In all other respects, Dakota stood in the midst of a perfect apartment. Not a dirty glass in the sink nor a newspaper tossed carelessly about on the sofa. No clothes lying on the floor.

"No semen. Coroner reports evidence of vaginal penetration. Tears on the walls."

"Post-mortem?"

"Both."

Dakota tried to feel the young woman's presence in the room.

"So she was raped before?"

"Medical Examiner thinks so."

"Hair or skin traces come off the body?"

Dakota approached the bedroom door. There were no screams that night. No neighbors awakened. No noise reported by aroused sleepy faces. Angela had died quickly, all too quietly.

"Zip. Wait...we turned up a few strands of hair which are not the victim's."

Dakota stopped at the threshold. See through the eagle's eyes. Soar above—silent and deadly—and take in all that exists without the hindrance of emotion. The words from so many years ago flooded back into his head. Words a shaman had instilled in him on one of his visits to the Mescalero reservation as a teenager. He went there seeking information about his parents; instead he learned of his people and their ways. Now he must become that which sees all, but feels nothing for what he must do.

"Stand down, Lieutenant," Washington said, in a tone all business.

Dakota turned.

Washington's thin lips formed a straight line across his face.

"This isn't your case. You don't belong here. You're on official leave of absence," Washington continued.

"Cap, I asked him to take a..."

"Detective Broncowski, I'm addressing Lieutenant Blackwood."

Washington's tone had become formal to the extent of sounding militaristic.

"Sorry, sir. I'll be grabbing a smoke outside."

Bronc breezed past Washington and took in the night air out of shouting range of his two superiors.

Washington removed his hat and tucked it under his arm.

"I heard what came out of the mayor's office," Dakota said.

"Screw the mayor. You're on leave and I don't want you here."

"But..."

"No buts. Can't you understand, man? Your wife needs you now. Not tomorrow or the next day. She needs you now."

"I've got somebody with her."

"That's not what I'm saying, Dakota. She's real sick. You gotta be with her."

"This is my case."

For a long moment Dakota became lost in the words. He knew what he would find in the next room. He knew the signature of the Boulder Hill killer.

"The bastard slithered away two years ago," Dakota persisted.

"That's right, Dakota. That was two years ago. This case belongs to the first detective on the scene. Bronc's the primary. We reactivated the task force and I've got a dozen detectives assigned to work this case."

"I know it's him. You know he's back. I'm not going to let that sonofabitch get away again."

"This isn't personal. It's procedure. You're not involved in this case. Go home, Dakota. Take care of your wife. She needs you now."

"Ten minutes, Cap. Give me ten minutes. I just want to look over the scene."

Washington nodded reluctantly. Ten minutes could be all that was needed for this case to permanently take root inside your head. Ten minutes that could ultimately destroy a detective's life.

"Ten minutes, then you're out of here. Bronc can keep you current on their progress. You just be there for your wife."

Washington squared his cap on his balding head and marched out the door passing Bronc on his return back to the bedroom.

Dakota stared into the chamber of horrors.

"For what it's worth, I agree with the Cap," Bronc said, not looking directly at Dakota, but past him into the bedroom.

Dakota just stared; then he pressed on to where Angela Walker lived and died.

"Man, nothing's more important than the people you love. You're just going to have to let this one go."

"Where did she die?" Dakota pressed.

Bronc indicated the bed.

Dakota penetrated deeper into the room. He studied the bed then scanned the room for the fifth time.

"No. She died here," he said, pointing to the floor at the end of the bed.

Dakota positioned himself where he believed Angela must have been the moment the killer snapped the weapon wrapped around her neck.

"Look closely at the angle of the blood hitting the television screen. She had to have been right here."

"I don't know," Bronc said, "A wire severing the carotid could cause blood to spurt quite far."

"No. The blood would then be more widely scattered. I figure she was within a few feet of the screen standing on the side of the bed."

Dakota planted his feet and rubbernecked the room: over his left shoulder the bathroom door and directly to his flank was a closet.

"He took her from behind. Splatters indicate she was standing as opposed to sitting on the edge of the bed. He may have come out of the closet or the bathroom and surprised her. If she were standing at this angle here watching the screen, he could have slipped out of the closet without her realizing it."

"So, we don't rule out a home invasion then. But look at the blood on the bed."

"Aftermath bleeding. First he strangled her where she stood; then he arranged her on the bed. See how there seems to be a blood trail on this side of the bed leading back to the pillow."

Bronc withdrew a photograph of a bloody body from the folder.

"And the note?" Dakota asked, even without seeing the photograph.

"Pinned to her panties. Exactly like before."

"Okay. What about traces of blood outside the killing zone?"

"Under the toilet bowl rim. Killer used the head to clean up and then flushed everything into the sewers."

"Type?"

"Victim's."

"He stayed around..."

"Long enough to sexually molest the body and clean things up."

"Prints?"

"Nothing useful yet. The tech matched all but one latent to the victim."

"Really? Great. We may have a remembrance of the killer."

"Could be. Tech said it's a long shot. He shipped it off to the FBI Fingerprint Identification Division. They're going to need time."

"You think our guy got sloppy?"

"Nope. Probably find the print matches the girl's mother or father, or a friend who stopped by or even the cleaning lady."

"Cleaning lady?" Dakota asked.

"Walker used one of those twice a week cleaning services."

"The kind that comes to your house while you're at work."

"Exactly."

Dakota swallowed hard. That meant a potentially long list of people had access to the keys to Angela

Walker's apartment. The employees of the cleaning service, their friends and acquaintances all could have accessed her keys.

"You got anything on the cleaning service?

"Nothing yet. I've assigned three detectives to work that."

"You're collecting prints from relatives, friends and anyone else who might have access to this apartment?"

"In process."

Dakota stood over the bed. The pattern of the blood seemed to indicate that the killer dragged the body from the foot of the bed to the head. Why? Why not leave it where it drops?

"Where you going from here?"

"Back to where the girl worked. Maybe somebody either knew or had seen the creep with the victim. Angela may very well have let him in and spent time with him before... We're going to find out."

Dakota stared at the body outline on the bed.

"Let me see the picture," Dakota asked.

He noticed the peculiar placement of the victim's hands. Palms up. Why did the killer take the time to place the hands palms up in such an unnatural way? What concerning the hands distressed the killer?

"Time of death?"

"Thursday, sometime during the night. Coroner thinks midnight is around as close as we'll get."

"What size wire?"

"M.E. believes a gauge similar to that found in a hardware store for hanging pictures."

"You find the wire?"

"No. We've gone over every inch of the apartment, and I detailed a dozen uniforms to do a circular search within a half-mile radius of the complex. He had to have taken it with him when he left."

"I don't know. Why carry the weapon with him? Traces of blood embedded in the strands would be enough to nail him. Stick with that for right now. I'm guessing he dumped the weapon. We just have to figure out where."

"We? I'll work on it. How about you take it back to your wife. She needs you now."

Dakota didn't argue. His left brain was faltering, his right brain beginning to feel. He had seen enough. It was the Boulder Hill killer, and he was back under Dakota's skin. Even without seeing the infamous note, Dakota knew it for sure.

As a cinnabar sun faded into the desert, somewhere in Albuquerque, a killer cruised in search of his next victim. Another woman. Another innocent person was about to fall prey to this demented mistake of creation.

Laurianne was pacing in the den when Dakota arrived. Dakota detected that she'd been crying though she hid behind hastily applied makeup.

"Grace's asleep. She tried some soup, but it came back up. You want me to stay?"

"No. Thanks for coming, Laurianne."

"I understand. I'll stay if you need me. Cole has a meeting that's going to run until after nine, anyway."

Dakota took Laurianne's hands into his.

"No. You've done so much already. I think I'll take the girls out for a treat as long as Grace's asleep."

Laurianne hugged Dakota, trying to find words that might somehow help. The pain of witnessing her sister-in-law's slow deterioration was growing too great for her to hold inside. She wanted to scream, to hit something—anything. But she couldn't. Neither Grace nor Dakota would talk to her—tell her the real prognosis.

Were they hoping to spare her? Silence is no way to spare someone. Laurianne witnessed Grace's suffering first hand, even though Grace tried to keep it beneath the surface. And there was no way to compare witnessing the ravages of cancer versus hearing about it. This time the cancer was worse. Grace failed to hide that fact. The pain was sucking all the fight out of her.

"I watched the news conference yesterday...."Laurianne said, collecting up her purse and sweater and wiping away the tear that worked its way out of her eye.

"You didn't say anything to Grace about it?" Dakota asked.

"No. She doesn't know then?"

"I haven't told her. She's too sick."

"I didn't think I should bring it up. She didn't say anything about it, either. Are you going to tell her?"

"Not right now. When she's better."

"What are you going to do?"

"I don't know...."

"Oh, I washed the girls' things and folded them. They're laid out on the dryer. I would have put them away, but Lauryn gets upset when I do that. She insists it's her job."

Dakota walked Laurianne to the front door, opening it without realizing it. A brisk wind slapped across his face.

"Looks like we may get some rain."

"Dakota, I want you to know we're here for you. Whatever you or Grace need. Cole and I are here."

"Thanks Laurianne, I know. I don't think I could handle this without your help."

Laurianne pecked Dakota on the cheek and then scurried down the stairs before he could see her tears. She ordered herself a hundred times not to cry in front of them. Grace was like a rock; now Laurianne also had to be.

Grace slept most of the next day, awakening in the evening. This time she kept down a bowl of clear chicken broth. A small but meaningful triumph. Dakota had heated it out of a can.

Then, with Lauryn and Heather nestled in their beds, Dakota settled beside Grace while she slept. The little that remained of her natural hair left blotches of red on the pillow. Occasionally, an unrestrained moan slipped out. Dakota responded by smoothing his hand over her hand to let her know he was there.

Dakota stared at the dying glow of the television screen he had switched off shortly before the beginning of the evening news. He realized his mind had been adrift for the past hour. He knew if there were any real progress in the Boulder Hill case, Bronc would have called him before the press got wind of it.

Dakota's mind drifted aimlessly. Only one thing mattered right now. Unconsciously, his hand slid gently along Grace's side. Nothing else could usurp his responsibility to her.

The doctors had always given it to them straight about Grace's condition. This time though, it was painfully straight. She was losing. Even a more aggressive treatment had failed to arrest the cancer's spread. This time the cancer progressed virulently, geometrically, Dakota thought, advancing like a brush fire more quickly than they had anticipated. Like an invisible predator, it crept through her—seizing vital organs as hostages. Now it threatened them with death....

Dakota jolted up in bed. Exhaustion wormed its way into every cell in his body. Yet when he closed his eyes, thoughts of Grace stomped about, pulling him out of sleep. And sleep was the one thing he wished for most; the one thing remaining the furthest from his reach.

Switching off the night light beside the bed, Dakota curled his body to meld with Grace's and covered her arm with his. Her skin was cool to the touch. She never felt his gentle kiss upon her neck.

Washington waved Dakota in the moment he appeared in the corridor outside the glass-paneled conference room. Bronc, Cal Sturges and Pete Rodman were sitting with their backs to Dakota and each turned at his approach. The round table discussion of the Walker case started at eight and it was now close to eleven. Washington left Dakota with an open invitation. He was very glad to see Dakota's arrival.

Agent Rodman rose from his chair, the only stranger in the room.

"Special Agent Pete Rodman," he said, extending a hand that had never seen the rigors of toil.

Dakota guessed Rodman to be an ivy-league graduate, whose father had strong political connections, which probably turned out to be determining factor in Rodman's position with the Bureau.

"Blackwood," was all Dakota said. Dakota detected a flash of disdain when he locked onto Rodman's eyes. The white man never could hide their contempt. No one ever told them contempt appears in the eyes long before the mouth opens.

"Agent Rodman's assigned temporarily to assist in the Walker investigation," Washington said. He, too, noticed an air of uneasiness between the two men.

Bronc nodded to Dakota but said nothing. The detective's face wore the strain of the Walker case all over it. Inadequate rest, pisspoor diet, and a half million people expecting him to find the killer before he killed again. Bronc had already tightened his belt another notch. He was the man under the gun. Turn leads into suspects and suspects into a solid arrest, he told himself a hundred times a day. And he had to do it yesterday. Tomorrow could be too late for the Boulder Hill killer's next victim.

"I know this is terribly short notice and I know the timing is shit, but Dakota could you prepare a full briefing for the task force on the Boulder Hill killer?" Washington asked.

"Sure. I just need a place to set up the files."

Cal stepped in to seize a pause that had filled the room.

"Lieutenant Blackwood, Mayor Bradley fully understands the gravity of your situation, and he would never ask this...."

"You told me we weren't going to open this up here," Washington said, rising out of his chair to cut Sturges off.

The vein in Washington's forehead pulsed with anger and his face turned ruddy.

"Damnit, Vance, this is serious," Cal quickly countered, rising slightly out of his chair to meet Washington over the table.

Bronc retreated out of the two men's line of fire. Rodman settled back in his chair and worked his fingernails with his thumb.

"We need to talk about his."

"Nobody's telling me how I run this department."

"These are grave circumstances. The clock is running, and we can't let this situation get out of control," Cal said, turning first to Bronc as if to apologize, then shifting his eyes over to Dakota, "we wouldn't be asking if we didn't feel it absolutely necessary."

"You don't have to tell us about the Boulder Hill killer. We've got four dead people from him. You think that isn't of the utmost importance on our minds!"

Washington was finished. He dropped his girth back into his chair. Sturges wanted him to react without thinking. Pressure was Sturges's strong suit. He had a knack for unearthing a person's hot button and then pressing the hell out of it until he got steam.

But Washington realized that and regained his composure, refusing to let the college boy manipulate him. His time would come; he just had to be patient. College boy over there was going to make a mistake and when he did, Washington would squash him like the bug that he was.

"Dakota, you're officially on leave of absence, and that's the way it stays. But we would like you to prepare a full briefing to update the task force on exactly what turned up on the three previous killings."

Cal shot Washington a cold glare.

"And that's it. You're not coming off leave."

Everyone in the conference room allowed the ensuing moment of silence to sweep the air clear of tension.

Sturges threw up his hands in an exaggerated gesture of surrender.

"Bronc, what's the latest?" Dakota asked.

"No substantial progress. We're still waiting on prints. We've questioned family, neighbors and co-workers. We've currently cleared a list of her acquaintances and anyone she was known to have socialized with. We're still basically in the middle of nowhere with Angela's murder."

"What about Walker's car?" Rodman asked.

"Clean—sitting in her parking space."

"Are there formal visitor parking spaces designated at the building?" Rodman pursued.

"We're compiling a list of the cars known to have been in the parking lot that Thursday, but it's slow going. Other than that, there are no formal visitor parking spaces identified at the complex. Each apartment is assigned a space and there are six extra spaces at either end of the lot for open parking."

"When do I brief?" Dakota asked.

"When can you be ready?" Washington pressed.

"Captain Washington," Rodman injected, "perhaps investigating the Walker case independent of the previous killings might prevent investigators from channeling their efforts into areas that were previously fruitless."

"What are you saying?" Bronc asked, with a rising glint of anger.

"Just that the previous investigation failed to produce the killer and briefing the men on the earlier cases might precondition them into following the same blind alleys taken two years ago."

"Dakota?" Washington said, turning from Rodman as if his statement lacked merit. This was exactly what Washington wanted to avoid—a hot shot, green agent a year of out Quantico with his own personal agenda. The Bureau must have decided to let the kid get his feet wet by stepping all over the locals.

"Tomorrow, eight A.M.," Dakota said.

"Great. Use the old third floor interrogation room to set up. Work with Bronc on anything you need. And Dakota, I'm serious, after the briefing you're out of this."

Cal just shook his head, muttering innuendoes about the mayor expecting Dakota to take charge of the task force.

Washington had already tuned out the mayor's aide.

The fact that someone else had the task of dealing with the mayor's office relieved Bronc. His stomach burned almost constantly and Bronc knew he'd have an ulcer before this investigation reached an end. Sturges was particularly adept at getting under people's skin. Maybe that's why the mayor assigned Cal the task of liaison with the police.

As the meeting adjourned, Rodman remained behind until only he and Bronc were left in the conference room. Standing side by side they resembled Laurel and Hardy. Bronc carried twice Rodman's girth.

Bronc busied himself returning reports and notes back into their proper folders.

"That guy Blackwood, he any good?" Rodman inquired, trying to downplay the question.

Bronc shot him a look. His eyes were answer enough.

"He Navajo?"

"Apache, Mescalero Apache."

"Oh," Rodman said, with more than just casual surprise.

Laurianne surprised Grace when she entered with a tray of tea and toast in the morning. But Grace asked no questions as to why Dakota had left.

Laurianne said nothing and as a matter of fact, avoided Grace's questions about what was happening in the news. The tip-off, however, came when Laurianne said that Dakota had taken the daily newspaper with him. Dakota never spent more than ten minutes with the paper. He scanned it over the breakfast table and then forgot about it.

"There's more tea if you're up to it," Laurianne said, as she sat in the chair beside the bed.

Grace consumed half her toast in small bites and sipped her tepid tea. She left the rest, fearing what she already ate would force its way back up.

"Girls got off to school without a hitch. How are you feeling?"

"Better. Not back to normal, but better."

"Have you thought...about what I said?"

"You mean Chimayo?"

"Yes. If you're up to it...I'll drive you..."

Grace said nothing, gazing off at the blue sky outside instead.

"Please."

"When?"

"Sooner the better. Right now's a perfect time. If you're up to it."

"Dakota wouldn't like... He's not real big..."

"That's why now is perfect. Dakota said he wouldn't be back for a while. We'd have enough time."

Grace detected the little glimmers of hope in Laurianne's emerald eyes. They were almost pleading.

"What about the girls?"

"We'd be back hours before the girls get out of school."

"I don't know."

"Please."

"Okay. It can't hurt."

"Great. I'll get your clothes."

Laurianne vaulted out of the chair and halfway to the closet.

"I don't know what we'd do without you."

"I'm here for you and Dakota. Anything you need, you just ask. Cole is ready to help out in any way he can."

"I don't know what's going to..."

"Grace, you just keep trying," Laurianne broke in. She avoided the words. Saying them might make them come true. She had enough keeping her awake at night.

"The girls are going to need you...to handle the changes in their lives...feminine times," Grace said. A sense of certainty rose in the way she spoke.

"Grace, you beat this thing before. You're going to be here for a long time. You're going to be here when Heather gets married."

Grace said nothing, staring out the window at the cloudless sky.

"I've always loved this place. Most people hate the desert, but I've always loved it here."

Laurianne swallowed with difficulty. *Don't talk like that*, she thought. Grace turned back from the window and centered her gaze directly on Laurianne.

"Laurianne, I know."

"Know what?"

Laurianne's innocent response failed to hide the truth. Grace could see it in Laurianne's nervous manner.

"I know why Dakota isn't here."

Laurianne hesitated for a long moment, keeping her back to her. She had to assess in that second whether Grace actually knew, or whether she was fishing. Dakota had insisted Laurianne say nothing.

"How did you find out?"

"Cable news. Dakota was out yesterday afternoon and I was flipping through the channels. It made the national news. He's back, isn't he?"

Laurianne held a floral print dress up for Grace's approval. Then she moved closer to the bed. She stared into Grace's teacup, while absently refilling it.

"You should try to drink more tea. The doctor said to pump you full of liquids. Dakota asked me not to say anything. He doesn't want you to know."

"Oh God. Are they sure? Are they certain it's the same?"

"Dakota said there was no mistake. The Boulder Hill killer is back working the city."

"Dakota's downtown, isn't he?"

"They asked him in for a few hours. That's why he left so early."

"Who's handling the case? Dunwoody?"

"Broncowski."

"Bronc. By all rights that case should be Dakota's."

"I know."

"God, why did he have to come back. Why is he killing again? I don't know if Dakota can handle the stress right now."

"Grace, what can I do to help? Tell me how to help you and Dakota. I'll do anything."

Grace took Laurianne's hand, clutching it so tightly that she mashed Laurianne's fingertips together.

"Just be here. Just be here to help Dakota take care of the girls. He can't do it alone. Not now. Not with what's happening out there."

"I will."

After helping Grace dress and make her way down the stairs, Laurianne settled Grace in the Jeep Cherokee. Within the hour, they were heading north out of Albuquerque.

Twelve men filed into the third-floor interrogation room. Twelve men whose jobs it were to sift through people's lives hoping to learn the identity of their murderers. Twelve men, detectives from Homicide, Violent Crimes, Vice, and both the Bernalillo County and Sandoval County Sheriff's Departments, sat before a four-foot by eight-foot corkboard filled with photographs, crime scene sketches and scribbled notes. One man killed the four people whose photographs were pinned on the board. Dakota was certain of it.

The usual morbid humor and detective banter fell silent the moment Dakota entered the room, which had now become the Boulder Hill Killer Task Force Command Center.

Dakota realized as he prepared for this briefing that everything he knew about the killer and his victims came flooding back into his head. Details he had meticulously collected two years ago returned in vivid color. He stared at the photographs with his back to the detectives for a long moment.

"Sheila Davis literally had her neck sliced in two," he started, coming about to face the task force, "the killer wrapped the wire so tightly that she never had a chance to scream. A scream that might have saved her life."

Dakota leveled his pointer at a stunning, twenty-three-year-old brunette with sparkling eyes and a smile so inviting that only a psychopath could bring violence against her. A crime scene photograph pinned next to her head shot displayed the body in the position police found it with a scribbled note pinned to her panties. Black blood saturated the pillow and sheets beneath her.

"The note pinned to her panties," he continued while pointing to scribbled writing that read: MERRY CHRISTMAS ELLIE, "is the one common element between the first victim found two years ago and Angela Walker."

Pete Rodman, sitting to Bronc's left, already slid back in his chair as if Dakota's dissertation bored him. As Rodman scanned the room, he considered the collective amount of time being wasted. This irritated the agent, and he made a mental note to add that to his report.

"This note has never been released to the public. Only the Boulder Hill killer and us are aware of its existence. Notice the handwriting—though crude and jagged, both notes match stroke for stroke. There is no doubt in my mind the Boulder Hill killer's back."

Bronc lifted a finger.

"Were you ever able to attach any meaning to the note?" he asked.

"Psychiatrist Sheldon Cinderman believes our killer is acting out his rage toward a person whose name is most likely Ellie."

"You're saying the killer believes he's actually killing someone named Ellie?" Rodman asked.

"Cinderman's saying that. And I, for the most part, concur. The problem is: Ellie could be short for Ellen or Eleanor. Furthermore, this Ellie could be the killer's mother, lover, wife, object of his perverted desires, or even a nonexistent fantasy character. If our killer is a psychopath, Ellie may very well exist only in his fantasy world. Or it could be a person in his real world but with a different name. The killer may have transferred the name Ellie to that person as a way of hiding his true connection."

"Did anyone ever connect a previous homicide where the victim's name is Ellie?" Rodman pursued in such a way that it hinted at condescension and caught stares from the other task force detectives.

"Two years ago we searched the homicide files from five states trying to locate this Ellie."

"Then you're saying she probably isn't a victim?"

"We just don't know."

Dakota shifted his pointer to the next photograph along the top row, ignoring Rodman's shrug that he caught out the corner of his eye.

"This was Janet Hegler. Victim number two. Her appearance is starkly different from the killer's first victim: lighter hair, smaller face with dark eyes. While we've concluded he picks his victims based on some factor other than physical, we, nonetheless, remain confident these two women had something in common. Whatever these two women shared had attracted the killer's attention. We're still trying to determine exactly what that is."

"Did the victims know each other?" a detective asked.

"No, as far as we've been able to tell."

"And you figure the link between those two victims two years ago is the same as for his latest killing?"

"Can't know for sure. But I was convinced then, and I still believe there was a reason these two women were singled out. He stalked them and gained their trust; probably just long enough to get them alone."

Dakota stopped for a moment, needing to refer to a set of notes he had scribbled on a legal pad the previous night. Now looking at them, he scratched his head over their meaning.

"You're saying then you believe beyond any doubt he is going to kill again," Rodman said, in what had become his grating way.

Dakota looked up, forgetting about his notes.

"Notice the similarities between Sheila Davis, the first victim in 1995, and Angela Walker. Yeah, he's going to kill again. And he's also going after a woman with the same general appearance as his second victim in '95: dark hair, smaller than himself and most likely shy and timid. That's all we could determine about Janet Hegler."

Dakota stopped. Something in the back of his mind struggled to get to the front. Something important about Janet Hegler was drifting below the surface. In that moment, he scribbled a note to review her file again.

Laurianne continued north out of Santa Fe. The car had been quiet for the past thirty minutes as Grace took in the rock formations rising up on their left. Strawberry cactus and pinions colored the otherwise lifeless landscape of grama grass, cholla and sand.

Grace followed the moving landscape with intense interest. Nothing anymore seemed insignificant in her life. She needed to take it all in before.... She never understood why she came to this place. Wisconsin was a different world compared to New Mexico. She just knew that once she did, she would never leave.

Thirty minutes outside of Santa Fe, Laurianne left the highway and followed the signs to the Sanctuaria de Chimayo. A place of miracles. A place where God would hear their prayers.

Laurianne drifted to a stop beside a battered old pickup. A handful of cars spread themselves across the expanse of the sand parking lot using rotted timbers to mark its border. The women waited until the dust cloud settled before leaving the car. With Laurianne's aid, Grace walked slowly through the hand-carved wooden gates into the green courtyard of the Spanish-Pueblo architecture shrine. The settlers to the area erected the small church in 1816 over sands they believed to possess miraculous healing powers. Grace had come to ask for a miracle.

A splintered wooden cross set in a sandstone block welcomed visitors into the heart of the courtyard. A courtyard where grave stones rose out of the sand on either side of the cobbled walkway.

Ahead, a crippled elderly woman with a horribly disfigured spine hidden beneath a black dress and shawl hobbled along at the arm of a fiftyish Indian man. She had just finished asking for her miracle. All races of people were welcome in this place. God does not discriminate.

Laurianne slowed, stopping Grace, while they their turn to enter this holy place. The low narrow chapel doors only allowed a single person to pass through the threshold at a time. Both women had to bow slightly as they entered. Only strands of bright midday sun found its way into the rear of the church once the doors closed.

Flickering rows of candles provided a sallow, dim light to illuminate the few pews that populated the rear third of the building. A single bright shaft of dusty light poured in through the roof opening to splay upon the altar and over a hole left in the floor intentionally to allow the faithful to touch the sand. There, it was said, those who truly believe could receive the graces of the sacred ground on which this place had been erected.

Laurianne settled into a retral pew, while Grace made the journey to the altar. Ahead of Grace, a women drew herself back to her feet, crossed herself twice and backed out of the way to allow Grace her time.

On the altar, a golden chalice and crucifix threw off the sunlight. There were no sounds in this house of God. No emanations to distract the Almighty from attending to the cries of His faithful; a spattering of which sat in the solitude of this holy place. Most of them were elderly and the crippled and they all sought the same from their Creator.

A handful of tourists stood off to the side, admiring the architecture and reading the placards that described the church's history. However, this was not a place for pictures or tours. Only the most callous and unfeeling would disrupt the sanctity of this house with such intrusions as flash photography, though there were no signs posted forbidding it.

Grace's presence seemed a stark contradiction to the others kneeling before the altar—she was too young and too vital to be in this place. She crossed herself thrice as she knelt before the altar screen painted in southwestern reds and browns.

In the low light, Laurianne slid to her knees, crossed herself thrice and began to pray. Let Him hear her voice, too. He could never deny them. Not after this.

Grace's eyes went to the crucifix suspended over the altar, and while touching the place meant to deliver miracles, she begged God not to turn His back on her. Her dry, cracked lips barely moved as she prayed with all her strength and faith. To receive a miracle, one had only to believe in them with all their heart.

To the right of the altar screen, discarded crutches and braces cluttered the wall in testament of this sacred land's power. A miracle had allowed the crippled to walk. Could another kill a demon raging inside?

Laurianne battled down tears fighting to erupt. Losing her fight, she fled—knowing she must leave this place because her thoughts had turned bitter. Feelings God would surely punish her for.

Minutes later, Grace emerged, squinting against the bright sun, wiping away the tears that came not from discomfort but from desperation.

Dakota neared the end of his briefing. He had emptied his brain of all his knowledge concerning the Boulder Hill killer. Yet in doing so, no one in the room felt any great sense of revelation that might help them find a killer. Now they all knew much more about the person called the Boulder Hill killer. But no one could say what he looked like, what his name was, or any marks that might aid in identification. No one knew enough to stop him from killing again.

"The FBI Behavioral Unit's profile makes our guy out to be five-six to five-ten with a slim build. Janet Hegler, victim number two, was five-three."

"Your reports two years ago stated the killer was sexually assaulting the women both before and after he killed them. So, if the killings are somehow sexual, why was the third victim two years ago male?" a detective on the end asked, scratching along his neck with his pencil.

"Good question. But look again at the medical examiner's report on the third victim: Steven Ashecroft. His genitals were mutilated post mortem. Another sexual assault."

"Any trappings of a Satanic ritual left behind at the scene? Those freaks use sexual mutilation as a way of keeping their followers in line."

"None found. As a matter of fact, none of the crime scenes turned up anything to indicate cult activity. And since we never uncovered any evidence of activity outside the norm for Ashecroft, we ruled out a ritual execution."

"Isn't it possible the man's murder might have been a copy cat?" another detective asked, rising out of his chair to get a better look at Ashecroft's photographs on the board.

"The signature by this time is undeniable. Notice how he repositioned the body in the room. Ashecroft died near the front door, possibly trying desperately to escape. The killer stabbed him four times in the back and chest. Yet the killer hauled the body back to the couch. Notice the constellation of stab wounds about the upper torso. Gentlemen, you are looking at the release of an intense rage. Yet the key remains in the body's display. Especially the hands. He displayed all three victims in exactly the same manner. In every case, he never abandoned the bodies where they dropped. Less than two months after Janet was found, we turned up Steven Ashecroft, a mild-mannered man with no apparent link to either of the two women."

"Why would the killer turn the hands in such an unnatural way?" a detective in the back row asked.

"Behavioral Unit speculates it's a sign of supplication."

"Supplication?"

"The killer might have wanted the victims to plead for their lives. When they didn't, either because he took them by surprise, or they refused; he posed them in supplication after he killed them."

"Suppose our killer's real target was this Ashecroft. Maybe they were gay lovers and the relationship soured. So he kills the women in order to make it more difficult for us to find a link between the killer and the victim. Maybe, in reality, there is no link between these three people," another detective said.

"Always a possibility. But from what we could extract from our victims' background, none of them were victims of random selection. They were selected, stalked, approached, lulled into believing they were safe, then brutally executed."

"Could there be more than just those three victims?" another detective asked.

"Most certainly. There could have been killings before Sheila Davis. We can only surmise that she was the first, since we haven't been able to match any other slayings to this particular killer's signature."

"So, we're looking for a lunatic. He shouldn't be difficult to spot."

"On the outside, our killer is anything but insane. He coolly and calmly plans out each murder. And he follows a ritual. You're looking for a man who appears and acts normal in every way. He could be your neighbor; the one you talk to over the fence. Or your barber."

"I have a woman barber," a detective injected, to lighten the moment.

"You'll never discern by appearance or actions that he's the killer."

"Where do we go from here?" Bronc asked.

Dakota's briefing offered up a whole lot of background, but very little useful information for the Walker investigation. When Dakota finished, the men sat in a hush, all studying the pictures on the corkboard. The feeling spreading from man to man was that it would take an army of fifty to crack this case. Every detective knew they had almost nothing to work with.

"Let's start with the time frame. The two-year lag between slayings may mean something. Let's get someone on the database and pull the names of all parolees recently released who served less than two years. Maybe our guy was doing time and just hit the streets. We need three of you to start working the psychiatric angle. Check with the psych wards to see if anyone who had been under inpatient care has recently been released."

"This is a significant cost in manpower," Agent Rodman remarked.

"Look for anyone who might have entered a treatment program as an inpatient or outpatient shortly after the Ashecroft murder. Talk to every psychiatrist in the state. Our guy may have been trying to get help and his doctor may have recently retired, dropped him as a patient, or died through either natural causes or an accident," Dakota said.

Their killer consistently sanitized the crime scene of incriminating evidence. A logically thinking psychopath was the toughest killer to track. They couldn't let the bodies pile up while they waited for him to make a mistake. And they all knew one thing without doubt: the killer had started the clock...and was intent on killing again.

6

Dakota sat behind the steering wheel of his Suburban reflecting on what he had gleaned from his two-year-old serial killer investigation. He felt something swirling out of reach inside his head, something he had neglected to give Bronc at the briefing, which was now three days in the past.

The clock was ticking—*death comes in threes.*

Right now he needed answers. He flipped through the notebook he had used in the original Boulder Hill killer investigation. There was so much there—no detail had been omitted or overlooked. Yet, in that mountain of jumbled information, Dakota was certain something was buried that might help narrow the search.

Dakota looked up when sounds of movement reached his ears. Parishioners began to emerge through the doors of the San Felipe de Neri Roman Catholic Church. He had parked down the street, in a clearly marked no parking zone, in such a way as to keep one eye on the doors.

Twin spires jutted high atop the adobe structure, flanking the roof peak where a twelve-foot cross cut a welcoming sign against the azure sky. From a distance, there could be no question as to the building's intent. A total of six towering crosses once greeted

weary travelers when the church was originally
erected in 1706. The very sight of the spires warmed
the hearts of those brave enough to cross the desolate and once forbidding desert. Welcome to the
peace and sanctity of this house of God was etched
against a once arid plain.

The adobe wall still surrounding this monument
to the Almighty no longer wore gates that might bar
those who seek her serenity. All were welcome here.
Even those who no longer believed.

Grace and the girls emerged through the massive
church doors amidst the other worshippers. Dakota
quickly stuffed papers back into his case and left the
car. Grace descended the stairs, weak and uncertain,
steadied by Lauryn's clinging hand. Over the past few
days, Grace's eyes had become dull and lifeless; the
sparkle Dakota had seen for all their married life had
fled. He feared gone forever.

Ill as she was, Grace insisted she attend mass
with the girls. And she insisted they drive into Old
Town Albuquerque to attend this centuries-old holy
place. It filled a need. But right now, it was too much
for Dakota to handle.

Dakota reached Grace as she stood at the bottom
of the steps waiting to speak with the priest, who
warmly shook hands with well-wishing parishioners.

"Morning, Father," Dakota said, feeling stilted
and guilty, as if he had just been caught ditching
mass the way he and Cole had done as teens twenty
years ago.

The priest took both Grace's hands in his, offer-
ing her cold flesh his warmth. He wished he had more
to offer her. His eyes searched hers as if he could
read the pain in her soul. His pleasant smile sought
to plant hope in her heart and it beamed with the
kind of contentment every young priest takes with
him from the seminary.

"I'm so glad you could make mass today, Mrs.
Blackwood. Keep God close to you through these dif-

ficult times. Your lovely daughters are getting bigger than ever."

The priest patted Lauryn on the head, which induced her to immediately shy away; resentful of being attended to as if she were a child. She tightened her grip on her mother's arm, hoping that might induce her to continue on.

Grace said nothing, though her eyes were crying out for more than a cleric's sympathy. Then she clutched Dakota's arm as if she were about to falter.

"You okay?" Dakota whispered, as they threaded through the crowd mingling about to greet the sandy-haired, cheerful cleric. He exuded such pleasure in doing the Lord's work—something that angered Dakota inside. There was no pleasure in police work. No pleasure in trying to hunt down a killer before he can kill again. No pleasure in watching someone you love being stripped of her life and vitality. It was easy to do the Lord's work—much more difficult to deal with the Lord's mistakes. Dakota knew something else was making him so angry inside.

"Maybe next week?" Grace asked softly as he settled her into the passenger seat. He kissed her before closing her door.

Dakota knew what she meant, but refused to answer.

Before returning home, Dakota detoured along the river to take in the cottonwoods with their leaves turning to shades of autumn gold.

Four more days passed—the investigation into Angela's death moved torturously slow. A hundred leads had been followed up, statements taken from every person even remotely connected to Angela and still the police were no closer to the killer than Dakota had been two years ago. And this investigation forged on without Dakota's expertise.

Bronc bowed beneath the pressure from everyone above him in the department. He skipped meals and sleep. His stomach burned and churned constantly. Aspirins and antacids became between meal snacks. He tightened his belt another notch. He dreaded the daily briefings with the captain. The chore only illuminated his shortcomings.

On a near daily basis, the media berated the task force in the papers and on the television for their lack of progress. That unsavory attention translated into heat from the mayor's office that funneled right onto the head of Captain Washington. Mayor Bradley pushed for outside consultants to be brought in. Washington countered with strong evidence that outsiders now would only bog down the task force. Not a day went by without someone from the mayor's office inquiring about Blackwood's status. Why couldn't he be brought in? they insisted.

As each day passed without a suspect, the city of Albuquerque grew more tense, waiting for the next victim to bob to the surface. After-hours business felt the shift the most. Nightclubs and bars saw fewer and fewer patrons as the days dragged on.

The bastard was out there, moving amongst the innocent and the unsuspecting...stalking someone...planning his next murder.

The public's appetite for information grew insatiable. They devoured file footage from the earlier investigations and relived the gruesome sights of bodies being uncovered by police. Count them—three victims in late 1995 were linked to the Boulder Hill killer. When task force detectives had nothing to offer, the media re-aired old footage again and speculated.

Ratings at KGGM soared as Lisa Roberts pasted image after image and ream after ream of information across the screen. Her fascination with the killer bordered on obsession. Her vividly detailed accounts of the investigation infected viewers. A columnist at the Albuquerque Tribune, eager to jump on the bandwagon, had labeled Roberts the expert; citing her almost continual in-depth and cohesive reporting. Roberts loved the attention and accepted her title and newfound fame with more than just a touch of grace.

Dakota spent most of his days helping Grace live from one day to the next. He worked with her daily to fight that desire to give up. The radiation treatments were zapping the life out of her and still the cancer grew instead of shrank. It was fighting like the devil to claim her soul.

The doctors spewed confidence at every turn, using as much toxin as they could risk, in hopes of killing the monster inflicting Grace's almost continual pain. But for all her struggle and suffering, Grace was losing her battle.

On Thursday, Dakota left Grace sleeping, albeit lightly, under the care of Laurianne and reported to headquarters at the request of Captain Washington. Vance's request had been cryptic and curt; something Dakota recognized immediately as trouble. The last thing Dakota wanted was to leave Grace, but the edge in Washington's voice indicated an urgency seldom expressed by his captain.

When Dakota arrived, Washington, Sturges and Rodman were in the conference room, sitting across from Detective Broncowski. But this time a new face had been added—that of Lisa Roberts. Lisa's presence struck an uneasy chord in Dakota. Never would a single reporter become privy to confidential departmental information.

There was something else wrong. Something Dakota saw in Lisa's searching eyes when she turned to him. Their eyes held for a long moment. These were not the sparkling eyes of an ambitious, self-confident news reporter. They seemed more the eyes of a frightened child.

"Thanks for coming, Dakota. We've got a big problem."

Dakota took the chair beside Lisa. A scrawled note encased in plastic on the center of the table snared his attention. The writing style matched, stroke for stroke, the previous notes.

"It appeared at the station...with my name on it. I don't know why the killer singled me out," Lisa said.

Dakota took the note and read it aloud.

> *Don't you want to play anymore, Lieutenant Blackwood?*
>
> *I can't believe you quit so easily. Yes, lieutenant, killing's a game and anyone can play—but only the best can win. Are you going to let me win? Too bad....*
>
> *The clock's running...tick...tick...tick.*

"Bradley wants you off leave and back on the Boulder Hill case," Cal said, exercising an authority borrowed from the mayor's office.

Dakota looked to Washington.

"He's one sick freak," Washington said, when no other words seemed appropriate. His eyes slid away from Dakota's as if to say there was nothing he could do.

"I'm really getting nervous. This creep is using me as a go-between. It's scaring me to death now. What if..."Lisa dared not finish her thought.

Dakota stared blankly at the note for a long moment. This squarely contradicted the way the Boulder Hill killer had played the game two years ago. Why the change? And why had he homed in on Dakota? Without so much as a clue, the killer struck down three people. Everyone expected him to act exactly the same way this time. But for some reason he changed tactics. He had established a physical and psychological link with an authority figure. As a result, Lisa might very well be in danger. This could be a new taunt. The killer may have named his next victim and was now intent on proving that he could still kill without being stopped. Or was it his intention to use Roberts as a way for the police to catch him?

Numerous psychiatrists had stated for the record, and FBI profiles concurred, that most serial killers had an inner desire to be caught—to have the authorities end their reign of terror because they themselves are incapable of ending it. Was this the killer's way of accomplishing this? Did he want Dakota to catch him when he tried to kill Lisa? Or was his plan to succeed in killing Lisa and then be captured?

"He's attained a level of confidence where he feels safe," Dakota said, staring at the words.

"And that means?"

"He's evolving his killing methods. He knows what he's doing is preventing us from hunting him down. It's his way of saying, 'you'll never stop me unless I let you.'"

Dakota avoided looking into Lisa's eyes.

"We'll assign men to you around the clock, Miss Roberts, and we'll monitor your phone, just in case he tries to contact you."

Lisa trembled at the thought. The killer might try to speak to her? Has the killer already contacted her and she failed to realize it. Had she become the mouse in this sick game?

"What about the note?" Lisa asked.

"For right now, Detective Broncowski stays as primary and Blackwood's officially on leave of absence."

Cal rose out of his seat at Washington's words.

"Maybe I'm not making myself clear here. The mayor is sensitive to Dakota's situation at home; we all are. But we've got a city with a half million people to think about. You put Dakota back on this investigation."

"I'm running this police force and Dakota's out of this."

Cal stormed out of the conference room.

Washington stood up then sat back down heavily.

"How did the note arrive?" Dakota queried.

"Nobody knows. The front desk security guard turned away for a moment and when he came back, the envelope was sitting there in front of him. The lobby was crowded at the time with a school tour group cluttering up the main foyer. For all we know, it could have been left by one of the adults on the tour," Lisa said. Her voice had become rock steady; like the Lisa people saw on the nightly news. Her eyes, however, searched Dakota's.

Less than two hours after the meeting's conclusion, Dakota was called back in to head up the task force in the Boulder Hill killer case. A press conference was scheduled in time to make the six o'clock news. Now, Dakota had to tell Grace before it became public knowledge.

Grace sat up in bed, flanked by the girls on either side while Dakota cleared away an untouched bowl of soup. She had said nothing since Dakota told her the news. A tear blurred her vision while she watched the television screen.

Lauryn, on the other hand, took the news in stride. All she said in response was that she'd help out by doing the dinner dishes. Heather was excited to see her daddy on TV, but had no real grasp of what the announcement meant.

"Time for bed, girls. I've already let you stay up later than I should," Dakota said, leading the girls away from Grace after their hugs and goodnight kisses.

At the door, Lauryn hugged Dakota for a long moment and then without saying a word, kissed him on the cheek and led Heather off to bed.

"What does that mean?" Grace asked. They were alone in the dark and laying front to back under the covers.

"It's window dressing. We're hoping it will have an impact on the killer. I'll be putting in a few hours a day with the task force and will be seen in a few routine press conferences, but the rest of the time I'll be here for you."

The silence grew thick in the air.

"Dakota, what does it really mean?" Grace persisted, while she stroked the back of his hand. It was difficult to believe the same hand that made her feel so good could hold onto Heather's little fingers with a tenderness that made her feel secure, and at the same time could close on the trigger of a gun.

"The Boulder Hill killer delivered a note to Lisa Roberts at the television station. He's turning this into some sick game. He wants me personally to come after him."

Just saying the words filled Dakota with a deep foreboding. Why him? Why was the killer so interested in him? His was the only name mentioned on that note. What was the real intent in sucking him into the investigation? Did Dakota know something? Again, a dark shadow rolled over in his mind. Something from two years ago?

"Is the task force making any progress?"

Grace's question stole away his thoughts. The shadow vanished.

"Nothing. We're no better off now than we were two years ago."

"Can Bronc handle it?"

"Can anybody?"

"He's going to kill again. Like he did two years ago."

"That's about the only certainty we have right now. We just don't have a clue as to who his next victim is likely to be."

"If anyone could find him, it's you..." Grace said, her voice falling off into a deep chasm of fatigue.

Neither talked. Finally, Grace fell off to sleep.

Both slept fitfully—Grace from the pain of a monster clawing inside her, and Dakota from the nagging notion that he already had what he needed to identify the monster outside him.

Laurianne took a leave of absence from her job. She availed herself to Dakota at a moment's notice, assuring him she would care for Grace in his absence, as his investigation demanded it. Cole had given himself flexibility in his position at the bank, as did most other vice-presidents, and offered to be there to help out in whatever way he could. Their presence gave Dakota a chance to clear his head of his problems at home, though he could never really put Grace out of his mind, and to focus his attention on what he hoped might help him—the Angela Walker crime scene.

Except for the body, not one thing had been touched in the apartment where Angela Walker died. And the body had been removed from the scene now more than two weeks ago. Dakota stood just inside the threshold to the bedroom and meticulously studied every inch of the space. To the trained observer, much of Angela's life was exposed in there; yet amongst all those scraps of living that people accumulate, there seemed not a single clue as to who had been in the apartment that night with her.

A western skirt and blouse in the closet, along with a pair of unblemished white boots, hinted that Angela liked country music, maybe so much so that she frequented the dance clubs. But no cowboy hat had been found in the apartment, nor did the soles of the boots appear worn.

Empty wine bottles in the trash attested to Angela's taste for alcohol, but nothing hard, since no whiskey, tequila or other distilled liquor was found. Had the killer picked up Angela at a dance club? Detectives had diligently worked Albuquerque's night life scene with Angela's photograph, but turned up nothing.

Clothes filled Angela's bureau drawers, but Dakota paid special attention to her lingerie. In one drawer, the top center, he stared at a collection of Vitoria Secret seductive, intimate apparel designed to tease and arouse even the most impotent man. Certainly their presence meant there had to be a man in Angie's life. Someone she wanted to excite with her intimates. Yet in all the statements taken from Angela's friends and family, no name emerged as a beau. Why?

Evidence technicians uncovered a single hair strand on the bed that did not match Angela's. Had someone else been in that bed with her? Or was it a stray left behind by the cleaning lady when she made the bed? And except for a latent print found on the front of Angie's lingerie drawer, the place was clean of a second person's presence on that night.

"Bronc, what about dishes?"

Bronc stood patiently in the living room, scanning for the least little clue.

"Sink was clean. Angela must not have been the type to let them pile up."

"Water in the sink?"

"No. If the killer put anything in the sink, he removed it before he left."

A thud from the next apartment came through the wall.

Dakota stopped. He and Bronc exchanged an optimistic look. If they heard that, maybe the neighbor had heard something that night.

"We already have a statement from...John Gimbel...Angela's neighbor."

"Let's go talk to him again while we have the chance," Dakota said. He was halfway through the living room by the time he finished his sentence.

Dakota knocked once at apartment 202. The noise from inside sounded like someone moving furniture. The door opened slightly at first, then more fully as John Gimbel's eerie eyes came into view. He was cautious in his stare and his manner. He exuded a Charles Manson quality in his eyes; opening the door only wide enough to see out. This kept the detectives from looking past Gimbel into his apartment.

"We'd like to talk with you, Mr. Gimbel, is it?" Dakota said. He wanted to waste little time on cordiality.

"About Angie again?"

John's penetrating hazel eyes held their stare, but not at either detective. Instead, he fixed his gaze on a point above their eyes or shifted them quickly downward.

Dakota became immediately suspicious of people unwilling to maintain eye contact. Were they attempting to hide something that might be visible in their stare?

"I told you people everything I know."

"I just want to clear up a few areas of your statement. May we come in?"

Gimbel hesitated. His eyes slid off Dakota's and landed briefly on Bronc's. That moment of uncertainty sparked further suspicion.

What was beyond that door? Dakota thought, waiting for an answer.

Gimbel raked his fingers through closely cropped cinnamon hair that lay flat on top of his head. His face carried an unpleasant demeanor.

"I'm moving things around inside. Place is a mess. Can't you just ask me now? Will this take long?"

"Not long. You said in your statement that the last time you saw Angie was on Tuesday, correct?"

"Around eight. I was leaving as she was coming home."

"You live here alone, John?" Bronc asked.

"Yes. In this apartment for four years now."

"Did you hear anything at all that Thursday night?"

"Not a thing. But I was out until about eleven."

"Where were you that night?"

John shifted uneasily. Dakota had asked for something inadvertently omitted from his statement.

"I was out...at a club."

"Which club, Mister Gimbel?"

Dakota was getting formal.

Bronc wondered if Dakota was on to something.

"The Palmaro," Gimbel said it as if it meant nothing. Everyone knew about the Palmaro. A so-called gentlemen's club. Perv city, Dakota thought.

"You like the entertainment there?"

"No law against it."

"And you returned here around eleven."

"Yeah. But that wouldn't have mattered much."

"Why's that?" Bronc asked.

"Angie was always very quiet. Kept to herself. You'd never really know when she was home and when she wasn't."

"In your statement you said you never met with Angie socially, is that correct?"

"Yeah. We didn't hit it off. We were friends but nothing more."

John shifted at the door, making sure he held it close so as not to offer the detectives a freebie of what was inside.

"You ever see Angie with any men? Anybody ever come home with her?"

"You mean besides her friends from work?"

"Any of them male?"

"No."

"Just her male friends."

"None. Well, there was one guy, but this was at least six months ago. I only saw him once."

"You know his name?"

"No. As a matter of fact, I just thought of it now that you asked. This wouldn't have been in my statement."

"What did he look like?"

"Blondish hair and a moustache. He had a Robert Redford kind of face, if you know what I mean."

"Was he taller than you?"

"About my height. I'm five-eight. But he had weight lifter's arms. You know, biceps that stretched his shirt sleeve."

"What about weight?"

"He was broad in the chest...but not fat."

"You ever try again with Angie?" Bronc asked. He shifted trying to catch a glimpse inside Gimbel's apartment. John shifted in unison to limit his view.

"God no. Not my type. We were good neighbors. She borrowed things from me, and I borrowed things from her."

"What kinds of things?" Dakota was back to asking the questions.

"Just things...sugar...flour...things."

Bronc stifled a guffaw.

Dakota raised an eyebrow. Seems friends that lend to their friends are more than just neighbors. John's response set up a wall of suspicion in Dakota's mind. Had there been something between John Gimbel and Angie Walker?

"When you arrived here Thursday night, did you notice whether Angie's car was parked in her spot?"

"As I told the officer before, I don't remember. That's not something I would think about at the time."

"Please, Mr. Gimbel, think very hard. It could be important to our investigation."

"I'm sorry. I really can't remember. If you want me to guess, I'd say it was there. But don't hold me to it, okay."

Dakota had run out of questions and still couldn't quiet the driving urge to push open the door and see what it was John Gimbel was working hard to keep out of sight. He knew to let the urge pass and come back at a time more advantageous to him.

Something about John Gimbel clawed away inside Dakota's mind. He had no idea what it was, but he knew he wouldn't rest until he uncovered it.

"When does the police tape come down?"

"When we've finished our investigation," Bronc said.

"Gives me the creeps."

"I'll bet it does," Bronc said, abandoning any hope of getting a look at what Mr. Gimbel didn't want them to see.

Dakota checked his watch, realizing it was time to get back to Grace. He had seen what he could see here and heard all he could. It was time to get back home, put the investigation out of his mind—if he could—and take care of his wife.

Corinne Schultz had two great attributes: one was her stunning pale blue eyes. Everyone said she smiled with her eyes. She had eyes that sparkled like precious gemstones. Hers were kind, attentive eyes. Her second attribute was her robust, well-rounded breasts. In high school, the boys drooled behind her back and were always willing to spend down to their last nickel in the hopes of copping a feel of Corinne's breasts. That was high school.... Now her body still offered the same attractions, and the men still spent; but relationships always seemed to fall apart shortly after making love.

Her looks weren't what kept men from returning to her door—her face could catch a man's eye as well as her body. It was her abrasive, and at times, condescending personality.

Corinne had little tolerance for incompetence; even less for shallow people. She unclothed her feelings as easily as she unclothed her body. So, it didn't take long for her to snap at her lovers until they could take it no more. On their exits, she bid them good riddance and each time swore off men for good.

In time, she acclimated to the solitude that superiority over others naturally brings. At twenty-five, she had grown accustomed to having herself as her own best friend.

But Corinne wasn't alone now. Love is something you just never gave up on permanently. What had started out casually had blossomed into something more. Slowly and patiently, like the roots of a great oak, it moved through her. Now she felt something deep inside. Something she mentioned to no one; not even the one who had stolen her affection. But then again, actions were the true heralds of the inner soul. At least more than any of those corny greeting card phrases you read. There was no need to actually tell someone you love them. Just show it every day by the way you live your life.

These past three weeks had meant more to Corinne than her entire twenty-five previous years on earth. And this was just the beginning. She could feel it.

Corinne tightened her terry bathrobe around her waist, feeling the chill from the open refrigerator as she shifted bottles and jars around. Her wet hair hung down like thick strands of black yarn.

It felt right. There was something about this night that just felt right to her. Her co-workers had talked about the woman taking the aggressive role; becoming the pursuer rather than being pursued. Corinne never thought she'd be able to do it. She'd never attempted it in the past and delayed a long time before forcing herself out of that protective shell she put on every morning before leaving the house.

Now she was glad she'd taken that step.

"Frankie, I've got a bottle of white Zinfandel. You said it's your favorite," she called back into the bathroom, where the shower had gone silent just moments before.

Corinne had something to celebrate, and someone to celebrate it with.

Dakota sat in his den. A cone of white light illuminated the photographs and files that covered his
desk. The case files were two years old, but still as
fresh in his mind as if the murders had occurred two
months ago. In a peculiar way, they had. The Boulder
Hill killer was now finding fresh kill. New victims to
feed his sick perversion.

A black, starless night looked in through the window. No wind stirred; no moon shone down from the
sky. Dakota felt alone. Alone in his struggle against
two monsters that had taken over his life.

Upstairs, beyond the reach of his thoughts, Lauryn and Heather slept soundly. Earlier, as Dakota listened at their door, Heather fussed about in her bed.
She had fought with Lauryn earlier in the day. That
wasn't unusual, as Heather was beginning to become
more and more independent, and she resented Lauryn's coddling. But today they fought more than
usual. And Lauryn was quick to fight back; eager to
inflict any measure of emotional pain upon her little
sister.

In the master bedroom, Grace clung to the very
edges of sleep. Her agony churned beneath the surface of drug-induced slumber. After a while, her
groans proved too much for Dakota to handle. Escap-
ing the room did no more than muffle her sounds.
They still rattled about inside his head. Even downstairs in the den, Dakota heard her groans in his
mind. Nothing could remove her torment from his
brain.

Work offered a moment of respite; a chance to
push his worries to arm's length. As the grandfather
clock struck a single chime, Dakota poured over the

moldering facts of three deaths; deaths haunting him both in sleep and every hour he was awake.

For the better part of an hour he stared at the smattering of papers. He saw nothing—felt nothing for what he had to do.

His mind was empty, his heart full. His gaze strayed to a photograph on his desk. A snapshot of them taken shortly after their marriage. She was so happy then, so full of dreams and hopes. There was such peace and contentment in those eyes. His hand went to the photo. His finger brushed her cheek. Fate had brought her to Albuquerque. Fate had arranged their meeting in that cafe so long ago. Her innocent smile had stolen his heart the moment he saw her. He knew from then on, she would be all his happiness. Nothing would matter. Fate had toyed with him. Given him something so treasured that no man could ever want for more. Now Fate sought to sunder the love they had nurtured from the very beginning.

The first tear splashed like a raindrop onto an open file folder. He had to stop it—turn off the hurt. The Apache endures—never cries.

Grace's face flooded his mind and erased all else. She was so beautiful in her wedding gown standing before the Sandia Mountains in their outdoor wedding ceremony. What were the words they exchanged, words that each held in their hearts despite their heritages?

Now you will feel no cold, for each of you will be warmth to the other. Now you are two persons, but there is one life before you.

Damn this! Nothing else could matter now. Nothing else could ever be more important than Grace.

Another tear fell.

Dakota wiped at his eyes. Stop! She's not going to... Tears rolled down his cheeks. At last he surrendered.

Hate something—something that will stop the pain.

"Damn you!" he scowled at anything that might listen, anything that might take empathy in what he felt. He no longer mustered the strength to fight; no longer wanted to maintain that struggle to keep it hidden inside.

Switching off the desk lamp, Dakota sought the safety of darkness. There in a world without witness, where he sat alone, it became his time to weep.

8

The following morning Dakota rushed to head-quarters. Bronc's call awakened him at first light. His heart pounded through his two-minute shower. He stuffed a piece of dry toast into his mouth, skipped the coffee brewing on the counter, and fled the house with no more than a hurried good-bye to the awakening girls.

Laurianne arrived within ten minutes of Dakota's departure to handle getting the girls off to school, though a still lethargic Lauryn insisted she had everything under control.

Bronc was pacing with cigarette in one hand and doughnut in the other when Dakota arrived. A smile would be premature. But Dakota could see a release of bottled-up tension in Bronc's eyes.

"Where is he?"

"Interrogation."

"Who's with him?"

"Childers and Wilder."

Dakota's mind raced faster than his heart. A suspect had been brought in for questioning. Routine questions led to a list of names. The list steered detectives toward one person in particular.

"Name?" Dakota asked, while they ascended stairs two at a time.

"Edward Cattrails. Boyfriend of a maid service employee Angela Walker used."

"Why is he in?"

"Bolted when detectives pulled up to his trailer. He lives in a rundown bucket in an isolated area just outside Cedar Crest."

"Rap sheet?"

"This you're going to love. Arrested in '93 for beating on a girlfriend. She spent three weeks in the hospital as a result. Never pressed charges."

"Let's hope," Dakota said, as he got his first glimpse of the suspect through the two-way mirror.

Edward Cattrail's pocked face turned toward the glass as if he somehow sensed Dakota and Bronc's presence in the next room. Thin, colorless lips remained a straight line across his face. He exuded arrogance in the way he placed his elbows on the table and positioned himself in the chair. Bronc and Dakota listened while the detectives grilled their suspect.

"Just tell us why you bolted when we arrived," Childers said, in a voice that always came across as meanspirited and callous.

So far Edward Cattrails was cooperating.

"I'm on parole. I thought you came to bust me," Cattrails said. His voice was grating. It seemed to match his ratlike face. His gray penetrating eyes bounced from one detective to another.

"Why would we be busting you?" Detective Wilder asked.

"I don't know. You fuckers bust anybody for anything."

"So you're dirty, then."

"I'm clean."

Cattrail voluntarily laid out his arms to illustrate an absence of needle tracks.

"You're probably shooting through your groin," Wilder said, as if to dismiss Cattrails' gesture.

"Tell us where you where Thursday, September Fifteenth," Childer prodded.

"Hey, what's this about? Why the fuck did you pull me in?"

"Hey, shit-for-brains, we just wanted to ask you where you were on the fifteenth. We didn't decide to haul your ass in until you bolted on us."

"Damn," Cattrails muttered.

Dakota stared through the glass.

"What can we use against him?" Dakota asked.

"Not much. He could have had access to the keys to the Walker apartment through the girlfriend. He's got a history of violence toward women. You want to take over the interrogation?"

"Not yet. Let them wear him down. If we still have nothing later in the day, you and I can take a crack at him."

Dakota left the observation room with an empty feeling in his gut. Something about the kid's actions dampened his excitement. He had little confidence that Edward Cattrails was the Boulder Hill killer.

Four hours later, detectives released Edward Vincent Cattrails. His alibi for Thursday the fifteenth proved ironclad. Three witnesses confirmed that Edward Cattrail could not possibly have been at the Silver Springs apartments. He was hustling University of New Mexico suckers at a pool hall across town.

Task force detectives scratched Edward Cattrail from their list of possibles. The excitement that had arisen earlier in the day had deflated. So far, the long tedious hours of investigating the maid service angle had come up with nothing.

Saturday morning Grace awakened with a new-found strength in her smile. Her eyes reflected the morning light like shimmering amethyst crystals.

Maybe the chemo had kicked in and beat down the cancer inside her.

Downstairs, Lauryn deftly answered the ringing telephone and the buzzing doorbell. The telephone call was her friend. Laurianne and Cole entered with Cole slapping Lauryn a high-five as he passed.

"You taking us to the zoo today, Uncle Cole?" Lauryn asked, after she hung up and delivered her expected hug.

"You can't know how much I wish I could take you to the zoo today, sweetie, but maybe next weekend."

Lauryn accepted his answer and dashed off into the kitchen. Heather ran up, kissed her Uncle Cole and without so much as a word, dashed after Lauryn.

"Hey, don't I get a hug?" Laurianne called.

"Later," Lauryn called back.

"Don't hurry...I'll take care of Grace. This will be good for Dakota," Laurianne said as she entered the kitchen and reached for an apron. She began extracting dishes from the pile crowding the sink.

"Yeah, well I'm not so sure this is so good for me," Cole offered, rearranging his glasses on his face as he rummaged through the refrigerator.

"Oh, I don't know. A good workout once in a while might remove that banker's paunch you've been carrying around," Laurianne said, with a smile, as she extracted the box of chocolate doughnuts from his hand and returned them to the refrigerator. "You need to get away from your desk and that laptop on occasion."

Laurianne playfully rubbed his stomach and kissed him; though his lips remained a rigid line.

"Very funny," Cole replied, taking a milk bottle out instead.

Cole failed to see the humor in her words. She had absolutely no understanding whatsoever of what was about to happen. She'd think differently if she had to play with these guys.

"Oh, come on, go have some fun. You take everything too seriously," Laurianne added, removing the milk bottle from his hand. "The girls' cereal."

"Fun, yeah right. You think basketball is fun. That's because you don't have to play."

Laurianne tossed a dish towel into Cole's face.

"I think it's more fun than cleaning a kitchen, doing laundry, and scrubbing the toilets."

"Okay, you win. Come on, Dakota, you ready?" Cole called up the stairs.

"Be right down," Dakota called back.

He stopped at the bedroom door and then returned to the bed for another kiss. Though Grace tried to hide it, Dakota could see the hurt in her eyes. As potent as the drugs the doctors prescribed were, the pain had a way of gnawing through.

"Would you be up to getting out of the house later?"

Grace hesitated for a moment.

"What did you have in mind, fella?"

"A surprise."

He winked.

"Then I'll make sure I'm up for it."

"Great," Dakota said, kissing Grace softly on her lips, "then it's a date."

Grace tightened her hand suddenly around his; Dakota stopped.

"I can stay. This isn't important," he said.

"No, Dakota, go. This will be good for you. Have fun and don't worry about me. Laurianne takes great care of me."

"Really, I can stay. I don't need to go."

"Dakota, honey, you need to go. You need to work off some of your frustration. I'll be all right here. I'm feeling a little better and I'll just be resting up for our date, anyway."

Dakota clutched her cold hand until distance forced him to release. Lately, she always felt cold. And she shivered more, needed a blanket constantly to keep warm.

"Be back in two hours tops."

Cole drove. Dakota stared blankly out the window. The silence seemed almost overbearing. Twice earlier Cole started to speak, only to stop himself before breaking the void between them. He had so much to say, and he needed to get at least some of it out. But Dakota's granite face bid that certain things remain unsaid even between brothers.

"How's Grace feeling?"

"Better today. I think maybe the treatment's starting to work."

"What'd the doctors say?"

"They're cautiously optimistic. But Grace's tough, she'll handle it."

"You're damn right. She beat it before. She'll beat it again."

Dakota offered no response.

Cole stopped asking questions; Dakota quit talking. Cole could just catch a glimpse every now and then of what churned behind Dakota's eyes, what lurked beyond his expression—what Dakota thought he hid from the rest of the world. There were two people Dakota never could hide from—his brother and his wife.

They had grown up together in the same house and fended off an alcoholic father together until the old man died from his own abuse. Neither could keep anything from the other. But Dakota was always the stronger one. He graduated top of his class at the University of New Mexico, and was always the one to come to Cole's rescue. Just once Cole would like to come to Dakota's rescue, and thereby, raise himself in his brother's eyes.

Why wouldn't he let Cole in?

"Do me a favor?" Dakota asked, as they wheeled into the half-full gymnasium parking lot. The accumulation of vehicles meant there was no way the game would be canceled due to lack of enthusiasm.

"Sure..."

"Take the girls for a while this evening."

"You got it."

Cole hesitated before leaving his Beemer. He didn't exactly love the game and had never been particularly adept at sinking baskets, which seemed to be the object of the exercise. He'd rather be in his office now, fiddling with numbers on his laptop. But there was no way out. They needed another man, and Cole had said he'd do it. Now he had to do it. He only hoped he wouldn't regret it.

"They're waiting," Dakota said, leading the way in.

Cole hurried to catch up.

The locker room reeked of sweat, used socks and moldy towels. Cole loathed the odor, an air that by its very pungency immediately transported him back to his high school memories, when jocks poked fun at his rippling physical form and snapped towels at his bare ass, hoping to provoke a confrontation.

During his junior year, Dakota had developed into an all-city contender at the 137-pound weight class on the wrestling team. Cole had made himself Dakota's unofficial groupie, running right beside him, and cheering him on when Dakota had to lose that last pound to make weight. Exhausted, sweating, and needing to shed another few ounces, they'd load their mouths with chewing gum and spit together, Cole turning it into a distance contest to motivate Dakota to expel every possible ounce of water. A mere two ounces of excess liquid could force a forfeit. Those desperate to make weight to the extreme destroyed their bodies by consuming Ex-Lax like candy; then paying dearly in the end for their decision—literally. But you did whatever it took to keep that balance bar from touching the top at weight-ins. And each time Dakota successfully stepped off that scale, Cole viewed it as a victory for himself.

After that all-important moment on the scales—that one solitary second for which you gave up eating for three days—you engorged on orange juice and candy to revitalize the energy pool necessary to wrestle the requisite nine minutes on the mat. Unless, of course, you pinned your opponent sooner, which Dakota often did. Attending every match even though his mother and father found excuses to miss all but the most important ones, Cole cheered from the bleachers; screaming with all the force his lungs could muster for Dakota to stick his opponent.

But for all Dakota's success and glory, (he ended his junior year with a 19 and 0 record) the school newspaper never doled out more than a single-sentence write-up; detailing either the point margin of his victory or forever recording the amount of time it took to pin his competitor.

Cole cringed while lacing his shoes as he relived that frozen moment in time when Dakota dislocated his middle finger during a match. The crowd had fallen suddenly silent. Dakota's digit had been bent backwards until it looked like a Popsicle stick broken at a right angle in the middle. Despite excruciating agony, Dakota silently grimaced as he held his hand rock steady while the coach snapped the bones back into alignment. Despite the pain, Dakota went on to pin his opponent less than a minute later. Yet for all his fierceness on the mat, he demonstrated compassion in his victories. He never employed holds or moves that could inflict pain or injury on his opponents. Victories could only be savored when they were earned with honor.

During that year, Cole had demonstrated the same commitment and determination as any member

of the wrestling team, but for all his effort, Coach Mu-
hinger simply replied they didn't want Roly-polies like
Cole on the team. The fatass butthead actually called
him a Roly-poly right to his face. Said he should go out
for the chess team, since he seemed more adept at
competing on that level.

Raucous shouts erupted on the courts beyond the
pair of doors with wire mesh guards and frosted glass.
Like it or not, it was time to play basketball.

Cole's stomach churned uneasily; he had a bad
feeling about this. He stared at his shoelaces for a long
time. Sweat rolled down his neck even before he left
the locker room. Something in Dakota's voice and
manner issued a warning. But Cole pulled his sweat
shirt over his hairy, soft belly and hurried to come
astride Dakota, who had already left the locker room.

Assemble ten police officers in a gym and basketball becomes not so much a game as a contest of wills.
And the game started off worse than Cole had expected. Everyone else had ample opportunity to go
through their warm-up and work on their shots. Dakota needed no warm-up. Cole got barely enough time to
stretch before the tip-off.

Being the only non-police-officer player on either
team, and being slotted on the opposing team, Cole
got the honor of guarding his brother. No one else was
crazy enough to take on that task. Somehow he
couldn't shake the feeling that he was being set up as
the fall guy.

Neither of these things sat well with Cole.

Cops play basketball not for recreation, nor exercise, but rather to vent aggressions on each other in a
questionably nonviolent competitive manner.

On the other hand, bank vice presidents, smart
ones that is, don't play basketball with psycho cops.
Especially when his teammates, other detectives Cole
had come to know through Dakota, badgered him
whenever Dakota scored. What did it matter anyway
that they were down by eighteen? It's only a stupid

game. The only one on the court more out of condition than Cole was Bronc, who kept pleading for a cigarette time-out.

This game's only redeeming grace was the rule that discussing police work was forbidden. You could talk about anything else: women and sex, or just sex, or just women. Anyone mentioning anything even remotely related to homicide, murder, death or the Boulder Hill killer caught a fierce elbow jab to the ribs or a knee to the groin. However, they used the more descriptive name for the target area.

Dakota, however, said almost nothing. His silence raised the intensity of the game to a level well beyond where Cole wanted to go. By the end of the second quarter, Cole opted to pass the ball off almost every time it came to him. The ridicule he endured with each missed shot had beaten down his ego to the point where he lost all confidence in his ability to even hit the rim. The laughter hurt even if it was only a stinking game.

By halftime, Cole wanted to call it quits. They were down twenty-four, and Cole had successfully missed six in a row. Only women missed so many in a row, his teammates chided. Cole thought his heart had reached its bursting point. Then he'd have a legitimate reason to quit. While the others were winded, they definitely had more stamina than Cole. Even Dakota refused to let up. Then again, how much stamina is really required for a bank vice-president to key up a spreadsheet on a laptop or analyze a corporate balance sheet?

Bronc being Cole's teammate, and sympathetic to Cole's plight, had been especially helpful during the third quarter in putting the brakes on Dakota's scoring drives. To Cole, this frivolous basketball game meant absolutely nothing. To the cops, it meant pride and determination. These guys had to win. Neither team would accept defeat. They had to win—just like in their professions—they had to win. All of them were conditioned to believe failure was not an option in homicide.

As a player crossed center court, he snapped the ball to Dakota and without breaking stride, Dakota pressed into the lane. When he went up to shoot, Cole smothered him, knocking the ball away. It hit an opposing player and caromed out of bounds.

Cole's arms vaulted in triumph. Finally, he had done something right.

"Foul!" Dakota yelled, fighting to take in oxygen.

"Bullshit! Clean block," Cole yelled back, frustrated by the game and having to shed the pride he had just felt for finally getting something right in this ridiculous contest.

"You fouled me, damnit!" an adamant Dakota charged. He waved for the ball.

Cole intercepted it.

"No foul. Out of bounds. Our ball."

Dakota ripped the ball from Cole's hands.

"Fuck you—foul," he yelled, then fired the ball into Cole's face, knocking his glasses off and sending a trickle of blood from his nose. Seemed no game could be considered complete unless blood was spilt.

"Hey, let it go, man, who gives a shit," Bronc said, grabbing Dakota's arm and drawing him away from Cole as they faced each other. Cole refused to yield; he refused to be intimidated.

"You fouled me, you shithead," Dakota blurted, losing control.

"Yeah, well fuck you!" Cole said, picking up his glasses.

"That's game," a frustrated detective called as the others wandered off the court. No one else spoke. The confrontation had caused onlookers in the gym to pause.

For a long moment, Cole stood there alone, wiping away the blood oozing out his nostrils.

"Fuck you!" Cole whispered, hating himself more than Dakota at that moment.

Cole arrived at seven sharp to pick up the girls. Dakota apologized for his outburst on the court. By then, Cole had shrugged the whole incident off. Pressure gets to everyone. Sometimes it even gets away from the best of them. No apology required. Difficult times, Cole told himself. Dakota just needed a way to release some pressure. Cole was prepared to do whatever was necessary.

Within minutes of the girls' departure, Dakota had Grace down the stairs and out of the house. His excitement quickly infected Grace and she felt her heart speed up.

"Mrs. Blackwood, you look ravishing tonight," Dakota said.

Grace's flowered dress with blue piped shoulder straps clung to her curves. Despite her gaunt appearance, she felt beautiful. She had splashed on a hint of makeup, just enough to highlight her eyes, and she carried a pale blue sweater to keep her warm in case the evening air chilled unexpectedly.

Dakota settled Grace in the passenger seat and without a word pulled out of the driveway and headed northwest. Grace knew better than to ask questions. She would learn their destination soon enough. Dakota had fumbled through preparing an egg dish for dinner, and though the girls hated it, Grace weathered the meal without serious nausea. Another small victory.

Quality time had become so precious to them that Dakota had to take advantage of every single moment. Grace's lull between the storms of her treatment might last only a brief time, so he would make sure each was a minute well spent.

"You taking me dancing?" she teased. She lacked the strength to move around a dance floor. She pondered over his secret destination. Certainly, he knew exactly where he was going, since every turn had been seemingly planned out.

Dakota only smiled that devious smile he used when he wished to heighten mystery and desire. His continued silence piqued her interest. However, once they had left Albuquerque proper behind and turned due north into the desert, she realized Dakota's plan.

A part of her began to feel again—a part of her the cancer and the radiation had dampened but could never kill. The stirrings of passion worked their way out of their hiding place. This time her goose flesh came from something other than the cool air.

Grace reached across the seat to take Dakota's hand. She brought it lovingly to her lap.

"We having fun yet?" she asked, a mischievous smile crossing her face.

"Not yet."

Neither spoke when they turned into a vibrantly orange sun descending toward the horizon. Dakota left the road at Cachanga wash and maneuvered over sand mounds to center the vehicle onto a traveled path. He crawled along, gravel tapping the quarter panels, until they reached the place where the sides of the wash rose to form rocky plateaus.

"Dakota, this is really sweet, but I can't..."

Dakota stopped her with a kiss. He grabbed a blanket from the back seat, left the car, and crossed behind it to Grace's door. He opened it and scooped Grace into his arms. She felt weightless.

The heel of his boot caught the door and kicked it closed.

"You're not?"

Dakota kissed her again. Her lips were warm and inviting. Her eyes became shimmering watery pools.

Cradling her ninety pounds only reminded him of how much of his wife he had already lost. Sweat bead-ed his forward and trickled down his cheeks as he trekked with her through the sand, finally climbing out of the wash onto a westerly-facing, narrow, jutting rock ledge. The feat left him breathless. The sheer majesty of the ocher sunset left Grace breathless.

Facing a swirling breeze, he stood for a long moment with Grace still in his arms.

"I love you," he whispered, as if they were in a crowded room.

The dying sun painted them in a rich saffron glow. Below, cast across the panorama as if some celestial hand had haphazardly discarded them, strawberry cactus, cholla, yucca and grama grass cast shadows across the rolling sand. Far off, etched against the sand, a lone windmill stood silent beside a rusted-out water tank. Here above the rest of the world, they could shut out everything and see only each other. Miles distant to their left, a train lumbered along the desert floor, pulling tank cars and a hundred boxcars.

The fading light continuously altered the colors of the rock bluffs at the edges of their sight. Behind them, the Sandia mountains rose up like great earthen walls, dappled with the deep greens of pinons.

It took a few minutes for Dakota to catch his breath after the ordeal. Afterward, he set Grace to rest on a flat rock seat while he spread the blanket near a pictograph of a bison left by his ancestors thousands of years ago. Then, together, they watched the western sky transform from the blue of day to the vibrant red of twilight and finally fade to the gradual slate of night.

The last rays of sunlight carved long shadowy images along the jutting sandstone rock formations in the distance. On its departure, it left behind dwindling hues of orange and red. The desert could be a beautiful place; if for only those last moments before darkness drew her into night.

Many miles to the north, black thunderheads lined in silver crowded the sky, pushed along by an arid desert wind.

"Dakota..."

"I just wanted you to enjoy the sunset."

Grace drew closer until his warmth became a part of her. She kissed him, and then curled up safe within his arms. The distant storm splashed its swirling wind across their faces, jostling Dakota's jet-black hair. No disease stole away the peace in this place. Here there were only two people whose love nourished them.

They had perched themselves on a land that long ago belonged to Dakota's people. A land isolated, if only thinly, from the white man, where he felt his heritage. Here he understood what it meant to be Apache.

Now this land belonged to no one.

Dakota had come to this place in his youth. A place of solitude and reflection; in this place, he felt close to his deceased parents. He knew only a few Apache words; words given him by elders during visits to his reservation as a teenager. He spoke them here, certain his mother and father would hear him. He thought of this place as their special place, though he never knew if Grace shared his feelings. Dakota had brought Grace to this rock plateau the night he proposed. Here they made commitments binding them together for all their lives. She had said yes without hesitation; without uncertainty. In the sand, they wrote out their promises: vowing to love each other forever and to never let anyone or anything tear them apart.

"How did you arrange that?" Grace asked, as lightning bolts crawled across the distant sky in beautifully jagged paths.

"Rain dance," he whispered.

For minutes, neither spoke. The light show consumed them. They felt the wind in their faces and the cool freshness that follows a sudden rain in the desert.

"When I was younger, I believed my mother and father talked to me in the wind, guiding me in the ways of my people."

"What did they say?"

"They said son, if you don't marry that wonderful white woman you are one stupid injun."

"You're going to make me cry," Grace said, and nestled into the warmth radiating off his chest. His arms engulfed her, holding her with a firmness that fostered security, yet a gentleness that she had come to relish. For a brief moment, while watching lightening splay across the darkening sky and feeling Dakota's lips upon her cheek, Grace had found peace. For that short time, her pain had vanished.

"Dakota, I love you," Grace whispered amid the rumbles of thunder. She intertwined her fingers in with his.

Dakota heard but could not speak.

With the next dawn, the demon inside her assaulted Grace with renewed tenacity. The radiation had sent it into hiding, but now the monster crept out from his hiding place and set the lower quadrant of her chest cavity ablaze. The following Wednesday, Dakota took her to the hospital for another radiation treatment. Each successive dose took more out of her. Dakota hated to witness what the disease and the cure were doing to the only woman he had ever really loved. But he felt helpless. Holding her made him feel like he had failed as a man. He had always taken care of problems. He always won.

Upon their return home, Grace spent her first hours retching in the bathroom until she thought her stomach would be ejected out her throat.

Dakota could only stand by, helpless and weak; the same way he felt about his investigation with the Boulder Hill killer.

Time seemed to accelerate against him; it raced twice as fast as it did in the past. He endured Grace's persistent decline as each day fell into night. They spoke less. Grace required more and more rest; ultimately spending most of her days in bed.

Through all this, Dakota waited for the next victim to turn up. He was running out of time—both at home and in the investigation. No task force detective gave less than fourteen hours a day—every day. They were rallying around Dakota. No one questioned his direction.

Except Rodman.

At four that afternoon, Dakota met briefly with the task force. No new leads had panned out, though they were getting more than forty new calls every day. Everyone in Albuquerque, it seemed, wanted to take a shot at identifying the killer. Yet, every call had to be taken seriously and investigated on the outside chance that one might be right. And the possibility existed that one of the callers could very well have seen or talked to the Boulder Hill killer.

None of the existing leads had shed any new light on the identity of the killer.

"I feel like we're trying to ride a dead horse out of the desert," Bronc said to Dakota, in private after the briefing.

Dakota asked him to go back and start from the beginning, talk to everyone all over again, and possibly find someone who might have information.

"The neighbor, John Gimbel, is clean in New Mexico. Maybe he's just a harmless flake," Bronc reported.

"Maybe not. Stick with him for now. See if you can find a way to see what's in that apartment of his. And compile a list of all the people who lived in the buildings surrounding the Walker crime scene. Compare that with the list of people living in the vicinity of the last three victims. Maybe our guy moved in the last two years."

"We're on it."

Dakota left the briefing struggling against a growing anger. He was losing control of his world. He couldn't help Grace; he couldn't unravel the identity of the Boulder Hill killer. He had to focus, though circumstances kept pulling his mind in different directions.

Consumed by his thoughts, Dakota crossed the main lobby of the headquarters building, oblivious to the policewoman hurrying after him. She snared him with a hand to his forearm just before the doors.

"Sir, I'm glad I caught you. There's a Chesney Winterthorne to see you."

"Chesney?"

"Yes, sir, that's what he said."

"Concerning?"

"The Boulder Hill killer, sir."

"Turn him over to a task force detective."

"I tried, sir, but he insists he must speak with you personally."

Dakota shifted with irritation. His movement elicited a not-my-fault shrug from the policewoman.

"Where is he now?"

"Outside your office. He's been waiting patiently for four hours."

Dakota did an about face and started back up the stairs.

"Where's Bronc? Have him meet me in my office."

As Dakota approached his office, a young, floppy-haired man rose out of a chair in anticipation. He wore oversized clothes at least three sizes larger than his frame and black-rimmed glasses that telegraphed *nerd*, as if he had written it across his forehead. His face lacked a smile and seemed all business.

"Lieutenant Blackwood," he said, extending a hand with fingernails chewed to the quick.

Dakota ignored the gesture, moving past him into his office.

"Lieutenant, you probably don't remember me...Chesney Winterthorne."

"You're right, I don't remember you..."

Dakota came about in sudden realization. The voice had an odd rasp to it. The sounds rekindled a long discarded memory.

"I tried to help you two years ago."

"The psychic," Dakota said, enduring an acrid rumbling in his stomach. He hated these people. But he cautioned himself to be patient. For all he knew, he might be looking at the Boulder Hill killer right now. These people all professed to have some kind of extraordinary power that ordinary people lacked, then used it to con people out of their money. This guy must be down from Santa Fe, the paranormal fruitcake center of the world, Dakota thought. The last thing he wanted was to run around town with some flake.

"Don't tell me, you know who the Boulder Hill killer is?"

"No, sir."

Dakota just stared at Chesney. Not the response he expected.

"Not yet anyway."

Dakota poked his head out of his office to his secretary.

"Where's Bronc?"

His secretary shrugged.

"Please, Lieutenant, I know we didn't hit it off last time. But just give me ten minutes of your time."

"Ten minutes and you're out of here," Dakota snapped, moving around his desk.

"And no access to investigative information."

"Thank you," Chesney said, taking the chair across the desk.

"That one," Dakota said, pointing to another.

"Sorry." Chesney moved.

Bronc ambled into the office, hands in his pockets, and looked over Dakota's visitor before taking the chair across the desk. His face remained rigid during the introduction, and though he removed his hands from his pocket during their introduction, he made no effort to shake Chesney's hand. Winterthorne shook off the indifference swarming over Bronc's face when he learned he was in the presence of a psychic.

"Hey, just give me a chance," Chesney added, "I didn't read anything in the newspaper about you guys making any arrests in the case."

"If your intent is to piss us off, Mr. Winterthorne, it's working," Bronc said.

Dakota settled back into his chair and checked his time.

"We're counting down from ten..."

Chesney leaned forward and bouncing his eyes back and forth between both men, finally settled on Dakota, the man he had to convince.

"Please, just hear me out. I went over to the dead girl's apartment."

"You what?" Dakota shot back.

"Did you break in?" Bronc accused.

"Yeah. Like I'd be dumb enough to come here and tell you that. No. I never went near the police seal on the door. But I felt something."

"You felt something?" Dakota asked, glancing at his watch. The crackpot still had seven long minutes to go.

"What did you feel?" Bronc asked sardonically.

"A vibration."

"Great..."

"I glimpsed Angela Walker in a car. A green car."

"A green car?"

"Yes."

"You ever think maybe she owned a green car?"

"No, no, please, I know you think I'm a loon. I got a flash of her sitting in a green car, on the passenger side."

Dakota looked at Bronc.

Bronc wanted to laugh, but knew he had to maintain his professional countenance, at least until Chesney left.

"So?" Dakota said.

"So? It might be the killer's car."

"You see the driver?"

"No. But someone was driving in my vision."

Dakota sucked in a breath of disbelief and fumbled with the files on his desk. Five minutes and counting.

"Please, let me help. If I had a chance to see the apartment or feel something the woman was wearing, I might get more. I know you think this is all bullshit. But I'm telling you, I felt something when I was standing at her door."

Dakota stood up.

"Well Chesney, I can see by my watch that your ten minutes are up."

Chesney refused to budge.

"Let me tell you something, Chesney," Bronc said, saying the name as if it were stuck in his throat and he needed to hack it up, "we've already interviewed more than a dozen of your kind. We take what you have to say very seriously. But at this point, we cannot allow anyone access to either the crime scene, physical evidence, or any documentation regarding this case."

"Please, I know you find it hard to believe, but give me a chance. I want to help you."

"Describe the car."

"A small car...compact. I couldn't see the model or make. All I saw was the girl."

"So, based on the notion that you saw Angela sitting in a green car, you want us to bring you in as a...consultant?"

"This is not about money."

"Please leave your name and number with the duty officer at the front desk. We'll be in touch," Dakota said, with a sense of finality that brought

Chesney up and out of his chair and reluctantly out of the office.

"Thank you for at least letting me have my say," Chesney said, shaking first Bronc's hand and then moving to Dakota's.

But when his hand met Dakota's, he stopped as if something had seized his insides. Dakota could feel Chesney's muscles tense. His face went slack; he stared into Dakota's eyes without flinching. It was like he could peer into Dakota's soul through his eyes.

Chesney said nothing. He quickly exited the office.

9

That evening Laurianne and Cole took the girls out for pizza and a movie. Dakota remained at Grace's bedside. There were few words to be said.

As the sun faded, Dakota allowed the room to be swallowed up in darkness. Sitting in a chair beside the bed, he listened to Grace's breathing and held her hand so tightly that after a while his forearm muscles cramped.

He turned over each piece of information he had on the Angela Walker death. Every shred the task force had gleaned now swirled around inside his head.

When Grace groaned in her sleep, Dakota dropped from the rocking chair positioned beside the bed onto his knees. Ever so gently, he smoothed his fingers along her cheek. The smoothness he had known so well and loved was gone now; her skin felt clammy to his touch.

Stabbing pains in his knees rekindled the memories of his youth, and almost automatically Dakota began whispering the words of a prayer he had so long ago given up on. If there were a God, would He even bother to listen now? Halfway through his stumbling rendition of the Our Father, Dakota buried his whispers into his own mind.

"I love you, Grace," he said, in a voice weakened by the suffering of a breaking heart. He kissed her gently upon her cheek.

Dakota presided over Friday's weekly task force briefing, a more formal one, in which each member delivered an oral progress report for Dakota and Washington. Progress was the wrong word for the occasion. Lack of progress might be a better way to describe this Friday's reports.

The number of leads under investigation climbed into the hundreds. Yet, when most were analyzed, investigated and documented, it turned out that no real progress had been made.

As lab and evidence reports trickled back from various forensic sites around the country, it became painfully clear that the Boulder Hill killer had systematically cleared the crime scene to leave no incriminating evidence behind.

"Still no ID on the latent print found in Angela's bedroom," a detective reported. "We've eliminated everyone: friends, family and the maid service. That leaves the killer as the most likely person to have left the print behind."

"We're bringing in the neighbor for fingerprinting," Bronc added.

"Voluntarily?" Dakota asked.

"Yeah. He's suddenly become very cooperative. Even let us have a look around his apartment."

"Anything?"

"Clean. Except for a half dozen dresses in the back of his closet."

"Seriously?"

"Seriously. He lives alone and must like to dress up on occasion. If you know what I mean."

The task force broke momentarily into cat calls and whistles.

Bronc assumed responsibility for coordinating the task force's efforts when Dakota was unavailable. In those isolated cases when urgency pressed for an immediate decision, Bronc made the decision on the spot; he would later apprise both Dakota and the captain so they maintained current on the investigation's status. No one questioned Dakota's devotion; all understood what he was facing.

Once the last detective finished his report, Dakota took the podium, still trying to digest the latest information about the case.

"We still don't know anything about the man in Angela's apartment that night?"

"Not a thing," Bronc responded.

"What about the woman who reported Angela missing?"

"She couldn't offer much. Seems Angela kept her private life private."

"Can we bring her in and question her at greater length? Maybe there's something she knows, but doesn't realize it."

"She's already been in once. But at the time she was still pretty shaken up."

"Okay. Let's hope she's settled down by now. Schedule a time to meet with her at her home," Dakota said.

"Can do. You want to be there?"

"Definitely. But I'll need time to study her statement before I question her. Can you make it for early next week? Say Monday?"

"What about Sunday? Maybe I could press her for Sunday?" Bronc asked.

"No. Monday," Dakota said.

Twelve detectives closed their notebooks and shuffled out for another twelve to sixteen hours on the streets. There would be little sleep and even less time off as each day passed without solid leads to follow. Every detective watched the clock—waiting and knowing the odds of preventing the next senseless death were getting too great to even contemplate.

Rodman remained behind in the briefing room until everyone, including Bronc, had left. Dakota knew the agent was waiting for him.

"May I have a minute, Lieutenant?" Rodman asked, moving to the front where Dakota stood stacking his reports and notes.

Dakota could feel the tension rise in the room from the way Rodman's eyes studied him.

"Sure."

"It's concerning the investigation. And this is all strictly on a professional level. I want you to understand that at the onset."

Now Dakota knew this was going to get difficult. He would have just as soon kept the Bureau people at a distance. But he had no voice in this matter.

"A lot of valuable time is being wasted," Rodman said, plunging right into the icy waters. "We're not focusing our efforts in the right directions."

"And what do you believe are the right directions?"

"You've got the Bureau's profile of the killer and you know that the FBI studies have indicated the killer is most likely someone living close to the victims. You've got your men spread out over the entire city when we should be doing door-to-door in the neighborhoods where the crimes were committed."

"Every detective is investigating every lead to its fullest..."

"Don't get me wrong, Dakota, I'm not saying the detectives are at fault."

"You're saying the leadership is?"

"Quite frankly, yes. I am aware of your personal situation and I feel for you. But you are in no way capable of managing such a large-scale investigation at this time. Detective Broncowski tries very hard, but he doesn't have the know-how to keep this investigation moving forward. We're stalled right now and time is running out."

Dakota fought to control the rage swarming over his insides.

"And you want the FBI to take over the investigation."

"Yes. We're far better trained to manage an investigation of this scope. Your people..."

"And who in the Bureau would head up the investigation?"

"I feel quite qualified to take charge."

"Rodman, I've got a dozen detectives better qualified than you. You couldn't find the shitter if you were standing in the bathroom. If you think this is your ticket to Washington, you can just..."

"Better qualified? Your men are down to relying on psychics and palm readers to get their leads. The Bureau uses facts and forensic data to catch killers. We don't have the time to chase after visions and premonitions.

"Listen, Rodman, if there's one thing I hate it's someone stepping over bodies trying to get to the top. You're part of the team. I'm running the team. You got a problem with that, then maybe we better see if the Bureau has another man to assign to us."

Rodman said nothing, staring deeply into Dakota's eyes.

"If you think you're going to rely on some Indian spirit to deliver you the killer..."

Rodman stopped himself. He had crossed the line. And he knew it. He stormed from the briefing room, realizing ambition had pushed him past where he had originally intended their exchange to go. There was no turning back. He had to play his hand to its conclusion, regardless of the consequence.

The press was getting antsy—and angry. That's what happens when too many days pass without feeding them something worthwhile. They had resumed their, at times, vicious verbal assault upon the police department, taking cheap shots at the task force on the nightly news and in the papers. Every reporter in Albuquerque had his or her own theory and failed to understand why the police refused to tailor the investigation to their ideas.

Every detective believed the killer would eventually be caught through facts and evidence...not psychics, nor crackpots nor unfounded, scatterbrained theories. That single thought kept them getting out of bed every morning and working the streets. Nevertheless, the ridicule and sardonic commentary over time eroded morale and dampened even the hardest-working detective's self-esteem. Somewhere, in a city of over half a million people, a vicious killer lurked and everyone expected the police to track him down—as if it were an easy task.

Dakota met with Cal Sturges and Washington behind the closed doors of the task force command center. The photographs of the Boulder Hill killer's victims provided a gruesome backdrop for their candid discussion.

"We need something to offer the media," Cal insisted, his eyes glancing involuntarily up to the photographs.

"Nothing to offer," Washington said.

"Angela Walker is dead. Another young attractive woman has already been sentenced to die. You've got to tighten a net around the city."

"But we don't know who we're trying to catch," Dakota said.

To Dakota, that two-year-old piece of the puzzle still eluded him. But he wasn't going to let it slip away again. And he wasn't going to allow his investigation to be steered by a City Hall official seeking to further his own political ambitions.

"I need to tell the mayor when," Cal Sturges said, as he rose. "You need to get something fast. We're sitting on a political powder keg. If you could make even some kind of arrest by the start of the campaign, the mayor would be extremely grateful."

"You'll be the first to know when we have something the mayor can use," Washington said, closing his file and pushing his chair back from the conference table, feeling as if they were pawns in the mayor's political gaming. Elections could be easily won or lost on the outcome of the Boulder Hill killer investigation.

10

Sunday morning sun streamed into the Blackwood house. The girls awakened early, and like they had done every Sunday in the past, dressed in their prettiest dresses. Lauryn needed no prodding, and even helped Heather get into her dress before coming down to breakfast. Their Sunday mornings had become almost ritual.

Though Grace lacked the strength, she pulled herself out of bed and dressed for church. Even in sickness, she refused to abandon her commitment to God. Now, she prayed that He would honor his commitment to her.

On Sundays, Dakota prepared breakfast and then drove them to church, where he remained in the car while they attended mass. Grace's sickness robbed her of her beauty, her vitality and her strength, but not that immovable resolve to pray to her God. She made her way precariously down the stairs with her arm wrapped tightly around Dakota's.

At 9:30, they left behind a table of dirty dishes and drove to the San Felipe de Neri Catholic church.

This morning, cars lined up before the church, off-loading fashionably dressed wives and children. Dakota never could understand why the white man had to get all dressed up to go to church. The clog at the steps forced Dakota to pull a few car lengths past the doors, park, and then scurry around to help Grace from the car.

Though she made no complaint, there was pain in her eyes and in the growing frailty of her grip.

Today, Heather held one of Grace's hands, while Dakota supported the other. In the past, Grace insisted she enter the church unaided, but that was then. Now it was different. Today, she lost some of her faith in her legs.

Lauryn dipped into the holy water and blessed herself as she crossed under the archway. Grace and Heather followed. Only a sparse gathering of the faithful, kneeling in prayer, were present this early.

Dakota maintained a steadying grip on Grace's arm until they reached that first pew directly before the pulpit. This was the place Grace occupied every Sunday for three years...praying for her miracle. She thought of it as her place; where she asked God to allow her to occupy it for a long time to come. So far, He had not said yes; neither had He said no.

Lauryn waited in the aisle while Dakota assisted Grace to her seat on the long oaken bench at least a half century old. Heather nestled in close to Grace on the side opposite Dakota. Lauryn stood waiting, smoothing her dress with white-gloved hands, and expecting Dakota to back out of the pew.

Not this Sunday.

This time, Dakota sat beside Grace, squeezing her hand and fumbling through the sign of the cross while watching Lauryn perform hers. He was fifteen the last time he was inside a church. Lauryn genuflected, slid into the pew beside her father, and then wrapped her arm under his. Her smile offered more than any words she might speak. She believed there was strength in numbers and figured that meant in prayers as well as deeds. Maybe now God would hear their voices and grant them what she so desperately prayed for.

Jessica Collins agreed to meet the detectives at her home Monday after work. Bronc and Dakota waited in their car until she pulled into her townhouse driveway. Jessica's first reaction was to scan the neighboring homes. How might it look having policemen in an unmarked car greet her?

After fumbling with her keys, Jessica showed the men into her living room, offered to provide them with something to drink, and when they declined, she sat across from them.

"I wish there was something more I could tell you, but I just can't remember anything else."

"Ms. Collins," Dakota started.

"Please, Jessica," she interrupted.

"Jessica, we believe Angela must have known the person in her apartment that night."

"I can't believe that."

"Why?" Bronc asked.

"Angela would never have let someone into her apartment, I mean, she wouldn't have..."

"It's all right. Can you tell us anything about Angela's social life? Did she date?"

"As I told the other detectives, Angela was a pretty private person. I know she dated a guy from the office about a year ago. I don't remember his name. He left the company, oh, at least six months ago."

"Was it serious between them?"

"I don't think so. Angie brought it up at lunch one time and never mentioned it again. When I asked her about him later, she just said the chemistry was all wrong."

"We have the company directory for the past three years. Two detectives have been going through it," Bronc said.

"Did you and Angela do anything outside of work? Parties..."

"You mean recently?"

"Within the last few months."

"Once we went to the Chaparral. Before that we went to the Palomino and Caravans."

"How long ago?"

The Chaparral was at least four months ago. Caravans was a couple of months before she... The Palomino was just maybe six weeks ago."

"Anything happen at the Palomino?"

"Not really. A few guys asked us to dance, but most of the time we just sat at a table in the corner and listened to the music."

"Angela like to dance?"

"Yes and no."

"She enjoyed dressing the part...but wasn't much of a dancer."

Dakota had already surmised that from a pair of unblemished white boots in her closet.

"But guys did ask Angela to dance?"

"Yes."

"Any of them hang around, or try to pressure her?"

"No. They all seemed real nice. Wait...there was one guy. He was tall and wore a black hat that covered his eyes. I remember him because his face was like you'd see on those television commercials."

"He danced with Angela?"

"Yes, maybe twice. I'm not real sure."

"Do you think Angela might have given her telephone number to him?"

"I doubt that. Angie was real careful and not the dating type."

"What do you mean?"

"I mean Angie didn't date much. I don't think she'd just give out her number to anyone who asked her to dance."

"Did Angie ever talk about that guy or any other guy after that night?"

"No...wait a minute."

Dakota shifted forward in his chair. He could feel his heartbeat quicken inside his chest.

Jessica held both detectives on tenterhooks while she bit along her lower lip for a long moment.

"There was one time."

"One time what..."

"Well, Angie didn't really mention him to me. I was passing her desk...and I heard her say 'Frankie.' She was talking to someone on the phone."

"When was this?"

"I don't know. I mean it was at least a month ago. Maybe in early August."

"How did she say it?"

"Kind of endearing. I don't know...excited...maybe a little surprised."

"Then it wasn't a business-related call?"

"No. I guess that's what struck me as funny. It sounded very personal, maybe even a little intimate."

"Did she ever talk to you about any man in her life named Frank?"

"No. I think that's why I just remembered it. Like I said, Angie didn't date much. She held this image of the perfect man, and she always tried to make the guy fit her image. Needless to say, her dates came with the changing of the seasons."

"You're sure it was Frankie? You couldn't be mistaken?"

"No. I'm sure it was Frankie, and I'm sure she said it with more than just a passing interest."

"How did she say it, exactly? Can you remember?"

Moments passed while Jessica pressed her memory for sharper detail.

"I don't know...is it important?"

"Right now, everything is of monumental importance. We believe Angela let the killer into her apartment. Either he met her outside the apartment and forced her to open the door, or she welcomed him in. Either way, he got close enough to Angela to take control without a struggle."

Jessica thought for another moment, feeling that accuracy had become paramount in her recollection.

"Frankie," she lilted, with her voice rising pleasantly at the end.

"Oh, Frankie," she said again, this time with a hint of unexpected surprise in the words.

"I think that's how she said it."

Dakota looked at Bronc—Bronc held his stare. Was it important? Was there a hidden connection between Angela and this guy named Frank?

Dakota rushed through his remaining questions, and Jessica's answers only confirmed statements she had made earlier. Before leaving, Dakota jotted in his notebook the three men that had passed through Angela's life; even if only briefly. Was he hoping for too much considering that the ex-employee from Angela's place of business might possibly be named Frank? That was the next thing for his detectives to check.

Thursday proved a terrible day for Dakota. Rumors ran rampant that a number of civic organizations were pressuring the mayor. Talk surfaced of turning the investigation over to a team of FBI agents.

Mayor Bradley insisted on a full briefing, which forced Dakota to spend the morning gathering updates from every task force detective. Viable information on the Angela Walker case was a precious commodity. They had still no shortage of leads. Facts that could point to the killer's identity, however, were still nonexistent.

Bronc reported that the man Angela had dated a year before her death was Wesley Williams. He left the company, as reported, six months ago and now resided in Los Angeles. He told the detective over the telephone that he and Angela just never could hit it off. He also said he left Albuquerque for a better job in California. His departure had nothing to do with Angela Walker.

After hours of effort, Bronc, however, confirmed that the man's alibi for that Thursday night held up. Leave no stone unturned, he told himself.

Another potential lead and a good bit of detective grunt work up in smoke. Bronc wished he had better news for Dakota, but not for one minute did he regret being kept outside the mayor's briefing. He could only imagine the fireworks set to go off in there.

"Anything from the phone records of Angela's telephone at her job?"

"Phone company provided records for June, July, August and September. Nothing out of the ordinary. Most of Angela's calls were directly related to business. She had a few personal calls to St. Joseph's hospital, her car insurance agent, the airlines and a travel agent. None that turned up any lead to somebody named Frank."

"Any way to determine where her incoming calls originated from?"

"I've got the phone company working on it. Their records are mainly for billing purposes, so they only capture and retain the outgoing call information. A supervisor's doing a database search to see if they can turn up an outgoing call that routed to Walker's phone. But it's a real long shot."

The afternoon briefing dragged on until evening and finally ended at eight. Dakota was drained of every ounce of energy and emotion. Everyone wanted answers; everyone wanted progress. Dakota offered neither. All he wanted was to get the Boulder Hill case out of his mind. He chewed at his guilt the entire drive home.

Thank God for Laurianne and Cole. Without their help, he'd never be able to split his time between Grace and this case. Dakota now had to swallow a tinge of remorse over his outburst toward Cole at the basketball game. It kept cropping up to haunt him. He could feel himself slowly unraveling under the pressure. He sought guidance in the sanctity of his vehicle. No voice came to his aide.

It was all just getting too much to handle. At least that's what Dakota tried to convince himself. But beneath the surface, it was something else.

Lights shone throughout the house on Dakota's arrival, but the place had an eerie silence to it when he strode through the front door.

"Lauryn, Heather, I'm home," he called. He scanned the mail on the bureau inside the front door and checked the answering machine for calls. But no answer came back to him. He scanned a neat and tidy living room.

"Laurianne?"

Dakota set his stuffed briefcase on a bureau beside the stack of mail and strolled through the house into the lighted kitchen. The table was clean, unused. No note on the refrigerator as an explanation for why he was standing alone.

"Hey!" he yelled.

Dakota checked the refrigerator. No dinner plate wrapped in plastic.

"Oh Jesus," he uttered, racing up the stairs. Grace...

Light seeped under the closed bedroom door. Inside, soft music sifted through the air. When Dakota threw open the door, Grace was lying in bed. Her smile erased the concern flooding through his head.

"Where is everyone?"

"Cole and Laurianne have the girls out for dinner."

"That's nice. I'm sorry I'm late. The briefing just wouldn't end."

He leaned down, and kissing her softly, filled his head with her wonderfully sweet fragrance.

"It's okay, I understand," Grace said, smoothing the blanket over her body.

Dakota again reached down to kiss her and felt her smile when their lips met.

"You look beautiful tonight," he whispered, before releasing her hand. He had to put this day behind him. Clear everything from his head and focus on what was important at the moment: Grace. Dakota pulled at his tie while emptying his pockets on the bureau with his back to Grace.

"They talked about you on the five o'clock news. Now that you're heading up the investigation, they're saying you'll break the case in a month."

"Don't believe those buttheads. He's playing us like the Keystone Cops."

Grace slowly slid out from beneath her blanket and rose out of bed, steadying herself momentarily with a hand to the night table.

Dakota turned, unbuttoning his shirt.

"Grace?"

She stood there naked before him, her arms out, and her eyes filled with something Dakota had not seen in months. He also felt something he thought had left him forever.

"Hold me," she whispered.

The tears gathering in her eyes glistened in the soft light as Dakota brought her close.

"Cole and Laurianne are keeping the girls overnight. Have you eaten?"

"I'm not hungry."

"I need you tonight, Dakota. I need you to love me..."

Dakota opened his mouth to speak.

Grace silenced him with a kiss wrought with desire. They struggled together to shed his clothes, and coupled, they fell into the warmth of their marriage bed.

Their lovemaking was slow and patient. Dakota's kisses and caressing hands washed away all her suffering—made her feel as beautiful as she once was. For these fleeting impassioned moments, she was young and pretty and free; exactly as she had been when they married.

Grace buried her pain beneath layers of exploding pleasure—a pleasure long absent from her. Her moans of ecstasy filled Dakota's head while together they reached for the pinnacle of their love.

Afterward, neither moved for a long time. Cuddled with arms wrapped around each other to share the other's warmth, each time one sought to speak, the other smothered the words with a kiss. This was a time to share what words could never convey.

In the shallow darkness breached by a gibbous moon peering through their window, in the afterglow of a love that could withstand anything, there was no pain and no disease. Only two people—one love.

At midnight, the radio station switched to serene mood music. Neither Dakota nor Grace slept. As they listened, Dakota brushed his fingers along the soft curve of her body. Vince Gill's "Just Look At Us" began, a country ballad that Grace loved and that rekindled memories of the earlier days of their marriage. Grace turned to Dakota. He could see a long-lost, giddy excitement in her eyes. At that moment, he felt like they had somehow returned to their honeymoon.

"Dance with me?" she asked, her voice barely above a whisper, her eyes begging him to say yes.

Dakota never believed himself much of a dancer. Regardless, he eased Grace from the bed, savoring the touch of her soft wonderful flesh against his. Nothing could ever take away what made her so beautiful to him.

Grace's shivers subsided as, wrapped within the warmth of his arms, they began to flow gently back and forth in the darkness. The lyrics meant nothing now; the music meant everything. She eased her hand teasingly over the granite curve of his shoulder, savoring the touch of his flesh, until she reached the tie band holding his hair in place. He had always had the power to excite her with his very contact. He could move her by just being beside her. She clasped the tie band in her fingers and slid it down, releasing his hair to spread upon his shoulders. Her fire began to rage. He was the kindest, most gentle man she had ever known. And despite her anger, she thanked her God in her heart for giving him to her. She clutched a handful of black hair while she kissed him. His lips and breathing told her he shared her passion in this moment. She slipped her hand from his shoulder to around his waist as she nestled her head up under his neck. Dakota's arms quieted her chill and steered her clear of the bed. In sync with the music, and in a voice flat in tone but rich with love, he sang to her.

11

Sunday night. Dakota endured a fitful, shallow sleep in his bed. Rather sleep seemed nothing more than an unkept promise. By two A.M., he pulled himself from the bed and dressed; all the while chasing after something that tugged at the shirt sleeves of his mind the way an insistent child begs for attention. Hoping something in his files might trigger recognition, Dakota tacked a scribbled note on the refrigerator for Laurianne, and then rushed through the deserted streets to the solitude of his office. There, beneath a cone of light, he poured over the files until his eyes burned. By five, exhaustion overwhelmed him, driving him to the meager comforts of a shabby couch in the corner of his office. Lying there he cast all thought from his mind. Whatever it was that had been toying with him needed a clean slate with which to create.

In sleep, his mind meandered back in time. He found himself sitting on a hand-formed chair of birch, staring into the soft, dark eyes of a white-haired Indian man. Ko-Na-Che was the Indian's name as Dakota recalled. Though the young Dakota voiced questions about his parents, he received answers having nothing to do with what he sought.

"In all Apache men, an inner spirit walks with them, meant to guide and instruct you as you journey through your life. It will speak to you words that will keep you safe—if you learn to listen and trust what the spirit offers you," the old man said.

"How will I know this spirit's voice?" Dakota heard himself ask.

"Your father would have instructed you in the ways of the spirit voice. Now, young She-Nay-Hay, you must learn to listen with both your head and your heart. Only when both are receptive will you hear the words of your spirit. He only whispers and never scolds you for the errors of your ways. Only you shall be responsible for your own discipline. Generations ago, young warriors would set out on a solitary journey to learn the ways of our people. Some would climb the great mountains; others would venture into the desert. Their spirit would guide them and those that listened with both heart and head returned as men."

"And those who failed to listen?"

"Lieutenant, the task force is assembled in the command center for the morning briefing," a policewoman said, shaking him gently.

For a long moment, Dakota stared into her eyes. Then he checked his watch. It was 7:30 and he had been asleep for two hours. But he realized what had been pulling at him from deep in his brain. He had strayed. Two years ago, his spirit had offered him guidance. He had listened then. Now the voice had returned. Dakota had to trust his instincts.

"Should I tell them you're unavailable, sir?"

Dakota shook his head, rubbing the sleep out of his eyes.

The note holds the key to the killer's identity. He believed that two years ago and nothing had surfaced now to quiet that feeling.

Before going to the task force command center, Dakota made a stop at the computer center. There, he assigned Mary Borlin to the full-time task of sifting through VICAP, NCIC and any other crime databases in all the western states. Something inside told him to go back to the beginning and dig.

"We need to find a link between our killer and a victim named Ellie," Dakota instructed Borlin, a self-proclaimed computer maven and ten-year department veteran.

Mary's eyes alighted. She loved both the challenge and the opportunity to aid the task force. But she suspected her digging might be a long shot at success.

"Sir, you're asking for a needle out of one huge haystack," Mary said, after Dakota finished his explanation. "We're tapped into VICAP and NCIC. I can start there and hope."

Less than two years earlier, they had gone through the very same exercise and came up bone dry. At that time, Borlin even searched the database for the victims of the Green River Killer in Washington and still came up with no match to the name Ellie. The very high probability that Ellie could also be a prostitute's alias meant Mary could be digging a long time with the same lack of positive results.

The fact that no victim named Ellie had surfaced forced Dakota to consider that maybe Ellie was a fantasy manifestation in the killer's sick mind. If that were the case, they could dig all they wanted and never uncover a link between the name and the killer. But if Ellie were real...she could be the key.

Find your killer's first victim, Dakota. Rage has its beginning, the spirit inside him whispered. The killer's internal rage may have forced him to strike out against someone close to him. Dakota suspected this Ellie might turn out to be the killer's mother or wife.

The other possibility—one Dakota feared consider-er—was that the killer might be redirecting his anger and violence. Instead of striking out at the real Ellie, the Ellie he loathed, the killer selected victims who reminded him of Ellie. Consequently, he then acted out his rage against the real Ellie. In that case, as was the situation two years ago, they would unlikely unearth a victim named Ellie.

On Tuesday, the Albuquerque press went into a frenzy. Another body had been found. This one, also a woman, had been dumped a couple of miles west of Douglas Road on the western edge of the city along a rutted strip that cut a meandering path into the desert.

The task force swarmed the area only seconds ahead of the press and camera crews. Police forced the press away, despite reporters' fervid objections, until no one other than Bronc himself could get a look at the crime scene. Police quickly set up a wide perimeter; wasting no time unrolling the yellow police tape meant to preserve the entire area.

Bronc doled out orders at the scene while they waited for Dakota's arrival. He ordered a police helicopter in to snap aerials within a quarter mile radius of the victim before allowing his men in. Every task force detective was to make absolutely certain the site remained untainted.

By four that afternoon, Dakota appeared in the wash. He and Bronc began the meticulous process of cataloguing every detail before them. They divided the site into quadrants and assigned each detective to a specific area within each quadrant, requiring them to sift through it until they were satisfied all possible traces of evidence had been uncovered. Afterward, they would widen their search pattern into the surrounding sand hills. Outdoor crime scenes required far more manpower to preserve and analyze than indoor. Yet this scene represented a distinct departure from the killer's previous pattern. Was he becoming smarter, more careful in his methods?

The body's display immediately raised a cautionary flag in Dakota. Previously, the killer took great pains to position the body a specific way. This victim had been dumped helter skelter in a shallow wash.

Multiple stab wounds to the chest, arms and neck indicated clearly that the victim had resisted. She actually fought off her killer before she died. Their guy had been smarter than that. Either the killer had misjudged his victim...or...

Clay, the lead evidence technician, immediately bagged the victim's hands, and once finished, he motioned Dakota away from the others.

"Lieutenant, I've got hair and skin on this one," Clay said.

Dakota raised a quizzical brow.

"My feeling exactly, sir."

"Get samples to the lab as soon as you can," Dakota said.

Three hours after Dakota's arrival, the fading sun forced detectives to call it a night. But no one was going home. They proceeded back to the command center to begin the tedious task of identifying the victim and setting up the strategy for the investigation.

At headquarters, Bronc switched on the small television in time to catch the nightly news in progress. Lisa Roberts described the scene where she believed another victim of the Boulder Hill killer had been found.

Dakota turned from the television to review the reports as his detectives finished typing them up.

"ID her as soon as possible. Where's Childers?"

The detectives around the room shrugged.

"Bronc, have Childers pull the latest statewide M. P. reports. Let's see if our victim has recently been reported missing."

A ringing telephone stopped Bronc before he could leave his desk.

"Dakota, for you."

Dakota snatched up the telephone, listened for only a few seconds and then returned the handset to the cradle.

"I've got to go, Bronc. You're in charge."

With nothing further, Dakota fled the command center. His face had gone slack.

On Wednesday, Grace became an inpatient at St. Joseph's Medical Center. None of the doctors treating her wanted to admit it, but the radiation had failed miserably. Her initial blood work-up indicated continuing liver and pancreatic deterioration. The cancer now threatened to shut down Grace's vital organs. They were losing the battle.

Dr. Rayorson, head of Oncology, approached Grace and Dakota with alternative treatments to try; more potent chemotherapy that just might make the difference. Dakota wanted to believe him. But Rayorson admitted it was still a long shot. The doubt in Rayorson's voice overshadowed any hopefulness in his eyes.

While Dakota arranged for neighbors to care for the girls until he returned, Cole and Laurianne remained at Grace's bedside. Despite everything, Grace wore her wig and her weak smile, refusing to let those she loved see her for what she had become.

In the room, Laurianne paced. Cole sat beside Grace with his arms tight across his chest.

"Coffee?" Laurianne asked Cole.

He shook his head, but started to rise.

"Why don't you get some coffee, Laurianne," Grace said, reaching out for Cole's hand. He returned to the chair.

"Go ahead downstairs. I'll stay with Grace until Dakota gets here, and then I'll meet you in the cafeteria."

"You sure? I can wait..."

"No, no, go ahead."

Grace smiled weakly at Cole once Laurianne had left the room.

"Thanks," she said. Her voice had lost all its vigor.

"You cold? You want a blanket?" Cole asked, trying to warm her hands with both of his.

"No. I wanted you to stay. I need to..."

"You don't have to say anything..."

"I know what you've been doing."

"What?" Cole replied, hiding behind a mask of innocence he draped across his face.

"The money...in our account. I know you've been taking care of things..."

"Now look, Grace, don't you start, too," Cole offered in his strongest sheltering voice, "you're going to beat this thing...like you did last time...." Tears crept up to blur his vision.

"I don't think so."

"Come on, Grace, you gotta fight this thing."

"Cole, please, just listen. I know you've been putting money in our checking account to cover all the bills."

"It doesn't matter. Only you matter."

"Cole, I need you to be strong. You need to be there for him now. You and I, and Laurianne and the girls, we're red hearts. We understand what it really means to be Apache. We are all Dakota really believes in. You know Dakota loves you. You and he have your differences, but he thinks the world of you. Dakota's not as strong as he wants everyone to believe. He will have a hard time. Outside, he's the toughest cop in Albuquerque. Inside..."

"Don't worry, Grace, I'm going to take care of them...I'll take care of everything."

"He's going to need you...I can't fight any...I can't win. Promise me you'll be there for Dakota and the girls. Help them get through this...don't let them feel alone."

"I promise," Cole said, crying now, clutching Grace's hands tightly. "I'll make sure..."

"I need to be alone for awhile. Go catch up with Laurianne."

"I'll be back up in ten minutes," Cole said, but found it impossible to relinquish her hands.

"Please, Cole, go now."

Cole kissed Grace on her cheek, wiped away his tears and cleaned his glasses before departing.

A second note appeared mysteriously at the television station addressed to Lisa Roberts. But this one she never opened. Using tweezers, a plainclothes officer collected the sealed envelope, secured it as evidence in a plastic bag, and raced it to police headquarters. Lisa lagged only minutes behind.

After dusting it for fingerprints, Clay opened the envelope and set the contents before Dakota, Bronc, Washington and Rodman on the conference room table.

The time draws quickly near.
You better hurry up Blackwood or
you'll be too late.

Dakota turned his attention to a three-ring binder holding a stack of black and white snapshots.

"How many of these people have we identified so far?" Dakota asked. He was flipping through the pages that showed each and every person who had come into contact with Lisa Roberts either in her job at the station or where she lived.

"About half. You really think the killer's in one of those pictures?" Bronc asked.

"He's must have some way of getting close enough to deliver these damn letters."

"But each time, he delivers these messages in the midst of a crowd and leaves the envelope at the guard's station," Rodman said.

"And the guard saw nothing?"

"Not a thing. No one hanging around the lobby. No one looking for an opportunity," the plainclothes officer, who had hand-delivered the envelope, said.

"How long before we can get still photographs off the surveillance camera in the KGGM lobby?" Washington asked.

"I've got a man working on it as we speak," Bronc replied.

"That may mean our man makes frequent trips to the station. If the opportunity doesn't present itself, he abandons the effort to try another time. Maybe after the fifth or sixth or seventh time he appears, he gets his chance and takes it."

"I'll get someone looking at all the video we can get from the surveillance cameras. We may just find a face that keeps popping in," Bronc said. Excitement began to infect his words.

"But why risk it?" Washington asked, thinking aloud.

"Because he's a sick bastard. He's sucking us into something. But what?" Dakota said, still staring at the words on the page.

"I don't buy it. This scumbag is willing to risk getting caught with the letter in his possession just to taunt us?" Rodman said. He tapped the envelope away with the flick of his index finger.

"Taunting me. He's taunting me," Dakota said.

The words stirred a disquieting feeling inside Dakota. A feeling that he already knew something that he couldn't focus on.

"I need to know what each of you think. Is Lisa Roberts in danger?" Washington asked, pulling the discussion into a sensitive direction.

"He's got to know we're watching her. He may have even seen our man lift the envelope at the guard's station. He's not going to try to kill her unless..."

"He wants to be caught," Rodman finished for Dakota.

"I don't think so."

"But our profile said the killer most likely goes through a period of guilt and remorse after the killings. Couldn't he be going through one of those periods right now?" Rodman insisted.

"I don't think so. But get this off to Quantico right away. For now, make sure every man assigned to Ms. Roberts understands the situation. If he's crazy enough to go after her, I don't want anything to happen to let him slip through our fingers."

"What's the status of our latest victim?"

"No ID yet. As long as she's a Jane Doe, we're going to have a hard time getting the investigation off the ground."

"How many men are working it?"

"All of them," Bronc said.

"Pull most of them off," Dakota instructed.

"What! Are you nuts?" Rodman insisted.

"I think a copycat did our Jane Doe."

Rodman made his anger obvious in his eyes. The crazy Indian was going off on his own again.

"Why?" Washington asked.

"Our man leaves his victim at the scene. Jane Doe was found at a secondary crime scene...a disposal site."

"Maybe the vehicle she was in became the primary crime scene. Maybe the victim panicked before our guy could get her where he wanted her."

"Our man takes his victims without a struggle. He sanitizes the primary crime scene very meticulously, and he leaves his signature. We know Jane Doe had the opportunity to fight off her attacker."

"I think you're way the hell off on this one, Blackwood. You and your goddamn crazy ass signature," Rodman moaned.

"I'm telling you in every previous killing the Boulder Hill killer positioned his victim post-mortem. Someone just dumped this woman."

"So maybe he forgot to sign his work. Maybe a car came by and spooked him."

"He would never allow that to happen. Every move is carefully planned and orchestrated. I'm still in charge, and I say we pull all but two detectives off Jane Doe. Have them get an ID and backtrack to the victim's family and friends."

Rodman crossed his arms over his chest and refused to listen to anything further.

Corinne shoveled the clutter on her desk into the wide drawer and fumbled with her sweater and purse. Standing up in haste, she snagged her nylon on a slightly open side drawer. She cursed; then a moment later she dismissed it as unimportant and the result of being in a hurry.

"Thanks for staying, Corinne. I hope I didn't ruin your plans for this evening," her boss said politely from his desk as Corinne passed his open door. He glanced up long enough to notice her preparing to leave.

She hated working late; especially when she had plans with Frankie.

"No problem, Mr. Graham, I didn't have anything pressing anyway," she lied, "I'll be leaving now. The spreadsheets for the last three pages you gave me are on the desk. I'll copy and bind them first thing in the morning. If you don't make any more changes, I can have everything ready for you by ten o'clock."

"Thanks so much, I'd never pull this off without your extra effort. Corinne..."

Corinne stopped and leaned back into the doorway in a polite gesture. She figured she had to wait until he finished his praise before bolting for the door.

Graham leaned back in his chair, grazing over her.

"I'll make sure certain people hear about all the hard work you've put into this project." Graham left her with his patented trust-me-babe wink.

Corinne smiled and buttoned the first few buttons on her sweater as she walked away.

"Yeah, right. That's what you said the last time, butthead. I got squat for all my long hours," Corinne mumbled low enough so that only she would hear.

Graham had been boobie-eyed over her since her first day on the job. Seemed like he never could take his eyes off her breasts. She had arrested his advances twice in the last few months and knew as long as she said no, there would be nothing extra for her in her pay envelope. Frankie told her she should go to the owner and scream sexual harassment. But she didn't. She wanted that salary increase he kept hinting at. From the way things appeared around here, the only way to squeeze more money out of these scuzbucket cheapos was to rip open her blouse and let them play kid in a candy store.

Dinner. Corinne was famished. She'd skipped lunch hoping to leave on time at the end of the day. *Yeah right!* All she wanted now was to meet Frankie and get some dinner. She had been anticipating this all day. Then when Graham said she had to stay to prepare the sales projections for tomorrow's meeting, her heart became a lead weight sinking to the pit of her stomach.

Corinne rushed across town, cursing each time a red light impeded her progress. Was everyone and everything out to sabotage her? Frankie had to wait for her. If she hurried, she could still get there on time. She was starving...and excited.

When Corinne rolled into Chez Paul's parking lot, she slammed the car into park, ripped the keys from the ignition and dashed for the front door. Inside, she scanned the entire breadth of the dining room, hoping. Her heart pounded; her mouth had turned cottony. She hadn't felt like this in a long time. It felt great. Was she too late after all? Damn those stupid lights! Why can't they time them to allow people to get somewhere instead having to stop at every other intersection!

Then she stopped. Frankie caught her eye while chatting with the waiter in a corner booth. Corinne wasn't too late after all.

Quiet consumed the hall outside Grace's room on the third floor of St. Joseph's. Dakota sat beside her bed; his hand locked in hers and his head resting on her mattress.

"It's late," she whispered, having to muster strength for each word.

"Shh, just rest," Dakota whispered back.

Outside, faint squeaks of rubber-soled feet rose then fell.

The latest treatment had been torturous and now the waiting began anew. Would this new round of radiation work? Could anything work?

"How did you get to stay?"

"Connections. Laurianne and Cole are at the house with the girls."

"You shouldn't..."

"Grace..." Dakota started. He paused until she became wide-eyed and attentive.

"I think it's time."

"Time? For what?"

"Time to call your parents. They have a right to be here..."

Grace grew ruddy with rage at the very mention of the word.

"No! You promised me the last time that you would not do that."

"I know. Honey, they're your parents, and they have a right to know what's happening to you."

"They gave up their rights. I don't want them here. You can call them after..."

"Grace, please..."

"Dakota, I never told you why. Please, I don't want them here. I don't want to see them. Promise me you'll respect my wishes."

"Grace, whatever happened between you and them is in the past. They'd want to see you. They'd want to be here with you."

"No!" Grace insisted; her anger had fueled a renewed strength in her.

"You're my world. You and our daughters. I never could understand how a mother could hate her own daughter."

"Grace, you have to listen to me. Put aside whatever happened between you and your parents. Give them the chance to make things right between you. Don't take this anger and hatred to the grave."

"I can't."

Tears seeped into Grace's eyes.

"Yes, you can."

"Dakota, you don't understand why I ran away at sixteen. You don't understand why I never went back.

I wasn't going to let him do what he wanted to do to me. I would never submit to his sick, vile acts. You also never knew I called them when we decided to get married. You made me so happy I thought I could try to mend our lives back together. I wanted to make things right between them and me. At first they were excited. But when they found out I was marrying you...an Indian...they told me not to bother coming home."

Dakota searched inside himself for words. He found none to counter her.

"I chose you fifteen years ago. And I've never once regretted that choice."

Dakota smoothed his hand along Grace's cheek. Her smile overcame her pain. Her grip had surrendered all its strength. She was letting go.

"Now it's your turn to listen to me. I need to get this out."

Dakota nodded, slid his chair nearer the bed so he could bring his face close to hers.

"I love you. I've loved you since the day you walked into that cafe. And I'm sure you didn't keep coming back there for the food."

Dakota wiped away the first assault of tears to breach his eyes.

"There is nothing you can do to help me now."

"Grace, don't give up..."

"Please, Dakota, just listen. You can't fix this. We both know it. I'm going to die. Neither you nor I can't change that."

As Grace spoke, her words revealed a growing strength. She had to focus everything left inside her to get it out.

"We can't fix this. What God has planned for me must come to pass."

Dakota turned away to hide the tears and the pain.

"Grace, don't give up...you've got to fight. You can beat this thing."

"Dakota, I can't. I can't fight anymore. I love you more than anything. You can't save me. But you can save them..."

Dakota turned back to Grace, probing her eyes.

"Them?"

"The Boulder Hill killer. Dakota, you're the best. You've got to find him. Save the others. Promise me you won't give up. Promise me you'll get him."

"Grace..."

"Please, Dakota, promise me. You can do it. You must get him before other people die."

"I promise, Grace. I'll get him. Now don't talk anymore."

"I have to. I have to say these things. I love you, Shee-Nah-Hay. I'm glad we could make love one more time. You made me feel beautiful. You made me feel like a woman."

Dakota squeezed tightly, holding on to her as if doing so could keep her from leaving him. Tears rushed into his eyes, overflowing down his cheeks.

"I'm tired now. But I want one more thing. Tell them I want to see our girls one more time. And Bring the envelope from my jewelry box on the bureau. I need to see the girls once more before..."

"I will. I'll bring them tomorrow. Just rest now, Grace. Go to sleep. I'll be right here in the room with you. In the morning, I'll bring the girls."

Dakota found sleep elusive despite the still of the hospital room. He listened to the sound of Grace's breathing and the occasional footfalls of night nurses at work in the halls.

With the dawn came doctors, the day shift nurses, and lab techs to draw more blood.

It was time. The doctors ordered Grace transferred to intensive care and set up a new, radical
chemo treatment plan for her.

Never give up. Never.

Dakota waited in the reception area while the doctors examined Grace. During that time, he called Laurianne and instructed her to keep the girls out of
school. Grace's doctor made no objection to Lauryn
and Heather coming to visit Grace, and Grace insisted
she remain in her present ward until after the girls'
visit. Grace refused to allow the girls to see her with
tubes and bags all around. That was not the lasting image she wanted the girls to have of her.

During those long empty minutes waiting, Dakota
contacted Bronc for an update on the investigation.
No new leads had opened up, and still they were working to identify the Jane Doe; each hoping her identity
might lead to a break in the case.

Dakota said nothing of Grace's condition; it was
hard enough for him to face what came next. Vocaliz-
ing it only made it worse.

When the girls arrived, Lauryn handed the envelope to her mother, which brought a faint smile to
Grace's withered cheeks. From the envelope, Grace removed two sets of sterling silver angel wings with
stick pin backings. She affixed the first pair to Heather
and the second pair to Lauryn.

"What are these?" Lauryn asked.

"They're guardian angel wings," Grace replied.
Heather stared at the pin in fascination. Lauryn's eyes
remained on her mother.

"They will watch over each of you for me and keep
you safe," Grace forced out, burying the agony of having to say the words.

Lauryn and Heather spent an hour with Grace at
her bedside. Heather asked when she would be coming home. Rubbing her finger along the silver wings,
Lauryn knew better than to ask. To signal the end of
their visit, the nurse entered and stood silently inside

the door, allowing Grace that precious few more minutes before asking if she were ready.

Grace acknowledged the nurse. She knew it was time to say good-bye. There were no tears from Grace; nor did she say she would be home soon. She sensed that somehow, in her own way, Lauryn understood. The kiss Grace bestowed on each of their foreheads would be the last contact they would have with their mother. And Grace made sure the last words they heard from her lips were 'I love you.'

Cole and Laurianne remained in the main lobby until Grace had finished with the girls and made the transition to intensive care. While Cole paced, Laurianne sat in a chair half listening to an elderly woman whine about her unending list of aches and pains. It was heart wrenching for Cole and Laurianne to have to see Grace in her current condition.

Dakota never left her side. They remained joined down the corridors and up the elevator from the third to the fifth floor.

The doctors admitted that Grace's organs had deteriorated more rapidly than they had anticipated. The cancer had virtually destroyed her liver, pancreas and spleen. Time became their fiercest enemy. If they had more time, they might find a miracle. Time becomes every man's enemy at one point or another.

With Grace settled in intensive care, the doctors pondered the potential benefits of a massive dose of chemotherapy. If it worked, it could buy a few more days; maybe even a few more weeks. Such an aggressive course of action, however, did carry greater risks. It could kill her. Yet there was little else to hope for.

No miracle had yet been delivered.

What had once been a woman full of life, quick to laugh and love, was now a shell of flesh. The disease had stolen her spirit and broken her will. The demon inside her had won. Now he need only claim her soul.

Grace placed herself in God's hands now. And never gave up praying for that miracle.

12

Bronc met Dakota at the hospital with the usual stack of daily reports filed by the task force detectives. The nursing supervisor arranged for Dakota to use the nurses' lounge. Anyone unaware of the Boulder Hill investigation and the task force detectives must have landed in Albuquerque from some other country. It became a subject of almost every newscast.

Dakota's face now appeared almost nightly on the television as a result of numerous segments replayed from his investigation two years earlier. He had yet to become a celebrity, but he did notice that glimmer of recognition from people passing him on the street or in the halls.

For the most part, Dakota refused to leave the hospital; he spent every possible minute at Grace's side, letting her know she would never be alone. As a result, Bronc carried in everything Dakota needed to stay in touch with the day-to-day.

"How's Grace today?" Bronc asked, as he poured himself a cup of steaming decaf coffee in the nurses' lounge. His hand shook visibly as he poured. It seemed like he had lost even the energy to force his lungs to breathe anymore. He needed time away from this thing. But this was not the time. Whenever self-pity crept in, he considered Dakota. That thought alone gave him the strength to press on.

"Holding her own. Doctors are trying a more aggressive treatment. And we're praying..."

"I'll manage the investigation. You just worry about Grace," Bronc offered, dropping his massive frame into the seat across the table from Dakota. He thought *he* looked bad. He had never seen his lieutenant looking worse. Reddened, sleepless eyes were rimmed with bags of swarthy skin. A constant faraway look consumed those eyes; a look that stemmed from unrelenting fear.

It was insane for Dakota to even think about the Boulder Hill killer now. But Bronc knew better than to question Dakota's intentions. A driven man, Dakota would let nothing break his spirit. Not now; not ever.

After perusing the latest reports, Dakota began the tedious process of backtracking into the Walker file to recollect older information; again seeking some link—some connection that might tell the team which way to go.

"Anything coming on-line from missing persons?"

"Not a thing. Jane Doe isn't helping us with this investigation."

"That's most likely where it will come from. Somebody's going to report the woman missing."

"You still think Jane Doe isn't his next victim?"

"No signature. He would have left his signature. Jane Doe's death isn't fitting into his ritual fantasy."

"Lisa Roberts is beginning to crack," Bronc added, after waiting for Dakota to finish the report under his eyes.

"What happened?"

"Some guy approached her in the station lobby; he just wanted an autograph. She flipped out when he touched her arm. She screamed and fought him off."

"Who was the guy?"

"An out-of-stater who thought she was a celebrity. We brought him in for questioning, but found no link to Angela Walker's death."

"Great. You think she can hang on a while longer?" Exasperation peppered Dakota's words. Lisa might be nothing more than another toy in the sick bastard's play world.

"I'd like to pull her off the streets for a time. At least until we have more to work with," Bronc said.

Dakota stared away, beyond Bronc, into the hospital corridor. A pair of nurses moved quickly past the open doorway. The distraction turned his mind back to Grace.

"What do you think?" Bronc persisted.

"I think you're right. Convince her to take a vacation. Preferably out of state and without anyone's knowledge of her whereabouts. And I mean nobody gets told."

"Got it. Any fresh ideas?"

"Keep searching for a connection to Angela; especially within the month prior to her death. The answer is there. Oh, and have Williams do a point-by-point work up between Angela Walker and the killer's first victim of two years ago. There's a common thread between them. We just have to find it."

"Could be a very thin thread."

"We've got to figure out why he chose them out of an entire city."

"I've already got Andrews on that. Says he'll have a complete profile done within the next three days."

Bronc emptied his cup and then rose to leave, taking the time to toss the empty cup into the nearest wastebasket.

"I'm here around the clock. Cole and his wife have the girls. Keep me current—any hour, day or night. And Bronc, have some men check out the university. Compare the violent incident reports from two years ago and any that are currently being generated. Maybe our guy's a student hiding on the campus and his eruption starts out slow and builds to murder. A violent incident on campus could be a precursor to his murders."

"Got it, Dakota. You take care of your pretty lady, and we'll nail that sonofabitch for you."

If only there were a sliver of confidence in Bronc's words.

Time. Time's pace never changes—only our perception of it. Fear can stretch a minute into an endless abyss. Pressure, on the other hand, propels it so lightning fast that we barely have the opportunity to witness it. And through it all, Time marches on a single second at a time.

Minutes dragged into lonely hours. Dakota tried to sleep in the chair beside Grace's bed. The room's wide window provided nurses continual observation from the central station. The wall-mounted cardiac monitor beeped off its barely audible tones. The drone signal repeated at the central station monitor.

Grace was never alone. Nurses monitored her vital signs while Dakota clutched her hand. As long as the monitor beeped, she clung to life at the other end of the wire. Grace had little trouble breathing; but on occasion, a groan would escape her throat from pains so severe, they penetrated the sea of drugs coursing through her veins.

Doctors said nothing to Dakota. They came and went with the hours. But Dakota understood. He no longer needed to be told his wife was dying. One hour eventually lead to the next. And, finally, the first dim rays of dawn spilled through the cracks in the drapes on the single outside window.

Dakota rubbed his eyes, listened to the heart monitor and thanked God for giving Grace one more day. The first thing he did was kiss her as she slept.

"Excuse me, Detective Blackwood, I'll need to draw blood from your wife," a young, plain woman with short, chestnut hair asked from the door. She wore a pristine white lab coat and held a rack of mainly empty test tubes.

"Sure. I need to move around anyway," Dakota said, trying to straighten cramped muscles. His stretching sent a shooting pain along his back. He rubbed the last remnants of sleep from his eyes as he passed the nurse on his way out.

"I'll just be a few minutes," the nurse offered apologetically.

Grace pulled open her eyes as if her lids were leaden when she felt a prick to her forearm.

"Feeling any better today, Mrs. Blackwood?"

"Not good...more blood?"

"Afraid so. I know we've been taking a lot, but it's really necessary."

"Sure. I've got enough stuff in me that I'll never feel it anyway."

"Good to see your spirits up. The doctors are going to take good care of you."

"You're not the regular nurse?"

"No, I'm Fran Hellstrom, Mrs. Blackwood. I'll be coming in and out to take blood. As a matter of fact, I'm pretty new here. I transferred to St. Joseph's two months ago. I hated Lovelace. Better people and better benefits here," the nurse said, as if she were sharing a secret with Grace.

Grace offered no reaction.

"But don't worry, I've been doing this for years. I won't mess up."

"You can't do anything worse than what's been done so far."

"That hurt?"

"No."

"I'm sorry. I'm having a little trouble hitting the vein...there, I've got it. Just give me one more second...and....there."

The nurse carefully labeled the test tube and placed it in her rack. She offered Grace a friendly smile.

"You can go back to sleep now." Then she collected up her rack of test tubes and left the room.

13

The Angela Walker investigation had crumbled into an endless rush to get to nowhere. Most of the time, task force detectives felt like the Keystone Cops; they dashed from place to place, stumbling over each other to uncover information from anyone who had anything to say about the Boulder Hill killer.

Every lead a detective worked led to a resounding dead end. Somewhere in the city another victim waited either to be found or, unknowingly, to be killed.

Dakota remained on the sidelines for days as the doctors struggled to arrest Grace's cancer. Each day, Grace slipped further and further away from him. Her periods of consciousness became less frequent.

Grace slept much of each day and most of the night.

Dakota awakened with a jolt when a duty nurse entered the room. He checked his watch: midnight. The rhythmic beep assured him Grace remained with them. The nurse first apologized for startling him then informed Dakota that a detective awaited him in the nurses' lounge.

A sleepy-eyed Dakota entered to find Bronc pacing with coffee and a cigarette in one hand and a doughnut in the other.

"That your dinner?" Dakota asked.

"We got it," Bronc said.

"Got what?"

"Jane Doe. Name's Melissa Sue Bryant and she's a local."

Dakota felt suddenly awake.

"What have you got on her?"

"Divorced. Lived alone. The car registered in her name is missing."

"Good work. Terrific work. Where are you going from here?"

"Family and friends. The girl's mother said Melissa went through a real messy divorce. We're going to talk to the ex in the morning."

"Get some sleep and update me in the morning."

Dakota could appreciate the smile on Bronc's face as he left.

Father Florentine arrived the following morning to administer Extreme Unction—the Catholic sacrament of Last Rights to Grace. Dakota removed himself from the room; he couldn't stand to bear witness to that Christian ceremony.

The doctors finally admitted that they had run out of treatments. Any drugs administered now were meant to stave off the pain of the growing menace inside her. The doctors accepted they couldn't win.

Dakota needed to get away. He needed to find a place isolated from the world. Hearing the words and knowing the truth in his heart somehow made the moment unbearable.

Cole replaced Dakota at Grace's bedside, while Dakota went home to have dinner with the girls. Two days had passed since he had seen them last. He missed them now more than ever.

Lauryn said little while they ate; she sensed what was close at hand. After dinner, Dakota held the girls while they watched something on television. Dakota had no idea what it was—nor did he care. Feeling Heather and Lauryn in his arms consumed his mind. Nothing else mattered at that moment.

Cole and Laurianne's handling of the household's day-to-day affairs relieved Dakota of everything except Grace. Bronc's handling of the day-to-day Boulder Hill killer investigation had, for the moment, kept it out of Dakota's mind. Dakota struggled to cope. He prepared for the inevitable. Right now, that was all he could handle.

Wednesday's sunrise washed across Grace's face as she lay in bed. She never saw it. Never knew it had come and gone. Dakota sat there watching her in the bed: knowing he would never hold her again, never kiss her again, or never tell her how much he loved her again. He dwelled obsessively now on their first few years of marriage and the smile he remembered on Grace's face when each of their daughters came into this world. He must remember her that way. Not the way she currently was in that bed beside him.

That evening after dinner, Cole and Laurianne accompanied Dakota to the hospital while the girls stayed with a neighbor. Through the glass, Cole and Laurianne caught a glimpse of Grace in bed. Tubes and bags hung from poles on either side of her head. She seemed at peace beneath her tightly-tucked tan blanket.

The nursing supervisor told Dakota that Grace had slept comfortably all afternoon. No one expected her to experience any more than a few moments of consciousness now and then. What she withheld from Dakota was that Grace might never wake again.

Cole and Laurianne left without a word; each feeling as if someone was squeezing their hearts until they could no longer breath. While they wished for that one more chance to speak to Grace, they both knew they had left nothing important unsaid.

As the floor grew quiet in the late hours, the nurse offered Dakota a second pillow when he settled into the chair beside Grace's bed. Dakota listened as the nursing supervisor's briefing for the night nurses coming on duty drifted into the room. Grace had become a 'no code.' The ominous ring to the words stripped Dakota of his voice and his spirit. There would be no effort made to save her if her heart stopped. Nothing would be done now to interfere with the plans God had made for Grace's life.

Shortly after midnight, Nurse Hellstrom returned with her little tray of test tubes and her sterile needles for drawing blood.

"Why are you taking more blood? What good could that do?" Dakota asked, with anger rising in his voice.

"Sorry, sir. Orders. I know this is difficult, but..."

"I'm sorry," Dakota said.

Failing to find a suitable position for sleep anyway, Dakota used the intrusion to stretch in the corridor.

Hellstrom poked around in search of a vein in Grace's forearm. This time, however, she was harsh in her probing; she intentionally inflicted pain with each jab.

Grace awakened, half opening her eyes. It took a long moment for her to focus. She saw a blur standing over her.

"More...blo...od?" she asked groggily.

Hellstrom leaned in close while she held a gauze pad in place. She brought her lips to Grace's ear and whispered words that only Grace would hear.

Grace's heartbeat accelerated, leaping from seventy beats per minute to ninety, and then to a hundred twenty. She widened her eyes; desperate to focus on the face so close to hers. But before she could, she fell into unconsciousness.

The nurse squeezed Grace's hand as if to assure her that everything would be all right.

Only Grace knew it would never be all right again.

Laurianne hit the snooze button on the clock radio a second time before accepting that she had to get up. Her stomach churned uneasily, and all she wished to do was hide beneath the blanket for another fifteen minutes. But she pulled herself out of bed after a near sleepless night. It was after seven—she was late—and she had to get the girls up and off to school. She rarely slept when she was alone in the bed. Cole had stayed at their house; he wanted to be up and out early for a meeting with a group of high-tech investors interested in Albuquerque's future.

Laurianne slid her hundred and thirty pound frame into a gray jogging suit and endured a sudden weakness in her stomach. It passed a few moments later.

She trudged listlessly down the stairs to begin the girls' breakfast. Within the hour, her pace hit fever pitch as she rushed about locating misplaced homework and finishing lunches in time for the girls' departure.

A laggard Heather descended the stairs with a glum expression.

"Heather, you can't go like that," Lauryn said, stopping her.

To which, Heather immediately plopped down on the last stair and began to cry.

Laurianne entered the hall to check on the state of the girls.

"I can't help it. This is all I could find," Heather pushed out between sobs.

"You can't go to school wearing socks that are two different colors. One's blue and the other is green."

"It's not my fault. I can't help it. That's all I could find."

Exasperated, Lauryn dropped her books on the stairs, fell to her knees and removed Heather's shoes.

"I'll find you two that match. Now just stop crying, will ya," Lauryn scolded, as she marched her little frame up the stairs.

"I can't. I'm trying to stop, but I can't. Stop yelling at me."

"It's okay, Heather. We'll get those socks to match," Laurianne said.

"You're going to make us miss the bus," Lauryn scolded from the upstairs bedroom. The words started Heather's crying anew.

Before Laurianne could start up the stairs to assist, Lauryn emerged from their bedroom.

"I found the blue. Now take off the green one," Lauryn said, descending the stairs with sock in hand. She knelt before her sister in such a way as to let Laurianne know that she intended to remedy the situation herself. Then she placed the errant sock back on Heather's foot, grabbed Heather's shoe when Heather tried to put it back on herself, jammed Heather's foot into the shoe, and re-tied the laces.

"It's okay. We're ready now," Lauryn said, in a voice meant to soothe her sister.

Laurianne scooped their lunches from the table and helped Heather into her sweater before leaving the house.

"I want you to have a good day," Laurianne said, wiping the last remnant of a tear from Heather's cherubic cheeks. "I'll be here when you get home. Maybe we can bake cookies together," Laurianne added, bestowing each with a kiss on the head as they marched off into the morning sun.

"Done," Laurianne said to herself, leaning against the front door after she closed it. They were off. One less hurdle to get over this day. Next would be the kitchen and the mess the girls left behind.

Looking over the sink of accumulated dishes, Laurianne sighed and poured herself a cup of the coffee. Coffee Lauryn had the forethought to put on for her even before Laurianne crawled out of bed. Sitting at the table, she stared into the cup for a time without drinking it. She wished she had children of her own. At thirty-five, she was running out of time. It had to be her fault, since Cole had tested out fine on his end.

Cole had promised he would leave the bank right after the meeting concluded. He would then come by and pick her up so they could go to the hospital together and still be back at the house in time to meet the girls.

The sound of the front door opening stole her away from her cup and her thoughts.

"Lauryn, what did you forget now?" she called, leaving the table to see what she could do to help.

Dakota stopped just inside the door; his jacket dropped to the floor as his arms went limp. Laurianne knew. No words need be uttered. Dakota's face confirmed it.

"Oh God, no," she cried, rushing to wrap her arms around him.

"During the night...I" Dakota stopped, burying his face into Laurianne's shoulder. He forced himself to control his tears, to rein in what struggled for release. But he failed.

They cried together for a long time.

14

The funeral home filled quickly with friends and neighbors the first night of Grace's wake. Most, if not all, of the police officers and their wives came to pay their respects. Bronc had arrived early and took it upon himself to play traffic control for the mourners. It gave him something to do. Some way to help. When chairs ran short, he, himself, lugged more in and set them up. Words could do little at a time like this, but actions would comfort the soul.

Seeing Grace there so young and attractive served to remind everyone of life's precious gift.

Laurianne cried in a corner, clutching Lauryn's hand.

Grace's frail form appeared as if she were sleeping, Lauryn commented. She stared at the body for a long time, trying to convince herself that her mother was not just sleeping.

Dakota said little, accepting condolences from those who came to see Grace one last time. In the midst of a crowd, he stopped suddenly. He knew who the woman was the moment he saw the red hair and small face: Grace's mother. She remained at the rear of the chapel, clinging to the door, waiting. A second later, a burly, graying man moved beside her and took up her arm. It was as if they needed to prepare themselves for what stood before them. Whatever rift had separated them from their daughter, Dakota accepted he would never understand.

The earlier telephone conversation between Dakota and Grace's mother lasted only a few minutes. But Dakota could feel the shock and hurt coming through the line. It had only taken an hour to track Grace's parents down. A single call to the Wisconsin State Patrol got him their telephone number and address. For a moment after he had hung up from their conversation, Dakota wished he had not waited then realized he loved Grace too much to have betrayed her.

The Logans made their way down the aisle; Grace's mother faltered at her husband's side and broke into tears when Grace's body became visible. They stopped a half dozen paces before the casket.

"You must be Rachel Logan," Dakota said.

The woman did not turn at once—the sight of her daughter held her eyes fast. She began to sob openly, left her husband's hand and moved to the casket, where she knelt and wept with abandon.

Dakota receded, opting to allow them a few moments with their only child. They had not seen Grace for eighteen years. Now they were seeing her only in death. Only in death had this family come back together.

Minutes later, Rachel brought herself under control. She touched Grace's clasped hands, hands that would clutch a rosary for all eternity, and pulled herself back to her feet. When she turned, her eyes settled on Dakota. David, Grace's father, rose a moment later, taking that extra moment for one last chance to gaze upon his daughter.

"I'm Dakota Blackwood, Grace's husband," he said, extending a hand that both Rachel and David refused. They were strangers who shared only one thing between them.

David said nothing. He seemed in shock. He just stared with tear-stained eyes that cried out for comfort.

"Did she suffer long...with the cancer?" Rachel asked.

She returned her gaze to Grace.

"Five years. She beat it twice but couldn't the third time."

"I never knew," David said.

"We have two children...girls, your granddaughters."

David turned about in sudden interest; Rachel's eyes remained riveted on Grace.

"Are they here?" David asked.

"Lauryn, our oldest, is."

Dakota pointed her out, hoping to coax them away from the casket.

Immediately following Grace's death, anger so consumed Dakota that he thought of a dozen vicious things he would say to these two. Berate them for what they did that drove Grace from their home as a teenager. Shake them violently for giving up something so precious.

Now he realized words meant nothing. And certainly now was not a time to speak in anger.

"Why didn't you call us sooner? Why did you wait until she..." Rachel couldn't finish the sentence.

Dakota had anticipated this; he had thought long about what he would say. But in the end he settled for the truth; even if the truth provoked confrontation.

"I respected her wishes."

"Why?" Rachel cried, "did she hate us that much? Did she think this would punish us?" There was pleading in her eyes. Dakota could witness the hurt tearing at her soul through those eyes.

"Grace never confided in me the why."

David remained silent, listening to Dakota but staring at his granddaughter.

"She has Grace's eyes and cheeks. How old is she?" he said.

"Eleven."

It took a few moments of persistence, but Dakota finally succeeded in coaxing Grace's parents to the rear of the chapel. Distance somehow made it less painful. From there, they could still see their daughter, but they were now shielded from the others.

"Why wouldn't she let you tell us she was dying?"

"It was her wish that I notify you after she was gone."

"She hated us that much?"

Dakota said nothing. The anguish in Rachel's eyes grew unbearable. He could only wonder what could have been so terrible that it drove this family forever apart.

"And you wouldn't betray her?"

"I'm sorry. I loved your daughter. I did as she asked."

"May I speak to my granddaughter?" David asked.

Dakota nodded.

"Her name is Lauryn."

David left without Rachel to meet someone he had never seen nor knew of before. Someone he would have to remind him of his only child.

Rachel seemed uncomfortable and unsure of what to do.

"Is it true all Indians hate their mother-in-laws?"

The statement stung Dakota as if she had slapped his face.

"You ask if I hate you? How could I? I never knew anything about you. How could you hate me?"

Rachel's face became ruddy. The words she had spoken to her daughter sixteen years earlier, when she learned of Grace's impending marriage to an Indian, flooded back to the forefront of her mind. Those words had slammed shut the door between them. Instead of tolerance and understanding, Rachel had delivered words that had, in reality, forever kept them apart.

Now Rachel could say nothing.

"I hold no objections to you visiting with your granddaughters before you return to Wisconsin. It would help them get through this time."

Rachel marched off without even acknowledging Dakota's last remarks.

Cole, who had been coordinating activities with Hilary Baumgrant, the funeral parlor director, entered the room, and with an ashen face, grabbed Bronc.

"You need to see this," he said.

Something clearly had seized him.

Cole led Bronc into the chapel foyer, far beyond the gathering. There he shoved a card into his hand.

Bronc stared incredulously at the card.

"Where'd you get this?"

"Those flowers over there," Cole said, pointing to a fanlike floral arrangement of yellow, white and red.

"Find that Hilary guy," Bronc said.

Bronc slipped unobtrusively back into the room, seeking out the funeral parlor director. Cole strode off down a hall in search of the funeral director's office. A few minutes later, without arousing suspicions, Bronc and Cole returned to the chapel to stand in the rear away from the other mourners. An unassuming Hilary joined them.

"Those flowers there—how'd they get in here? Who brought them?" Bronc fired the questions.

"I don't know," Hilary stammered. His eyes sought clemency.

Bronc's had none to offer.

"We need to know. It's very important."

Dakota locked on to the fierce look in Bronc's face, then moved his eyes quickly to Cole and realized something was terribly wrong.

Cole advanced to intercept Dakota before he could reach Bronc.

"It's nothing, Dakota, just a mix-up in the flowers. We're taking care of it."

"I don't think so," Dakota said, and moved past Cole to get closer to Bronc.

"What is it?"

Bronc handed Dakota the card.

We all die sometime...even Ellie.
You're running out of time Blackwood.

"Where'd this come from?" Dakota asked, his manner unusually cool and level. If the killer meant for the note to shake Dakota, it had failed. Dakota's eyes scanned one by one through the gathering. Could the killer be standing in this room right now watching them?

Bronc identified the flowers in the corner.

"I told the detective that I didn't see who brought those flowers in. There were at least a dozen delivery men in here this morning and early in the afternoon. I don't keep track of them," Hilary Baumgrant offered in defense.

Bronc dismissed the director, who quickly and gratefully returned to his cubicle of an office at the end of a hall between chapels.

"What do you make of this?" Bronc asked.

Cole, feeling out of place and useless, left to be with Laurianne and Lauryn. This had escalated into something he wanted no part of. The ominous meaning in the card sent a sick wave through him. Cole figured it had something to do with the serial killer. But why?

Dakota stared at writing that exactly matched the notes in evidence for the murders in Albuquerque.

"He knows too much about you...I'm getting uncomfortable with this, Dakota," Bronc said, drawing him further away.

"Identify every person who comes in here," Dakota ordered. His eyes moved over the mourners sitting in the rows of chairs before the casket. Would the kill-er be bold enough to show up here?

"I'll get somebody on it. This guy's one sick bas-tard."

Dakota said nothing. He moved back into the chapel with the others. The killer obviously followed the obituaries; he knew of Grace's death. But more im-portantly, why was he tracking Dakota's life?

It rained the day of the funeral. Not a heavy rain, but a light mist that appeared like morning dew on the mourners at the grave site.

Members of the Albuquerque police served as pallbearers. The task force detectives surrounded Da-kota and his daughters as they stood staring at the flower-draped casket.

Bronc had offered to be a pallbearer, but even in this time of grief, Dakota instead assigned him to watch over the gathering at the cemetery. Even at such a moment, they had to be alert for signs of the Boulder Hill killer. The possibility existed that the killer might show up as part of his game.

From inside a sedan parked a fair distance from the grave, a detective used a long lens to snap clandes-tine photographs. Everyone in or around the cemetery during the funeral services had to be identified. An unmarked car at the cemetery gates recorded license numbers for every car entering and exiting. No one passed unidentified.

Detectives stopped and questioned anyone out of the norm after the service ended. They had orders to detain any person failing to produce satisfactory iden-tification.

Heather never saw her mother again. Dakota ordered the casket closed at the chapel prior to Heather's arrival. As a result, she had no real understanding of why she stood before such an ornate box in the rain. She cried when she saw her aunt and uncle crying.

Lauryn remained strong, clutching her father's hand until her fingers ached. Both girls would remember their mother with treasured memories of when she was alive, loving and beautiful.

"I know this is a difficult time for you, Dakota, but we have to talk," Cole said the day following the funeral. They were alone in the den. Laurianne had taken the girls out for a walk—and what had to be said, had to be said. Grace was gone now. Dakota had to accept that and move on.

Cole stumbled starting out, always at a loss for how to start sensitive conversations with his Indian brother, so as usual, he plunged right in and hoped for the best.

"You've got to back off," Cole said, like a rational banker evaluating a loan application with a cold eye when he knew the risk was greater than prudence dictated.

"Back off?"

"Yeah. Back off this serial killer case. You're all the girls have now. You've got to be here for them."

Dakota said nothing, staring at the floor for a long time.

"You know it's the right thing to do. You can't be the hero anymore."

"Don't tell me what I can't do. That's my job. That's what I do."

"And who's going to take care of the girls? Dammit, they just lost their mother. You've got to be here for them."

"I can't back off. I can't let it go."

Cole was hurt and confused. He saw a fire in Dakota's dark eyes. He wasn't getting through Dakota's stubborn Apache head.

"You have to. Let the other detectives work the case. Sit behind a desk."

"I can't...I promised."

"Man, there's no getting through to you, is there? Screw the promise. What about your promise to take care of your daughters? They need you more than ever. They've got to know when they wake up in the morning that you're going to be here."

"I promised. Don't you understand?"

"You promised? That's ridiculous. Who did you promise?"

"Grace."

Cole's mouth fell open. He dropped into a chair across from Dakota. He did the only thing he could think of. He looked away when Dakota looked up to him.

"Cole...I promised Grace. She asked me to get that bastard. She said I couldn't help save her, but I could save the others."

Cole ran his fingers through what remained of his hair. Someday he'd learn to keep his mouth shut more. Nothing he could say now could undo what he had said.

"So, what are you going to do?"

"I'm going to get him before he can kill again."

"What about the girls?"

Dakota looked at Cole for a long moment.

"I want you to take care of them for me...if anything happens. I've made the appropriate arrangements."

"Dakota, this is crazy. They're your flesh and blood. They're part of you, man. You can't let that go."

"You and Laurianne love those kids just as much as Grace and me. You're great with them. I know you'll take good care of them."

"Dakota, this is crazy. You're talking nuts."

Dakota said nothing.

"You know I love those girls. But this is still crazy. Just back off. Grace would never have wanted you to die over this."

"Will you take care of them?"

"You know I will."

Dakota spent the next five days in mourning, during which time he was out of communication with the task force. Bronc took charge in his absence. But Dakota followed the news daily, and since no new bodies had been reported, and Bronc had not called him to say the killer had struck again, Dakota believed the Boulder Hill killer had yet to strike. Was he waiting intentionally for Dakota to return?

Lauryn and Heather stayed out of school during those five days and Dakota spent every waking minute with them. They talked about Heaven and peace and all the good things they wanted to remember about their mother. However, still too many of the hours were spent in silence, but when they talked, Dakota made certain they spoke only of good things. No more talk of pain and suffering.

At the end of the five days, it didn't hurt as much...but it still hurt.

For Dakota, times were worst when he climbed into an empty bed. In the darkness and solitude the night brought, he thought about the intimacy they had shared. Grace must have known her fate that night they made love for the last time. He could still feel her in his arms as they danced. That had been her way of making their final act of love the best that it could be. He would have to live off that memory for the rest of his days.

Come Friday, Dakota took the girls away for the weekend, but he kept in touch with the city through the nightly news and arranged for Laurianne and Cole to take care of the girls upon their return.

On Monday morning, Lauryn had a difficult time preparing herself to return to school and Heather cried in her bed instead of getting dressed. But Dakota's gentle coaxing brought both girls to the breakfast table and soon afterward into the car for the ride back to their everyday life. They would go on, though life could never be the same.

Returning to the house that now seemed without life, Dakota donned suit and tie, strapped his 9mm Beretta under his arm and headed for police headquarters. It was time to return to what he had to do.

He had said his good-byes to Grace; he had grieved her passing, and he missed her so much that it ripped apart his insides. But now he must bury his pain and accomplish what he had promised. He could let nothing deter him from this.

Bronc was waiting when Dakota entered his office. Sitting squarely on the center of the desk, someone had placed a deer head mask, replete with antlers, fur and ornate feathers.

The Apache sign of the hunter. A century old symbol of prowess.

"How did you know about that?" Dakota asked. He picked up the mask with both hands.

"A trip to your reservation. One of the elders on the council told me about the mask and its meaning. Welcome back. I did get it right, didn't I? That is how it's supposed to be said?"

"Close enough."

The mask, a long forgotten symbol of Dakota's heritage, meant he had been accepted as the Hunter. The one the tribe would depend on and follow. He became more than a leader—he became a warrior. He accepted his responsibility as the one who must never quit in the quest to ensure the tribe's survival. The one, who against all odds, would never acquiesce.

"Just give the orders; we're ready to go."

Rodman stopped at the door, staring quizzically at the deer head on the desk.

"Heard you were back."

Dakota detected disappointment in Rodman's eyes.

Rodman moved on.

"Let's start with an update."

"First of all, you were right about our Jane Doe. We brought in the ex-husband for questioning. When he refused to let us take hair and skin samples, we advised him to retain an attorney. The slimebag confessed when we started turning up the heat. Melissa Sue Bryant died at the hands of her enraged ex-husband. He thought he could get away with it by making it look like a Boulder Hill slaying."

"Any chance he's the real killer?"

"Not a chance. He was in the drunk tank the night Walker died. The couple moved to Albuquerque from Rhode Island less than eighteen months ago. His previous employer confirmed he was there two years ago."

"So, we're still waiting for the killer to take a second victim."

"That's exactly what we're saying. You think he's waiting for Roberts to return to work?"

Dakota said nothing. He set the deer head atop his credenza and opened the stack of reports waiting for his review.

"If he is, we'll nail him."

"Other than that, our leads have dropped to nil. We chased down every male acquaintance of Angela Walker and can't find one viable suspect. Now that you're back, where do we go from here?"

"Stay with Lisa Roberts for now. I don't know why, but this creep seems to be real interested in her and me. Maybe there's a connection there that we're unable to see."

"What are you going to do?"

"Talk to her again to see if there isn't something we haven't thought of yet. You assign two men to go over the Walker crime scene again and let's plan a review of crime scene evidence at the end of the week."

15

Cal Sturges perused the stack of paperwork that had lain idle for days. He never realized how taxing his liaison with the Boulder Hill Task Force would become. He had come to realize, however, just how much media exposure accompanied the assignment. And media attention kept the mayor's office in the public mind. As long as the coverage remained positive and supportive, it would assist in the upcoming election. If, on the other hand, it turned ugly, somebody would have to run damage control and, likely, heads would roll. Cal had to make certain his would not be one of the bouncing ones. He relished the kind of interest the media poured over him. Even though he viewed himself more a behind-the-scenes player, he received equal time on the screen and in the papers.

Suddenly, what Sturges had to say was quotable. Reporters were actually asking him what he thought, and then writing it down. He saved clippings of every story that had made it to print and videotaped the evening news nightly in the hopes of assembling a video montage of all his coverage. Political careers were made or smashed to bits based on what appeared before the populous. For the first time, Cal could see himself attaining a level of political power in his career.

Outside, night settled over the city and the lights of Albuquerque glittered against a background of the blackened Sandia mountains. Inside, the automatic timers kicked in, extinguishing all but a few of the corridor lights to conserve energy. Cal's antique desk lamp with its frosted crystal shade lent a clandestine air to the room.

Across his office, on a wall of rich mahogany shelves, a small television flashed red and blue off the darkened walls. Cal had muted the sound at the end of the news bulletin and only glanced up occasionally, anxious for the next news update to take over the screen.

Pete Rodman's soft rap on the open door brought Cal up from his work. Rodman strolled in without invitation, after confirming with sidelong glances that Sturges was alone. His freshly-shined shoes clicked smartly over the tile floor, and there was not a wrinkle discernible in his dark blue suit. Rodman could have easily been the face on an FBI recruiting poster.

"I missed the afternoon task force briefing," Sturges said, kicking back in his chair while he rubbed fatigue out of his eyes.

"Hardly worth attending, if you ask me," Rodman said, settling into the chair across the desk. He straightened his suit sleeves before smoothing hair that was already neat and orderly.

"I take it that's what prompted this meeting?" Sturges probed. He glanced out the window at the night sky.

"I suspect you and I are on the same wavelength when I say Albuquerque's finest are incapable of apprehending your Boulder Hill killer. The question you have to be asking yourself right now is how many more deaths are the people of Albuquerque willing to tolerate?"

"We can skip past the small talk," Cal said, with a smile creeping onto his face. He smelled blood in Rodman's presence and became eager to get a taste.

Rodman's smile was almost imperceptible.

"That's what I thought. You know your Indian chief is doing more to botch this investigation than to solve it. He's making your men run in circles most of the time. From my viewpoint, there is no focused effort."

"And you're proposing?"

"That someone exert the right amount of pressure on the mayor. Get him to bring in real experts. The longer this investigation drags on, the more it reflects badly on the mayor's office. I don't think you want this to turn into a Green River killer fiasco."

"And I take it somehow you have a way to prevent that?"

"We both know the Bureau has the depth and the experience necessary to track down this lunatic and stop the senseless killing. And our tactics can be much more effective than your police department."

"And this is not about personal ego?"

Cal worked his fingers along the desk surface as he spoke. His mind already raced ahead, assembling details for what he thought might be useful.

"If anything, it's that damn Indian's ego that is keeping the killer out there."

In a ruminative stare, Cal focused for a long moment on a point across the room.

"But what does Pete Rodman get out from this? I mean how do you expect to gain from such a move? Right now you are a background player with about zero visibility."

"We nail this killer, and I become the local hero. I'd be the one coordinating the efforts with the team of agents here."

"And you see that as..."

"My ticket out of Albuquerque and into the soft leather in Washington."

"And what do you see for me? I'm assuming it's my influence with the mayor that has brought us together tonight."

"Look at it this way, Sturges, your Indian gets lucky and snares the killer. He becomes the hero. You and everybody else gets pushed into the background. Is that what you want in an election year?"

Cal offered a noncommittal shrug.

"I'm still having a problem seeing exactly what I come out with in all this."

"I could make certain you're involved with the federal team when the arrest is made. You could be the one who controls the flow of information to the public. You could be the one who calls for the press conference that announces the end to the fear. Your face is what everyone in Albuquerque sees when we announce we've taken down the killer."

Cal shifted forward in his chair. This he liked. Imagining his face on the television screen for a change instead of Blackwood's brought on an involuntary glance to the television on the shelf.

"You can guarantee that?"

"We both end up with some pretty impressive coverage. Maybe even enough to launch a political career for yourself. How far you run with what I feed you is completely up to you."

Cal's eyes sparkled at the thought.

Delivered with the glow of salesmanship, Rodman's skillfully crafted presentation had baited the hook. Now he intended to reel in his trophy. Alone, Rodman knew he lacked the political moxie to bring about Blackwood's removal, but with City Hall's help, he could kick that Indian back to the reservation where his red ass belonged.

Rodman had stumbled upon Cal's hot button—and he knew it.

"I can make sure certain media figures know who you are and the role you played in helping the Feds. You get the grand coverage, then it's up to you to let the right people know you're a mover and a shaker in the mayor's office that made it all happen. Cal, I believe I'm waving in front of you your ticket into the mayor's office in say, two years."

"So, what do I have to do?"

Rodman shifted closer to the desk.

Lisa advanced as close as she dared to the burning Paxton hotel near the Amtrak station. The blaze erupted shortly before seven and by nine, firefighters were still struggling to bring the blaze under control. It felt good to be back behind a microphone. The forced vacation accomplished nothing for her. Probably damaged her career in the process.

The big question crowding both Lisa's mind and the minds of the nightly viewers was: did all the residents get out? The Paxton served that near invisible class of people in Albuquerque—a narrow slice just barely above indigent, but a significant number of notches below poverty level. The kind of drifters and low-lifes that good citizens look away from when they pass on the street. A subclass no one ever really thinks much about.

"Zack, swing over there," she instructed.

Zack swung on cue, zooming in as a pair of rescuers pulled a rotund, scraggly-haired woman out a window and onto the waiting ladder. Her charred face and terrified eyes conveyed more of the story in the blink of an eye than any words Lisa could ever conjure up.

Zack, iron-shouldered and professional, had a flare for homing in on the core of human drama in everything he shot. Zack loved working with Lisa; he saw the two of them as pros out to make names for themselves. He never took it personally when Lisa barked orders at him. Actually, he liked the way she took control of every situation; he figured her to be a real ball-buster in the sack. He'd lay down a month's pay to be permanently assigned to her—to have a chance to be this close to her every day. And Lisa was the only woman at the station willing to see beyond the pocks that marred Zack's face, the thinning hair he pulled across the top of his head and the alcohol that occasionally tainted his breath at work.

"Come on, back it up, Roberts, you know better," the fire supervisor scowled, approaching them with his own flame in his eyes. Newspeople habitually cared more about the stories than the people in them.

"Give us a chance to get this thing under control. You'll get a closer look in a while."

Lisa backed away as the yellow-jacketed fireman lifted his arms to form a moving barricade.

Zack ceased filming, but never stopped working. He pulled the camera eyepiece from his face to soak up the scene and plan his next shot.

"Come on..." the fireman moaned.

"We're moving," Lisa said, though she slowed intentionally, looking for one more opportunity. She was always after that one more shot at the big time. The one to make her famous and get her onto one of the big three networks. Lisa had beaten the other reporters to the scene by at least three minutes, but she had gained only a few seconds of usable footage as a result.

As they retreated, Zack motioned Lisa to a desolate stretch of sidewalk away from other reporters. He tipped his cigarette pack her way, which she declined; then he placed the crinkled pack to his mouth and after many clumsy attempts, drew one out clamped between thin, colorless lips. With the same difficulty, he struggled to light it while balancing the camera on his shoulder. After three failed attempts, Lisa took the lighter from his hand and lit the cigarette for him. Zack smiled, relishing the personal contact between them while she brought the flame to his cancer stick.

"I think we got some good stuff. You're quite the celebrity," Zack commented in a casual tone, though his eyes delivered a conspiratorial glint.

Lisa stared at him quizzically.

"How so?"

"Heard our Boulder Hill killer has taken a shine to you. Been said your little vacation came as a PD request. I half-expected to find Donovan out for this story. Rumors around the station are you're running scared."

"And I shouldn't be?"

"Didn't say that. But I figure you've got something none of those other buttheads standing over there have."

"And that is?" Lisa said, watching nascent flames churn over the roof of the hotel as the fire returned to life unexpectedly. A ladder with a fireman and nozzle craned toward the rising shafts of yellow.

"Inside track on the killer. You, Lisa, have the scoop of a lifetime staring you right in the face."

Lisa narrowed her eyes at Zack as her mind raced to form some connection. She gave up, lost in his cryptic words.

"The way I see it, the reason our killer sent you those letters is because he's taken a fancy to you. Hell, you may have even talked to him without realizing it."

"And you figure that's good..."

Lisa glanced over her shoulder to dispel the sensation of eyes staring at her. A shiver rattled her spine. There were eyes watching her that very moment. But they were the eyes of two detectives recessed far enough from the scene to keep onlookers from detecting their presence.

"Sure. You've got the opportunity to do what the entire police department hasn't been able to do."

"Zack, I don't get it."

"Hear me out on this, Leez," he said, crushing out his cigarette prematurely under foot. He had snared her interest and he knew it. Time to go for the close.

Lisa detected no jest in Zack's eyes; she already had a suspicion regarding what he would say. Zack knew how to work angles.

"For whatever reason, our Boulder Hill killer is interested in you. All we've got to do is find a way to make this guy commit himself. Bingo, we snap a picture and offer it to police. You become Numero Uno."

"Zack, you didn't drink your dinner before coming here, did you?"

"Come on, Leez, it's perfect. I'd be right behind you every step of the way."

"I still don't follow."

"Okay. Let's say our killer's watching you and he's not those two bumbling Mayberry dicks in the car down there. Those numb nuts make it so obvious. Anyway, he wants to approach you, but he never gets the opportunity because you're never alone."

Zack motioned to the black sedan parked down the block.

"So, you're saying I should offer myself to him."

"Yeah. But not with Laurel and Hardy around."

Lisa revealed the first glimmer of interest in Zack's proposition. The idea of getting close to the killer intrigued her. Everyone would know her name if she became the one who delivered the identity of the killer to the police.

"This guy isn't stupid. He's knows the cops are watching you. He's not going to move unless he's convinced the cops are out of the picture."

"Let me see if I get this straight. You figure our killer's stalking me and waiting for a chance to get me alone. So, you're suggesting I set myself up as a decoy. And when he comes after me...then what?"

"I'm there to protect you and get a shot of this guy."

"You're going to protect me?"

"Yeah. You'd be the hero of the day...or should I say heroine."

"Zack, this guy's a psychopath. How are you going to protect me?"

"You probably didn't know I spent six years with a Marine unit."

"Doing what?"

"Navy corpsman."

A long silence took over the air. Lisa shifted, leaning against a parked car. Her eyes never left his. He was dead serious. The question of whether he could actually protect her from the Boulder Hill killer pulsated inside her head.

"Think about it. It's not nearly as dangerous as you think. The guy would never get real close to you. I'd handle all the details. I'd set it up with at least two back door escape routes for you. All we have to do is shake the cops and you have car trouble or something. When he comes out of hiding—bang! We've got him."

Lisa said nothing; she envisioned herself on the cover of Time with an inset of Zack's photograph of the Boulder Hill killer. New York... She moved off the car and started back toward the burning building.

"Think about it, Leez. We're talking '20/20' now. You'd be Number One in New Mexico."

Dakota caught up with Lisa Roberts at the scene of the smoldering Paxton hotel fire. Once the flames had been doused, the onlookers quickly drifted away. During the initial assault of men and equipment on the building, firefighters rescued twenty-eight people. That, however, still left five unaccounted for.

Lisa had been on site since the initial fire call crackled over the radio and had filed a number of brief reports over the airwaves; each report keeping viewers up-to-date on the firefighters' progress. So far, all but five of the transients that could afford the few dollars a day it cost to keep a room in the run-down century-old building came out alive.

With a quick nod, Lisa acknowledged Dakota's presence. She needed no words to know that he was there to see her. From the look on his face, she also knew he had not come with the kind of news she longed to hear.

Zack eyed Dakota for a long moment before returning his eyes to his camera, where he set Lisa in the foreground and the fire trucks in the background. As he rolled tape, she delivered two minutes of well-rehearsed commentary on the possible causes of the fire. Arson was certainly the one looming in the back of everyone's mind. She concluded her piece by dangling a teaser before viewers that promised more information loomed just moments away.

Just off screen, two plainclothes officers stood around working very hard to make themselves unobtrusive on the scene. They also never acknowledged Dakota's presence.

When Lisa received the 'all clear' in her earpiece, she signaled Zack to stop the camera. While he reached for another cigarette, she slid the microphone under his arm and stepped away.

"You'll have to light that one yourself," she said.

"I'll be over by the van," he said, giving her one of his clandestine, think-about-what-I-said looks.

Obscured by a baseball cap and jacket, Dakota canvassed the street, wondering just how effective his men were under the circumstances. Was the killer watching right now? Just how clever was he? It wouldn't take long for someone to realize that the same faces kept showing up at every scene Lisa showed up at.

Certainly, the Boulder Hill killer had to know they were protecting her. Could he still possibly be entertaining thoughts of making her his next victim? That is, if he hadn't already taken his next victim.

There was no doubt in Dakota's mind that the Boulder Hill killer's next victim would be an attractive young female. For now, the killer held the city on tenterhooks—a city waiting—a city frantic for police to turn up some clue before he killed again.

"Lieutenant, sorry about your wife," Lisa said, as she motioned him away from the commotion of the scene to a nearby car.

Her words fueled a momentary pang deep inside. Dakota swallowed it and forced himself to focus on what now became a matter of utmost urgency.

"How are you holding up?"

"How would you expect me to be holding up?" Lisa said. An edge of sarcasm clung to her voice. "I nearly flipped over backwards when your people arrested that guy. Then it all crashed when it turned out he was a copycat murderer of his own ex-wife."

She wiped away her sarcasm when she saw the pain in Dakota's eyes.

"I'm okay for now...no...I'm terrified. I can't sleep; I can't eat. I'm afraid to do my job," she continued.

Dakota gently took Lisa's arm to escort her into his car parked down from the fire scene. He said nothing until they were safely ensconced inside away from other reporters and the few remaining onlookers.

"I understand how you feel."

"Do you? Two weeks ago some guy took my arm to ask for an autograph and I freaked. I started screaming and swinging."

"I know, I read the report."

"He was just some nice man who saw me on television. I thought he was the killer and I went berserk. I don't think I can handle this."

"Lisa, we're doing everything we can right now. We've got two men on you 'round the clock."

Dakota caught the glint of a tear finding its way out of Lisa's eye. Her brief vacation did little to relieve the strain of her situation. There existed only one way to permanently remove the terror consuming her life in much the same way the flames had consumed the old hotel.

"I haven't been able to come up with a reason why the killer contacted you? Can you think of one?" Dakota asked.

"Just from the television. Those reports I ran might have cut him to the bone. That's the only reason I can come up with."

"Lisa, there's something else I need to talk to you about. It's very important. Are you up to it?"

Lisa nodded, staring pensively out the window.

"We believe you may have met the killer. Or at least seen him."

"What?"

"It is possible the killer has a fixation with you, for whatever reason. If he does, he may have set up a situation where you and he would bump into each other. He may have even talked with you over the last month."

"Oh great. Now you're telling me this lunatic walked right up to me and started a conversation."

"He gets a thrill out of such a situation. It's like he knows a secret and he gets off in the knowledge that he's that close and you don't realize it. It's a form of psychotic control."

Lisa said nothing. Her eyes went to Zack, who was blowing smoke rings across the street.

"Can you recall any unusual exchanges over the last two months? Anything out of the ordinary."

"Like how out of the ordinary?"

"Like a strange man approaching your door saying he had the wrong address? Maybe someone coming up to you on the street just to meet you?"

Lisa sat for a long moment gazing beyond Dakota to the scene in front of the hotel. Zack had crushed out his cigarette and taken up his camera. He was at the moment filming a crowded scene at the rear of one of the engines. It looked like a perfect fluff piece to run with the late night newscast.

"I've had at least a dozen instances where people have stopped me on the street or at the station. Could he have been one of them?"

"Very possibly. But I believe he's feeling fairly secure right now. He's convinced we're still without any solid evidence that might give up his identity. So, I'm guessing his exchange might even be more deliberate."

"Do you have anything that might tell you who the killer is?"

"Off the record?"

"Off the record."

"No."

Lisa's stare turned distant.

"What if you had something..."

"We're working every possible angle. We could use your help. You're sure nothing out of the ordinary comes to mind? Nobody stopping you at the station?"

"Nothing. And certainly since your men have been watching over me, I haven't noticed anything that might help you. Shoot straight with me, Lieutenant, do you really believe the killer might approach me?"

"The FBI profile indicates otherwise. The Behavioral Science Unit thinks our man is an introvert and takes a long time to approach his victim."

The words made Lisa cringe.

"And what do you think, Lieutenant? I want to know what you think. You know this creep better than the FBI, the Behavioral Sciences Unit or anyone else."

"Off the record?"

Lisa shot him her patented, are-you-serious look.

"Off the record. I think the profile's wrong. I think our guy is willing to risk everything for the thrill he gets out of killing. And I don't think he's killing simply out of opportunity. His killings are well-planned and executed. He knows exactly what he's doing every step of the way."

"He's a textbook psychopath then. Let me ask you something. I've been doing enough reading on serial killers to make me go bug-eyed. They share a lot in common with one another, don't they?"

"Yes. I've studied the files of every known serial killer in the country. They share a lot."

"Well, right now, I'm most interested in just one. I read that the majority of serial killers, in reality, want to be caught. Is that true?"

"I'd say seventy-five percent are relieved when they're arrested. Most begin confessing to the killings before you can finish reading them their rights. By the time you get them to the station, they've unloaded at least three or more killings, if they've gone uncaught for any length of time."

"What does that tell you about them?" Lisa asked.

"They're usually suffering from deep-seated guilt and remorse that finally breaks to the surface."

"Yeah. But more important, they can't stop themselves."

"Lisa, what are you trying to say?"

Lisa paused to collect her thoughts. It had become increasingly difficult to concentrate on any one thing for very long without thoughts of the killer clouding her mind. A terror-induced hesitation crept into her voice when she began again.

"What if he's stalking me...knowing your men are watching me. And he wants to be caught...wants to end this sick perversion of his...."

"Lisa..."

"Hear me out, Lieutenant. He's going to try to kill me, even though your men have me covered. You understand what I'm trying to say?"

"Lisa, we'll get him before he gets you."

"Give me a guarantee, Lieutenant." Lisa paused. Those were the wrong words. "You can't guarantee that. This guy could be watching us right now. Your men might be too late. This guy might want to kill me and get caught..."

"Lisa, I understand how you feel. Trust us. We'll get him before he can get to you."

Lisa said nothing for a while.

Dakota stared out the windshield at a smoke curl rolling out a fifth floor window of the hotel.

"You want out of this? We can put you in a safe place until..."

"Until when? Until he kills another woman instead of me? Until you catch him? He slipped away from you two years ago."

Lisa stopped herself suddenly. How deep did that cut him?

"He's back and you still have no clue who he is."

"Lisa, just say the word and you're off the streets. You don't have to risk your life."

"I gotta go, Zack's waving me back."

Dakota took her arm before she could leave the car.

"Think about it," Dakota said.

"I will. And I'm really sorry about your wife. She must have been a wonderful woman."

For the next forty-eight hours, Dakota buried his face in the volumes of reports filed for the Angela Walker investigation. Every task force detective put in sixteen-hour days trying to solve this one. The clock was ticking. Still they had yet to get a break. And a break was what they needed most. It seemed regardless of how hard they tried, they could not force a break in the case.

Dakota sat with Bronc, Agent Rodman and three other task force detectives in the conference room planning their next move. Rodman forced every man on the team to address him by title—he detested detectives addressing him as Pete because he felt it lowered him to their level. Their next move would be to anticipate the killer's next victim.

"How are we doing on the incident reports from the university campus?" Dakota asked Bronc.

"Slow. We've tagged three problem students who had violent incidents on campus two years ago and have recently generated incident reports now. One's a habitual and the other two seem pretty innocuous."

"Keep some men working on them."

"How does that fit into our killer's profile?" Rodman interjected.

"Everyone with any reported violent incident fits our profile, Rodman. Bronc, let's bring in the habitual for some questions. But keep it one-sided, I don't want him starting rumors on campus that we suspect the killer to be one of the students."

The task force knew if they released too much information, letting the public know whom they suspected and how the killer executed his plans, the city would panic. So they had to move quietly and quickly.

But Dakota had new problems to contend with. Problems created out of personal intent.

The sudden appearance Thursday morning of three high-ranking Bureau specialists from Washington, with Rodman in tow, put every detective on edge. Word floating through the station inferred they came at the mayor's request. A need for independent professionals to scrutinize the Boulder Hill crime data and make certain the task force had not somehow derailed itself over the past few months. Their very presence led to rampant speculation: Blackwood would be yanked and the FBI would take full control of the investigation. Rodman would be named lead investigator. Most figured Washington and Blackwood would be the ones under fire. The detectives were just the grunts who did what they were told. It was the leadership that had fouled up the investigation.

Careers were on the line.

But Dakota had nurtured his own clandestine sources in the mayor's office; sources who leveled fingers in the direction from which the usurpation had arisen. In an all-too-formal memo, the mayor informed Captain Washington that the whole process was strictly routine and that he expected the full and complete cooperation of every man assigned to the Boulder Hill case. He concluded that no malicious intent whatsoever should be read into this situation.

Only someone's plan backfired.

Dakota's sources informed him of a low-key, closed-door meeting between the mayor and a consortium of representatives from the 225 neighborhood associations that watch over Albuquerque. The Office of Neighborhood Coordination set up the meeting and hand-selected the representatives to attend. And as usual, the affluent neighborhoods like Sandia Heights and Tanoan received the most significant representation. The neighborhood associations sought to exert their own pressure on the mayor and hopefully induce the task force to work more diligently to catch the killer. Association meetings in the neighborhoods were growing angry over the amount of time the police had squandered away so far. On the surface, the meeting had seemed innocent enough. Below the surface, one man was manipulating the Office of Neighborhood Coordination to do his bidding. Dakota had just enough forewarning to assemble all his ducks in a row before the federal inspectors arrived.

The Bureau team exhaustively interviewed task force detectives, including Dakota himself, and spent countless hours reviewing every document generated in support of the investigation.

The specialists knew going in that the police professionals would be edgy concerning intimations that they failed in any way to perform their jobs properly. As a result, the team tread lightly, skillfully avoiding any direct confrontations with task force detectives. After all, they all wanted the same thing: remove the killer from the streets before he kills again.

In the end, the Bureau team member who specialized in understanding serial killer behavior typed a neat, fourteen-page report praising the efforts of the men assigned to the task force and offered unequivocal recommendations that nothing need change. Afterward, as quietly as they had arrived, the team departed. Rodman was livid.

The only positive result of the exercise: it killed someone's personal attempt to have Dakota removed from the investigation. Dakota, Bronc and the other detectives were still there...still staring at a blank wall and still determined more than ever that they would catch the killer. Dakota had his suspicions as to the traitor's identity and soon he would have it con-firmed.

By noon, the five of them—Bronc, Dakota, Wash-ington, Sturges and Rodman—had gone over the lat-est Bureau report, concluding that a sweep of the neighborhoods surrounding Angela Walker's apart-ment complex would yield very little.

The Bureau profile again projected the strong belief that the killer would live close to the victims. But the four victims were actually spread out over the entire city of Albuquerque. Staring at a map with a pin to indicate where each victim had been found, it became intuitively obvious that the killer could live anywhere in the city limits. He could even be an out-sider, coming to Albuquerque only to kill then flee to the safety of some distant abode.

Dakota was having trouble concentrating. He reread whole paragraphs over and over in order to gain information. Still, he had to be here; he had to force himself to work on the case. If he didn't, Grace's memory would shred his mind until he could no longer think.

"The killer's second victim two years ago..." Bronc said, thinking out loud.

Dakota lifted his eyes from the report.

"Quite the social butterfly, frequented dance clubs and liked to go out with her friends."

"Yeah, so?" Rodman asked.

"So, how come none of those friends could point us toward the killer?"

"What's your point, Bronc? We're rehashing two-year-old information. You're not going to nail this guy by trying to figure out what he did two years ago," Rodman said.

Bronc calmly turned from Rodman, directing his eyes and question to Dakota.

"That's exactly how we're going to nail this guy. How could this guy come into these women's lives without being noticed, kill them, then disappear with-

out so much as a single person being able to identify
him?" Dakota said.

"My guess," Bronc said, as if something were falling into place in the labyrinth this case had assembled in his mind, "is that the victims kept secret their
association with him."

"Oh Jesus," Rodman moaned, "this is doing nothing to lead us to the killer."

"It will...if we can find a reason why these victims
knew the killer and yet kept their relationship secret."

"I say we break for lunch," Rodman said, in such
a way that it came across as an attempt to dismiss
Bronc's statement.

Rather than lunch with detectives, Dakota took
the walkway overpass on Third to meet Cole at the
bank. Dakota's earlier call to his brother had been
curt and cryptic; asking Cole to keep his lunch open
and that he would be there as soon as he could make
it.

Cole cut his phone conversation short when
Dakota arrived. He grabbed his jacket as he maneuvered around his desk. Leaving the bank, they walked
to the Crossroads in silence. Cole ruminated over
Dakota's intent. After stopping for burritos with the
works, they ate their lunch sitting on a bench in the
Civic Plaza.

Dakota said almost nothing, which caused Cole
to question why he had wanted to meet in the first
place.

"How are the girls?" Cole asked, to break the
silence.

"Okay. We take everything one day at a time right
now."

"That's great."

Clumsy as it was, Cole's conversation greased the wheels.

"I know what you've been doing," Dakota said at last. He stared blankly at a woman walking a newborn wrapped in blankets in a stroller. It reminded him of Grace when Lauryn was first born. Everything reminded him of Grace.

"What?"

"The money...I checked our account. There's about three grand in it that I didn't put there."

"I just wanted to make sure you could cover any expenses that might come up."

"I can handle it just fine."

Cole finished off his burrito and crumbled the wrapper into a tight ball to harness his frustration. Dakota seemed to oppose him at every turn.

"Can't I help you out?"

"No."

"Why not? What the hell am I supposed to do with my money? If I want to give it to you, the least you can goddamn do is take it."

"I don't need it."

"I just don't want you to...you think it doesn't hurt me...you think I sleep at night.... We grew up together...Grace was special to me, too. You want to know how many fights I got into in the dorms over you and Grace?"

Cole stopped himself; instead, he tossed his drink cup into a nearby trash receptacle. There was a moment when he just wanted to keep walking right back to the bank before he said something that would put them against each other.

"Dakota, I just don't want you to have to worry about money right now. This is the only way I know how to help. We're brothers—in here!" Cole said, pounding his fist over his heart. "Let me be your brother for Christ's sake!"

Dakota said nothing.

Cole stormed away and crossed the street to return to the bank. He never looked back to see if his brother followed.

Even before Dakota could rise to cross the street, his beeper sounded. Bronc's code appeared on his LCD display. Dakota pitched what remained of his lunch into a nearby trash receptacle, all the while enduring a sick rumbling in his stomach for the way he had acted. Weaving through the midday traffic, he headed back toward City Hall.

God, let this be the break the task force has been praying for, Dakota thought as he threaded his way through the crowd clogging the sidewalk.

16

Dakota arrived out of breath and with a racing heart to find Bronc shifting nervously outside a witness room. The strain of the investigation had begun to emerge in Bronc's mannerisms. The way Bronc's eyes danced back and forth he knew something might have finally turned their way.

"Tell me it's good," Dakota asked. There was more than just a glimmer of hope in his eyes.

"Could be. We've got Tracey Kendall inside. She's frightened half to death. Says she saw some guy hanging around her apartment. She noticed him standing alone in a nearby children's playground."

"Where does she live?"

"An apartment complex on Taylor Ranch Drive."

"Fantastic."

Dakota entered the glass-paneled room with a table and three chairs. The woman's appearance sent cold shivers up his spine. Janet Hegler, Dakota thought. This Tracey Kendall resembled the killer's second victim of two years earlier.

Ms. Kendall even hesitated in a timid way before beginning her story to Dakota. Exactly the personality trait the FBI said the killer would be seeking in his next victim.

"I know you've told the other detective your story, but I'd like to hear it from you, if you could."

"There really isn't much to tell. Like I said, a few days ago I noticed this guy with scraggly hair and an army jacket hanging around my apartment complex. At first I didn't think much about it..."

"Is he a white man?"

"Yes, kinda."

"Not Hispanic or Indian?"

"No. Definitely not. He has a darker complexion, like he was from the Mediterranean. He's got black hair."

"How old would you say he is?"

"Thirty, I guess."

White male, twenty-five to thirty-five.

Dakota slid his eyes off Ms. Kendall to Bronc's. Could this be it? they seemed to be saying.

"At first, I didn't give it much thought. I just figured he might have been with someone who lived in the complex. But later that night, I noticed him there again. He was staring at my apartment window. I live on the second floor, so he really couldn't see in."

"And you're absolutely sure you've never seen him around there before."

"No. Well, I don't know."

"Could he have been waiting for someone?"

"I don't think so. When I checked a while later, he was gone. The play area was deserted."

"Could he have seen you staring back at him?"

"I don't think so. Maybe with this serial killer story on the news so much I'm just being paranoid. But he was there the next day."

"In the same place?"

"Yes...almost. This time he was concealed partially by the trunk of an old tree...like he was hiding. He thought I didn't notice him, but I did and I got concerned. When I looked out the window not two minutes later, I saw him staring at my apartment. We made eye contact."

"Then what happened?"

"I backed away from the window, and when I went back, he was gone."

"Did you call the police?"

"Well, no. At first I thought maybe my seeing him frightened him off."

"But it didn't?"

"No. As I was leaving for work this morning he was standing across the street. He watched me pull out of the lot. I'm sure he was waiting for me to leave."

"Ms. Kendall, do you live alone?"

"Yes."

"Could you have met this man or might he have known you from some previous meeting?"

"No. I don't think so. He doesn't look familiar at all. And I would have remembered him. He has real scary eyes. They pick you apart."

"Why do you say that?"

"I don't know exactly. He stared so deeply at me that...just his stare gave me the willies. Those eyes looked right into you. He was a good thirty feet away when our eyes made contact, but I could feel something in the way he looked at me."

"Ms. Kendall, do you think he might know you're here? I mean did you ever notice him following you?"

"I don't know. I don't think so."

Dakota rose, motioning Bronc out of the room.

In the corridor, they moved a few steps down from the door. Bronc could see Dakota's mind churning behind his eyes.

"You think this creep's our man?" Dakota asked.

"She's a dead ringer for the type he'd be looking for. Her description could fit a psychopath. We shift some men onto her?"

"No." Dakota thought for a moment. "Here's what I want. Slip an undercover policewoman into Kendall's apartment. If he's our man, I want to make sure we get him before he makes his move."

"You want in on this?"

"You bet. Assign two detectives to watch her for the twelve hours you and I are not on her."

"What about back up?"

"Not until we get an ID on his guy. We don't want to spook him with unusual activity. Keep everyone away from the surveillance."

"So, we're going twelve on/twelve off surveillance."

"Exactly. And because we don't have anything damning on this guy, I don't want him picked up. Let's just make sure we can ID him and follow his every move. There's no way we'll bring him to trial unless we can get something on him or the bastard confesses."

While Dakota sketched out his plan to Ms. Kendall, Bronc had a duplicate house key made. They saw no way to remove Tracey from the situation without losing the suspect, so it was imperative that Tracey agree to participate. Dakota assured her that at no time would her life be placed at risk.

Within the hour, a policewoman had been assigned twenty-four protection for Tracey Kendall. Since there were no women detectives on the task force, Bronc pulled a female officer out of Vice. Officer Carrie Martin had eight years on the streets and jumped out of her chair at the chance to be part of the Boulder Hill team. Her sergeant informed her she was in the right place at the right time. Carrie believed otherwise. Her scores from the pistol range attested to her deadly accuracy.

The trick now was to get Martin inside the apartment unseen; then have her remain out of sight until they had at least identified the creep in the army jacket.

While Bronc drove Carrie to the apartment, Dakota continued to question Ms. Kendall regarding the man. Her proffered description was less than desirable and Dakota knew that unless they actually saw him and snapped a few pictures, they wouldn't have much to go on.

Forty minutes later the call came. Officer Martin was in place. Previous to that, the area had been covertly swept. The man in question was nowhere in the area. Phase one had gone off without a hitch.

Dakota released Tracey, which set their plan into motion. He instructed her to drive straight home just as she did every other day in her life. Above all, he cautioned, make certain her actions did not arouse suspicion. He also instructed her on what steps to take should she encounter the man. He emphasized again just before she left that at no time would she be left vulnerable.

Dakota's heart raced out of control. This could be their man. This kind of break comes once, so Dakota knew they had better not blow it now. Dakota, himself, chose to follow Tracey home. He would continue past the complex once Bronc reported picking up the surveillance.

From here on, Tracey was to act normally and let the police do their job. Do nothing that might spook the suspect.

From his car phone, Dakota contacted Martin, instructing her exactly how far to go in her assignment. First priority was to protect Ms. Kendall and herself. Above all else, she had to insulate both of them from the suspect. Second, identify the man without compromising the surveillance. Third, and only if the situation could be kept safe, allow the stalker to incriminate himself before apprehending him.

Dakota had engraved the killer's profile so deeply into his mind that he would know immediately if he had caught the Boulder Hill killer. Or so he told himself as he watched the Kendall car turn right, leaving the main artery of rush hour traffic behind. The street she turned onto was quiet and residential.

In a sick puzzle of psychotic life and death, the Boulder Hill killer always varied the murder weapon used from victim to victim. No doubt at some time it was a conscious effort to keep the crimes from being linked together. But as the ritual fantasy became more real, the crimes became easier to link together. That is, once you knew the key elements of the killer's fantasy.

On a deeper, subconscious level, the killer was nonetheless leaving behind a signature that, once Dakota uncovered it, clearly demonstrated the victims all died at the same hands.

The Boulder Hill killer's first victims were strangled using picture wire. Wire that never turned up. The repetition supported Dakota's theory that the killer was reliving his fantasy over and over.

The killer bludgeoned his second victim two years ago, then severed the carotid causing the victim to bleed to death. Dakota believed the blood was a significant symbol in the killer's psychosis. Since the unconscious victim was already helpless, the killer became free to choose any number of less execution-style measures at his leisure. Yet, the killer specifically chose to open the artery and drain the victim's blood. Perhaps the killer himself had spilt his own blood during some violent act with a women and that caused him to fantasize revenge by spilling her blood in return.

The precision with which the incision was made on the neck led investigators to speculate that the killer had some level of medical training. A military corpsman, a doctor or possibly a medical student who failed to make the grade.

The murder weapon used on the second victim greatly complicated the task force's strategy. It could be any weighty object close at hand, which was then removed with the killer after the crime. The killer could approach his intended victim without a weapon on his person. If—and Dakota knew this was a long shot—if the killer carried on his person a surgical blade, they might have the evidence they need to get the case into a court. But any blade would do—even a common kitchen knife.

In all cases, though, Dakota concluded the victims had been taken without a struggle. Therefore, if the man they were hoping to see shortly was the killer, he must have some plan for getting into the Kendall apartment without arousing the woman's suspicions.

At this point, the pieces still failed to fit together, and Dakota couldn't force them. He had to keep turning them over in his mind until they all came together of their own accord.

Was the guy at the apartment the Boulder Hill killer? And if so, what would be his method of gaining Tracey's trust? She seemed much too suspicious a person to allow him to fool her.

Dakota snapped his attention back to the Toyota in front of him. Tracey had flipped on her left turn signal.

Ahead, Dakota spotted Bronc's car—but no Bronc.

"What the hell..."

Tracey slowed to cross a speed bump at the apartment complex parking lot entrance. She pulled into the space she always parked in just below her apartment door.

Dakota noticed quickly that the entrance to her apartment lacked seclusion. Anyone approaching the apartment door became visible to the street or to neighbors.

The Boulder Hill killer craved isolation...

Tracey left her car a dozen paces from the stairs. She scanned the walkway, the breadth of the parking lot, and especially the playground area thirty yards from where she parked.

A swing fluttered in the breeze. There were no children playing today. And he wasn't anywhere in sight. But shadows filled the thicket of trees just beyond the play area. An overcast sky, coupled with a thickly crowned canopy of branches, kept light out. He could be standing in a shadow...watching her right now.

Tracey sucked in a breath before moving to the stairs. Her mouth had gone bone dry; her heart pounded in her chest. Could he discern what was writ across her face? Was he sensing, from some unseen vantage point, the trap she had initiated for him?

She had to mask not only her fear, but also the fact that she was no longer alone. That meant suppressing the urge to seek out the men protecting her as Dakota had instructed her to do. It took all her will to keep from glancing back at the cars in the lot in search of the one containing the detective assigned to watch over her.

Tracey released a pent-up sigh of relief, the way pressure cookers vent excess force, when she opened the door to a policewoman's badge catching the light. The woman stood akimbo in jeans and a black shirt across the living room at the doorway to her bedroom. Her hand rested on her weapon.

Tracey hesitated slightly before entering and closing the door.

"Nice place," Martin said, "our guy out there?"

"All clear for now. It's small but homey. You want the drapes closed?"

"You usually close the drapes?"

"No. I like the natural light."

"Leave them open. The last thing we want is to raise suspicion. He may have been monitoring your habits hoping to uncover a moment of opportunity. Do everything just as always. For now, though, avoid the front window. We'll get a call if the man is spotted on the grounds. When we do, you give us a nod as soon as possible. Once you're sure it's the guy, we'll take over."

"I understand. The other detective...Black-wood...is his name? He instructed me about what to do."

"You mind?" Martin said, before dragging an easy chair from the living room into the bedroom.

"No. Fine."

She then settled into it, shifting her revolver as she sat down.

Knowing a gun was in the apartment and some-one capable of using it calmed Tracey. She looked forward to sleeping soundly tonight. Something she had missed over the past two nights.

"Did you want to sit out by the television?" Tracey asked.

"No. I remain out of sight in case he passes the window."

The words sent a shiver through Tracey. The thought of looking up to find him staring through the glass at her only reinforced her conviction that she had not overreacted and had done the right thing.

"I'll turn the television up so you can hear the news. I guess I should have told the detective I'm vegetarian. I don't keep meat in the house."

Tracey caught a low grumble drifting out of the bedroom.

"I'll have a pizza brought in later," Martin said.

Dakota and Bronc put Tracey Kendall to bed at ten-thirty. With Martin on the sofa and the two detectives that came on at eleven outside, Bronc and Dakota retired to get some rest of their own.

The evening hours had been fruitless. A few children played on the swings after dinner and a dozen couples strolled the walk between the buildings. But no one appeared around the complex fitting the description Tracey had provided earlier.

Back at police headquarters, three detectives burned the midnight oil running the names of every male living in the complex through the computer. By one that morning, they had compiled a profile list of every tenant in Tracey Kendall's complex, along with the apartments down the street, and every single family residence, duplex or townhouse within six square blocks of Tracey Kendall's place.

On the outside chance that the killer did live in the immediate area of his victim, Dakota had assigned half the detectives on the task force to investigate every male within the six square block area of the Angela Walker murder. And now they were to work the Kendall area the same way, just in case.

While Tracey Kendall slept, twenty men tugged at their collective investigative gray matter, trying to turn up a lead that would pan out; all the while hoping the killer had already made a crucial mistake.

An exhausted Dakota was glad to get home. Thinking about the Boulder Hill killer case kept him from thinking about the pain. The girls were already in their beds, but Lauryn was still awake. Laurianne had retired hours earlier, drained of energy from the rigors of managing two households, two children and two men.

Cole sat over a kitchen table layered with computer printouts.

"How's the investigation going?" Cole asked, without looking up at his brother.

"Okay...we may have finally gotten a break in the case."

Dakota opened the refrigerator and pulled out the milk carton only to find it nearly empty. Then he spied the empty milk glass on the table.

"That's great. Oh, speaking of break."

"How are the girls? They get to bed okay?"

"No. That's what I was supposed to talk to you about."

"What happened?"

"The girls were fooling around when it was time for bed."

"They get hurt?"

"No. They're fine. But Lauryn broke her dream catcher above her bed, and now she refuses to go to sleep."

Dakota felt relief rush into his veins.

"She wouldn't let me touch it. Said only you could fix it for her. You know, the Indian legends."

Dakota trudged up the stairs and opened the bedroom door to find Lauryn sitting up in bed with her arms wrapped across her knees. Her face beamed in the hall light falling into the room over Dakota's shoulder.

"Daddy," she chimed, opening her arms to welcome him.

"Uncle Cole tells me you have a problem," he whispered.

"Sorry, Dad, it broke when I jumped into bed."

Lauryn held up the hand-sized hoop with feathers strung along the bottom and a leather mesh similar to a tennis racket strung across the interior. A section had broken free, leaving a gaping hole.

"I can't go to sleep," Lauryn began crying, "the nightmares will come...and mommy will..."

"It's okay, princess," Dakota said, squeezing her tightly in his arms. He kissed her gently on the head while he kept her close to him.

The dream catcher had been so much a part of Dakota's childhood, yet he had forgotten the role it now played for his daughters. The mesh trapped the bad dreams, keeping them from entering the sleeping child's head. It held them prisoner until dawn when the morning sun caused them to evaporate. The strategic hole located near the center of the mesh, however, allowed only the good dreams, dreams that knew the way, to pass through.

The tear in Lauryn's dream catcher had terrified her so much that she refused to sleep until it was repaired. And only Indian hands could properly weave the mesh of the dream catcher.

Within a minute's time, Dakota returned the dream catcher to its perfect form and suspended it on the wall over Lauryn's head.

She kissed him and hugged his neck.

"Thanks, Dad."

All was well now. It was safe to sleep. Lauryn no longer had to fear the nightmares that hung in the darkness to torment her.

For a long moment neither spoke. Words were the furthest things from their minds. Holding each other said more than any words could ever say.

"Tell me about *O'zho* again, Daddy," Lauryn whispered, stuttering over the Indian word. She wiped away the tears that wet both her face and Dakota's shirt.

It took a moment for Dakota to tuck away his pain and find the strength to speak.

"Do you remember a year ago when we flew to that place in the middle of the ocean. You watched out the plane window and it frightened you because all you saw was water."

Lauryn moved her head against his chest.

"Remember outside our little hut, we had that beach almost all to ourselves. There were only six or eight people on that whole stretch of white sand. And you and Heather played all day, and your mother and I just laid under the sun."

"Mommy was so happy there."

"Your mommy wished she never had to leave that place, with the waves rushing up and the sun shining and the breeze in our faces. And she...didn't have to hurt then..."

Dakota stopped abruptly, fighting to display his courageous self, hiding that part of him rushing to get out.

"That's Heaven, Lauryn, O'zho...it's where Mommy is now. She'll be waiting there for us."

Lauryn seemed to draw up her tears, pulling out some inner strength that she must have held in reserve. Knowing that her mother was safe and free of her torment helped Lauryn. At least for the moment.

"Can you go to sleep now?" Dakota asked, smoothing a hand along her hair.

"Will you be here when I wake up?"

"Yes, I will. I will always be here for you and Heather."

Lauryn pulled herself away from Dakota, found warmth and solace beneath her blanket, and looked up at her dream catcher once more before turning to her side.

"I love you, princess," Dakota whispered as he set a kiss upon her head. She smiled with eyes already closed.

Before leaving the room, Dakota tucked Heather in, ran his finger along the dream catcher above her bed and left her with a gentle kiss on her cheek. He tasted tears. Were they his or Heather's?

Back in the kitchen, Cole had shoveled up his printouts and stuffed them into his briefcase when Dakota returned.

"Heather cried for a while before going to bed. Laurianne laid with her for an hour or so. Then she seemed better and fell off to sleep. Lauryn's problem all fixed?" Cole asked.

Dakota nodded while he rummaged through the refrigerator for anything of substance. His surveillance had forced him to skip dinner.

"Sorry about the milk. We're worried about Lauryn. She's got a lot of anger built up inside her right now. I, ah, I don't know what to do or how to handle it."

Dakota came over to put his hand on Cole's shoulder.

Cole looked up. Dakota never accepted the need for personal contact. Cole was at a loss for how to react.

"You and Laurianne are doing a lot by just being here for the girls. I expected Lauryn would have some difficult times. I talked to her. She's going to need more time—and someone to be there when she reaches out. I need you to be there.... I've got to be on stakeout. It could be the break we've been desperate for."

"Okay. We're here. The girls will have whatever they need."

"Thanks Cole..." Dakota said, "thanks for everything you're doing," his voice trailed off as he left the kitchen and retired to his den.

Dakota felt like he had just fallen asleep when the clock's third chime woke him. No, it wasn't the clock. He had tuned that out when he shifted to sleeping in the den while Cole and Laurianne stayed upstairs. It was something else. A thump had filtered down from upstairs. Then he heard it again. Were the girls awake? He listened. The house was quiet.

Moments ticked away. Dakota lay perfectly still while a foreboding chill crept under his skin.

Fatigue jabbed at Dakota to return to his blanket, but another thump drew him up off the leather sofa. He stumbled in the darkness to reach his desk. His inner voice urged him to take his gun. Something inside his head issued a warning. Dakota didn't know what it was; only that he had to remove his Beretta from the locked desk drawer.

After fumbling with the key, he finally opened the drawer and felt around in the darkness—the gun was gone. Dakota swallowed the bitter fluid rising into the back of his throat. He thought about one thing—the girls upstairs in their beds.

Someone was moving about upstairs.

Then a heavy thud came—like someone falling out of bed. Dakota tried the light switch outside the den door.

Nothing.

When Dakota breached the hall leading to the stairs, a cold wind cut sharply across his face. He turned into the fierce flow. The front door was wide open, banging against the wall. Moonlight poured in.

He had come.

Without thinking, Dakota raced up the stairs, slapping the hall light switch when he reached the top. Again nothing. The house was without electricity.

But the window at the end of the hall allowed sufficient moonlight in for Dakota to discern that both the bedroom doors remained closed.

Something was wrong. Black smudges glinted off the handle of the girls' door. Dakota touched the marks—his hands came away wet. Blood wet. The marks were bloody fingerprints.

He reached for the knob, his heart hammering inside his chest. Something warned him not to open the door. He turned the knob anyway.

A dismal light from the window fell upon the two beds with the girls asleep beneath their covers.

Dakota entered. He reached for Lauryn and turned her. As he did, her head flopped loose at her neck. Blood soaked the sheet and pillow.

"I've come for you, Blackwood!" a throaty voice issued from behind.

Dakota spun about. Cole stood in the doorway with a bloody knife clinched in his right fist.

"Noooooo!" Dakota screamed.

His own scream catapulted him out of his sleep. He sprang up on the sofa in the den. An icy sweat drenched his body, causing him to shiver. Or was it the nightmare? He shook off the terror, realizing the vision of two years ago had come to visit him again.

17

Dakota's first stop in the morning was to meet with those detectives on the task force available for an update briefing. He had learned that no man had shown up at Tracey Kendall's apartment during the night and she had left for work just as she had done every day for the past five years. Only now, Dakota asked her to make certain not to deviate from her pattern in any way. If their man were watching her, any changes in her daily routine might spook him.

While Dakota sat with his detectives, Mary Borlin slipped into a seat in the back of the room. Though she did nothing to attract Dakota's attention, Dakota stopped speaking and turned his attention to her.

"Anything useful, Mary?" he asked.

There was so much hope in his voice. It all died away when she began her report.

"No, sir. No link between the Ellie mentioned in the notes and a homicide victim named Ellie."

"What about an outstanding M. P. report?"

"Negative, sir."

"Can we broaden the computer search to cover more than just the western states..."

"Already did, sir. No matches in either California, Oregon or Washington. How far East should I sweep?"

"Everything west of the Mississippi. What about NCIC?"

"Nothing yet, sir, but I've written a background program to monitor all NCIC updates, and I'm doing the same on-line with VICAP. There's a lot of states out there just starting to put their historical crime data into the national database. I figure it's a long shot, but you never know."

"Very good, Mary, let me know if we get any hits, no matter how remote they may be."

Despite what he had just heard, Dakota still believed locating the mysterious 'Ellie' was the key most needed in this case.

"What's the status on Lisa Roberts?" Dakota asked the room.

"Nothing new," a blurry-eyed detective said, as he rose clumsily out of his chair. "We've finally identified every person who has come into contact with her since she received that first message. I'm afraid...all dead ends."

"How many open leads are we currently following up on, Bronc?"

"Eleven now. Not counting Tracey Kendall. Or any old leads pending relative to Lisa Roberts."

"Gentlemen, where can we go from here?"

A hush fell over the detectives. All of a sudden they were concentrating on their notebooks in their hand.

"Why don't you ask your psychic?" Rodman sniped from the back of the room.

"What about forensics?" Dakota asked at last.

"Still waiting for reports on the physical evidence. The state lab promised us something in the next two weeks."

"Get an update from the labs today. And Bronc, announce a press conference for later in the day. Let's appeal to the public for help. Maybe someone will come forward."

"Got it. How's three sound? We'll make the evening news."

"Perfect. Let's hit the streets. Somewhere out there is someone who can help us find this bastard. Let's dig him up."

"Where will you be, Lieutenant?" a detective asked, scratching at his hair that had grown wild as a result of his lack of attention to it.

"With Bronc on the Kendall woman. I want two of you on standby throughout the night. I want to be able to bring you in on a moment's notice if we get lucky."

Luck is something you never get when you need it. Don't count on it because it just won't happen. Even when the stakes are life and death. You want luck? Go make your own luck.

There is no Apache word for luck. Dakota substituted tenacity. Tracey Kendall returned home following a short after-work stop at a local market, with her shadow in tow. Bronc and Dakota sat out of sight throughout the evening, communicating by radio with Martin, who was enduring the long, lonely hours inside the apartment. Cabin fever was what she called it.

But as Tracey retired that night, there was still no man skulking around the apartment complex. Dakota feared their presence had spooked him. Maybe they screwed up. Maybe somehow the suspect sniffed out the police and abandoned Tracey as a victim. That meant another woman could be falling into the killer's sights.

In the silent still, Dakota rehashed the details in his mind, trying to isolate where they might have gone wrong. The only way the suspect could have become suspicious is if he had seen their plant slip into Kendall's apartment. Both Bronc and Martin were confident that no eyes had been watching.

The waiting scraped Dakota's nerves raw. It forced him into too many empty hours with which to fill his mind with thoughts of Grace. And all this time was lost if the suspect never showed and had moved on to another victim. It was entirely possible they were waiting for the wrong man. Another body from the Boulder Hill killer could prove them wrong.

Despite all the uncertainty that clouded the investigation, they waited—and they hoped.

Relief arrived at midnight. Dakota turned the surveillance over to task force detectives and returned home. This night, however, he only slept a few hours in the den. Sleep was a whip that tortured him. He saw Grace when he closed his eyes. He tried to block out her image and force himself to rest. But...

Then the faces of the Boulder Hill killer's victims appeared. In the past, Dakota had always been able to separate himself from the crime scenes. Leave them at the office was what he had conditioned himself to do over the years. But lately, the scenes kept spilling into his mind, stealing away his thoughts and robbing him of the rest he desperately needed.

What secret did Angela Janine Walker share with the other victims?

Usually, Dakota forced himself to remain on the den sofa until first light. But this morning he was up, showered and out of the house before the girls or Cole and Laurianne had awakened.

Something was driving him out of the house and toward the Kendall apartment. He thought about nothing else. Far beyond his reach, something toyed with his subconscious, tricking him into thinking too deeply about the case. *Find the missing piece.* He knew he had to find that piece to go forward. But what that piece was, he still had no idea.

The killer was exhibiting more than just a passing interest in him. He had taunted Dakota into coming back onto the case. Then he made it sound like he knew he would never be caught. Why? Was he someone with knowledge about evidence processing and/ or police techniques? Did he know how to execute his crimes with relative certainty that the police would be unable to nail him?

Dakota rolled to the curb two blocks before the apartment complex. Today, he dressed in blue overalls. A laborer...the perfect cover for an Apache. No one looked twice at an Indian in dirty overalls slinging a pick and shovel.

Dakota withdrew a wheel odometer and a clipboard from his trunk. Then, he pulled his Atlanta Braves baseball cap down over his eyes and started walking. Just another dumb injun, he hoped, taking those first strides at a quick pace. His heart surged inside. Each day offered a new opportunity. Today could be the day.

The drowsy sun crept over the eastern horizon, splashing new light down the street as Dakota strolled with his little wheel clicking off the feet. Whistling, he checked his clipboard every few seconds, pretending to be engrossed in his task.

A lone, battered pickup cruised down the street. Dakota had at least another thirty minutes before the yuppies in the complex headed out for their daily grind.

Dakota never broke stride when he passed a cream-colored van. From inside, however, came a flinch of recognition. Somewhere, and even Dakota failed to spot him, a second detective watched over the complex.

Dakota marched past the complex entrance, intent on his clipboard, leaning forward as if to check the reading on his equipment. Only after he cleared the line of sight of the interior of the complex, did he stop to write and scan back over his shoulder. Just another normal day...until...

The detective in the van perked up, moving a hand to become visible through the windshield. The rest of him remained hidden in the darkened interior. The movement caught Dakota's attention. Dakota immediately trained his eyes on the front of the apartment complex. From his vantage point, nothing unusual presented itself. But he was too far off to see directly into the thicket beyond the play area. If the suspect were there, Dakota appeared not to notice.

As Dakota watched, a camera slid into sight inside the van. He had to be there! But the lens caught the morning sun, throwing it at the building in a flaring burst.

Dakota tossed clipboard and odometer, racing down to the next building. Damn! Had the suspect caught the reflected light?

Dakota turned into the parking lot and furtively made his way down the walkway toward Tracey's apartment. They had to maintain radio silence this close to the area where the man had been reported. In the quiet, Dakota listened to his thumping heart. Adrenaline fueled his muscles. He focused on a single thought. Sweat rolled off his face even though a cool morning breeze swirled between the buildings.

Could it be he was about to get his first glimpse of the Boulder Hill killer?

Dakota stopped at the building's northeast corner. Leaning against the wall trying to make himself invisible, he expended a precious moment to catch his wind. Then he inched forward, knowing what awaited him around the corner.

The play area entered his field of vision.

Nothing. A swing luffed back and forth, but Dakota detected no skulking form ensconced in the trees beyond it.

Motionless, Dakota waited.

A slim fiftyish woman wearing a shiny, tight jogging suit paused in the play area to limber up. A minute later, with a splash of sand, she began her run.

Dakota made a mental note to track her down later and question her, hoping she might corroborate Tracey Kendall's story. Maybe the runner had also seen the man and could provide a more exacting description than they currently had.

Dejection flooded Dakota. False alarms dashed fragile hopes. Dakota returned to his car with his equipment, where a detective stood smoking a cigarette.

"Thought we had something," the detective said, crushing the cigarette out.

"I saw the camera go up," Dakota said, tossing clipboard and odometer into the back seat.

"Thought I saw something in the trees. Sorry."

"Nothing overnight?"

"Not a thing."

Bronc arrived fresh and ready to begin another day of surveillance. Every one of them suspected the killer might be playing a game with them. Could he have staged this little episode to lure the task force here while he killed elsewhere?

Sooner or later, though, every scumbag makes a mistake. And Dakota and Bronc would be right there to nail him. They were all just hoping it would be soon—very soon.

The radio crackled, announcing in a sleepy feminine voice that Tracey Kendall was ready to leave and all was clear outside. Carrie Martin concluded her transmission with something about being held prisoner and needing to either be set free or be given bacon and eggs.

The detectives laughed. Even Dakota allowed a slight, almost meaningless, smile to show through his granite jaw.

Dakota and Bronc picked up Tracey as she pulled out of the Occidental Insurance building parking lot for the drive back home. Nine more hours had expired without progress in the case.

"We need some luck. At times, I get fed up with trying to ride a dead horse out of the desert," Bronc moaned, as they maintained a safe distance behind Tracey's Toyota.

"All we can do is keep kicking that dead horse until we can get our chance to put that scumbag away. He plans his every move so carefully that we can't get close to him."

"You ever think maybe he's right under our noses...but we keep forgetting to look down?"

"We'll get him no matter where he is."

"You think anything's going to come out of your news conference the other day?"

"There's only one thing I really want to come out of that conference."

They drove on in silence. Tracey must have been daydreaming, as she almost went through a red light. She slammed on her brakes just in time to avoid a calamity.

Dakota laughed. People are supposed to drive better when they know there's a cop behind them.

"I've got a red pickup falling in behind her," Bronc reported.

"You see it before?"

"No, you?"

Dakota slid to the right lane to close the gap. They fell in one car behind the pickup. When Tracey turned at an intersection she normally went straight through, the pickup followed.

"Wow, maybe we got something," Bronc said, leaning forward for a glimpse of the plate.

"I've got the last three...675..."

But just as Bronc grabbed the mike, the pickup veered right and careened into a liquor store parking lot.

"Coincidence..." Dakota said, easing off the accelerator to widen the gap between them and Kendall's car.

Three and a half miles later, the Toyota pulled into the apartment complex parking lot. Dakota radioed Martin of their arrival. She, in turn, took up her position just beside the apartment door with her finger opening the drapes enough to allow a look at the play area. She reported no suspect in the area.

It was Dakota's turn for foot patrol, so he left the vehicle while Bronc slid over behind the wheel. Dakota approached the complex from the north, which was the side furthest from the Kendall apartment.

At first, Dakota looked right past the man. A scrap of army jacket disappeared around the far corner of the building adjacent to Tracey Kendall's.

Dakota watched Tracey leave her car, but this time her preoccupation precluded her ritual scan of the area. She closed the car door without even looking toward the play area.

Dakota held his position, though an inner voice screamed for him to move. If the man Tracey thought she saw days ago was back, they couldn't risk spooking him now. Dakota continued to the next building, and ran its entire length hoping for a vantage point to observe the children's play area.

"Bronc, you got 'em?" Dakota risked in a whisper into his radio.

"Not yet...he's in the trees..."

"Notify Martin."

Dakota stopped at the edge of the building. The moment they had been praying for had arrived. Sweat rolled down his cheeks—his breathing came in gasps.

"Please be him," he whispered to himself.

"Dakota, in the trees. I can't make out a face."

"Get a picture of him," Dakota whispered to himself.

"Anything from inside...." Bronc asked into the radio. No reply came.

"All I get is silhouette," came from inside the Kendall apartment.

"I got Tracey's nod...she thinks he's the guy. The hair and the jacket."

"Bronc, you got..."

"He's spooked! Move in, move in! Back up get your asses in here now," Bronc burst over the air waves as he bolted from his car. The arrangement of the parking lots for the various buildings made a chase using the vehicle extremely difficult. The mike banged the door on his departure.

Dakota exploded around the corner in time to lock on a green blur dashing out of the trees just beyond the swings and climbing bars.

"He's running toward Mojave. Cut him off—I'm on foot. He's bolting for the canyon. Somebody cover Homestead west of Taylor."

The suspect had a dozen possible escape routes available to him and all could avoid the street traffic. If he got into Boca Negra Canyon, he could easily make himself invisible. The deeper southwest he went into the canyon, the harder it would be to track him. Dakota tried to call for a K-9 unit but 'dog' was all he could force out between gasps. The next block over was fifty yards to the west and the residences were arranged like a maze.

Dakota rolled over a six-foot fence like a high jumper and held his Beretta in check while he scanned the houses hoping for a glimpse of the suspect. He had to be here.

Bronc careened around a corner, slid sideways to a stop and ran from his car pointing to the shadowy gap between two buildings.

Dakota was off again, weapon skyward as he searched for their prey. They had to find him...

A second surveillance car turned down Tesuque Drive, scanning yards. A black and white waited where Mojave spilled onto Homestead Circle.

"I've got him coming out on Pojoaque Drive!" came through the radio with a blast of excitement.

"Which way?" Dakota yelled.

"South. Dakota, he's heading toward you..."

"Bronc, come up on Montano," Dakota commanded, racing through a wide gap between houses and emerging onto a quiet street.

Bronc emerged half a block down, fighting to suck in enough oxygen to keep from passing out.

"Damnit..." Dakota cursed, spinning around, praying for something—anything to indicate the suspect's last direction.

"All available backup converge on Unser Blvd and Montano. Now!" Dakota barked into his radio.

Bronc bolted across the street, cutting an angle in Dakota's direction. Exhaustion kept him from talking; he had only enough strength to point toward a two-story house with a three-foot high hedgerow running along its left side.

Dakota spotted a runner slipping between that house and the one beside it.

"I got a bead...cut him off! Cut him off at Montano west of Chimayo."

As Dakota cut north through a yard, the suspect veered left, taking a straight-line track for the canyon. Dakota adjusted to intercept him after Tesuque, but before he could reach Mojave and the canyon.

"Freeze, police!" Dakota yelled, leveling his Beretta on the back of a stained army jacket as the man rose out of a crouch from between a parked Grand

Cherokee and a black Camaro ten feet away. Their breathing sounded more like bulls snorting.

The suspect's right hand went to his jacket pocket.

Dakota tightened his finger his 9mm's trigger.

"Don't do it, man!" Bronc commanded, leveling his revolver to rest on the hood of a Taurus. He centered the shaggy head of hair in his sights.

For that suspended moment, nothing else existed in the universe. *Hold until the very last second*, Dakota thought. The truth; they need the truth. Dakota ceased breathing, never feeling the river of sweat rolling off his face. Even his heart fell silent—waiting.

Bronc's gasping broke the still.

The suspect turned slowly, his black eyes coming about to stare through Dakota. The man was unsure...hesitant.

Dakota cocked back the trigger. He was on automatic now. React and neutralize the threat.

Bronc's finger began a deadly draw on the trigger.

The hand drew away from the pocket without going in.

Dakota returned the hammer.

The suspect's hands rose skyward.

Dakota breathed once more. The last thing he wanted was to kill the suspect. They needed the truth. They had to be sure this olive-skinned man with black hair and dark eyes really was the Boulder Hill killer.

Bronc came up from behind, grabbed the man's hands in a lock behind his neck and slammed him onto the trunk of an old Chevy Nova.

"That's for making us run, you shithead scumbag," he snarled as he cuffed him.

"He's taken," Dakota announced over the air waves.

"Boy, you must be bug-eyed stupid if you thought you were going to outrun us," Bronc added for good measure.

18

Tracey Kendall had little trouble picking the suspect from the lineup populated with officers and clerks who shared the same complexion and hair color. It took less than three minutes to positively identify Mr. Mervyn Delaney.

"Take your time. Please make sure," Bronc coached.

"I'm sure that's him. He's even more frightening close up."

Dakota thanked Tracey for her courage and released her with the assurance that everything was all right now; she no longer had to fear this man bothering her again.

The suspect never so much as flinched during the lineup. When asked to step forward, he did so, staring out as if he could see through the mirror. Never once did his eyes go to the men on his flanks.

"Is he the serial killer?" Tracey asked, before leaving.

"That we don't know yet," was Dakota's response.

Mervyn Delaney carried nothing more on his person than an expired Colorado driver's license and claimed he had lived in Albuquerque for the past four years.

Probably on the streets, Bronc surmised.

Mervyn said nothing else.

Detectives moved Delaney to an interrogation room where he sat unattended. Mervyn never made a sound, nor left his chair.

"We got us a Frank, Dakota. Mervyn Frank Delaney, no priors, no record in New Mexico. You think he goes by Frankie rather than Merv?" Bronc said, fingering a printout. "Where do you want to start?"

During the next two hours, Dakota and Bronc looked on through a two-way mirror. They had put the pot on to boil. They were waiting...waiting for time to erode Mervyn's street-hardened resolve. They hoped to see signs of the first cracks before going in.

"We got an address on him?"

"According to this we do."

"Get a warrant and send a team to his place of residence. Go through everything."

"Can do."

"Anything about arson?"

"Nothing here, but I'll have his name run through the Colorado computers, NCIC and VICAP."

"Juvenile. Particularly violence."

"It'll take some time to work his name through the juvi system. Maybe a long time."

"Turn it over to Borlin. She can cut through the crap. Have her wash this guy through every computer she can get into. I want to know who he is and what he's been doing for the last thirty years."

"Mary already has the information. You think it's time we talk to him?"

"Not yet. The longer he's alone, the more he's thinking. I'm going home to have dinner with my daughters. You wanna come?"

"No. I'll have something brought in. Can I give the task force a break?"

"Bring them all in for dinner. Order pizzas or whatever. It's too soon to celebrate, but we definitely have finally gotten something to go our way."

Two more hours passed. Dakota entered the interrogation room first. Bronc followed, holding a file two inches thick that had nothing to do with Delaney but in itself appeared intimidating. Neither detective spoke as they took up chairs on either side of Mervyn Delaney.

Delaney never looked up and never acknowledged their presence. He fixed his eyes on tightly interlaced fingers planted on the table. His knuckles had paled.

"You understand why you were arrested?"

"No," was his razor-sharp retort.

"You acknowledged to the two detectives who read you your rights that you understood them."

"Yes."

Mervyn's eyes never moved.

"Why did you run, Mervyn?" Bronc asked in a tone of genuine concern. Only Bronc and Dakota knew otherwise.

Delaney lifted his head and stared into Bronc's eyes for a seemingly unending moment, then he returned his gaze back to his hands.

"Why did you arrest me?" Delaney asked in a coarse, almost surreal, voice.

"Why did you run?" Dakota persisted in a calming tone, all the time studying the man's gestures. This one would prove tough. He had obviously been through police interrogation before by the way he controlled his gesturing.

"Had to."

"Why were you there in the first place?"

"Wanted to."

"Why?"

"It's no crime. I can be there if I want to."

"I don't think so, Mervyn. I think you were there for a very specific reason...and that reason is the woman living in apartment 2-K."

Mervyn shifted his eyes in an unnatural way, like he sought to hide recognition from the detectives.

Both Dakota and Bronc caught it.

"Wasn't there for Miss Kendall," he said.

Dakota swallowed hard. Delaney acknowledged her by name. A rising excitement caught in Dakota's throat. Too soon, he thought, don't move too fast.

"So, you were watching Miss Kendall," Bronc offered in a nonthreatening way.

"No law against that?"

"Yes there is, Mervyn, you can't do that..." Bronc said, saying the suspect's name with a hint of disdain in his voice.

"Says who?"

"Mervyn, how do you know Miss Kendall?"

"I just do. I know where she lives."

"Well, Merv, why were you watching Miss Kendall?"

Mervyn's eyes shifted again. He stared beyond Bronc's eyes, as if he could tunnel his way into Bronc's soul. Delaney never smiled; he never frowned. His face remained devoid of emotion.

Was his soul devoid of guilt? Another trait of the serial murderer.

After an hour of working diligently to evade the detectives' questions, Delaney's hands remained tightly clasped together and firmly in place on the table. He had made no gestures that could even remotely be misconstrued as offensive in nature, and thereby give the detectives no cause to smack him around.

"I don't have to say anymore..."

Dakota pushed his chair back. They still had nothing of use for their investigation. Dakota decided to take a chance.

"We're going to need hair and blood samples from you. Will you do so voluntarily?"

Delaney said nothing. Dakota gave the words a few minutes to take hold. Both he and Bronc knew samples would be useless in their case, but the question itself became pivotal. A guilty man would refuse to risk it. If Delaney refused, it could heighten suspicion that they had gotten lucky.

"I know my rights. You can't make me do anything I don't want to."

"Who is Ellie, Mervyn? Is she your mother?" Dakota asked, stepping further out onto that fragile limb.

Mervyn held his unflinching gaze still focused on his hands. Nothing about him acknowledged the name Ellie.

"I don't know anyone named Ellie," he offered finally.

"Sure you do, Mervyn. C'mon tell us who she is...she your girlfriend?" Bronc said barely above a whisper. He was very close to Mervyn's face now.

"Merv, can you tell us where you were on Thursday, September fifteenth of this year?"

Delaney snapped up.

Dakota felt a rush fill his head.

Bronc could barely contain his excitement.

"Just tell us where you were on Thursday, the fifteenth of September."

"Why?"

"Because we need to know."

"I was with a friend."

Delaney answered too fast, keeping his gesture in check, Dakota thought.

"With a friend?" Bronc persisted.

"A friend, Mervyn? A girlfriend?" Dakota pressed. He just needed this scumbag to say the words; to open the flood gates and let it all out.

"Who was she, Mervyn?" Each time Bronc said his name, he delivered it with the vicious sharpness of a stab wound.

"He...Willard."

"Willard who?"

"Willard Bendenning...fishing."

Bronc and Dakota felt their hopes deflate. They took the information out into the hall, leaving Mervyn to think about what he had just said.

"Get this to Mary right away. Have her see if there is any link to anyone named Ellie through this Bendenning. Could be a relative, neighbor or a co-worker; check for an alias. In the meantime, assign two men to dig up this Willard Bendenning...if he exists."

After Bronc left, Dakota watched Delaney through the window in the door. Mervyn at no time displayed any overt signs of nervousness. He sat with his back facing the door and his head tilted slightly forward. He never moved. And he never altered the position of his hands on the table. The same way an insecure person might withdraw into the safety of the fetal position, Dakota suspected this was Mervyn's position of maximum security.

Dakota endured the acid churning in his stomach. Not only had the task force blown the stakeout at the Kendall apartment, but now questioning Delaney was leading nowhere. If he were the Boulder Hill killer, Dakota had to come up with some way to link him back to Angela Walker. And even more important, he had to find a way to keep him locked up.

Then it struck him with a sudden flash. Had Angela placed any calls to police about a man watching her? Dakota pulled a detective off the phone, issuing instructions to check the records. Maybe Mervyn had watched Angela's apartment before she died?

Certain aspects, though, were failing to follow the pattern the FBI and most psychiatrists believed about serial killers. Mervyn Delaney did not live close to either Angela Walker or Tracey Kendall. Nor did he live near any of the three victims of two years ago. Was Mervyn a cruiser? Maybe when he saw Tracey Kendall, something inside his sick brain went off, and he began to watch her—to familiarize himself with her habits. Was he waiting for that one time when she would be vulnerable?

Mervyn also wasn't spilling his guts to police. If he were the Boulder Hill killer, he, for the present, kept that inside.

But the part that really stuck in Dakota's head was that Delaney, if he were the killer, would never have given a potential victim the opportunity to place him in jeopardy. Serial killers are control freaks. Their intent is to maintain absolute control over the encounter with their victim.

Mervyn's actions just about guaranteed that the Kendall woman would notify police....

Bronc returned, and after a brief strategy discussion, the two again entered the interrogation room.

Mervyn never looked up. But this time he shifted his eyes side to side as the detectives took their chairs. Sweat on Mervyn's neck became more apparent. Delaney revealed the first subtle signs of cracking.

Dakota saw something new in Mervyn's dark eyes—fear. Fear of exposure could trigger something inside Delaney. Fear could induce him to tell the truth.

"I'm not who you want me to be," Mervyn offered with an air of arrogance. Yet the words failed to erase what he must have been feeling inside, for it poured out his eyes. But Mervyn had spoken first, rather than wait for either Bronc or Dakota to resume their questions.

"Well, Merv the perv, who do we want you to be?"

"The Boulder Hill killer."

"Why do you say that?"

"You know why. But I'm not the one you're looking for."

"Then why were you hanging out at that apartment complex? Why were you staring at Miss Kendall's window, you sick, fucking pervert?"

"Doesn't matter why. You have to charge me with something or let me go."

"Oh, we've got something to charge you with, Merv the perv," Bronc delivered as coolly as if he were holding a smoking gun.

"You've got nothing."

Time to shift gears.

"Don't fuck with us, Mervyn," Dakota said, rising out of his chair to close in behind Delaney.

"We know you were stalking Miss Kendall. What were you doing in those trees, beating off? Is that the way you can get your kicks, Merv the perv?"

"No."

"Then what were you doing there?"

"Watching her."

"Merv the perv likes to watch?" Bronc stabbed in.

Dakota eased in right next to Delaney's ear.

"She was your next victim, wasn't she? You were getting ready to do her, just like you did Angela Walker on September fifteenth and like Janet Hegler two years ago. The same way, weren't you?"

"I'm not a killer. I wouldn't hurt Miss Kendall."

"Why did you hurt Angela Walker?"

"I didn't hurt no one. I never hurt no one."

"I don't believe you, Mervyn. I think you killed Angela Walker. I think you killed Sheila Davis, Janet Hegler and Steven Ashecroft two years ago," Dakota said, all the time watching for subtle gestures from Delaney that might indicate he was lying. Something as simple as an increase in the number of times he blinked his eyes, or in Mervyn's case, simply shifting his hands on the table could betray him. The right side of the brain hates to lie, and as such, offers up clues to the astute observer.

"I didn't kill anyone. I'm not who you want me to be. You can't make me be someone I'm not."

"Who made you be someone else? Ellie? Who is Ellie, Mervyn?"

"I don't know any Ellie."

"Where were you on that Thursday night, September fifteenth? Were you watching Angela Walker from outside her apartment? Did you see her go in alone and you decided it was the right time for you?"

Mervyn said nothing. He tightened his fingers until the blood ceased to flow.

"How did you get in? Did she forget to lock the door? Did you tell her you were from building maintenance? Come on, you shitbag pervert, tell me how you got into Angela's apartment; how you took her by surprise."

Dakota grabbed Delaney's jacket collar and pulled, forcing Delaney to look directly into the detective's eyes.

"Fuck you, injun. I was fishing."

"You want to hit me, Mervyn? You want to bash in an Indian skull? Come on, take your shot."

"Why, so you can scalp me? Take my head back for your whore squaw."

"You don't want to play cowboys and Indians with me. It wouldn't be a pleasant experience."

Dakota released him but never completely let go of the hold he had on Delaney's eyes.

"I bet you were fishing. Fishing for your next victim; fishing for some innocent woman to kill. You bastard, you were there that night. You planned to kill Tracey Kendall. She was to be your next victim, wasn't she?"

"I wouldn't hurt anyone."

Dakota sat back down in the chair.

Delaney carefully and meticulously reassembled his hands squarely on the table in front of him. Then he tilted his head slightly forward and focused on his fingers. He was making every effort to control his gesturing. Something that reinforced in Dakota the notion that Delaney had been through intense police questioning before and had grown wise enough to conceal those telltale visual clues which mirrored his inner psyche.

"Come on, Merv you perv, we think you were there to hurt Tracey Kendall. Isn't that true? If you're sick, we can get you help," Bronc said.

"Not true."

"Then tell us why you were there. Give us a reason to believe you aren't the Boulder Hill killer."

"Not true. I wouldn't hurt anyone. I can go anywhere I want."

Dakota sprang from his chair, sending it crashing to the floor, and stormed from the room. Delaney never even flinched.

"You know, Merv the perv, you're really starting to fucking piss me off."

Bronc lingered a moment more in hopes that Mervyn Delaney might change his mind and offer up the truth. Bronc was too tired to push any harder.

19

Midnight. Corinne never stayed up past eleven, but tonight was different. Tonight she would remember for the rest of her life. Earlier she had overindulged in the wine and had let the spirit of the moment take her. But now she didn't care. Nothing mattered really. The moment was what counted most. Seize the pleasure and excitement of the moment.

Frankie had taught her that.

The drapes were left parted just enough to allow a slice of silver moonlight into the bedroom. Corinne wanted candles; Frankie dashed the idea. The white light cast an eerie glow over the furnishings.

Maybe she'd skip work tomorrow. Sleep in. If the weather was mild, a picnic at the Crossroads sprang to mind. Tomorrow was going to be a great day.

The words were in her throat. They filled her mind, yet she still had difficulty bringing them out. Should she say it? Was now the right time?

They were in bed together; they had shared something very beautiful. But something buried deep below her excitement and contentment held the words in check. Too soon, she told herself.

Corinne lay facing the edge of the bed, feigning sleep. Say it, she told herself. Say it before it's too late.

The bed moved. Was she going to be alone now?

She turned; the words sprang to her lips.

A black shadow obliterated the light filtering in through the window. Corinne looked up. She gasped to breathe when a cold hand seized her throat. Before she could expel her exploding scream of terror, a stone statue whacked the side of her head at the temple. The dull thud fell into her ears. Blood splattered her pillow as she surrendered consciousness.

Corinne never got to say the words that were in her heart at that moment. She never suspected that love and hate could coexist in one heart at the same time. Corinne never felt the blade carefully open her carotid, as she never knew she had just become the Boulder Hill killer's next victim.

20

The following morning, Dakota turned the interrogation of the suspect over to Bronc and the task force. They had forty-eight hours to sweat something out of him before having to file formal charges. And Dakota considered filing charges just to keep Delaney off the street.

But for right now, Dakota needed some time away from the case. He needed time with his daughters.

Rodman insisted the task force was again wasting their time on Delaney. He contradicted the profile; ergo, he couldn't be their killer, and the FBI agent concluded the detectives instead should be out on the streets searching for the man the FBI Behavioral Science Unit said was the Boulder Hill killer.

Dakota felt otherwise. In fact, Mervyn Delaney *didn't* fit the FBI profile of the killer. But that's what Dakota had been saying all along. Two years ago, when Dakota first received the killer's profile, he suspected the FBI had overlooked something and now he was even more confident in his feelings.

They had the Boulder Hill killer in lock up. Dakota knew it. He could feel it inside, where there was only truth. Outside, you can stretch truth, twist it to fit your own desires, fabricate facts to support anything, or even lie. But inside, the truth remains the truth.

Dakota treated the girls to a pancake breakfast. Cole and Laurianne hastily made plans of their own...something about getting away from Albuquerque. They were grateful for some time strictly for themselves. Caring for two rambunctious girls had become quite an adjustment. And though they were holding up well under the circumstances, they still needed that private time they had grown accustomed to over the ten years of their childless marriage. It seemed there was always something that had to be done.

Laurianne never complained. She enjoyed the work, knowing how important her support was to Dakota, who was totally consumed by such an important case. In her own way, she was doing her part to help police catch a crazed killer.

Besides, caring for the girls kept her busy from morning to night, and as long as she was busy, she had no time to think. Switching her brain to autopilot kept the tears buried inside. At least for now.

To the girls, Laurianne remained as solid as those rock walls they saw in the desert. She never wept in front of them. And never spoke of Grace with them. Instead, she afforded herself a few minutes after everyone had left and the house had become tranquil. Then she cried. She cried until it hurt. Like a sudden rain, her tears cleansed away grief; if only for a short time.

After their breakfast, Dakota and the girls took in the zoo and spent the day strolling through one smelly animal house after another. He noticed Lauryn smiled more and spoke of things Laurianne had done for her and Heather. A growing sense of acceptance seemed to now crop up in Lauryn's voice. They had to go on. Though there were still moments when she withdrew suddenly and sought solace in her private thoughts, Lauryn was beginning to understand that she would go on.

Dakota and the girls returned home late in the day to find Cole and Laurianne preparing a dinner close to fruition. The savory aroma of chile and steamed rice greeted them at the door. Along with an anxious Cole, who couldn't wait to hear about their day. He missed them.

"Come on in, find yourself a seat at the table. Dinner's almost ready," he said.

"Look what I got, Uncle Cole," Heather said, lofting a stuffed animal of some endangered species Cole guessed was some kind of marsupial.

"What did you get, Lauryn?"

"I didn't want anything."

Cole exchanged looks with Dakota.

"Laurianne's got dinner on the table. Did you want us to stay afterward?"

"Could you? I need to check on some things," Dakota said. The aroma of the food rekindled difficult memories for him.

"I figured you would. I heard on the radio your guys are questioning a suspect."

"What!" Dakota's face flashed a melange of surprise and anger. Another leak. Delaney was supposed to have been kept quiet. Washington said he would be the one to break it to the media when they had something they could rely on. Did Bronc break the case open during the day? A rush worked its way through Dakota. Could it all be over?

Dakota sat quietly through dinner while Heather recounted their day detail by detail. He heard little; he fought the urge to call for an update on the investigation. He decided it could wait—the girls were more important right now.

As soon as he finished, though, Dakota changed into a tie and prepared to leave.

"Will you be home late tonight?" Lauryn asked, standing in the doorway to his bedroom. She sounded so much like Grace.

"Not too late," he said, feeling a knot rise in his throat.

"I'll wait up for you," Lauryn offered.

"Okay. Did you enjoy your day?"

"It was great."

Lauryn drifted in to sit on the end of the bed watching Dakota put the finishing touches on his tie.

"You okay, sweetheart?" he asked when he noticed the faraway stare in her eyes.

"Do you have to go?"

"Yes, I do. But I'll get back as soon as I can. You understand, don't you?"

"I guess. Mom used to say you had to go so other people would be safe."

Dakota turned from the mirror, dropped to one knee and hugged Lauryn.

"Your mother was right. How about I make us some tea when I get home. We can sit together before you go to bed."

"Okay."

"Help your aunt until I get back."

There was more to say. So much more in his heart. But he left it there and pulled himself back to his feet.

A near carnival atmosphere buzzed through every floor of police headquarters. Even though it was after eight in the evening, every detective on the serial killer task force, along with most of the uniforms that had been temporarily assigned to work the case, and the local FBI agents, were milling about the third floor.

Bronc's face had lost its luster; his eyes were red and tired. But he smiled as if he were about to take off and fly when Dakota walked in.

"We chose not to disturb you, boss," Bronc said, "but things are starting to pop."

"What have we got? Anything turn up at his residence?" The excitement infected Dakota; something he usually resisted. He had been down this road many times before. There was a right time for celebration. As a result, Dakota conditioned himself to believe a homicide was solved only when it was solved. And it's solved when the State's Attorney has the evidence to make an ironclad case in court. When it's a done deal and the bad guy has no chance of evading conviction. Then it was time to celebrate.

For a moment, the excitement rekindled memories of the false hopes he had cherished two years ago. No, this time it wasn't solved until the killer either confessed or the State's Attorney turned back flips in front of the district judge.

"Not exactly. The guy's a filthy pig. But other than the garbage, his place was clean."

"Delaney confess?"

"Party-pooper," Bronc replied, losing his smile. "How about...Merv the perv's alibi for Thursday, September fifteenth took off for the desert."

"No shit?"

"God's honest truth. Old Willard Bendenning headed for the cholla and the rocks. We've issued a bulletin for him. If he's stopped or spotted, he'll be ushered in for questioning."

"Have you told Delaney yet?"

"Not yet. I tell you, that guy is one tough nut to crack. We've been going in and out on him for the past twelve hours, and we can't get him to open up."

"What do you think, Bronc? Is it time?"

"Lab says it's a no-go between Delaney's prints and the latents found at the Walker scene. But that doesn't necessarily mean anything."

"But his alibi is real shaky?" Dakota said.

"That's our only trump card right now. Once we play it, he might know we've run out of material."

"How much time's left on the clock?"

"Roughly twelve hours. DA says either we charge him or spring him. I'm all for going in with everything we've got right now and sweating the confession out of him. If that don't work, we try a midnight polygraph. Sooner or later that scumbag has got to break."

"The lab turn up anything more than the prints from the Walker crime scene? Fabric, blood, anything?"

"Zip, zero, nada, squat, bupkus. The latents were our best shot with physical evidence."

"You forgot zilch."

"Zilch."

"Where are we going with the prints right now?"

"FBI fingerprinting division is our best shot with that."

"Then let's see if we can bluff our way through this. If we get anything of value out of him, I'll convince the DA to keep him in custody."

Dakota and Bronc reentered the interrogation room. Their faces revealed to Mervyn Delaney that they had just learned something incriminating. Their revived exuberance unnerved their suspect.

Mervyn's position remained exactly as it had been when Dakota had last seen him. His eyes, though, were darker and rimmed with ridges. His skin had turned to parchment. Bronc had reported that Delaney had refused to eat and accepted only a glass of water.

Dakota stared into the troubled emptiness in Delaney's eyes. Eyes that peered back at Dakota with a flash of hatred. But Mervyn's hands had not moved from their place on the table. He kept them clasped as if nailed to the surface.

"The time for bullshit is over, Mervyn," Dakota said, taking his chair and moving it right next to Delaney. Dakota sat down—an inch separated their faces.

"Get your fucking injun face out of mine," Mervyn said.

The words ignited a fire inside Dakota. Mervyn was starting to lose it. Delaney hated having an Indian control him.

"Tell us where you really were on the night of September fifteenth. The night Angela Walker was strangled and mutilated."

"Why don't you go fuck your squaw."

"Your good buddy Bendenning rolled you over."

Mervyn's eyes moved up to Dakota's face. They searched Dakota's eyes. Was there truth in there or bullshit cop trickery?

"Bullshit. You know where I was that night; you're trying to bullshit your way through it. You know I'm clean, injun. You ain't got shit on me."

"You listen, shitbag," Dakota said, rising out of his chair and taking a fistful of Mervyn.

"We know you weren't at the river fishing that night with your old buddy Bendenning. We know you got this sick perversion for young women. We know you spent a year on a juvi farm in Pueblo, Colorado for beating up a girlfriend."

Delaney stared into Dakota's eyes. He never flinched at Dakota's accusations.

"You believe Bendenning?" Mervyn said coolly.

"I'd rather believe you, Mervyn. But you're not giving me anything to believe."

"I'm telling you the truth."

"If it's the truth, then you won't object to a polygraph."

"You mean a lie detector?"

"Yeah."

"Right now?" Mervyn said. His voice showed fine cracks of concern.

"I bring in the machine, and we'll know in ten minutes if you're telling the truth."

"Then do it. Hook me up, and I'll prove I'm not who you want me to be."

Bronc left the room and returned a few minutes later with a square black box on a cart. He stopped it so Mervyn could see the needle resting on a roll of graduated paper the width of adding machine tape. The device resembled the old-style machines used to record electrocardiograms. With an expression as flat as a rock, Bronc slowly unfurled three long wires. One he wrapped loosely around Mervyn's neck, the second he wound multiple times around his right index finger, and the third he attached with masking tape to Mervyn's temple.

"The test is very simple," Bronc instructed while he fiddled with a row of dials above the resting needle.

After plugging the power cord into an outlet, he turned the machine on. Paper began moving very slowly off the roll. The sleeping needle left a straight blue line in the center.

"Merv, you tell the truth, this line stays straight. You lie—the line jags back and forth. The more serious the lie, the more the needle jiggles. You understand?"

Mervyn barely shook his head. His eyes refused to stray from the line on the paper that now stretched almost to the floor.

"I'm going to ask you to lie intentionally, so we can make sure the machine is properly calibrated. When I ask you your name, I want you to respond with Dick Nixon. You understand?"

Delaney nodded.

Bronc glanced up at the two-way mirror.

Dakota pushed his chair away from Mervyn and the equipment.

"Okay, we're starting. I'd like you to state your name for the record."

"Mervyn Delaney."

The line remained straight.

"Mervyn, am I going too fast for you?"

"Sorry."

"Please state your name for the record."

"Dick Nixon."

The line jittered a third of the way along the graduations on either side of the center line.

"See. The machine detected your lie. Now, Mervyn, do you know Tracey Kendall."

"Yes."

The line remained straight.

"Mervyn, do you know Angela Janine Walker?"

"No."

The needle jittered to create spikes, then settled back into a straight line.

"Were you in the apartment of Angela Janine Walker on the night of September fifteenth?" Bronc fired off with rising emotion in his voice.

"No!"

The needle scraped full tilt in both directions, leaving behind a jagged spike.

"Did you kill Angela Janine Walker on the night of September fifteenth?"

"No!"

The needle went crazy, bouncing back and forth to the ends of the paper.

"Your fucking machine is bullshit!" Mervyn yelled, pulling the wires off his finger and temple.

Bronc quickly unplugged the machine and tossed the wires onto the cart. Ceremoniously, he ripped the strip off the roll and folded it into his hand.

"Just relax, Mervyn, it's all over. Have a cigarette. We'll be right back."

Bronc and Dakota left the room, bursting into laughter as soon as they were beyond the window in the door.

"Where did you come up with Dick Nixon?" Dakota said.

"Spur of the moment."

Detective Wilder emerged from the observation room with a hand-held model airplane remote control unit. The telescoping antenna scraped the wall as he joined Bronc and Dakota.

"How'd I do?" Wilder asked, flicking the lever back and forth.

"Perfect," Bronc said.

"You think it worked?" Wilder asked.

Bronc and Dakota shook their heads in the negative.

"I think he was testing us. He almost tripped us up at our own game," Bronc said, peeking back into the room.

"Let's give it one more try before we call it a night," Dakota said as he composed himself for his return.

Dakota and Bronc reentered the interrogation room with somber faces. Messengers of Doom, come to tell Delaney the bad news.

"It's not good, Mervyn. Our polygraph expert read the results. You lied to us, you pervert scumbag," Bronc said while staring coldly into Mervyn's eyes.

"Fuck you."

"No, fuck you, asshole. I believe you're sick and you have to kill innocent men and women. I believe we've got the Boulder Hill killer in our hands. And you better believe that we're going to nail you and see you rot on death row," Dakota said with a conviction meant to unnerve Mervyn; his last-ditch effort to bring about a confession.

It was too late to keep trying. Dakota was dead tired, but he knew he had to go that one step further. He glanced at his watch and for a split second thought about Lauryn in her bed, staring at her ceiling, wondering when he would be home.

A gentle rap at the window on the interrogation room door brought him out of his thoughts.

The face on the other side of the glass had disaster written across it. Dakota needed no words to know something was up. Bronc rose and left the room. As he listened, he waved Dakota out.

21

Dakota stood in the doorway to Corinne Schultz's bedroom. The crime scene remained untouched. The first officer upon the scene stood guard at the sealed home until the task force arrived.

The tedious process began anew. Study every inch of the scene. Dissect everything in sight. Pray for something the killer left behind. And hope it's enough to lead to an arrest. Above all else, don't look at the victim. Don't see her as a person. Don't feel.

For hours, Dakota and Bronc stood just inside the bedroom, recording every detail until their fingers holding their pens cramped. No one approached the body; no one invaded the sanctity of the scene of the Boulder Hill killer's latest victim.

Dakota identified the signature within ten minutes of examining the corpse from a distance. The killer left the body face up on the bed. Blood splatters supported the theory that a weighty object crushed part of Corinne's skull. Then the throat was severed. The pillow and sheets became drenched in Corinne's blood. Her eyes were open and clouded. In death, they delivered a glimpse of the terror the young woman must have felt.

This scene was near identical to the one burning in Dakota's mind. Corinne had been bludgeoned while in her bed. Then the killer positioned the body with the hands in supplication. Afterward, a blade opened the carotid to drain the blood. His undeniable signature.

Dakota would not make it home tonight nor tomorrow; not until they had wrapped up the complete crime scene processing. Lauryn would be disappointed; no, she would be terribly hurt that he failed to be there for her. She needed this time with him. And he had let her down. Somehow he would have to make it up to her.

There had to be something left behind. Had to be some clue to what really happened, Dakota thought, as his eyes swept the room for the twentieth time. Miss nothing, he commanded himself. The piece is here—find it.

Bronc and Dakota took turns pointing out to each other things that might later prove important. Each collected an independent set of notes to compare back at the station against one another.

Outside, task force detectives worked the grounds surrounding the house with flashlights, hoping for evidence the killer might have overlooked. No criminal, regardless of how careful he was, could erase every single trace of his presence at a crime scene.

Bronc assigned four uniforms the unsavory midnight responsibility of awakening surrounding neighbors in search of someone who might have seen the killer enter or exit. Someone had to have witnessed something. Someone had to have been curious enough to notice something.

Preliminary information surfacing became painfully redundant.

"Who reported the body?" Dakota asked the officer who handled the initial call.

"Girl's mother. The young woman missed a dinner engagement with her. In anger, the mother drove to the house and used her key to enter. She said Miss Schultz could be absentminded at times."

"Was there a car around?"

"Yes. The mother became concerned when she saw Corinne's car in the garage."

"Where's the mother now?"

"St. Joseph's. Could be a heart attack. Unfortunately, she pushed open the bedroom door and saw her daughter before realizing that the terrible odor was itself enough to know there was death inside the house."

Dakota and Bronc withdrew for a break. Evidence technicians and a photographer invaded the crime scene to do their jobs; something they trained themselves to perform devoid of emotion. Two dozen pictures would be snapped before the body would be touched.

The coroner arrived and scratched his head when he came upon the body.

"Time of death?" Dakota asked.

"Still some residual rigor...I'd say within the last twenty four hours, but don't quote me on that," the coroner offered, "I'll know more later."

That confirmed Dakota and Bronc's worst suspicions; they exchanged sidelong glances and retreated to the hall.

"If he's right, we've got to cut Merv the perv Delaney loose," Bronc said, scratching at the hair on his neck. He needed a haircut, but that would have to wait at least another three or four days now. No one would get time to even eat until they had some solid leads to work on.

"We hold Delaney until our time is up. That will give the coroner a chance to establish time of death conclusively."

"Where do we go from here?" Bronc asked with a blank face.

The Boulder Hill killer was playing the game his way and keeping the task force groping for straws in the dark. Somewhere, someone was laughing at their buffoonery.

"We've got to pull something out of this crime scene. That scumbag had to have left something behind."

While inside the Schultz house, Dakota and Bronc returned to the bedroom, satisfied now that the technicians had extracted everything possible; across the street, detectives gathered in the living room of Maranga Jenkins' house.

Frail and friendly Maranga Jenkins, who at seventy-eight could hardly be considered a credible witness, told the nice officer in uniform that she remembered seeing a small red car in Corinne's driveway a few days prior. She couldn't recall the make or model—said she knew nothing about automobiles—she could only say it was boxy and small. She paid no more attention to it than that; at least, not enough to remember any of the digits on the license plate. She was certain the car was a compact with a New Mexico plate, but aside from the color, it was unremarkable in every way.

Between the three detectives, Maranga endured more than forty questions, and she stated for the third time that she saw no vehicle in Corinne's driveway the previous evening.

Maranga also commented that she did not hear anything unusual. Of course, the detectives had to speak quite loudly for Maranga to even hear their questions.

"I can tell you there were no lights on in the front of her house when I looked out my window around ten last night. The whole block seemed so dark. I asked the city to put in more street lights because it's so dark here, but they never did."

"Did you ever see Miss Schultz with any men? Coming home with them or leaving with them?" the detective asked, not expecting to gain anything useful.

"You mean men she was seeing?"

"Yes. But even a delivery man or a man in a worker's uniform."

"I'm no busy body. Corinne kept pretty much to herself. There weren't men coming and going, if that's what you mean."

"Did you speak to her often?"

"Occasionally. I like to work with my flowers and she had asked me about them a few times. She used to work in her front there, putting in perennials, but she never really had much luck. I guess you just have to have a green thumb."

The detectives thanked Maranga Jenkins for all her cooperation despite the late hour. They left with a glimmer of hope no brighter than a distant star. Plucking a small, red car out of a city of half a million, without the make, model or license number, was going to be a tough assignment. More than tough—literally impossible. But at least they had a starting place.

Dakota took in the detective's report concerning the car. He then assigned two detectives to return to Angela Walker's apartment complex to ascertain if anyone in the complex owned a red compact. Failing that, they had to hope to find someone who might remember seeing a red compact in the lot the day or night of Angela's murder.

Possibly someone in the apartments might have seen Angela with a companion that drove a red car. Everything, no matter how remote, had to be checked out and checked out fast.

Time was running out. *Death comes in threes.*

Dakota hadn't seen his daughters in over twenty-four hours. Guilt scraped at his insides. He called regularly to check on things at home and could only promise Laurianne that he would try to get back home that night to sleep.

"It was on the five o'clock news," Dakota said without his usual energy and spirit. It wasn't so much what he said that worried Laurianne; it was what he didn't say.

"You're sure it's the Boulder Hill killer?"

"Without a doubt. I wanted another twenty-four hours before the press got wind of it, but there was nothing we could do."

"Lauryn asked about you when she heard the story. They showed stock footage of you at an apartment complex."

"Tell her...tell the girls, I'll get home as soon as I can and we'll spend some time together."

"Dakota, they understand...they're real troopers."

The next twelve hours sent every available detective scrambling in every conceivable direction to shake up every contact they had on the streets. Somewhere in the city someone had to know something. Nobody could move about so freely without being noticed. It was almost like the Boulder Hill killer was invisible.... Or the victims were being careful not to publicize their relationship with the killer. Or the killer had a way in and out of these people's homes. The bottom line, though, remained the same: these women had something in common that linked them to the killer.

Dakota's investigation of the Schultz crime scene reinforced the notion that the killer knew the victim

before he killed her. Detectives unearthed no footprints around the house and neither entry door
showed signs of forced access. Corinne knew the man
that killed her. As did Angela Walker. Both women,
for some reason still unknown to Dakota, let the
killer into their homes.

Forty-eight hours after arriving on the scene of
the second murder, preliminary reports trickled in to
Dakota from the state crime lab in Santa Fe. Technicians turned up no prints in Corinne's home other
than the victim's or the victim's mother. That meant
the killer remained behind long enough to clean all
the places he might have touched.

For a long time, Dakota did nothing but stare at
the photographs tacked on the board in front of him.
The perverse pattern of brutal death had been maintained. Corinne Schultz bore a striking resemblance
to Janet Hegler, the Boulder Hill killer's second victim
of two years earlier. Same hair color and same short
styling, same eyes and similar build. Why? What did
the killer see in these women? Why single them out?

Even without a complete psychological profile on
Corinne, Dakota guessed the victim would turn out to
be an introvert who kept to herself. Just like Janet
Hegler. They were both single and not currently
involved.... Dakota was still guessing.

He suddenly sprang forward in his chair and
began a voracious search through the Hegler file. His
eyes raced from page to page looking for that bit of
information that seemed to set a fire in his mind.

Corinne wasn't romantically involved.... He saw it.
Janet Hegler was not involved with anyone at the time
of her death.

Was the killer someone who showed up suddenly
out of these young women's past? A previous lover
forgotten. Could each of them have dated the man
casually for a brief time and then moved on? Perhaps
the killer stalked them so carefully they never knew
he was still bordering on the fringes of their lives.

Dakota caught four hours sleep on the battered old sofa in his office. The brass had asked him to get rid of it, but it was comfortable and it provided Dakota with a place to crash while he waited for feedback from his task force out on the streets. When the brass sprang for a new one, he'd discard this old one.

Six-thirty came. Bronc set a box of doughnuts on Dakota's desk along with a steaming cup of coffee.

"Look, I made you breakfast," Bronc said, selecting the largest chocolate doughnut for himself.

Dakota's eyes felt like a thousand needles were stuck in them. His mouth felt like it was filled with grit.

"Any startling revelations overnight?" Bronc asked, though he seemed more interested in an eclair he set on a napkin. "Screw the diet, screw cholesterol, screw everything," he mumbled.

"No. You?"

"Zippo, but I did..."

A dreary-eyed detective leaning against the door frame cut Bronc off.

"Cap wants both of you in his office," the detective said, his eyes widening at the inviting box of doughnuts.

"Help yourself. Spread 'em around to the others as they come in," Bronc said, after he took another for himself.

"Keep everyone here until we can have a briefing," Dakota added, scraping together the reports and notes sprawled across his desk.

Washington, Sturges, Rodman and Lisa Roberts were waiting in the captain's office, all looking fresh from a shower and a decent night's sleep. Washington, though, had a look of dread in his eyes. Lisa's ashen face looked as if she had seen a ghost.

"Bad news," Washington said, even before Dakota and Bronc could take up the two empty chairs awaiting them.

Sturges handed over a scrawled message encased in plastic.

"This guy must be invisible," he said, anxious for some response from either Dakota or Bronc, who were at the time reading the note.

Rodman fiddled with his tie in an I-told-so gesture.

By now, Dakota and Bronc had learned to ignore it.

It's as easy as one-two-THREE!
I thought you were better at the game,
Blackwood...You'll have to do much better
if you want to win....

"How'd it arrive?"

"We don't know?" Lisa said, her voice no longer hiding fear.

"What do you mean, you don't know?" Dakota harped, allowing fatigue to dampen his self-restraint.

"I don't know!"

Dakota looked across at her with apology in his eyes.

"I'm serious. My mailbox was empty when I left the station last night around ten forty-five. When I got in this morning—it was there."

"What did security say?"

"No one entered or left the station unaccounted for."

"This is crazy," Sturges blurted out, "you mean to tell me someone got into the station, slipped this envelope in your mailbox and then walked out without anyone noticing him."

"No. Our security would have noticed anyone out of place at the station. And they swear no one was out of place during the night shift."

Sturges left his chair, clearly angered. The killer was playing them for fools. And Blackwood was the biggest fool of all.

"If your people are that certain, it means only one other thing," Dakota said, going back to the note a second time.

"What's that?" Washington asked.

"Someone entered the station during normal business hours, say part of a tour, or a messenger, or a temp. But instead of leaving at the end of the day, he remained inside the building overnight. When things were quiet, he located your mailbox and put the envelope in it. Then he returned to his hiding place until morning and walked out amid the commotion of people coming to work."

"Okay, let's say you're right, Blackwood. Let's say this nut can sneak in and out of the building unnoticed. The question is: what are we going to do about it?" Cal queried, pressing for concrete answers as opposed to Dakota's 'Sherlock Holmes' supposition.

"What's his next move?" Washington asked, ignoring Cal's ranting.

"The killer's third victim two years ago was male and Caucasian. Assuming he sticks to his pattern, he's going after someone like that next."

"Then I'm safe, right? He won't be coming after me?" Lisa said. Her eyes were searching Dakota's for affirmation.

Dakota said nothing. He wanted to agree, wanted to confirm her relief, wanted to say the killer would act exactly the way Dakota believed he would act. At that moment, Grace popped into his mind. He had wanted to tell her that before.... But he couldn't.

"You want me to be straight?"

"Please."

"There is always the possibility that we missed a victim two years ago."

"What do you mean missed a victim?" Sturges pounded out with an accusatory tone.

"I mean the third victim we found that we could positively link to the Boulder Hill killer was Steven Ashecroft, a twenty-four-year-old single Caucasian male. But there may have been one or more killings between victim number two and the one we called number three. We may have failed to find them."

"But he wants you to find them. Doesn't he?" Lisa asked, seeking reassurance.

"We can't know that for sure."

No one in the room wanted to face the reality of what Dakota had just said. There were always unsolved missing persons cases on the books. One or more of them could have been victims of the Boulder Hill killer.

"No, he wants them found. Isn't that why he's been sending these messages, and why he leaves his victims exposed the way he does?" Lisa said.

"Yes, but each time he kills, he changes his method a little bit. He evolves as a murderer. We may have overlooked something in a murder investigation two years ago and not linked it to the serial killer."

"What does the FBI say about this? Have you talked to Quantico about this?" Cal said. He shifted his eyes to Rodman.

Rodman's face turned smug. They had their chance and they blew it. Why was everyone now looking to the Bureau?

Sturges grew angry. His temper only heightened Lisa's already towering fear.

"I wasn't involved in the investigation two years ago. But I'll back up the Bureau's profile," Rodman said unctuously.

"The Behavioral Unit in Quantico agreed with my thinking on the number of victims. There may have been a third female victim in between the time the second victim was found and what we are calling the third victim. We just have no way of being sure two years later," Dakota said.

"So what do we do, Dakota?" Washington asked. He knew Dakota had no answers.

Dakota looked at Bronc. That was the question.

22

Hours slipped away quietly like a thief in the night. Only afterward, did anyone realize they had come and gone. Even with twenty committed detectives working the two homicide cases, progress was torturously slow.

No names out of Corinne Schultz's past matched names collected from friends and family of Angela Walker. The man they held in common—the identity of the Boulder Hill killer—they kept secret right up to their deaths.

Everyone had questions—answers were at a premium. Each answer, however, spawned a dozen new questions. Was the killer well known to both victims? Or was he known to one and a passing acquaintance to the other?

So far, Dakota had failed to link the two recent victims of the Boulder Hill killer to each other. Whatever they shared that had brought the killer into their lives, they carefully concealed it from their families and friends. Was there a dark secret these women shared or an innocuous intent that now baffled police?

Bronc assigned three detectives to intricately dissect the lives of Angela Walker and Corinne Schultz. He ordered a side-by-side, point-for-point comparison of the two women with their respective victims of two years earlier: where they went, how they spent every dime they earned, who they spoke with, and who spoke with them. Every little detail had to be collected and scrutinized under a microscope. With the lights still burning well toward midnight, the detectives had come up dry. None of the three detectives had been home in the past twenty-eight hours. Not a single shred of information brought to light why the killer had singled these women out. Exhausted, edgy, frustrated and mired down by information, the detectives abandoned the files for the night, promising to be on time for a six A.M. briefing.

In the dead silence of a now deserted floor, Dakota and Bronc sat in the squad room; their eyes blurry from hours of pouring over police reports. Task force detectives documented every detail uncovered in their investigation and nobody went home until all the dailies were in.

After the men had left, Dakota and Bronc looked over each and every report as a prerequisite to the next day's activities.

A few die-hard stragglers slogged into the squad room to put up their feet and relax before calling it a night. No one stopped off for a drink at the end of the day as had been the custom in the past. That would come only after they finally nailed the Boulder Hill killer.

Dakota closed the files, more frustrated than fatigued, and prepared to leave when a NEWS SPECIAL banner flashed across the television sitting atop a file cabinet in the corner of the squad room.

"The following is a rebroadcast from an earlier presentation," a monotone voice said.

The opening sequence delivered its irresistible hook: THE BOULDER HILL KILLER—WHY HE KILLS. A SPECIAL REPORT BY LISA ROBERTS. The local networks were squeezing every nickel they could out of this.

Dakota settled back while Bronc cranked up the volume. A shift detective abandoned his paperwork and swirled toward the television.

An unsmiling, calm and somewhat aloof Lisa Roberts filled the screen.

"Police remain baffled as yet another woman is found brutally murdered in Albuquerque, the second victim of the Boulder Hill killer's latest reign of terror. Why does he kill? Tonight we'll focus on what is known about this bizarre man and attempt to take you inside his head."

The detectives booed, throwing paper and pencils at the screen.

"But first, let me sell you some crap..." Bronc said when a commercial spring-boarded off the intense lead-in for television's real purpose.

At last, the screen returned to Lisa and then dissolved to police wheeling a bagged victim into the back of a coroner's wagon. A gruesome image to present to someone just before retiring.

Bronc flipped through the latest reports, seeming to lose interest in the story.

"Have we run down a common acquaintance between the two women? Someone who knew them both through say, where they bank, or where they get their hair done?" Bronc asked.

"So far that's been a blank," Dakota responded.

"All right, try this one on. Our man's a fly geek out at the air force base. Two years ago he does a psycho tailspin and starts killing. But then he gets transferred to another base and the killing stops here, but starts somewhere else. Only we don't know that so we think the killer's gone. And the police in the new area think they got a new killer because they don't know the history of this creep."

"So how do you explain the revival?" Dakota pressed.

"He got discharged and decided to come back where he felt safe. Where he felt he could kill again without getting nailed."

Dakota ruminated over Bronc's theory. That could explain a two-year absence.

"Get a team of three over to Kirtland first thing in the morning. Have them work with the base security on that angle. Flag anyone who was stationed here two years ago and could have recently been discharged. And while they're at it, get the base police to compile a report of all violent incidents for the last six months. Let's make sure we're not dealing with a GI getting off on the locals when he gets pissed at his commander."

"Can we get access to base psychiatric reports? We may get a lead from one of their people?" a detective across the room asked.

"I'll make some calls in the morning," Bronc offered.

"The Air Force wasn't helpful two years ago," Dakota muttered, recalling his conversation with Air Force officials during his initial investigation.

"You make sure someone from our office persuades them to be helpful this time."

Lisa Roberts returned.

"Two years ago, Detective Dakota Blackwood linked three murders in our city to the same killer. Newspapers quickly labeled their lead story the Boulder Hill killer. His second victim lived in the Boulder Hill subdivision and it was then that police first suspected one man might be responsible for both murders. But after a third victim, the Boulder Hill killer suddenly stopped. Speculation surfaced that police were close to an arrest and that had sent the killer underground. Insiders believed the killing stopped because the Boulder Hill killer was already in jail, arrested on some other charge."

The screen went to a black silhouette with a question mark over it.

"But now he's returned and taunts police with written communications mysteriously delivered to me at this station. Two years ago, homicide Detective Blackwood had the highest clear rate in the department. Yet even he failed to catch the Boulder Hill killer."

Bronc and the other detectives laughed as two-year-old footage rolled across the screen. Dakota looked no younger, but certainly looked less seasoned than he did now. The laughing continued. So much so, that everyone missed Dakota's statement back then that they were closing in on a suspect. The words had been borne out of political pressure at the time rather than evidence. Of course, back then they had no idea the killer would disappear after his third victim.

"The leads dried up and the investigation ground to a standstill. Everyone appeared ready to accept the notion that the Boulder Hill killer, for whatever reason, was gone. Now we know without doubt he is back and killing again."

While the screen showed pictures of the first victims, Lisa continued.

"The FBI Behavioral Science Unit in Quantico, Virginia, which studies serial killers, provided a profile of the man known as the Boulder Hill killer. According to them, the killer is most likely a white male between the ages of twenty-five and thirty-five. He is most likely shy, introverted—a quiet resident of Albuquerque—and sexually impotent. He may exhibit antisocial behavior and could even become belligerent when provoked. Most psychiatrists agree with the notion that serial killers, in general, exhibit Jeckyll and Hyde personalities."

The screen cut to a well-dressed man in his forties sitting before a seal of the Federal Bureau of Investigation. His name flashed across the bottom of the screen, but none of the detectives paid particular attention at the time.

"Serial killers are control freaks. They seek out weak victims; targets they can easily gain control over. The act of killing to them is like a high or a sexual release. As a result, they are unable to stop themselves—only the authorities can stop them. The killing will continue unabated until the serial killer is finally caught."

The agent's voice came across with that deep resonance that exudes authority and confidence. Who would argue with someone like that?

"Serial killers are incapable of compassion and guilt. Killing to them is simply an act; their reflex response to some stimulus. Research has demonstrated again and again that most serial killers grew up in violently abusive environments in which the constant application of pain and suffering instilled an indelible sense of propriety. Serial killers know only violence as a means of dealing with the adversity in their lives."

The screen returned to Lisa. The detectives cheered.

The program doled out mountains of wonderful fluff for the uninformed viewers, but afforded no real substance that might aid police in their search.

"The FBI warns that men like the Boulder Hill killer are walking time bombs capable of violent explosion at the slightest provocation."

"Okay, everybody, it's past our bedtime. Let's turn off that television and go to sleep now," Bronc said, trying to bring the room back to life.

Everyone there shared a responsibility for Corinne Schultz's death. The longer it took to find the killer, the more people would die.

"Was any of this cleared through the department?" Bronc asked Dakota. They both now sat spellbound.

"No. I had no idea she was airing that."

"Can it hurt us?"

"Politically?"

"Yes."

"Probably."

"Where did she get that stuff?"

"Sturges..." they said in unison.

Two nights following her famed Boulder Hill killer broadcast, Lisa exited the station parking lot in a rush. Rolling through a red light, she turned right at the first intersection, as she had done every night she worked for the past month. At eleven-thirty, there was no traffic to deter her.

In her rearview mirror, she watched a pair of headlights come to life and a dark sedan accelerate away from the curb. Just as the sedan moved out, a rust-bucket VW van pulled out, sputtering and bucking. It stalled in such a way as to block the sedan's passage. Behind the wheel of the van, Zack Krieger raised his hands at the two detectives in apology.

The sedan ground to a halt and the detectives waited patiently while Zack pumped the accelerator and cranked the lethargic engine. The machine droned on and on as the battery gave up its meager supply of power. Zack stopped for a long moment, slammed the steering wheel in mock anger then began cranking anew.

"Want a push?" the detective behind the wheel yelled, more in jest than in anger.

Zack waved him off, then he cranked it again. Only after he made certain Lisa was out of sight, did the van miraculously restart. Zack revved up, spent another moment turning on his headlights before shifting into gear and lethargically pulling away in the direction opposite the two detectives assigned shadow duty for Ms. Roberts.

Zack vaulted an arm in success, watching the sedan speed away to catch up with its assignment.

But it would be too late.

Zack rounded the block and found Lisa cruising at twenty-five miles an hour on a prearranged alternate route. While the detectives hurried along the river to make up their lost distance, Lisa traveled away from the river.

She drove slowly, training one eye on her mirror. Her heartbeat quickened when headlights fell into her wake. A single vehicle followed her, a vehicle whose headlights appeared very different than her shadow's. Zack had succeeded in stalling the detectives. Now he had become her shadow. She hoped soon there would be another in her wake also.

A part of Lisa never really believed Zack's crazy idea would work. But he could be persuasive when it came to her career aspirations. Besides, if his plan failed, they would have spent a few hours for nothing. That was their job—investigative reporting. They had to be the aggressors to get to the top. They had to take chances to earn the reputation.

A part of her prayed it would work. Because if it did...

The thought sent icy chills through Lisa's veins.

Checking her mirror, Lisa spied the familiar VW van headlights with the right side parking light out. Zack had removed the bulb to distinguish his vehicle from any other on the road that night. This would be the only signal of recognition between them. The game was on. They had to hope they would get lucky.

So far so good with Zack's plan. Everything had worked exactly as he had planned.

Zack had laid out every detail and assured Lisa repeatedly that he would be there and ready when, and if, the killer showed. He even factored in an emergency abort routine should she lose her nerve at the last minute.

But visions of a network anchor spot cemented her resolve. She'd go through with it...he just better be there.

Lisa kept reminding herself of the celebrity status out there waiting for her. Despite that future admiration and adoration, Lisa felt an acrid fluid back up into her throat.

Do everything exactly as I say and this will work like sliding on pig grease. Zack's words suddenly popped into her head.

"Okay, Zack, you better be right," she said aloud, while she watched his van move ahead on her left and continue into the distant darkness. This was it. For a short time, she proceeded unguarded, vulnerable. Under no conditions should she stop or even slow. Stay with the plan and everything will work just fine.

The next three miles clawed at her nerves. She was totally alone on the road. At a steady forty-five miles an hour that meant four minutes of exposure. The only four minutes when the Boulder Hill killer could get at her without her backup.

Lisa scanned her mirrors for other vehicles. A pair of headlights trailed a good two blocks in her wake. Was it him? Was the Boulder Hill killer following her, seeing her alone for the first time since he began sending her those messages at the station?

Suddenly Lisa thought about the ramifications of actually being alone. All the businesses on the boulevard had closed for the night. In another half mile, the lights of the strip would fall behind her and she'd be alone on a dark road leaving the city.

Zack had said he needed three minutes to position himself.

Lisa checked her dashboard clock. Only two minutes had passed. She slowed as the buzzing neon of the sleeping businesses fell behind her. She checked the clock again, keeping her eyes off the road for more than a few seconds. Her Saab drifted over the line. She jerked it back.

The next turn...

"Settle down, Lisa," she warned.

An oncoming truck flicked its brights. Lisa found herself easing off the accelerator for no good reason except that she was frightened. The headlights in her mirror maintained a safe distance. He was in no rush to close the gap on her. He probably knew where she lived, could trail her until she reached her home, then make his move. Still enough time to back out, she thought. If she didn't, she had to hope those weren't the lights of her shadow. They would disrupt the plan if they showed up on her tail now.

Ahead, the road curved right, skirting a rock formation set there a million years before. As she made her turn, Lisa's headlights washed over the turnout on her left with its wide gravel shoulder.

Twenty seconds to D-day.

Zack had instructed her exactly what to do.

Lisa reached the critical decision point. If she left the road as planned, she was committed. If not, she should continue on—Zack would understand and abort the plan.

Slamming the accelerator to the floor in quick jabs, Lisa forced her car to lurch forward then buck abruptly back. She slapped down her turn signal and bucked her way onto the turnout across the road. A pitch-black curtain of desert met her. She killed the engine, allowing the vehicle to coast to a stop. Her headlights faded at a drop-off into the sand and cholla below.

To her right, an impenetrable wall of pine reflected the light back. Lisa carefully scanned every inch, failing to detect Zack's location. Was he even there? She extinguished her headlights, counted to five, then brought them back to life. Without lights the pure ebony night engulfed her, still and spooky.

Leave the keys in the ignition, the transmission in park and all doors except the driver's locked at all times, Zack had instructed her earlier, but do not restart the engine until...

Lisa responded exactly as instructed.

Something inside warned her to remain in the car. But Zack wanted her out of the car so the killer could make her out under the wash of his approaching headlights.

Lisa had come this far. She had to go all the way now.

Silence clung to the air. Lisa thought for a moment. The headlights she had seen behind her earlier must have turned off because the car should have been upon her by now.

First she drew in a couple of deep breathes to calm her trembling, then Lisa stepped onto the gravel and stood looking at the front of her car. Her eyes moved across the brush before her. Zack had better be there, she thought to herself when nothing seemed to move.

Headlights splashed across the vegetation as a car rounded the bend.

Lisa reached back, finding security in the cold steel of her car. She remained within two steps of safety. The door hung open at arm's length. She fought down the urge to dash back to the Saab's interior. Something inside blared a warning.

The car slowed. A faceless driver stared from across the lane. But the car continued around the bend and quickly out of sight.

Lisa experienced both an outpouring of relief...and failure. Was that the killer? Did he sense a trap and continue away?

Then headlights approached from the opposite direction. The same car that had passed a few moments before now slowed onto the turnout.

"Zack, you'd better be ready," Lisa said aloud.

Her hand clutched the open door. She needed one step to be safely inside.

As the car crept closer, Lisa tightened on the door handle. Her heart pounded at the inside of her chest. She waited. Don't panic...safety remained close enough.

It takes real courage to get to the top. Don't be a chicken shit.

Her hand slipped off the handle from the sweat in her palm.

A twenty-something woman with short, chestnut hair and deep, staring eyes leaned across the seat to roll down the passenger window.

"Trouble?" she asked.

Lisa drank in a swarm of relief.

"Car just went dead."

"You want a lift back into Albuquerque?"

"No. I already called a tow...car phone. He said he'd be here any minute."

"You want me to wait around? Just in case."

"No. My husband's on his way. I'm just going to lock myself in the car until he gets here."

"Suit yourself."

The woman closed the window and rolled her car in a wide circle. Her dust cloud cascaded around Lisa as the car accelerated back onto the road.

Alone again, Lisa's heart slowed. She needed a drink, something with a real kick. Minutes ticked away. Lisa waited. Another vehicle rolled onto the turnout. This one a red full-size pickup.

Lisa could discern a man's features as the vehicle approached. She didn't wait. She slid back into her seat and closed the door. The truck, however, circled, stopping with the driver's side inches from Lisa.

"What's the trouble, pretty lady?" he said in a slow, smooth drawl.

"Damn thing stalled."

The driver, in his forties, with gray-flecked hair and bushy eyebrows, offered a smile that seemed innocent enough. His tobacco-stained teeth, however, made the smile unappealing.

But Lisa knew better than to trust a smile.

"You want me to have a look under the hood?"

Lisa hesitated. Zack said no exchanges between anyone.

"No. I've got a tow on the way."

"How 'bout a ride, pretty lady. I can take you anywhere you need to go."

The man's eyes drifted off Lisa to scan the road in both directions. When they returned to her, Lisa detected temptation's ugly head rearing to the surface in those eyes.

The truck engine stopped.

Lisa checked that she had locked her door.

"That's all right. I've already called my husband and gave him my location. He's on his way."

She held up her phone in witness to her statement.

The driver looked her over once more then restarted his truck and crept slowly away.

No other cars came down that stretch of road. If the killer had followed her, he surely had ample opportunity to observe her alone and vulnerable.

Lisa opened her door and leaned halfway out of her vehicle. Another twenty minutes passed. No other cars showed.

Then it hit her like a lightning flash. Her headlights had been on all this time.

She jumped into her seat, slapped the light switch to turn the lights off and turned the key.

"Come on," she pleaded as the engine at first clicked. The Saab then groaned like a dying elephant, cranked weakly twice and stopped.

"Fuck!" Lisa said. Now she really was stuck. She rested her head on the steering wheel.

"Real smart, Ace. Zack, you better get over here. I'm really stuck now." Her voice carried into the nearby pine trees.

In the darkness, the undergrowth came to life, but she had no idea exactly where the commotion emanated from. Her head went side to side searching for that familiar face.

Then Zack emerged from a thicket and pounded his way in the sand to the car. Relief flooded through Lisa. What a stupid plan, anyway. Lisa unlocked the passenger door, allowing Zack to slide into the seat beside her.

"I got a decent shot of the guy in the pickup. He looked too old to me. What do you think?"

"Definitely."

"Either the scumbag decided to abandon you—or he was too chickenshit to risk making an approach."

"I can't start the car," Lisa said.

"I know. You left the lights on too long. You should have turned them off after a few minutes."

"You see, Zack, you didn't tell me that. Besides, I didn't want to be standing alone in the dark."

"Leez, I stayed within fifteen feet of you in those bushes the whole time. He'd never have been able to even get close to you."

"So now what do we do?"

"It's all right. I'll pull my van up and give you a jump," Zack said.

But he made no move to exit the car.

Lisa glanced over her shoulder back at the road. No headlights shone nor were the sounds of any approaching cars apparent.

"Well?"

Zack took Lisa, covering her breast with his hand.

"Zack! What are you..."

His other hand knifed between her legs just above her knees before she could intercept it. He worked it up under her skirt.

"Zack?" Lisa said, with a frightened, incredulous look taking over her face.

"No Zack... don't do this."

But Zack said nothing as he forced himself onto her, pushing her down until her legs were doubled beneath the steering wheel.

"Oh God, no!"

Zack clinched his jaw while he probed deeper up Lisa's skirt until he forced his way into her apex.

"No, Zack, no please," she whimpered, unable to fight him off. His wet lips worked down her cheek onto her neck. His breathing came in gasps. He fumbled with his pants, attempting to thrust himself between her legs.

Blaring floodlights cut through the rear car window as two sedans careened around the bend and skidded to a stop a few car lengths from the Saab.

Zack pulled his face away from Lisa's, withdrew his hand from inside her panties and struggled to get his genitals back into his pants.

"Motherfucker!" he snarled.

He ripped open her blouse, exposing a miniature wire taped to the inside of her bra.

"You fucking bitch!"

Zack wanted desperately to slap Lisa—to shove his fist halfway down her throat. But he had been had. He bolted from the car, but got no further than three steps before lights and guns overwhelmed him.

"Freeze, asshole!" Bronc yelled, planting his feet and leveling his revolver to fire.

"Police!" Dakota yelled, lowering his Beretta over the roof of the car.

Krieger stopped mid-stride and clamped his hands together on the rear of his head. He had been through this before. He knew the routine.

"To your knees—right now!" Bronc yelled.

Zack complied.

A uniform approached from behind with revolver trained on the back of Zack's head.

"Interlock the fingers," the uniform ordered.

With Zack cuffed, the officer removed the .45 from Krieger's jacket pocket. Krieger said nothing, obeyed every command police made and never looked back into the Saab.

Lisa never moved inside the car. She couldn't comprehend what had just taken place. It all happened lightning fast, though that minute Zack spent clawing her stretched out for an eternity while she waited for police to arrive.

Dakota helped Lisa out of her car.

"You okay?"

Lisa nodded. She held her torn blouse closed while struggling to get her footing.

Her eyes met Zack's as he sat inside the police car. His were empty...no remorse...no guilt. What was his real intent? Could he be the Boulder Hill killer?

"Car won't start," Lisa said, falling into Dakota's arms and crying into his shoulder.

"It's all right, Lisa. It's all right. He's not going to hurt you."

"Bronc, get a tow for the vehicles. The van's got to be parked in the trees somewhere. Get a team to go through it thoroughly."

"I can ride in with the black and white. You can take Ms. Roberts home," Bronc offered.

Lisa's face had paled; she trembled.

Dakota moved Lisa to his vehicle, where they sat while Bronc settled into the black and white.

"How did you know?" she asked, watching the police car pull away with Zack in the back.

Dakota waited until the car disappeared from sight. The central dispatcher's broadcast request for a police tow to their location came over the radio. Those moments helped Lisa recover.

"Krieger had called himself in as too sick to work the night Angela Walker died. And he had access to the station, so it would be easy for him to leave notes for you without drawing attention to himself."

"You really think he's the Boulder Hill killer?"

"By any chance is your middle name Ellen?"

"Patricia. Why?"

"Nothing. Forget it."

"Could Zack be the killer?"

"For right now, he's our number one suspect."

Dakota wheeled the sedan around and spun the tires to get out of the gravel and back onto the road.

For Lisa, it was over and she was glad.

Instinct being the wise, persistent teacher that it was instructed Dakota to maintain his guard. When they arrived at Lisa's home, an upscale two thousand foot ranch house with a view of the desert, situated on the western edge of Corrales just off Loma Larga, Dakota first did a walk-around on the grounds. Lisa's house was the last structure on an unlit street and as such, left vast expanses of darkness on three sides. Places where eyes could watch unseen. Only after reconnoitering the area did Dakota wave Lisa out of the car and meet her at the steps.

She clutched a fistful of blouse as they walked up the flagstone stairs. Home was a truly warming sight for Lisa.

The tight material drew Dakota's eyes to her instead of the dark wall of green beyond her residence.

"You always leave lights on?" Dakota asked, noticing a light in the kitchen and another upstairs.

"Timers. Ever since the first letter. I put all the lights on timers. They go on and off all night long."

Dakota took her keys, opened the front door and while she waited, he swept the rooms with his Beretta in hand.

"This mean you're not sure Zack's the killer?"

"This means we don't take chances. I'll stay with you until backup detectives arrive to watch over you."

"God, I wish this would end."

A living room light popped on.

Lisa spun and grabbed for Dakota's arms. She moved into him until her body pressed against his. Panic drained from her face. She lifted her eyes to meet his. Her hand released her torn blouse to allow her breast to show.

Before he realized it, Lisa kissed his lips, slipping her hands around his shoulders. Her warmth encompassed him in a way he yearned for. When at last their lips parted, Lisa searched Dakota's eyes while the moment lingered. She wanted him to kiss her again, to validate what she had just done.

"Thank you for what you did," she whispered, pressing her breasts against him.

For a moment, Dakota did nothing. Her soft inviting flesh against his crept into his head. He wanted to wrap his arms around her and lose himself in her body. His own excitement pressed back against her.

When Dakota opened his mouth to speak, Lisa kissed him again, moving her hand down.

"Don't say anything," she whispered in a voice fraught with need. "I know how terribly difficult it must have been for you. I can make you feel better."

Dakota took her shoulders, easing her gently away. His eyes never went to her exposed breast. What she said was true. His needs were knotting up his mind. He wished, at that moment, that he could hold Grace one more time. But this was wrong. He couldn't do it. He couldn't betray...

Lisa couldn't avoid the anguish in his eyes; she realized how deeply she had just hurt him.

"I'm sorry," she cried.

She left him standing in the living room for the next fifteen minutes—the time it took for another car to arrive and assume responsibility for Lisa Roberts.

They said nothing to each other.

Dakota never looked back into the house on his departure.

Lisa never came to the window to see him drive away.

13

Chaos reigned at police headquarters. But the commotion had come from a most unlikely source. Mr. Von Johannson Strickwold, the keynote speaker at the fall convention for the Association of Professional Psychics held in Santa Fe, had urged his fellow practitioners to put their powers to use for good. As a result, a hundred psychics, clairvoyants and soothsayers made the drive down to Albuquerque and promptly presented themselves to the police in the most sincere hopes that one of them could be the one to break the Boulder Hill killer case.

The fact that police had Zack Krieger in custody and considered him their prime suspect was, at this point, not for public consumption. The task force meticulously picked apart Zack's life. The more information they uncovered to support a hypothesis that Zack could be the killer, the more credible a case they could assemble for the District Attorney. Zack, however, understood the gravity of the situation and held nothing back during questioning.

The onslaught of paranormal volunteers, all wishing to aid in the Boulder Hill investigation, greatly complicated matters for the task force. Detectives knew all along that the killer may try to inject himself into the investigation as a way of gaining information about what the police had on him. Therefore, it became feasible that if Zack Krieger proved innocent, the Boulder Hill killer could try passing himself off as one of these psychics. As a result, every so-called psychic entering the station had to be checked out thoroughly.

For the psychics, getting police to take them seriously became another matter altogether. Interviews began innocently enough, but later they unfolded into extremely well-disguised interrogations.

Within two hours, every detective and uniform available had been tied up with a psychic and the routine administration of police business had ground to a halt.

Upon his arrival, Dakota surveyed the mass of confusion, realized the true gravity of the situation, and, within minutes, concocted a solution. By noon, the headquarters had returned to the peace and routine of daily affairs and nary a soothsayer lingered in sight.

"Okay, how did you swing this?" Bronc asked, witnessing order come out of chaos in a matter of two hours.

Dakota's mischievous smile conveyed more than any words. He walked Bronc down the stairs into the police headquarters basement and ushered him into a large open waiting area where an odd assortment of men and women had gathered. Some were clad like gypsies; others in beards and overgrown hair resembled hermits who had descended out of the Sandia mountains. All professed to have some cosmic knowledge of the Boulder Hill killer. And all wanted to help police.

A woman rose from her chair to approach the men the moment they entered the room. Her wrinkled smile covered toothless gums.

"You don't understand. I can help you, but we must hurry. You're wasting valuable time."

"Ma'am, if you'll just be patient, we'll have some-one available to take your statement. For now, please just remain seated."

Bronc turned when the door to a lone office opened. Agent Rodman escorted a white-haired woman who resembled a witch out. She wore all black and her hair looked like spun silk the color of alabaster.

"But don't go there before Thursday. He'll show up at exactly six forty-seven in the evening. You'll know him by the snake tattoo on his right forearm.

"Thank you, ma'am, we'll be checking out your information."

Rodman glared across to Bronc, then shifted his eyes over to Dakota. Loathing poured out.

"You, you're next," Rodman growled, his face a lifeless slab of granite as he leveled a finger at a her-mit-like man sitting in the chair to the right of the door.

Dakota waited while the next in line rose and stepped into the office. Rodman refused to look back at Bronc or Dakota before closing the door.

"There is a God after all," Bronc said.

"Two problems, one solution. I think this should keep our Agent Rodman busy for a while."

"I'll say."

Dakota and Bronc climbed the stairs. Neither noticed Chesney Winterthorne rise from among the group to follow in their wake.

"Excuse me, Lieutenant," Chesney said, stopping at the door to Dakota's office after he and Bronc had entered.

"Psychics are being interviewed downstairs. Ask at the desk, someone will direct you."

"I know. I just came from there. I spoke with you a while back...maybe you don't remember."

Dakota suddenly remembered the strange look that Chesney's face wore when they shook hands at the end of his last visit.

"The red car guy..." he said.

Bronc looked quizzically at Dakota.

"If you'll just go back downstairs, someone will..." Bronc said.

"Wait," Dakota said, waving Chesney into the office.

"I've got to get back to Krieger," Bronc said, leaving Dakota with Chesney.

"The last time you were here, when you took my hand, what did you feel?"

"Why do you ask?"

"Just something in your face that..."

"I'm sorry. I'm usually better at hiding my reactions."

"Reactions?"

"My visions are spontaneous. They come like a flash in my head. They last only a second or two. I can usually maintain a poker face."

"What did you see when you shook my hand?"

"Sir, this is usually something I don't like to talk about. I rarely understand what I see. Sometimes I only create trouble by telling my visions."

Dakota motioned Chesney into a chair while he took his own behind the desk.

"I sensed death. A woman's death. I could feel your pain when I touched your hand."

"What kind of woman?"

Chesney hesitated. The sickness he felt whenever he had to confront one of his visions rose up into his throat.

"A woman with red hair, but not her own hair. A white woman, not Indian."

Dakota pushed back in his chair.

"Tell me again what you saw at the Walker apartment."

Chesney recounted detail for detail what he had told Dakota in his previous visit. This time, however, Dakota wiped away his skepticism.

"If I were to take you there, would you see the vision again?"

"I don't know. If I touch something belonging to the victim I might. But I can't be sure. I can't control these flashes inside my head."

For a brief moment, Dakota questioned whether he was losing control of the investigation. But he couldn't shake the feeling that persisted from their last visit. Chesney's eyes had conveyed something; something that inspired faith in what he had said.

"Leave me your number. Can you be available if I need you?"

Chesney shot out of his chair.

"Yes, sir. I can be here in an hour. I live in Santa Fe.

Dakota walked Chesney out, realizing that if the Krieger interrogation failed to produce results, he may very well have to bring in this Winterthorne kid.

Mary Borlin strummed her fingers on a stack of computer printouts while she waited for Dakota in his office. For a while, she thought her efforts would be wasted since she heard an arrest had been made and officers outside the task force speculated that the Boulder Hill killer had been taken down. Most were ready to celebrate. Mary convinced herself to wait for the official word and continue with her assignment until instructed otherwise.

Exhaustion aged her face ten years. Nor did it help that she had hastily pulled her hair back into a loose bun and had forgone the subtle touches of makeup she normally wore. But, by regulation, she wore a uniform crisp and neatly pressed despite the long, arduous hours.

"Sorry to keep you waiting, Mary. I'm sure by now you've heard about our Psychic Fair downstairs."

"Yes, sir. I understand, sir. I also heard about the arrest. Just figured I should give you the information anyway."

"What have you got?"

"I hope it's unnecessary. I hope the suspect in custody is the killer and this will all finally be over with."

"Me, too. But until we know for sure, we keep a full head of steam behind the investigation."

"Yes sir, that's why I extended my checks on the crime databases. California, Oregon and Washington came up empty.

"But..."

"I got a hit in Salt Lake City."

"What kind of hit?"

Mary frowned.

"It's a real long shot."

"Mary, we're living on long shots."

Mary shifted to the printouts on her lap and flipped through the pages until she reached the one she had marked.

"I mean, at least it's a place to start. Six years ago, an unknown assailant killed a young woman named Ellen Hellstrom in a rural area north of Salt Lake City."

"How old was she?"

"Twenty-four."

Dakota shifted forward in his chair. His eyes never left Mary's.

Self-consciously, Mary went back to her computer paper.

"When was she killed?"

"September the tenth. No wait. Police discovered the body September tenth. The database doesn't pin down the time she was killed."

Mary moved her stream of computer printouts from her lap to Dakota's desk. Then, to avoid having to read upside down, she came around the desk.

"Why couldn't we get this sooner?"

"Because it wasn't on NCIC. Utah just recently started a statewide program to input their violent crime data into VICAP. They must have been loading up the older files within the last two years. That's probably why our last search returned no record of any homicide victim named Ellie."

Mary caught a glimmer of excitement in Dakota's eyes. It made her feel as if all her effort had not gone to waste.

Find the first victim raced through Dakota's mind.

"You think you'll need this information?"

"As far as I'm concerned, until we get a confession or physical evidence linking the suspect to either murder scene, this is a wide open case."

"I've contacted Salt Lake City, but the crime occurred outside their jurisdiction, so we'd have to contact the Davis County Sheriff. They're actually the department that handled the investigation."

"Is the case still open?"

"Yes, sir. I know it's a long shot, but...well, it's the only shot I've found that might bear relevance to the note at the scene."

"Leave this with me. I'll assign a man to it."

Mary rose and began to leave.

"And Mary...thanks for this. I know your job isn't easy or exciting. Thanks for your hard work. Let's pray we won't need this information."

Bronc was still in the interrogation room with Zack Krieger and had been for the last three hours. Dakota decided to hold on to Mary's find until he got Bronc's update.

At present, all they could dangle over Zack Krieger's head was his documented history of violent behavior while in the Navy: two violent outbursts against superiors. That fit the profile of the killer.

And Zack's Naval Enlisted Code of 8404 meant he served as a corpsman, which gave him medical training. But Krieger had no criminal record in New Mexico. Not so much as a traffic ticket.

Before Dakota could turn his attention to the stack of reports cluttering his desk, Captain Washington entered his office and closed the door. He sat down across the desk with a grim, official face.

"What the hell kind of goofy crap went on last night?" Washington said, leaning forward to place his elbows on the desk the way he habitually did when angered.

"We were playing out a hunch," Dakota said, lifting his eyes from the paperwork. He picked out both grave concern and disappointment in Washington's eyes.

"A hunch? My understanding is Roberts almost got raped in the process."

"We had it under control. She wore a wire. We were hoping Krieger might say something. Obviously, we had to delay as long as we could."

"I understand the scumbag was packing."

"Yeah."

"How much danger was Roberts in?"

"We had it under control. Had we moved sooner, we would have came away empty."

"Blackwood, you don't have a goddamn thing. Krieger's lawyer is screaming entrapment. Says she stuck her hand between his legs. He just reacted to her advance."

"I don't give a shit about the attempted rape. I need to know if he's the Boulder Hill killer."

"I told you from the get-go that plan was too far-fetched to work. Fine, he could have been the one dropping off letters to Roberts at the station. But did you ever think him and Roberts concocted the letter scheme as a way of drawing attention to themselves for their own purposes?"

"I had the handwriting checked. Our guy believes the notes could have been written by the killer."

"Could have?"

Dakota shifted in his chair. He took warning from the way the words had come off Washington's tongue.

"And?"

"Bronc updated me thirty minutes ago. Krieger's got a whore to alibi him for the night of the Walker murder."

"Verifiable?"

"Solid as a fucking rock. She took him back to her sleazy apartment where the neighbor saw them and confirmed his alibi."

"What about the night Corinne Schultz was killed?"

"Bronc's got two men running down Krieger's story. But let's face it, Krieger isn't your man. No match either to the latents or the hair found at the Walker apartment.

"He gave samples?"

"Jumped over backwards to cooperate."

Washington left his chair and shifted his weight to the side credenza. He stared right into Dakota's eyes.

"That foolhardy stunt puts Roberts in a bad position."

"She going to press charges?" Dakota asked.

"What do you think? Without a way to stick the serial murders on him, he'll be out before day's end. All we've got is Roberts saying no and Krieger claiming she stroked him to tease him. It's not going to hold up in court."

While Dakota waited for Bronc to finish up the Krieger interrogation, he switched his mind back onto the Boulder Hill killer. With Krieger's alibi holding together for the night Angela Walker died, they'd have to abandon him as a suspect. At least for the present. Dakota decided to assign a man to keep tabs on Krieger's whereabouts for the next few days. He doubted Krieger would bother Lisa since two detectives still maintained surveillance on her around the clock.

After reviewing again every report accumulated for the Schultz homicide, Dakota called in the evidence technician who had worked the scene that night.

"What did we get back on prints?" Dakota asked, even before evidence technician, Clay Morgan, sat down in front of the desk. Morgan looked haggard and tired, but snapped to a straight-back position when Dakota spoke.

"Nothing. Place was clean. We picked up a few latents; they turned out to be the victim's."

"Is there anything we might have missed?"

"I don't believe so. I went over the bedroom and the bathroom without missing an inch," Morgan said with a defensive edge.

Now was not the time to protect fragile egos.

"What about the kitchen?"

"I dusted all surfaces...the refrigerator, the faucet, and everything on the counter tops. All clean. Our guy must be a cleaning freak."

Even before Morgan finished, Dakota began rubbing the side of his forehead with his index finger trying to force his brain to work harder. There had to be something they were missing. The killer had to have made a mistake. Nobody's perfect. Nobody. That's the basic axiom of all criminal investigation. That scumbag had to have made a mistake.

So, if nobody's perfect—the Boulder Hill killer slipped up in some way either at Angela Walker's or at Corinne Schultz's. From the signature, they knew the same killer murdered both women. So, if the killer slipped up...

"Sir..." Morgan said when Dakota seemed to be staring off.

"What about inside the kitchen cabinets?" Dakota asked.

"Inside the cabinets?"

"Yeah...what if..."

"There were a couple of glasses on the counter and a few utensils in the sink. I checked them, but I didn't go inside the cabinets."

"Go back to the Schultz scene today. Dust all the plates, glasses, bowls, and anything that might yield a print."

Morgan, smiling, jumped out of the chair and was on his way out the door.

"Report in by the end of the day. No matter which way it goes."

Alone once more, Dakota began to ruminate over the crime. The killer enters Corinne's home. Maybe they were friends. Maybe he picked her up in a lounge and they dated once or twice. He comes to her house. They sit in the living room and talk for a while. Corinne likes him...why? He's kind, gentle and soft-spoken. Mr. Wonderful. He treats her really special. He comes across so timid and shy that no woman would ever dream him capable of such violence.

They have something to drink. Maybe he even brings a bottle of wine that he takes with him when he leaves. Maybe Corinne had him get the glasses out of the cabinet. They spend time together; maybe he kisses her and tells her he's crazy about her.

Dakota placed his mental conjurings on hold when a uniform stuck her head into the office.

"Lieutenant, Bronc asked me to tell you he's finished with Krieger and he should be here in twenty."

Dakota nodded, returned to the scene playing inside his head.

Corinne and the killer have sex. Or do they? Again, no semen found at the scene either on or inside the body. That puzzles Dakota. Would Corinne have gone to bed with him if they were casual friends? But the autopsy indicates sexual activity. So, if they had sex, he doesn't achieve orgasm. Not unusual, since many serial killers are incapable of reaching a climax during the sex act. Their climax comes from the violence.

Then he bludgeons her with a heavy object. The weapon eventually leaves the scene with him. But maybe Corinne comes back around...to see the object strike her again.

She's unconscious on the bed, but not dead. Then the killer removes a knife and severs the carotid. But does he sexually molest her while she's unconscious? Before he kills her?

Afterward, the killer backtracks through the house, cleaning everything he's touched. The killing must have been silent. He's in no hurry...but why?

"How can he know no one has seen him enter?"

Dakota stopped; he was speaking aloud.

"Surprise!" he said to the room.

The killer appears at Corinne's door unexpectedly. It's very dark, so nobody notices him walking up to the door. He parked his car blocks away from the scene.

Dakota began meandering, getting lost in his own thoughts. Too many unknowns...too many variables to account for.

Bronc strolled in wearing a suit desperately in need of pressing. He scratched at his hair while he scanned for something to eat.

"Did I hear someone say dinner?" he said as he sat down before Dakota.

Dakota's eyes were hopeful.

"Krieger's going to walk," Bronc said.

"I heard. His alibi's holding up for the night of the Walker murder."

"Ain't that the shit. I figured we had the sonofabitch," Bronc commented.

"Well, don't let it get you down. We may have another break."

Bronc lurched forward in the chair.

"For real?"

"It's a long shot."

"Hundred to one?"

"More like five hundred thousand to one. Borlin turned up a victim named Ellen."

"Thank you, God," Bronc said with his eyes Heaven's way.

"I said it's a long shot. A six-year-old rural case outside Salt Lake City."

"You want me to go?"

"You up to it?"

"A clean suit, an hour with my wife, that's about all she can stand anyway, and I'll be on my way."

"There's a flight in the morning. Mary has the details. See her before you go."

"You going to tell Roberts?" Bronc said from the door.

"Yeah. The version I heard is the attempted rape isn't real solid right now."

"Worse. After ten minutes with his lawyer, the puke changed his story. Said he wasn't exactly accurate with what he said earlier."

"What's the lawyer's angle?"

"Now Krieger's claiming Lisa was jacking him off. All he did was submit."

Dakota bit down on the bile in his mouth. They were without physical evidence that would dispute Krieger's claim. The scum said nothing that could break his version of the incident.

"I'll report in as soon as I get a look at the case file in Salt Lake," Bronc said, then exited.

They exchanged a glimmer of hope. A gossamer hope with the tenacity to rise above the murk of their desperation. They had played out a thousand dead ends since the investigation started anew. They needed something to go right instead of wrong.

Dakota felt uneasy with the idea and now he wished he had talked himself out of making the telephone call in the first place. Had they become this desperate? he wondered, as he unlocked the door to Angela Walker's apartment.

Chesney Winterthorne hesitated before following Dakota inside. He sought a vision of Angela as he crossed the threshold, but his mind remained vacant.

"Do you have to touch anything?"

"Yes. It's how I get an image. You'll have to trust me," Chesney added.

Dakota worked his hands through his pocket for a pen while he waited. He wondered just how valuable such speculation could possibly be.

Chesney moved very slowly through the living room. He studied everything, yet shook his head to Dakota's hopeful inquiry.

"Anything?" Dakota asked, wanting to get this over with. He had already wasted half the day waiting for Chesney to show up. He would rather not waste the other half while the amazing Bongo fondled a dead woman's personal things.

But even Dakota's skepticism took a jolt when Chesney stopped at the door to the bedroom. He brushed the closed door lightly with his fingers.

"She died in there. It was dark...I mean night."

"Okay," Dakota said, being noncommittal. He opened the door with his gloved hand.

"You're sure you can't get those vibrations wearing gloves?"

"I'm sure."

Chesney stared into the bedroom for a long time.

"She never made a sound."

"What are you getting?"

"Just a feeling."

The manager of the Silver Springs Apartments had been after Dakota to release the crime scene so the apartment could be renovated and returned to a state of cash generation. Dakota reassured the owners that the moment they solved the case, he would release the apartment...but not until then.

"May I?" Chesney asked, as if he needed permission to enter.

"That's what we're here for."

Winterthorne went right to the bed and smoothed his hand over an area of the mattress free of blood.

"I'm not sensing anything on the bed itself."

"So?"

"So, I think she was already dead before the killer placed her on the bed."

"Look, Winterthorne, I didn't bring you here to play Sherlock Holmes. You said you got a vision of a car, remember?"

"You think I control this? You think I just say abracadabra and the vision appears?"

"Sorry," Dakota said.

Chesney next went to the closet, where he fingered the clothes on the rack. He stopped for a long time on a western blouse with rhinestone buttons. Then, shaking his head, he continued on until he reached the end of the rack. He withdrew from the closet only after he had touched every piece of clothing in attendance.

Dakota checked his watch. This was taking longer than he hoped. But he resolved that he would remain until Chesney had his shot.

Winterthorne crossed to the bureau and stared at the reflection of the bed over his shoulder. He felt some psychic energy there, but evidently not enough to generate an image. He then opened the center top drawer—Angela's lingerie drawer.

"Why did you select that one?" Dakota asked, when it became apparent that Chesney intentionally bypassed the drawer closest to his hand.

"I don't know. I just felt I should open this drawer."

Dakota held himself in check.

Chesney worked his hand through the lacy panties and bras, touching each garment in the drawer. Then he removed a pair of red, low-cut panties and put them up to his face.

"What are you doing?" Dakota snapped, grabbing Chesney's arm.

"Leave me alone," Chesney scowled back, for the first time unleashing anger.

"It's a green car. She's in the passenger seat. Someone is driving.

Dakota released Chesney's arm and stepped back.

"Give me a license number."

"I don't see it. The driver has dark hair."

Chesney suddenly dropped the panties from his face. His voice fell in dejection.

"It's a woman...driving. Sorry."

"Great. You see anything else?"

"No. A woman with short hair was driving. She was smiling. Sorry, I thought it might mean something."

24

Dakota arrived home later that evening with the girls. Stopping for ice cream after dinner had given him a chance to find out everything that happened at school that day. The answering machine blinked insistently at him. He considered letting it wait. It was late. Tomorrow would be a better time. Whatever it was could wait...or could it?

"Dakota, I think you need to get up here right away. We may have hit upon something," Bronc's recorded voice said, while trying to remain objective. Only the slightest hint of excitement slipped through. Bronc refrained from any inflection that might raise hopes until he was more certain of what they were dealing with.

Dakota dialed the number for the Salt Lake City motel. Their conversation was brief, but Bronc believed a potential connection existed between the victim in Utah and the cases they were working.

The news erased the fatigue Dakota had been feeling since dinner. Before, he wanted nothing more than to flop into bed and remove everything from his mind. Now he knew he'd never sleep. He had to know more about the Salt Lake City murder case.

Before retiring, Dakota called Laurianne, apologized, though it was unnecessary; then asked if she

could be there at five in the morning—Dakota had a
flight to catch.

Bronc picked Dakota up at the airport with a
smile as wide as a boy who had just been given an all-
day sucker. He confessed he'd slept only a few hours
the night before; having spent most of the night
going through the reports filed back in '91. They
drove directly to the Davis County Sheriff's office
located twenty miles outside the city to the northeast
of the great Salt Lake.

Davis County Sheriff, Jerome Kinsey, rose to
greet the two detectives as they entered his office. He
knew of the Boulder Hill killer in Albuquerque, but he
never dreamed Davis County might have anything
that could be even remotely connected to those cases.

Dakota detected a glint of surprise in Jerome's
eyes when he saw that Dakota was an Apache police
lieutenant.

In anticipation of Dakota's arrival, Kinsey had the
file for the Ellen Hellstrom investigation accessible
and spread before him on the desk. He had mulled
over the detective's reports in advance, since he had
no real recollection of the original investigation six
years ago.

But something else caught Dakota's attention the
moment he entered the room.

Kinsey withdrew a scribbled note encased in plastic that had been buried under a stack of moldering,
typed reports.

"Detective Broncowski said you'd be most interested in seeing this," Kinsey said, moving the note to
the top of the stack.

MERRY CHRISTMAS, ELLIE.

"Killer had it pinned to the woman's underpants when we found the body."

"Prints?"

"None."

Dakota fingered the note. He was here. This could have been the killer's first victim. This could be the place where they had the best chance of uncovering the killer's identity. The killer's original rage had been released upon this victim.

Dakota's heart quickened—he thought of Grace and the promise he had made her before she died. His eyes locked on the careful strokes of the writing; he analyzed every nuance of every angle that formed each letter. One hand had fashioned all the notes. One hand had written the note pinned to Sheila Davis' underpants two years ago, Angela Walker's panties three months ago and the lifeless corpse of Ellen Hellstrom. The Boulder Hill killer had left his first calling card on Ellen Hellstrom's body.

"What do you have on the killer?" Dakota asked, finally pulling his eyes from the writing and directing them to the sheriff.

"Not much I'm afraid. Detective Broncowski here says you've got five victims from the same killer."

"This makes six," Dakota said.

"Can we have complete access to all your homicide reports for the same year Ellen...Hellstrom died," Bronc asked.

"Sure. What are you looking for?"

"Two more victims."

The sheriff picked up the phone and issued orders.

"You realize what this means?" Bronc asked. He fingered his way through the yellowed reports to get at the victim's photographs.

"We've finally found the link. This had to be his first victim. This had to be where it all started. Now we've got to find out who wanted Ellen dead. Who did Ellen know that was capable of this gruesome act...and why?" Dakota pondered aloud, seeing the picture of Ellen Hellstrom for the first time.

The resemblance sent shivers through both Bronc and Dakota.

"When we find the why...we're going to nail that bastard once and for all."

"If we're on the right track, there's going to be two more victims linked back to this Hellstrom woman."

"How are you going to know?" the sheriff asked.

"We'll know," Dakota said, as his mind raced ahead, reassembling the pieces they had used to define the Boulder Hill killer's signature.

Dakota and Bronc sat with a uniform in a dust-laden file room searching through stacks of other moldering reports. Lives that, except for loved ones, had long been forgotten.

After hours of fruitless searching, they were still without a single case matching the second victim of the Boulder Hill killer in Albuquerque. Dakota believed the killer had killed two others along with Ellen Hellstrom. At this point, his hypothesis had yet to be substantiated. But neither he nor Bronc would give up hope.

That evening over dinner, Dakota and Bronc discussed strategy. They had let their initial excitement cloud their right brain processes, and they realized they were drifting. They needed direction. And that direction now was to investigate the original Ellen Hellstrom killing. Attack the obvious. Even without the other victims, their confidence swelled that they had found their link. Now, the best course was to backtrack into the case to see if they could get a line on the killer from the original investigators.

But six years is a long time. Clues vanish quickly over time. And witnesses may no longer be living.

After dinner, Dakota spent an hour on the telephone with Lauryn and Heather, assuring them he would be back in a matter of a few days. This was the first time he had to leave them totally in the care of Cole and Laurianne. Lauryn made it obvious in her voice that she was less than pleased with the situation.

Bronc spent an hour on the telephone also. But his calls were to Mary Borlin in Albuquerque. The Davis County Sheriff's office provided both password and authorization codes to run whatever data searches they felt appropriate. If crucial information were locked in their computers, Mary would dig it out.

In a short time, the Utah authorities realized Dakota's people were much better equipped to handle this investigation and the best thing for them to do was to just stay out of the way.

Sheriff Kinsey was more than willing to cooperate; especially if a six-year-old murder case could finally be solved. Though he had his doubts that Ellen Hellstrom had died at the hands of a serial killer.

For the first time since the discovery of Ellen Hellstrom's body, Sheriff Kinsey actually entertained thoughts that the case might be solved. Not one of his detectives could ever nail down a suspect at the time of the murder. The primary detective assigned to the Hellstrom case concluded the killer must have been a transient and long gone by the time they launched a full-scale investigation. And that would fit a wandering serial killer's random pattern. Now, from what Dakota had told him, there seemed a chance more than just that one case had a shot at getting resolved.

Dakota and Bronc were less than fully awake when they entered the squad room for the county sheriff's office. But their enthusiasm overshadowed the residual aftermath of near sleepless nights.

They returned to the Ellen Hellstrom case file and reread everything page-by-page. Six years had passed. The trail had grown glacial. Worse, the primary investigating detective had retired from the force and now resided somewhere in south Florida.

Sheriff Kinsey tried to fill in the blanks. And that responsibility had kept him awake much of the night rereading the official reports and the scores of notes taken during the lengthy investigation.

"Says here Ellen was home alone when the murder occurred," Dakota said.

"Yes. Mother worked nights at a truck stop on the interstate," Kinsey clarified.

"Any other family members living in the house at the time?"

"No. Father was long gone. Been gone seven or eight years. Younger sister was away at college."

"Was Ellen married at the time?"

"Divorced. She'd been married only a year when she filed for divorce. We cleared the ex. He was serving two years for possession with intent to distribute when the murder occurred."

"What drug?"

Kinsey flipped through a stack of pages.

"Cocaine."

"Any connection to the ex-husband through his drug involvement?"

"None my detectives could make."

"What about boyfriends?" Bronc asked.

"Turned out Ellen was a very sexually active woman. So was her mother, from what I understand. The only prudent one was the sister."

Questions and answers droned on and on. For all their back and forth, they were getting nowhere, so they decided to break for lunch. Afterward, Dakota asked to visit the crime scene. Neither Dakota nor Bronc held out any hope of gaining anything from a scene that old. But they had to leave no stone unturned in this investigation.

A gravel road led off County Road 71 and cut into a field of overgrown weeds for about a quarter mile before ending at the Hellstrom farmhouse. The road sloped downward for about an eighth of the way. The lower plane and overgrown weeds made the structure unobservable from the county road.

"Hellstrom sold the place two years after the murder. She died of alcoholism about four years after losing her daughter. Far as we know, the sister never returned after finishing college. A local attorney handled the sale. The new owners were informed of the house's history, but they didn't seem to mind when they took ownership," Kinsey recited, as if reading it verbatim from the case file.

Dakota walked slowly around the grounds, his eyes taking in the entire scene. In his mind, he tried to reconstruct how the murder might have occurred that night.

"What could he hope to find?" Kinsey asked Bronc, wiping away the sweat rolling down his neck. His eyes never left Dakota.

"He's not some Indian psychic, is he?"

Bronc refused to even acknowledge the sheriff's question.

"Can't see the farmhouse from the main road," Dakota commented as he watched for signs of traffic in the distance. "Can't know for sure if that's the way it was back then."

"Yeah, so?"

"So, the killer most likely didn't choose the house at random. Unless he came down the road, he wouldn't have known the farmhouse even existed."

"Preliminary investigation indicated the detectives thought the Hellstrom girl was just in the wrong place at the wrong time," Dakota said, his eyes still roving over the grounds.

"That's the way my men figured it."

"You don't see it that way?" Bronc asked, raising a brow.

"No reported signs of forced entry. The girl wasn't alone at the time—she was with her killer."

Dakota returned to the car and leaned against the door.

"If she were alone at...what time?" Dakota stumbled.

"Midnight," Bronc inserted.

"And someone came to the door, why would she let him in?"

Kinsey shrugged.

"What was the time of death?"

"Between ten and two—closer to midnight," Kinsey said, deriving his answer from an official coroner's report.

"This report states there were no usable prints, other than the family's, nor any other physical evidence at the scene."

"So, that meant the killer either wore gloves, touched nothing, or had to take the time to clean the place up before leaving."

"Maybe he wore gloves."

"But when would he have put them on? He wouldn't have worn them upon arrival. He'd have to have put them on afterward. Even after the brutal murder, the killer made certain there were no usable prints anywhere in the house."

Both Dakota and Bronc raised a brow.

"How did the killer know he would have sufficient time to clean the place up before leaving? Why was the body left at the scene? He had no view of the main road from the house. So, he wouldn't have seen approaching cars."

"You think maybe the killer knew the mother was a night waitress?"

"Most likely. When did her shift start?"

Kinsey went thumbing through the stack of reports he juggled in hand. He stopped at the mother's statement.

"Mother left for work around ten."

"How far is the truck stop from here?"

"About twelve miles...right off the interstate."

"So, let's say the mother left at ten."

"When was the body discovered?" Bronc asked.

Kinsey flipped back to the front of the stack.

"Four in the afternoon on Sunday."

"Where was the mother?"

"Ah...with a friend. Verified by detectives. She was boozing it up with a guy and they took a room."

"You think the killer knew enough about the family to know that Ellen was going to be home alone that night?" Bronc asked.

"Had to. He could have arrived shortly after the mother left for work. He knew he had all night... Mother at work, sister away at college."

"What if the killer had intended both the mother and the daughter to be victims, but the mother left before the killer went in?" Kinsey queried.

"Doesn't make sense. If the killer had approached the house before the mother left for work, he might have been spotted. Besides how did he get out here?"

"Our detective surmised that the killer parked a car off to the side of the county road and hiked through the field to get to the house."

"That then assumes he knew the house was here."

"What's your scenario, Dakota?" Bronc asked.

Dakota panned the stack of detectives' reports, looking for glue to hold his theory together.

"The killer knew Ellen Hellstrom personally. At least well enough that when he appeared at the door, Ellen let him in. And well enough that he was able to strangle her with the wire without her putting up a fight."

"He surprised her," Kinsey said.

"She never saw it coming," Bronc said.

"Therefore, she trusted him," Dakota said.

"Maybe an old boyfriend or maybe one of the mother's boyfriends. Did your men check to see if Ellen slept with any of the mother's boyfriends?"

"I'm not sure. I remember that every man on the list the mother gave us was cleared. Except for a few long-haul truckers."

A crackling police radio interrupted their conversation. The county dispatch passed on a message for Dakota to contact his office as soon as possible.

"You want me to patch you in?" Sheriff Kinsey asked, still holding the microphone in hand.

"No. Let's drive back in. I think we've gotten enough from here for now. What about you, Bronc? You think of anything we can get from here?"

Bronc shook his head, but at the same time, he wondered what, if anything, useful had been gained. So far, Dakota was fitting information concerning Ellen's death into the preformed mold of the Boulder Hill killer in Albuquerque. Just because something could be made to fit didn't make it true.

There was no real evidence to anything that Dakota had theorized. Still, the note and the strangulation using picture wire were consistent with the first victims of the Boulder Hill killer. Bronc agreed that if Ellen were the killer's first victim, then she had to have had some kind of relationship with the killer. That much became clear out of the case file. Bronc suspected the original detectives were merely going for the quick close by pointing a finger at a transient.

Now all they had to do was tie the relationship between Ellen Hellstrom and the killer together.

Back at the sheriff's office, Dakota called Albuquerque and put Clay Morgan on the phone's speaker to allow Bronc to be privy to the conversation.

"What did you find?"

"You were right, Lieutenant, I picked a partial print off a wine glass in the cabinet to the left of the sink."

Dakota felt a sudden rush of adrenaline in his veins.

"Tell me it's what I'm thinking," Dakota said, his fist clinched on the desk.

"Yes, sir, I had that print checked against the print we extracted from the Walker apartment."

Dakota and Bronc exchanged hopeful looks, listening to the crackle of the open telephone line.

"They're a ten-point match."

"Are you sure?"

"Yes, sir. The print extracted off the bureau in Angela Walker's apartment matches the print found on the wine glass in the Schultz home."

"You're sure? You couldn't have made a mistake."

"I'm sure. But I've also sent the print on to the state lab for independent confirmation."

"Bingo! We've just made the physical evidence that is going to put that scum away forever," Bronc said.

"Now all we do is find the hand that left those prints."

Dakota turned to Sheriff Kinsey, motioning with his hand toward the Hellstrom file.

"There were no prints recovered at the scene," Kinsey whispered.

"Sir," Morgan interrupted, pausing long enough for the silence to return, "we've checked the latents against every known person to have visited either of the women's residences. No matches."

"What about the maid service the Walker woman used?"

"We're still checking."

"Has the FBI had any luck yet in identifying the print?"

"No, sir. We're their top priority, but they still don't have a name to put to the prints. They said it could take months to go through every possibility."

"But, Clay, you're absolutely certain the prints are from the same person?"

"Yes, sir. Ten points says they're from the same finger."

"Great work! Stay on top of things until I get back."

Dakota switched the phone off.

Bronc left his chair. What was surging through his veins would never allow him to sit. He stood staring out the window for a long moment.

"How'd you know?" Bronc asked.

"Groping for straws. I'm guessing our killer is in each of the places long enough that he forgets something."

"That's the first good piece of news we've gotten since the killer started up again."

"So, all along he's been making fatal mistakes. It's just taken us a while to dig them up."

25

Dakota sat behind Sheriff Kinsey's desk staring at the reports and photographs of the Ellen Hellstrom case. They had come this far. Now, Dakota felt very close to the source.

He studied the array of photographs that detailed Ellen Hellstrom's murder. Slowly, he began to pick out elements of the killer's fantasy. Ellen had been strangled as she sat on a sofa. Her body was then moved to the floor, and later transferred to a bed. Why? The killer must have been fantasizing, and he was adjusting his victim to match his mental picture of the crime.

Little by little, Dakota began to absorb how the killer's fantasy had been refined over the years. There was clearly confusion in the Hellstrom murder. Much less confusion than in the Walker and Schultz murders. Hellstrom's body presentation was crude compared to the killer's later victims. Here, he was just learning how to deal with his psychosis. In Albuquerque, he had mastered it. Or had it mastered him?

That tenacious spirit voice inside Dakota's head told him the killer's identity was in Utah. He surrendered completely to that voice now. And Dakota clung to his theory. If he were right, then the next two victims must have been somehow linked to this first one.

"Sheriff, did your detectives check to see if the Hellstrom woman's murder fit into any pre-existing serial killer pattern at the time?"

"No. We only get a handful of homicides in this county. We never did go beyond the Salt Lake City area to determine if there were others."

"Where do we start, Bronc?" Dakota asked.

"If we assume the killer of Ellen Hellstrom and our victims is one and the same, and he is killing according to a definitive pattern, then there's another woman and a man murdered in this area around the same time. But maybe not in this county."

"Let's get Borlin into the Utah computers and let her dig around for all homicides or missing persons reports occurring within six months of the Hellstrom murder."

"That may not be a small list," the sheriff said, with a whistle.

"If we're right, our list will get short real fast, because our killer had to have a tie with both those victims. Or all three—if we can find them.

Cole and Laurianne had finally gotten the girls into bed and settled themselves in the den to watch television. The days seemed unending. Laurianne appeared exhausted. Cole wanted to watch the Leherer report while Laurianne wanted to switch to a Patrick Swayze movie on cable. Laurianne had been pensive since dinner, and now chose to sit across the sofa from Cole rather than under his arm.

"Look, if it's that important, I'll skip the Leherer report tonight. Just let me finish this segment on what's been happening on Capitol Hill. Those damn politicians can cut the rug right out from under the banks if they keep screwing with the foreign policy decisions.

"It's not that."

"What's the matter then?" he asked.

"Nothing..."

"C'mon. Nothing. You sure?"

"It's just Lauryn. She's withdrawing more and more. There's a lot of anger bottled up inside her right now. She snapped at me today for straightening up her room. She told me, and I quote, 'stay the hell out of my stuff. You don't belong in my things,' end quote."

Suddenly, Leherer didn't seem so important. Cole had no inkling how to handle something of this magnitude. Lauryn was succumbing to the rage that consumed her.

"She said that? She told you to stay the hell out of her things? She's just trying to adjust. Dakota really needs to be here with them. We can't take the place of her mother and father."

"I know...it's just I don't know what to say or how to act when she gets into her moods. I want to hug her, but she pushes me away. If I try to discipline her, I might end up doing more harm than good."

Laurianne began to feel her defense mechanism crumble.

"Who knows what's right under these circumstances. Just give her space. Let her know you're here for her. She knows you're only trying to help. She's angry at life. She's not angry at you."

"I can't any..." Laurianne had been as stoic as she could for as long as she could. She could hold up no more. She faltered and began to cry. First in whimpers then bursting until she wept out of control.

"It's all right. You're doing the best you can."

Cole was quick to take Laurianne into his arms, though he knew in his heart there was nothing he could say to ease he pain.

"Why did she have to die?" Laurianne forced out.

A ringing telephone stole Cole's attention. He stood for a moment torn between Laurianne's sobs and the telephone. It could be Dakota. He dashed to the phone just in time to beat the answering machine.

"Hello," he said.

"Lieutenant Blackwood?" a soft voice said.

"I'm sorry, he's not here. This is his brother."

Cole turned to angle the phone away from the sounds emanating from the den. He had to cover his ear to be able to hear.

"When will he be there? It's important I speak with him." The voice was urgent—more than urgent— it bordered on frantic.

Cole turned back to Laurianne on the sofa. He needed to get back to her.

"He's out of town right now. I don't know for sure when he'll be back."

"He asked me to call him at this number. It's vitally important. I must speak with him," the voice persisted.

"I'm sorry. But if this is police business, call the downtown headquarters," Cole said, growing irritated with the woman's tenacity.

"Where did he go? There must be a number where I can reach him...don't you understand it's urgent." The woman's voice spewed panic.

"He's in Salt Lake City. The police department will know how to get in touch with him. That's all I know. Who's calling, please?"

The woman's voice went silent. Then a dial tone. Laurianne lifted her head from her hands. Her eyes rained tears.

"Who was that?"

"I don't know. She insisted on speaking with Dakota. I told her to contact police headquarters if it was important. Then she hung up on me."

Dakota and Bronc spent the day at the headquarters for the Salt Lake City police homicide section. For hours, they sat with a computer operator who punched in command lines that searched the homicide database for murders occurring in 1991. Dakota was convinced that if he could duplicate the killer's pattern here in Utah, he could hone in on the killer's identity. The information they had intentionally withheld from the public was sufficient to reduce the chances of a copycat killer to nil. Only the Boulder Hill killer knew the note existed. They had never made it public in New Mexico. Now, the very same note turns up on a woman named Ellie in Utah, connected to a murder six years earlier.

"Sir, I've got one," the demure policewoman said, waiting for Dakota to return to the present.

Dakota stared at the computer screen, without comprehending the data placed in the green boxes sprinkled about the glass.

"A twenty-five-year-old male named Clete Randall was murdered three months following the date in question."

"Status?"

"Open...detectives never found the killer."

Dakota grabbed his pen and scribbled the case number displayed on the upper right corner of the screen.

"Where would I find his case file?"

"Central records storage downstairs. What would you like me to do, sir?"

"Continue searching the database. I'll need any unsolved homicide falling inside that window of time."

Dakota and Bronc waded through the overstuffed case file for one Clete Randall. Seemed there was no shortage of people who would have liked to see Clete dead. Not only was he a lousy gambler, who lost regularly, with a half dozen statements on file that indicated he owed significant sums of money, but he also made barroom brawling his Saturday night pastime. Clete, alone, had four arrests for battery in his last year of life. And though Clete had never been arrested for anything more serious than misdemeanors, he was suspected of being involved in a stolen-car ring.

Even given a list of a dozen potential suspects, the detectives investigating the homicide never made a case against any one of them. And after close examination, Dakota knew why. Marked similarities between Clete's murder and the male victim of the Boulder Hill killer two years ago buoyed to the surface. In both cases, there was post-mortem genital mutilation. Both died from multiple knife wounds to the chest. And as had become the trademark for the killer, Clete's carotid had been opened. He bled to death inside of minutes.

"Where's the connection?" Dakota asked, after he and Bronc had both thoroughly reviewed the file.

"Beats the hell out of me," Bronc said. "They lived seventy-three miles apart. He was killed on the other side of the city from where Ellen died."

With case file in hand, Dakota and Bronc returned to the county sheriff's office to place the two murders side by side. Sufficient physical evidence surfaced to suspect these two murders were the work of the Boulder Hill killer. Now they needed to understand why the killer had selected these two victims.

Hours passed without progress. Dakota grew blurry-eyed trying to read the reports for the third time.

"How old was the guy?" Sheriff Kinsey asked.

"Twenty-five," Bronc said.

"And how old was Ellen when she died?"

"Twenty-four," Dakota said.

"Maybe they were lovers at one time?"

Sheriff Kinsey was becoming an irritant.

"Not confirmable. Even if they were, we're unable to determine that."

"Okay...what if they went to college together?"

Dakota flipped through Randall's file. The kid worked in construction after high school. There was nothing to indicate he ever went on in school.

"Where's he from?" Bronc asked.

"Salt Lake City, I guess."

Dakota stopped and turned his interest to the Ellen Hellstrom case.

"Where did Ellen Hellstrom go to college?"

"UNM," Bronc offered.

Dakota swallowed hard. That put her back in New Mexico. Did she meet the killer while she was in college? Dakota had to shake off that eerie feeling and get back on track with this investigation in Utah.

"What about high school? Where did Hellstrom go?"

Kinsey leaned forward in his chair.

"Brighton, why?"

"Where did Randall go to high school?"

"I don't know..."

It took more than an hour for a sheriff's deputy to dig up the high school yearbooks for 1988 through 1992, the four years Ellen had attended Brighton High

School. It took another forty-five minutes for detectives to locate the picture of one acne-faced, scraggly-haired and rebellious-looking Clete Randall.

Clete's face wore arrogance like a badge of honor. He looked like the kind of kid who would never amount to much in life. A prison sentence waiting to be delivered. And from what they could gather from the murder file, Clete achieved nothing noteworthy before he died. If he had dreams, they died with him.

But most important of all, Clete Randall had attended Brighton High School for three years. There was no picture for him in what would have been his senior yearbook. However, he was in the same year as Ellen because he had repeated the tenth grade, and both Dakota and Bronc knew they had just turned over something of crucial importance. But they were still shaky as to what it meant.

"You thinking what I'm thinking?" Dakota asked.

"That one of these photographs is going to be victim number three?" Bronc said.

"Without a doubt. I also think one of these pictures is our killer," Dakota said. His mind was so numbed from all the intense effort that he could barely think straight.

"Let's get some dinner," he said, rubbing the strain out of his reddened eyes. He wanted to allow the latest discovery to breathe exhilaration into his soul. He knew, though, it was still too soon.

"Gentlemen, dinner is on me," Sheriff Kinsey said.

After a dinner that consumed more speculation than food, Dakota spent two hours on the telephone back in his room before retiring. He split his time equally between Lauryn and Heather.

In the next room over, Bronc spent two hours on the telephone with various detectives on the Boulder Hill Task Force. A half-dozen more leads had fizzled, and with both Dakota and Bronc absent, the task force was starting to flounder. The good news was that no new victims had been discovered. So for now, Bronc felt they still had a shot at the killer.

But how much time was left? Would the killer disappear again after his third victim?

In a quiet lounge downstairs in the motel, Bronc briefed Dakota on the progress in Albuquerque while they had a drink. Both men returned to their rooms hoping tomorrow's efforts would bring them one step closer to the killer.

A bright-eyed Sheriff Kinsey met the detectives for breakfast and probed their brains while they ate. Dakota had already picked out so much from the reports that until now, had gone unnoticed. The detectives investigating the Ellen Hellstrom murder never determined how the killer got into the house or how he left the house that night. There were no tire tracks nor footprints. Tires always left tracks on dirt roads; yet there were none.

Dakota was right in the middle of a mouthful of watery eggs when his mind began to clank and click. More of those elusive pieces were falling into place.

"Was there evidence to indicate Ellen was raped?"

"No," Bronc said, trying to unearth the meaning of the question.

Kinsey stopped a forkful of biscuits and gravy inches from his mouth.

"Is that important to your cases?" the sheriff asked.

"Why was there no sign of rape?"

Bronc and Kinsey exchanged looks. What was Dakota trying to say?

"In all subsequent victims, there are signs of sexual assault and rape. Yet, his first victim he doesn't rape. Why?"

A pause endured.

"Because he had no intent on raping her. He wanted to kill her. But he had no desire to rape her. His fantasy originally must have been all jumbled at that time. It was after Ellen Hellstrom that he somehow got hung up on the sexual perversion."

An elderly couple sitting in the booth across from the three looked over, then hurriedly collected up their plates and moved away.

"So what does that mean?" Bronc asked.

"I don't know...yet."

Dakota and Bronc plowed into the stacks of homicide records piled on a long table in one corner of the records room. The overhead light was barely adequate.

Kinsey offered uniforms to assist them, but Dakota knew only they could pick out the subtle details that would give them the information they needed.

They lunched on deli sandwiches at the table where they worked, and abstained from getting up except for necessary trips to the coffee machine or lavatory.

The answers to Dakota's questions had to be here. He had to be on the right track—he no longer had time for wild goose chases. Death comes in threes. And he was one victim away from the killer slipping beneath the surface of normal life again. He had to find the answers here. He had a promise to keep.

A uniform delivered a large sealed manila envelope while Bronc sat alone, comparing two reports laid side by side. Dakota had left minutes earlier to see if sunlight really existed.

"What's this?"

"They told me to deliver it to you. It originated out of St. George, Utah, on special request from a Mary Borlin of your department. You know her?"

Bronc's eyes widened. He slit the seal and withdrew a brown case file filled with photographs and reports. A second later, he flew out of his chair clutching the brown file folder with a dozen facsimiles stapled to it.

Dakota was deep in thought as he walked down the aisle to return to the table. The fresh air and sunlight did lift his spirit, albeit only slightly, and only for a short time.

In the file Bronc spread out on the table, a photograph portrayed a young woman bludgeoned to death. Her neck had been sliced open and her body lay grotesquely contorted in death. The dead woman's hands were positioned unnaturally with the palms up.

"Colleen O'Connor," Bronc said, slightly above a whisper.

Dakota pushed files away on the table, making more room for Bronc's discovery.

"Murdered in St. George, Utah, less than three months after the death of Ellen Hellstrom."

O'Connor's hair color matched those of both second victims of the Boulder Hill killer in New Mexico. And this victim was killed with a more recognizable signature, a signature Dakota and Bronc knew so well.

"Where'd you get this?"

"Borlin had it shipped in," Bronc said.

"Mary, you are wonderful," Dakota said to himself, just before stopping a passing clerk. "How far is St. George from here?"

"About three hundred miles dead south."

Dakota grabbed the old high school yearbook containing Ellen Hellstrom. Colleen O'Connor was in the same year as Ellen.

"They were both in Spanish club," Bronc said, staring over Dakota's shoulder at the picture of the two girls smiling.

Dakota set the book on the table and pushed his chair back.

"We got him," Bronc whispered.

"We damn well got him," Dakota said, as if a great load had come off his shoulders.

After a quick high five in celebration, the elation deflated.

"We just have to figure out who," Dakota said, returning to the faded black and white pictures of six years ago.

"Look at this," Dakota started, with the excitement of a kid, "Ellen Hellstrom was the first. Colleen O'Connor was the second and Clete Randall was the third. All three attended Brighton High School at the same time. They were possibly even friends."

"But it doesn't make sense," Bronc said, rubbing at his neck and scratching the hair hanging over his ears.

"Look at the dates...the killer murders Ellen Hellstrom first. Then he travels three hundred miles to kill Colleen O'Connor. Afterward, he returns to kill Clete Randall. All within four months of each other."

Dakota left his chair to exercise his legs and his brain.

"That does make sense. All three were murdered far enough apart geographically to reduce the likelihood of linking the murders together. All three remain unsolved to this day," Dakota said.

"So, these three all had something in common with their killer."

"That's where we now branch off into a different direction. All three of these people must have been involved with the killer. These were not random selections. These three people were the reason the serial killer started killing."

Dakota stopped. Saying the words further unraveled the mystery lurking in the darkened corners of his mind. You can think about some things all you want, and never get them straight until you hear the words out loud. Then everything falls into place.

"These are the three people the Boulder Hill killer destroys over and over every time he goes on his rampage."

Dakota suppressed a schoolboy's excitement inside as he collected up the three files for the cases he now knew for certain were his link to the Boulder Hill killer in Albuquerque. Now to nail down the link, he had to study the three people before him.

Dakota left behind two stacks of records on the table; he had more than he could handle at the moment. There could be more killings in those stacks that might be linked to the serial killer. But he had no time to spend with them. He had to take what he had and squeeze every drop of information out of those three files. Somewhere in all those reports and pictures existed the clues vital to identifying the killer.

Now, Dakota relished the assistance of two detectives from the county sheriff's office. Together, they were going to analyze every piece of the three murder cases until they uncovered what the killer was desperately trying to conceal.

There was no longer any doubt that the killer had set out in 1991 to kill only these three people. And he had a reason for selecting them. In one or more of those reports, there had to be information that would put them on the trail of the killer.

Dakota assessed his findings.

For some time in the early nineties, the killer lived in Utah, at least long enough to have acquired his hatred for the three people whose files Dakota held in his hand. Afterward, the killer left Utah and migrated to New Mexico.

Dakota was sure the answer lay somewhere in that old high school yearbook. But for now, he had no place with which to start probing.

"Where do we go from here?" Bronc asked.

"We go after every long shot."

Dakota and Bronc returned to the policewoman sitting at the computer terminal.

"Can you do an arson search for me?"

"Arson? Sure..."

"Search all records for any cases of suspected arson occurring prior to 1991."

"1991? How far prior?"

"Start at ten years. Look between 1981 and 1991."

Bronc stared, with a puzzled look on his face.

"It's a long shot, but more than half the serial killers cut their teeth in arson. Let's hope."

Dakota returned his attention to the files for the three victims.

"Right now, we have to believe the killer had something in common with the three in this yearbook. Let's have every name in this book run through New Mexico vehicle registration. We'll see how many names out of here are now living as New Mexico residents."

"That's going to take some time," Bronc said.

"I know. And it's possibly time we don't even have."

26

After two days of interviews with detectives who had worked each of the murder cases in question in 1991, Dakota wanted to go home. The vast myriad of information quickly led nowhere. The cases each had their share of potential suspects, and the detectives each had their own theories about the murders, but none of the theories had resulted in an arrest. And because no one before had tried to link the murders together, no investigation into a serial killer was ever even remotely suspected.

Anger swelled inside Dakota. He had been away from the girls too long. They needed him and he needed a break from the case. He needed time to be away from the killing and the death. Grace haunted his dreams by night and whispered encouragement in his ear by day. He felt her watching over his shoulder, hearing everything he heard and seeing everything he saw. Then, as he slept, she would come to him. But her words made no sense. She said something like she's the one, which Dakota could only interpret to mean that Ellen Hellstrom was the key to the Boulder Hill killer.

Just give up, he heard his inner voice repeat again and again each time he came up empty. Her voice inside him, however, urged him to stay. The answers he sought were here. The identity of the killer was in this state, not in New Mexico. In these murder files he would find the answers; not in the ones in New Mexico. Stay! his spirit commanded in his native Apache tongue.

Weary and drained, Dakota and Bronc sat across from a gray-haired detective who claimed to be familiar with the Hellstrom case. Dakota asked the questions, while Bronc thumbed the yearbook almost absentmindedly, looking for anything that might bring a sense of order to their investigation.

"Tell me about the sister," Dakota asked, his voice empty of spirit and drive.

"Not much to tell. She was away at college when Ellen was killed. She came home when she learned of the death. She was nineteen at the time."

"How long did she stay?"

"I don't know. A week, I guess."

"Did she take it hard?"

"Difficult to say. Frances was a strange girl. Didn't like people much. Shy and introverted. You'd have to pry things out of her to get her to talk."

"She didn't stay with the mother?"

"I don't believe she did. If I remember right, she returned to school not long after the funeral."

"Didn't that seem strange to you?"

"Well, yeah...I guess."

"Did Frances ever pressure police to find the girl's killer?"

"No. As a matter of fact, I don't think Frances ever contacted the police department again. Even the mother faded away. But it was the booze that took her out of the picture."

Bronc suddenly sat forward in his seat. He no longer listened to the detective; instead he stared intently at a picture in the yearbook.

"Damn!"

Dakota looked over, needing to see what had snared Bronc.

"Look at this."

Bronc slid the open yearbook in front of Dakota.

Dakota stared at a snapshot. In the foreground, a group of students clowned around on the grass. But it was the background that had snared Bronc. Ellen Hellstrom and Clete Randall were sitting on a picnic table holding hands. The school building served as a backdrop. But even more significantly, half of Colleen O'Connor's face appeared in the picture on the right side.

"See what they're doing?"

Dakota looked up at Bronc.

"Holding hands..."

"They were more than just classmates. Ellen and Clete were, at the least, involved."

"Did you have anything more to ask?" the detective asked, feeling forgotten.

"Not for right now..." Dakota said, his voice trailing off.

As the detective left the room, the policewoman who had been working the computer terminal for Dakota stood in the doorway.

"You were right, sir," she said, venturing in with a computer printout in hand.

"About what?"

"I've got a suspected arson report dated April 24, 1991."

Dakota glanced at Bronc. He reached for the report, but failed to make sense out of it even after staring at it for a few seconds.

"Sir, that's the Hellstrom address. The fire took place on the rear porch."

Dakota's eyes left the printout.

"No parent home at the time. Arson investigator believed it could have been a juvenile, though he had no hard evidence."

Like a safecracker listening through a stethoscope, Dakota heard another tumbler in the case fall into place.

"Thanks," Dakota said.

"Will there be anything else, sir?"

Dakota assigned a uniform to get all the information he could on the sister—one Frances Hellstrom, now age twenty-five.

"What do you make of it?" Bronc asked when Dakota returned to the table.

"We've got three close friends in high school. From this, we can assume Ellen and Clete were dating. Someone singled those three out and systematically executed them."

"So, we could be looking at a revenge motive," Bronc said aloud, without giving the words any direction.

"Or hatred, plain and simple. Since each went in a different direction after high school, the act that sparked the killer's desire had to have taken place while the three were together in school."

"But why five years later?"

Dakota shook his head unconsciously.

"Incubation. The hatred or anger grew over a period of dormancy until it took over the individual."

It was Bronc's turn to shake his head.

"More importantly, the killer had to have kept track of his prey; waiting for the time he would get even or get close enough to one of the three to know what had become of the other two."

A clerk in a county uniform rapped on the door and waited until Dakota motioned her in.

"Lieutenant, your office line seven. They said it's urgent."

Dakota's heart sank. Had they been too late? Did the task force just turn up another victim in Albuquerque? He put the receiver to his ear and listened. He said nothing. Within a minute, Dakota hung up and started shoveling files and papers into his case.

"Time to go. The computer just spit out a name. You get us on the next plane out. I have one more stop to make before we can leave here."

27

Dakota's first stop upon returning to Albuquerque: home. Lauryn and Heather ran into his arms and hugged him so tightly they almost knocked him out of his squatting position.

"You should have let us know you were on your way back," Laurianne said, when the girls at last released their father.

"We were rushed. There was no time to call."

"Are you going to be here for dinner?"

"I'll try. There's been a big break in the case. I need to get downtown right now. But I just had to come home to get a hug from the girls."

Both girls groaned at the news of Dakota's imminent departure.

"You're leaving again?" Lauryn moaned.

"I just need to go to the office, princess. I'll be back in a few hours. I promise."

There was more than just disappointment on Lauryn's face; rejection poured out of her eyes while tears gathered in Heather's.

"I'm sorry. But it's very important. We'll all go out when I finish."

That announcement lessened the girls' frustration, but only slightly.

Laurianne saw an excitement in Dakota's eyes—something that had died along with Grace. Now it had returned. She knew immediately what it meant, so she coaxed Lauryn and Heather back into the living room and walked with Dakota to the stairs.

"Your shirts are clean and in your closet. I'll take care of your suitcase after I get the girls distracted with something."

"Thanks, Laurianne, I'll try to get back as soon as I can."

"Dakota, you do what you have to do."

With that, Dakota went to the bedroom, where he talked to the girls through the door while he changed. He apologized four times, but that still failed to remove the pang in his chest.

Lauryn had so much to say; she barely stopped long enough for Heather to squeeze in a few words. Dakota listened, smiled every time he looked at them, and fumbled with his shoes while sitting on the edge of the bed.

Before he could return to his feet, Lauryn and Heather were hugging him again. But neither urged him to stay. They understood he had to go. They understood that his job was important to other people. Finally, as he prepared to leave, Lauryn took Heather's hand and moved out of the way.

"Promise you'll be home for dinner, Lieutenant," Lauryn demanded with a maternal ring that she had acquired more and more since Grace's death.

"I promise. And you two decide where you want to go."

"Any place we want?"

"Any place you want."

The Boulder Hill Task Force shifted their nerve center into Dakota's office. Four men had been dispatched to watch over one Paul Allen Copley. He graduated Brighton High School the same year as Ellen Hellstrom, attended the University of New Mexico, then settled in Albuquerque where he made his living as an actuary for a prominent insurance firm.

Bronc headed up the surveillance and reported that since their arrival, there had been no movement from the home where Paul Copley lived with his wife and three young children. He also reported that a red Toyota Camry sat in the driveway. But otherwise, there had been no signs of life inside.

Dakota looked up from his desk when the radio crackled.

"We've just snapped a dozen of Copley taking out the trash. He hasn't changed much from his high school picture," Bronc reported.

Washington entered the control room with Cal Sturges excitedly in tow. Sturges's cold look penetrated Dakota.

"I don't understand why we're waiting if you're so confident this guy is the killer?" Sturges said, in a voice capable of grating nerves.

"We're hoping he might somehow slip. As long as he doesn't know we're watching him, there's a chance he'll do something that will help the DA later. We have no physical evidence right now on this guy. If we pull him in and he clams up, we're going to blow it."

"Haven't your men turned up anything that links Copley directly to either of the victims?"

"Not yet. We're going to need at least forty-eight hours before we can know if we're on the right track."

"I wish the hell you'd get on the right track. The press is tearing us apart," Sturges said.

"What about the FBI?" Washington asked.

"They're pulling everything they can on this guy. But Rodman's convinced Copley doesn't match the profile. Says we're wasting our time again."

"Yeah, but don't you have someone who saw a red vehicle in the second victim's driveway?"

"I hardly think an eighty-year-old woman's reliable," Dakota said.

"I don't give a rat's ass if you think she's reliable," Sturges put in.

"We're not going to jump because Copley owns a red Toyota."

"I think you have to. And I think you can't wait until another body turns up."

"Handle it by the book," Washington interjected, his words meant to quiet Sturges.

"What are you going to do?" Washington asked, after his comment sent Sturges storming from the control room.

"Watch him for a while. Then pull him in for questioning. There's a chance if he's the killer, and if we sweat him, he just might confess. Otherwise, we'll just have to watch him and see if that, in itself, doesn't stop the killing."

Dakota turned complete control of the surveillance over to Bronc before leaving the office to have dinner with his daughters. Everything appeared quiet for the moment. The suspect was sitting in his living room watching television.

Dakota still had one more card to play. Only time would tell. Time he wished he had. He trusted that Bronc and the other detectives would do their jobs, and they'd know soon enough if Copley made any suspicious moves.

Dakota was glad to be home, and glad to have the time with his daughters, but the emptiness of his bed that night brought back the pain he had been trying so desperately to purge from his mind.

Having to sleep in the den while Cole and Laurianne stayed to care for the girls had been therapeutic. Alone on that lumpy cot gave him a sense of being out of place. Being away from that part of his life.

Now he was sleeping, or rather lying awake and staring at the ceiling in the bed he had shared with Grace for fifteen years. She was beside him there beneath the blanket; her head on his shoulder like she had done for so many years.

He had left no words unsaid between them. He never once gave her reason to doubt his love. They knew only happiness together. Now the time for tears had passed. She would dwell in his mind and his heart, and he would see her beauty every day in the faces of Lauryn and Heather.

Where she was now, there was no pain. Her spirit, now free of the body, could explore and experience all the vast reaches of the universe.

Dakota closed his eyes, telling himself they would find each other again...someday.

A persistently ringing telephone pulled a lethargic Dakota out of his shallow sleep. Even before reaching the receiver on the table beside his bed, he noticed that it was four-thirty. No light filtered in through the windows.

"Dakota," he said, keeping his eyes closed. It seemed like he had just fallen asleep ten minutes earlier.

"Sir," a soft, feminine voice said.

"Yes?"

"It's Borlin, sir, I think you should come down here right away."

Dakota opened his mouth to speak, but her words cut him off.

"We've got the match you've been looking for."

Dakota became immediately alert.

"Stay right there. I'll be downtown in twenty...no make that thirty minutes."

Dakota dressed in a flurry, wrapped the girls in blankets and carried them out to the car. Fifteen minutes later he jostled a less-than-excited Cole out of a deep, restful sleep. But Cole understood.

By five twenty, Dakota stood beside a blurry-eyed Mary Borlin as she typed away at a computer terminal.

"How long have you been here?" Dakota asked.

"Nineteen hours," Mary responded, never looking up.

As the screen filled with data, Dakota sucked in a deep breath.

"Jesus..." he murmured.

"It's all here, sir. Frances Hellstrom registered a vehicle for the first time in New Mexico three years ago. A green Taurus. I went poking around the state licensing computer and it spit this out."

Mary tapped in a string of characters and rubbed her eyes while the computer flashed a message along the bottom of the screen.

"She's a registered nurse. Works at the same hospital your wife..."

"Did you get the print card?"

"Sir?"

"The fingerprint card I brought back from Salt Lake City."

"Oh yes, sir. I turned it over to Morgan just as you instructed."

"And?"

"That's what I meant by the match, sir. The prints on the card you gave me match the latents taken from the Walker crime scene."

"You're sure?"

"Ten-point match. The Hellstrom woman's prints match the latents taken from the crime scenes."

"Don't you ever sleep, Borlin?"

"Not tonight, sir."

Bronc strode into the room stirring a cup of vending machine coffee.

"This stuff tastes like mud. We must all be crazy around here," he moaned.

"You get any sleep?" Dakota asked.

"Two hours. Borlin called me before calling you."

"I didn't know if I should disturb you."

"Mary, can you print out everything you have on the Hellstrom woman?"

"In process, sir."

Bronc pulled Dakota from the computer terminal.

"You think?" Bronc asked.

"We don't have to think. The Davis County Sheriff's office fingerprinted Frances when her sister was killed. They wanted to eliminate her fingerprints from the crime scene. In doing so, they failed to realize that they eliminated her as a suspect."

Bronc looked incredulously at Dakota.

"She registered a green Taurus in New Mexico with a local address. I brought the fingerprint card back with us and had them check her prints against the latents found at the two crime scenes."

"Jesus...a woman?"

"It all fits. She would have known the three victims in Utah."

"But you're saying she killed her own sister..."

"She killed her own sister first. There was a reason for that and we're about to find that out."

"Ellen Hellstrom died on a Saturday night," Bronc said.

"Yeah. That gave Frances sufficient time to leave school and come home for the weekend. Except no one knew she was going home. My guess is she stayed out of sight of her mother and sister. And she would have known when her mother was leaving for work that Saturday night."

"And Ellen would have let her in. Little sister just popped in for a quick visit home."

"Frances knew her mother would be working all night, so she was in no hurry to..." Dakota felt the final pieces falling into place.

"What about the car? Hellstrom owns a green car," Bronc said.

"Green..."

"The old woman's color blind," they both said in unison.

"But what about the indisputable signs of sexual molestation on the Hellstrom girl's body," Bronc said, puzzled.

"That's the key," Dakota said. Already his mind was turning that final piece of the puzzle so it would fit in with the rest.

"If Frances killed her sister, she had to have a motive. Something happened between them; something violent enough to cause Frances to go off into a black world of psychotic behavior."

Bronc shook his head.

"What's the update on Copley?"

"Sound asleep. I checked with the night shift watching him. He went to bed at eleven and there's been no movement since. What do we do now?"

"Assemble the task force, but leave some men on Copley."

Their wait lasted less than four hours. By nine A.M. the state evidence lab called. Dakota put the call on the speaker. Bronc and Washington were sitting with him in the command center...waiting.

"Right on the head, Lieutenant," the voice said calmly, as if the words meant nothing to anyone.

"I also get a ten-point match between the latents at the two murder scenes and the print for one Frances Hellstrom."

Dakota had had to endure the hours of waiting for official corroboration. Nothing was official until the state crime lab confirmed it. He needed more than just one opinion to justify his actions. The lab's corroboration of the fingerprint identification put Frances Hellstrom at each of the scenes.

The roar from the room shook the glass panes in the neighboring offices. Everyone—every person on the third floor of the headquarters building stopped what they were doing and gazed in the direction of Blackwood's office.

"We can, without any doubt, place the Hellstrom woman in both residences," the voice finally got in after the noise settled.

Dakota struggled to find words. No one knew but him what this meant. His thoughts turned briefly to Grace and the promise he had made. He would stop another innocent person from dying. He couldn't save Grace, but he could save someone else. Who it was didn't matter now. All that mattered was they had the identity of the Boulder Hill killer. She was out there right now...

Twelve men crowded into the third floor interrogation room. The same room where photographs of five victims over the last two years were tacked to a cork board. But now, a new row had been added above the others. The first photograph in that new row was Ellen Hellstrom—young, attractive, with the hope of a future in her green eyes. Beside her Colleen O'Connor, and then Clete Randall. They were Frances' first victims. They, for whatever reason, had been the focal point of rage that had sent Frances over the edge.

The full briefing complete, Bronc divided the task force into five teams. He dispatched one to the Hellstrom house on the east side of Albuquerque. Two teams were being positioned as back up—to be ready to help out in either location. And two teams were preparing to go to St. Joseph's hospital, where Frances Hellstrom worked.

Secrecy became paramount now. Frances Hellstrom had to be taken down fast and hard before she could learn that the police knew the identity of the Boulder Hill killer. They had to prevent her flight, not allow her to be free for one more day.

Dakota, Bronc and another pair of detectives left the interrogation room for the hospital. The computer showed Frances Hellstrom had transferred to St. Joseph's hospital from Lovelace seven months ago. They concluded she would most likely be either at home or at work.

Both Dakota and Washington felt in control now. For the first time in two years, they actually had control over the Boulder Hill killer case. They were standing on the doorstep of ending the killing.

That was until Dakota and Bronc exited the headquarters building.

Lisa Roberts stopped them dead in their tracks. She had the most uncanny sense of timing and persistence.

"Looks like some excitement this morning," Lisa said, fishing for an exclusive.

"Just routine. Nothing to report on the investigation," Dakota snapped back, sidestepping her to get moving again.

"Sure, Blackwood, a dozen detectives come flying out the doors, all of whom make up the Boulder Hill Killer Task Force, and it's strictly routine. Come on, you guys," Lisa pleaded as she matched Dakota stride for stride.

"Our investigation is continuing. We're following up on every lead," Dakota delivered mechanically.

Bronc stopped, grabbed Lisa's arm, and held her back while Dakota continued to the car.

"Listen, why don't you take some time off. Okay? We'll have a statement to make later in the day. For right now, you need to be someplace else. You understand?"

"Then you let me break the story, Bronc. You owe me big time."

"We'll make sure you get all the details."

Bronc winked, then left Lisa standing on the sidewalk.

"I want an exclusive. You owe me that," she called.

Whatever they had was big. Big enough that it took twelve detectives to handle it.

Lisa watched as a pair of black sedans turned north, while Dakota's car and another white sedan turned south.

She had a fifty-fifty chance of guessing right.

Dakota focused all his mental energy on one thought: get Frances Elaine Hellstrom in cuffs and in a cell downtown. Nothing else mattered. They had the evidence they needed. She was the Boulder Hill killer. It no longer mattered how Frances came to befriend the women and men she murdered. Nor did it matter at that moment why she killed. Taking her down was all that mattered.

If luck were with them, Frances Hellstrom would be at home in her bed or just stepping out of the shower to ready herself for work. In minutes, it would all be over. If luck went against them, Frances Hellstrom would be at her job at the hospital and somehow sense the approaching task force detectives.

The situation was more delicate than butterfly wings.

Dakota held no doubts that if Hellstrom suspected the police were closing in on her arrest, she would fly.

Whatever it was, Frances had motive back in 1991; a motive that sent her over the edge. Dakota suspected that once Frances was in custody, she would spill her guts all over the interrogation room. As intelligent as she is, she would not be able to resist talking about her crimes. It would take Dakota and Bronc little time to uncover her motive. Dakota also knew that motive would be intimately linked to Ellen Hellstrom.

Two sedans rolled into the hospital parking lot, coming to rest at the outer fringes. The detectives, however, made no move to exit their vehicles. They observed nurses and doctors clad in characteristic hospital garb enter the building through the main revolving doors. One of them could be Hellstrom. Or perhaps one of the women in white leaving the hospital could be their killer.

Patience.

There existed potentially two ways for this to go down: one by storm. Dakota mulled over that method with distaste in his mouth. Hospitals were modern mazes with more hiding places than he had men. Once Hellstrom realized police were in the building en mass, she'd find a hole to crawl into and wait for the authorities to flush her out.

The second method was to slip in quietly and clandestinely. Though they could never prevent the internal grapevine from passing the word of their presence on to Hellstrom, they could slow it down long enough for them to corner her. Not knowing exactly where in the hospital she worked meant they had to question someone to determine her likely location. Asking questions brought attention to her and sent the word through the floors. If she worked on say the third floor and was in the cafeteria having coffee when word reached her that men were asking about her, she'd be able to slip away. Hospital security could work against them, so Dakota decided they must be kept in the dark as to the police operation. Make-believe cops like to impress people with their tough talk, and if Hellstrom had cultivated a contact in security, that contact might unwittingly tip her off to police presence.

Every detective in the car, save for Dakota, chain-smoked their cigarettes. They sat minutes away from breaking the biggest case in this decade. Don't get impatient, Dakota realized. This had to go down exactly right. They might likely get only one shot at her. They had to wait. And the waiting gnawed at Dakota's mind and his resolve.

First objective: locate the suspect. Dakota's team held their positions; waiting on radio confirmation from the second team. Four minutes earlier the second team radioed their arrival at the house of Frances Elaine Hellstrom on the northeast side of the city. Authorities would first blockade all possible escape routes. If she attempted to run, she'd run right into custody.

Would she be there instead of at the hospital?

The second team had to find out. Nobody would move in unless the suspect exhibited overt signs of flight. They concluded Frances would know immediately when police moved in. She might very well try to bolt—having already devised a plan to evade a police net. The standing orders were to apprehend only on Dakota's orders.

"All your backup in place?"

"Ten-four."

"Confirm she's inside the house before you approach," Dakota ordered.

"Please be there," he whispered, staring at the multistory building beyond his windshield. A thousand employees, all similarly dressed, populated those floors. Even sealing off the entire building might not guarantee Hellstrom would be unable to find a way out.

A hospital was too unwieldy a place to take Frances down easily. They'd be on her turf. They'd be hunting her in her forest, where she felt strongest and knew the terrain. Silence right now was paramount. If Frances were tapped into the hospital grapevine, the slightest slip could spook her.

The Bravo team leader double-clicked his mike. A few seconds later the report came.

"We've got four black and whites on scene. A county vehicle is two minutes away. We're ready now...we have no sign of the suspect inside the house. I repeat, there is currently no movement coming from inside. The front drapes are open along with the drapes to the upstairs windows. There appears to be no movement inside."

Dakota checked the time: seven-twenty. Was Hellstrom at work? What time did hospital shifts change? Could she possibly slip out while the detectives were moving in?

Dakota and Bronc waited, listening to the sounds of anticipation playing out in their car. Bronc ran his hand along his gun, checking for the third time that his clip was full.

"If we go in fast and hard, she'll be down before she even realizes we're on to her," Bronc said, more for himself than for Dakota and the others.

"Please, let us take her at her home. I've got a bad feeling about the hospital. She knows that big maze better than we do. There's got to be a dozen ways for an employee to slip through."

"Assuming we go in hard, how much time do you think we would have?" Bronc asked.

"Two, maybe three minutes at best."

Bronc shook his head.

"Grapevine's that fast?"

"As soon as we move in, word will start flowing up to the other floors. The upper floors will know we're there before we get to the elevator."

"Let me go in alone," Bronc said.

"Too risky. She'll know our faces thanks to the media coverage over the past few months."

"Send in one of the other detectives."

"Where's he going to go? As soon as anyone starts asking about Hellstrom, she'll get the word."

"He can do a floor-by-floor."

"Take too long. We can't give her time to react."

Bronc acknowledged another unmarked police car as it rolled into a parking slot just down from them.

"We've got the manpower we need to cover every exit, but we'd need fifty cops to do a room-by-room."

"We've completed a scan of the parking lot, lieutenant, and the Hellstrom vehicle isn't parked here," a voice crackled over the radio from the other vehicle.

Bronc's eyes scanned up the floors to the top of the hospital. Going in there after her gave her all the options.

The moment Dakota had been hoping for was at hand. However, it was contrary to the way he imagined it in his mind. Two long years. Now it was all about to come crashing to an end, if they didn't screw this up.

"We're going to get her, Grace," Dakota said in a whisper.

"What?" Bronc said, returning his gaze from the hospital.

"It's time," Dakota said in response.

Bronc heard something different, but let it pass.

Sitting in his vehicle, waiting for word from the second team, Dakota knew they were poorly prepared to control this situation. Frances could easily blend in inside the hospital. That was her jungle. She would feel safe in there. She could move freely and she knew every closet and storage room on every floor. She could transform herself into a patient or a visitor. Or she might make herself invisible by holing up in a place few knew existed. She would have prepared for this eventuality. She would have taken precautions, worked out escape routes and rehearsed in her mind how she would evade capture if it came to this.

Bronc trained his eyes on the hospital front doors. All kinds of people: Hispanic, Anglo and Indian—women and men—continued to flow in and out. Bronc studied the faces of all departing women in white. He kept reiterating to himself that surprise was on their side. She couldn't know they had uncovered her identity.

"She may look very different than her high school picture," Bronc advised the others in the car.

"We'll know her the moment we see her, and you can bet she'll know it's over the moment she sees us," Dakota said.

Dakota long anticipated that moment when their eyes would meet for the first time. He would see the recognition in her eyes when she knew she had been taken. For Dakota, the recognition in her eyes would be all he needed to know she was the killer. She would see his eyes and, in that moment, know the killing would be over.

"Suppose she's altered her appearance and hair color, or had plastic surgery to keep us from recognizing her?"

"Doesn't matter. She's living under her real name. If she's on duty, she'll be wearing a name tag and other nurses will know her. She can't know we're on to her. Only the task force and Borlin know we've made the link."

"Anybody see Roberts around here?" Dakota asked.

Eyes scanned, heads shook. Lisa Roberts must have chosen the alternate course to follow.

"I'm ready to do it now," Bronc said, getting antsy to advance to the next step. Waiting gnawed at the nerves.

Dakota sat for a long moment, staring at a painted sun creeping over the Sandia Mountains. He switched his gaze to a pair of nurses leaving through the revolving doors. Then he grabbed the mike.

"Bravo team, give me an update."

"Negative on the suspect. There's no sign of activity in the home. Give me two minutes...I've got an idea."

Dakota rubbed his finger unconsciously along the mike switch. His gut burned. He was losing faith that luck was on their side. They would not find Frances Hellstrom at her home. The building in front of them would have to be sealed off until they had Hellstrom in cuffs.

"Alpha, we just staged a ruckus and still no movement inside the residence. Lieutenant, I don't believe she's inside. Please advise. We're standing by."

"Is the location secure?" Dakota asked.

"We've completely surrounded the place and blocked off any potential escape routes."

"Send a man up. If she answers the door, take her down."

"Ten-four. We're moving in."

The next two minutes droned on without end.

Bronc smoked another cigarette while Dakota watched people move in and out of the hospital.

"We've got nothing, lieutenant. I repeat. There is no answer at the door."

"Hold tight for now. We're going in. We'll be off the radio for approximately twenty minutes. Maintain radio silence while we're inside. Alpha team, everyone going in turn down your radios before entering the hospital and no communications unless you're calling a sighting."

"Ten-four, we're standing by," said Childers, in the car next to Dakota's.

"We could try running a ruse on her. Use something like a flower delivery or package delivery to learn if she's in there."

"Anything out of the norm will make her suspicious. If she's never received packages or flowers before at work, she'll realize we're on to her."

"What about having a hospital administrator call her for a meeting?"

"Still too risky. Any break in her normal daily routine and she'll know."

"This ain't going to be easy, is it?" Bronc finally concluded.

"Let's hope she's here," Dakota said. He tossed the mike onto the seat and pulled his Beretta from its holster.

They now faced their worst case scenario. If they waited, and she caught wind of them, she might fly away. If they went in, they had to go in hard and fast. It was unlikely she'd be carrying... Dakota stopped himself. Her victims died from a blade to the throat. Frances Hellstrom would be armed and dangerous.

"Dakota, you want an officer to call to confirm she's on duty," Childers asked over the radio.

"Negative," Dakota shot back, "we can't risk any form of indirect reconnaissance. Anything out of the ordinary could spook her."

"Dakota, she knows you," Bronc reminded him, "she sees you coming and she's going to know it's over."

"Doesn't matter. We'll make sure she doesn't see me until it's too late to do anything about it. I'm not missing this for anything."

Two additional unmarked vehicles rolled into the hospital parking lot. One contained Rodman. If there had been anyway to include the FBI on this without including Rodman, Dakota would have allowed it. However, the one guy he wished most to keep outside the situation was staring coldly at him from two cars over.

Dakota deployed two men to cover each exit to the building, which included the loading dock and the maintenance doors in the rear. Each man held a picture of what Frances Hellstrom looked like in high school with instructions to stop anyone even remotely matching the picture.

Every man understood his role in this operation. Frances Hellstrom was the Boulder Hill killer and must be arrested on sight. The first four detectives dispersed to cover their assignments. Two vice detectives followed Dakota and Bronc through the revolving doors. Once inside, however, they stopped inconspicuously to either side of the doors while Dakota and Bronc continued on.

Within two minutes, plainclothes officers and detectives had covered all hospital exits. France Hellstrom was going to have a difficult time getting out.

Dakota and Bronc strolled through the main lobby at a pace neither hurried nor laggard. Neither spoke while their eyes roved over the expanse of the main lobby, missing no one. Dakota forged on through a momentary shiver, hearing his steps on the shining gray tile floors. The men paused at the door marked ADMINISTRATION to exchange an cryptic glance. Having spent so much time here, Dakota knew certain sections of the hospital better than the people who worked there. He could only wonder about the hospital grapevine's efficiency. How much time did they really have between the moment they inquired about Frances Hellstrom and word reached her that men were in the building to talk to her?

People flowed through the lobby in both directions. Many were seniors or mothers with children in tow. Hospitals always seemed busy, crowded places. Especially hospitals serving large chunks of the population.

Dakota pulled the door open. He had entered this particular office so many times before, but for a reason on the other end of the spectrum from why he was here now.

A silver-haired woman lifted her eyes from her desk and, removing pearl-framed glasses, began to speak.

Dakota felt his heart quicken and his palms start to sweat. Bronc stood right behind him, allowing the door to close in his wake.

"Can I help you?"

Dakota at first said nothing, waiting until the door to the administration office closed completely. His smile failed to mask the intent in his eyes.

He stopped before the woman behind her battle-ship gray, metallic desk. She shuffled stacks of paper from one side the other; as if to offer an appearance of importance.

"Ms. Johnson, is it?" Bronc said, reading the name on black plastic pasted to the back of her terminal screen, "Could you tell us if you have a nurse named Frances Hellstrom here?"

Both knew the answer. The question was nothing more than a prelude to the real information they sought.

"I'm sorry. We're not allowed to give out that information," the raspy-voiced Ms. Johnson replied. Her eyes bore a glimmer of power.

"Police business, ma'am," Bronc responded, producing his badge.

During the exchange, Dakota watched the others in the office. Two desks away a middle-aged, black-haired, rotund woman paused to listen; all the while appearing busy by tapping on her keyboard at her terminal screen. But Dakota could see that she caught every word exchanged between Bronc and Ms. Johnson.

Dakota moved swiftly when she reached for the telephone.

"If you could just wait to make that call," he ordered her, dropping his shield in front of her face with one hand and returning the telephone handset to the cradle with the other.

She withdrew her hand and lifted her eyes to meet Dakota's. He detected that all too familiar disdain people flashed when an Indian told them what they could or could not do.

Ms. Johnson hesitated, studying Bronc's badge for a long moment.

"I think you should speak with a supervisor," she said, her hands frozen on her desk.

"I think you can help me. I need to know where in the hospital Ms. Frances Hellstrom works. Now!"

Ms. Johnson cast a sidelong glance for assistance. She found herself all alone.

A dozen finger strokes brought the desired results to Ms. Johnson's computer screen.

Dakota moved in close to read the information for himself.

"She's an oncology nurse on Four West," he said.

Dakota and Bronc exchanged looks.

"She on duty right now?" Dakota asked.

"Can't say," Ms. Johnson replied, "I'd have to check with her immediate supervisor on the floor."

Bronc's delivered glare served as an inducement for Ms. Johnson to rethink her answer.

"I'm sorry. We don't keep that information here. Shift schedules are maintained in the department. You'll have to check with the nursing supervisor on Four West. All I have here is that Nurse Hellstrom is on a four-specialty rotation. There's no way we have information on her shift schedule here."

"Fine," Bronc said, but he made no move to leave her desk.

This was the part of the plan that unnerved both Bronc and Dakota. The hospital grapevine could get to Hellstrom before them. A telephone call could give Hellstrom the time she needed to escape. And the caller would never know she had just inadvertently aided the Boulder Hill killer.

"A detective's stationed right outside this door. It is imperative no one be made aware of our presence, understand?"

Ms. Johnson seemed too shaken all of a sudden to answer.

Dakota and Bronc rode a half-filled elevator to the fourth floor. Dakota knew where to go. He had walked that corridor so many times in the last four years that it felt as familiar as his own home.

Dakota's eyes roved the expanse of the floor the moment they stepped off the elevator. To their right was the east wing; to their left, the west wing.

Thirty paces down the corridor from them, a nurse crossed from one room to another. She appeared much older than Frances Hellstrom and offered Dakota no more than a casual glance.

With each step, Dakota and Bronc peered into rooms for a glimpse of a nurse. Vacant rooms had neatly made beds. Occupied rooms were where nurses performed their duties. About half the rooms they passed were occupied.

Dakota felt Grace each time he saw a patient lying beneath crumpled white sheets. A black nurse turned and stared. Their footsteps were hard and determined. The slightest noise caused them to react. They intentionally created more noise than those of a more typical considerate, soft-footed visitor. Their emanations were meant to bring the nurses out of their rooms in order to give them a chance to ID their target. At all times, their hands remained inside their jackets resting on their weapons.

She had to go down.

Bronc completed his scan of the entire nurses' station twenty paces in advance of their arrival. A Hispanic woman sat beside the phones while another nurse entered a room at the rear of the station. Bronc's hand tightened on his weapon.

Be here, he said to himself as if commanding it could make it become true.

The black nurse approached from their flank, passed them and shuffled through a rack of metal charts. She tilted her head toward them as Dakota and Bronc came to a stop; intimating they were an intrusion in her domain. She said nothing.

"Lieutenant Blackwood," a soft, soothing voice said from somewhere behind the two.

Dakota spun around, his weapon half way out of his pocket.

A nurse who had cared for Grace had recognized him. Dakota failed to recall her name; he couldn't, at the moment, allow his concentration to wander even for a second.

"Hi. Supervisor around?" Dakota asked, all the while slipping his Beretta back home. There was no smile on his face; no glint of recognition or friendliness.

Bronc trained his eyes to snare any abrupt changes in the surroundings: a head popping out of sight or a body turning about suddenly. Was Frances Hellstrom within range of the nurse's greeting? If she were, she made no sudden move to flee.

Bronc, however, didn't wait for an answer. He moved past the nurses' station to scan the remaining rooms in the wing.

"I'll get her for you," the nurse said, affronted by Dakota's coldness.

Within two minutes, nursing supervisor Jennifer Coffelt stood before Dakota. She knew him well from when Grace was under their care. They had even spoken briefly when the time of Grace's death became imminent. Jennifer's memory had lost the essence of that conversation that night, but it would never erase the sadness she saw in Dakota's dark eyes.

"We need to speak with a nurse under your charge," Dakota said. As he spoke, his eyes slid off the nursing supervisor's to an open storage room, then to the nurses' lounge just to the right and rear of the nurses' station. Dakota detected a flash of white pull back from view inside the lounge doorway.

He darted the three steps to reach the doorway, slammed the door full open and prepared for an assault. A petite nurse sprang from her chair at the table. She looked nothing like the Hellstrom woman.

"What's this all about?" Jennifer demanded.

Dakota returned to the supervisor and at the same time flashed a glance to Bronc, who was returning down the hall.

Bronc shook his head.

"Who are you looking for?"

"Hellstrom, Frances Elaine Hellstrom," Dakota said. The change in the supervisor's expression sent a convulsion through his stomach. Was it surprise?

"Frankie...I'd like to speak to her myself. She's missed two shifts without so much as a phone call."

A slur of four-letter words raced through Dakota's mind.

Bronc quickened his pace. A sudden change swept over Dakota's face. Dakota's eyes moved in a twitch of panic—something Dakota rarely revealed to the outside world.

"You haven't seen her?"

"Going on four days. Her normal days off are Tuesday and Wednesday. She hasn't been back to work."

Dakota and Bronc were already backing away and turning toward the elevator.

"Thank you," Dakota called over his shoulder.

Once back on the first floor, Dakota and Bronc split up to round up the other detectives and return to their cars.

This couldn't be! How could Frances have gotten wind of the investigation? No one outside of Dakota even knew she was being considered as a suspect until they had confirmed it back in Albuquerque. Dakota tore apart in anger the thoughts flooding his mind. Could someone back in Utah have contacted the Hellstrom woman?

"How in the goddamn hell did she find out?" Bronc muttered. They were back inside their cars in the hospital parking lot.

"Bravo team, we're clear of the hospital. Hellstrom's a no-show for the last two days. Any visual contact with the suspect yet?"

"Negative," crackled back. There was no mistaking the depth of the defeat in the transmission.

"What about a vehicle?"

"Negative as far as we can tell. She's tacked cardboard over the side garage window. All we get is a sliver of opening to peek through. No vehicle. Our bird's gone."

Dakota looked at Bronc.

"Fuuuck!" Bronc yelled, pounding out his anger on the dash.

There was no explanation for how the Hellstrom woman could have possibly known that the task force had uncovered her identity. And there was no time to waste trying to figure that one out. Four people knew it in Albuquerque; one person knew in Utah.

Dakota started the engine, slamming the accelerator to the floor. The motor roared like an angry lion, and the screeching rubber sent rooster tails of white smoke in their wake. He tossed the mike over to Bronc.

"Call in a warrant for the Hellstrom residence. We need it approved by the time we get there. Issue an APB for her vehicle. And let's get somebody digging up all the possible places she might go."

By the time Alpha team got within five miles of the Hellstrom residence, the warrant to enter the premises had been signed. Dakota prayed they would find the woman sick in bed, but deep inside he knew better. Somehow the Hellstrom woman had learned she was their prime suspect. Was it possible that someone inside the department had leaked the information? How could anyone in the police department have done that? For a moment, Lisa Roberts popped into Dakota's mind. She had been there outside the headquarters building waiting. What had she been waiting for? Did she know? The whole idea seemed preposterous.

Bravo team, already in place at the Hellstrom residence, waited until Dakota's vehicle reached their location. Then the stream of cars roared around the corner and came to screeching halts in and around the Hellstrom driveway.

Men spewed in all directions. Four circled the house on the right, while another two detectives with two uniforms in tow circled on the left. Every gun was out and ready.

Once the lead uniform battered the door open with a forty-pound steel ramrod, Dakota and Bronc poured into the Hellstrom house.

At any given moment, at least four guns remained trained on anything that might move during their initial assault.

A bright morning sun illuminated every corner of the front half of the house. Down a narrow hall they could see part of the kitchen.

There was no movement—not a single sign of life. Yet rumpled clothes lay over the arm of the sofa and a pair of black low-heel shoes had been tossed into one corner near the foyer. Dishes cluttered the kitchen table.

Dakota and Bronc raced up the stairs while the two uniforms proceeded toward the kitchen. The uniforms dropped to their knees, leveling revolvers when the six-panel door next to the refrigerator opened. A task force detective with gun ready came through the door that led to the empty garage.

Dakota and Bronc stopped; one on either side of the first closed door at the right side of the hall. Another door a few feet further down remained wide open.

Dakota held his breath, leveled his revolver and moved quickly around to stand beside the open door.

"Police!" he issued, in a tone meant to frighten.

No voice answered him.

Dakota peered into the room from the angle that allowed him to see a third of the space. Then he rolled across the opening, his gun ready, his eyes missing nothing. The room was empty save for a stack of boxes in one corner.

By now, two more detectives waited at the top of the stairs. They nodded their readiness. Bronc and Dakota prepared to open the closed door.

Bronc tightened on his trigger before reaching for the doorknob. On Dakota's signal, he twisted and flung open the door.

Boom!

The shotgun's blast tore the swinging door nearly in half. The two backup officers dove down the stairs for safety while Dakota and Bronc fell to become one with the floor. Smoke curls and a shower of wood splinters infested the narrow hallway.

Dakota rolled over and emptied a full magazine into the room. He held up suddenly, spying the shotgun taped to a chair. The neighbors must have thought a gang war had broken out in the house. Dakota and Bronc invaded the smoked-filled room, holding their guns in the low ready position.

Dakota's eyes took in a mattress on a pallet, a scratched-up dresser and a shabby '70s decor lamp sitting on a night table. Dakota wondered if this was all that remained of her life in Utah. Like a sleeping snake, a curled line lay on the floor between what remained of the door and the chair.

The room resembled a monastery with only the simplest of adornments. No pictures on the walls, no unnecessary furnishings and a trail of hastily discarded clothes littered the bare wood floor from the closet to the edge of the bed.

"Fuck!" Dakota yelled, moving to the closet and sweeping his revolver from left to right.

Frances Hellstrom was gone.

29

"She knew..." Bronc muttered. "She knew we were coming. How the *fuck* could she have known?"

The bedroom, as well as the rest of the house, displayed signs that Frances Hellstrom lived a very simple and unpretentious life. There were no snapshots nor portraits anywhere. She either took them with her or never had them in the first place. But then again, she was a woman whose father had abandoned her at a young age and whose mother and sister were both dead. She had no one in her life worth remembering.

Dakota surmised that consistent with the serial killer profile, Frances Hellstrom had little family and probably no friends. The only friendships she established were the people selected to be her victims.

By now, all the detectives had crowded around the bedroom entrance, each of them wondering, like Dakota and Bronc, how the woman could have learned of their discovery.

"Downstairs is clean, lieutenant," a detective said, while he peered in where Dakota now stood.

But Frances left one thing behind—a pair of sheer, black panties spread on the pillow of her bed. She pinned to them an envelope in the same way she had pinned the note to her victims.

362

Seeing it there, as a perverse sign of triumph over Dakota, sent an acrid fluid up into the lieutenant's throat. He had come so close this time.

"I figure it's for you," Bronc said from the other side of the bed. Neither looked at the other.

"Or whoever came in to clean up after the shot-gun blast."

"Sir, bathroom's clean," another detective said, while standing outside the bedroom in the hall.

Dakota pulled tweezers out and carefully separated the flap from the envelope. Hellstrom hadn't taken the time nor the effort to seal it. With that same care, Dakota removed a folded sheet of paper. He opened it at the corners and began reading to himself. Then he abruptly stopped and pulled his eyes up from the paper to scan the room.

"I think you all need to hear this."

30

Within a minute, every task force detective had shouldered his way into the bedroom. Here was the lair of their killer.

Using a pencil, Bronc opened the night table drawer only to find it completely empty.

Dakota waited a moment longer to allow word to spread down the stairs, so anyone lingering on the first floor could come up.

Pete Rodman shouldered his way to the front of the crowd.

Silence ruled until Dakota began to read aloud.

"You play the game well, lieutenant. Of all the bumbling idiots in law enforcement, you were probably the only one capable of catching me. I don't think you realized it two years ago, but even then you were beginning to put the pieces together. I'm guessing it has something to do with your Apache blood. You understand how hate affects people better than most men. But as you can see, in the end, even you failed."

Dakota eyes never left the page, though his pause lasted longer than expected.

"Since our paths shall never cross again, I thought it only fair that you understand a little bit about your nemesis. You were right—Ellen was my first victim. Actually, she's the reason I started killing. Her and her friends.

"Ellen always hated me...treated me like I was vermin and I never knew why. But that wasn't why I killed her. It wasn't that she hated me...it was what she did to me. I'm four years her junior...but you already know that. I shouldn't stray too far from the point at hand. After all, you still have a serial killer to catch.

"Ellen and her boyfriend, Clete, thought it would be fun to use me...you know...they made me do things to them. I was twelve at the time, and Ellen and Clete were both drunk the first time they raped me. I hated Ellen for it. They both thought it was fun. I never forgot the pain and the blood from that first time.

"But they didn't stop after that. They said if I told anyone what they had done to me, I'd end up dead in a ditch out beyond the bridge.

"You see, Blackwood, both of them were guilty...but it was Ellie who initiated the abuse. It was her idea. She was the one who held me while Clete...she did things to me, too. But she wouldn't stop there. Later, she and her fatass girlfriend Colleen used things to abuse me. Even when I cried for them to stop—they continued. It went on for more than a year, and I never told anyone about it. My mother already blamed me for our father's abandonment. After that, Ellie graduated from Brighton and went to college. Clete tried to continue his little fun with me, but I fought him off and that seemed to put his fire out.

"When I went away to college I thought I had put that nightmare behind me. I figured that was why I wanted to be a nurse. It gave me a way to remove other people's pain, even though I was unable remove my own. Blackwood, can you understand that kind of pain? The kind that never goes away. The kind that wakes you up in the middle of the night and forces you to scream until your stomach's pulled up into your throat. Can you understand that pain?

"It dawned on me late in my freshman year that little by little my mind was being torn from my being. It would never be over inside my head. Even though Ellie and I were hundreds of miles apart, what she did still tormented me.

"I began thinking about what I would do to her if I ever had the opportunity. You'd be surprised how well the mind can conceive a plan when it has hours and hours to contemplate it.

"By the beginning of my sophomore year, I began thinking of nothing else. I think what triggered it for me was when I got a letter from Ellie detailing the list of extravagant things she wanted for Christmas. She actually expected me to pick something off that list. But I had decided on my own special Christmas present.

"It didn't take me long to realize that if I killed her at Christmas I was sure to get caught. So, I planned a little unexpected visit home one weekend. I knew Mother worked the night shift, so I'd have plenty of time to kill Ellie and leave without a trace. The only thing I couldn't be sure of was whether Ellie would be home and if she'd be alone. Ellie usually screwed anything willing to put their arms around her, so that became the only variable out of my control."

Dakota paused for a long moment to recapture his breath. The words put everything into place in his mind. Not a soul in the room moved. They were peering into the darkest corner of a serial killer's mind. They had become privy to the killer's most private, most secret world. Most of all, they were learning why Frances Hellstrom began a life of seemingly random killing.

"I waited until Mother left for work that Saturday night. From down the road, I watched her car pull out of the drive and down the path away from me. Ellie would be alone. So I drove just into the drive and parked the car. Ellie was really surprised to see me. Of course, she didn't know at the time that I was going to be the last person she'd ever see alive. We talked for almost an hour before...and I skillfully inquired what had ever happened to Clete and Colleen. Ellie revealed everything I needed to know. She also told me about her failed romance and her plan to move to New Mexico and start her own business. I laughed.

"It only took a few seconds to kill her with the wire, though she struggled more than I had anticipated. A woman's neck is so much easier to snap than a man's. Afterward, I did...well, you know that now anyway. Colleen was second and I decided to render her unconscious before slitting her throat. I didn't want to have to struggle with her. Clete I saved until last. I figured I would need my wits about me when I met up with him. You could say I practiced on Ellie and Colleen.

"So now, Blackwood, you know why I killed them. Can you figure out why I killed the others? Can you make that connection yet?

"Is that it?" Bronc asked.

Dakota shook his head.

"It started when Ellie wanted to touch me. She made me what I am. She turned me into something vile and disgusting with her sick desires. The others wanted to touch me, too. I gave them a test and they failed. They wanted to touch me. They were infected with the same sickness Ellie had. I had to stop them before they could hurt someone else. Do you understand that? I couldn't let them live. I couldn't let them turn someone else into the monster I had become.

"You think I'm bad. But I'm not. I'm helping you. I destroy the bad seeds before they can bring forth the monsters sleeping within.

"I can only guess at how much you were able to figure out on your own. But I know as you read this, you have to be wondering how I learned that you had uncovered my identity. If you think one of your detectives slipped, you'd be wrong. You probably didn't know that I had been calling your house on occasion to check up on you. Lauryn sounds like a wonderful child. That's how I knew your wife was in the hospital. That's why I transferred to St. Joseph's when I learned your wife was taking her radiation treatments there. You and I, we passed in the halls many times. You never even noticed me. I wanted to be close to her. Did you know I talked to her before she died? You didn't, did you? You didn't know that I whispered in her ear that I was the killer. You see, Blackwood, she knew the Boulder Hill killer's identity, but she was so drugged up, she'd never be able to tell.

"I called your house last week. I had worked up the courage to actually talk to you myself. But instead, I spoke with a man who said you were in Salt Lake City. That's how I knew you were going to discover me. Once you connected my murders to Ellie, it wouldn't take you long to question my relationship to the victim.

"Too bad for you he slipped. Otherwise, we'd be speaking face to face right now and you'd have spared someone's life. You see, Blackwood, I still have one more to go before I've fulfilled my commitment...

The letter ended. Unsigned and with no clue as to where the Hellstrom woman might have gone. Was she still in Albuquerque? Had she already moved on to another city?

Dakota held the paper in his hand for a long time after falling silent. No one had words to say nor questions to ask. They had failed. The Boulder Hill killer had eluded them once more. The United States had thousands of cities where Frances Hellstrom could disappear. She'd become another face in the crowd until the need to kill drove her again to seek out innocent women and men.

"Where do we go from here, lieutenant?"

Dakota looked up. The question seemed foreign to him at the moment. He was incapable of forming an answer.

Washington read the letter twice while sitting at his desk. Dakota sat across from him while Cal Sturges, holding his thoughts inside, paced back and forth on Dakota's flank like an agitated ten-year-old. He waited until Washington finished the letter and lifted his eyes to stare at the two.

"I can't believe after all this you allowed her to get away from you," Sturges burst out, coming around to face Dakota.

"I didn't allow her to get away," Dakota shot back.

"Come on, she said it in black and white. Someone at your home told the killer that you had gone on police business to Salt Lake City. She put it together right away."

"Dakota, when could she have made that call?"

"I don't know. I've haven't been able to reach anyone at home. Cole is on his way to the bank and Laurianne is out. I should have an answer soon."

"The hottest case of the decade and you blow it."

"Listen, Sturges, I've taken just about all I'm going to take from you," Dakota said, his eyes bearing down on Cal, who was less than an arm's length from him.

"What's done is done. We can't undo it," Washington forced in, hoping Sturges would shut his mouth and Dakota would return to his chair and in the process let Cal's asinine remarks pass.

"We've got an APB out for the Hellstrom vehicle and we're putting her face on the six o'clock news. The problem is if we go public with what we know now, we're going to frighten a lot of people."

Dakota said nothing. For a long moment, he stared past Washington into thin air.

"Everything that can be done has been done. Dakota, go home and get some rest. Spend some time with your daughters. Let Bronc monitor the traffic. We'll update you with anything that comes in."

Dakota agreed. He missed his daughters terribly; he missed Grace even more. There was little he could do now. Frances Hellstrom had slipped out of their grasp. She was free to kill again. But only for the present. It wouldn't take long for the calls to start coming in, once her face appeared on the news. Someone, somewhere will have to have seen her.

Dakota planned on going home, but first he had to make a stop. It was not something he felt good about doing.

Cole was at his desk. His feet were up and he was on the telephone with a venture capital firm when his secretary buzzed him that Dakota was coming down the hall. Cole terminated the call prematurely and slid aside the papers he had been holding.

"I heard through the grapevine," Cole said.

"Heard what?" Dakota asked.

"Your guys are ready to make an arrest in the Boulder Hill Killer case."

"Grapevine's not always right," Dakota said, taking the chair across the desk from Cole.

"You look worn out," Cole commented.

"I am. Been up all night. The arrest went bust. We lost the suspect."

"Sorry to hear it."

"We cracked the case, but the suspect was one step ahead of us."

"Damn. What are you going to do now?"

"Go home...sleep until the girls get home from school and take them out for dinner and a movie—a Disney movie."

"What about the Boulder Hill killer?"

"We'll get her sooner or later."

"Her? The Boulder Hill killer's a woman?"

"The Boulder Hill killer's a woman named Frances Hellstrom. We're going public with everything on the six o'clock news. It will be just a matter of time before we run her down and put her away."

"A woman...that's really bizarre...." Cole's voice trailed off, as if some startling realization had just come to him.

"I dug up the link we needed in Salt Lake City."

Cole swallowed hard.

"You going to take some time off?"

"Yeah. Nothing more we can do now. The killer's on the run. But I doubt she'll get far."

Dakota rose, a bit unsteady at first.

"Dakota, you did your best. If anyone was going to catch her, you were."

"I know."

At the door, Dakota stopped and turned back to Cole, who was staring blankly up at his Indian brother.

"What?" Cole asked, his face shadowed in guilt.

"Nothing," Dakota said, then continued out of the office and down the hall.

31

Dakota slept more peacefully than he had slept in months. That is, until three o'clock when the persistent telephone ringing brought him out of his dreamless sleep. He picked up at the same moment the answering machine kicked in and had to endure the ten second announcement.

"Dakota, we've located the car. She abandoned it about fifteen miles outside Flagstaff," Bronc said, without a greeting.

It took a moment for the words to register in Dakota's mind. But when they did, he swung his feet out of bed and stared out the window.

"Any sign of her?"

"None. She's out of our state now. At least we can sleep at night. Hey, did I wake you?"

"It's okay. I wanted to get up anyway. The girls are due home from school in half an hour. When was the vehicle found?"

"Arizona State Police found it mid-afternoon. But they couldn't tell us how long it might have been there. They assigned an investigator to find out."

"You sending men?"

"They're on their way. We should have a full report from the authorities processing the car soon. There is no doubt it's the Hellstrom car."

"We get anything out of it?"

"We got zip, zero, zilch, squat, bupkus. Not a trace of evidence we could use against her."

"Make sure our men report in within the next twenty-four hours."

Dakota was fully awake now. The house was completely silent...empty. Laurianne had left to do shopping and wasn't expected back until later. The girls wouldn't be getting off the bus for another ten minutes. The emptiness pervaded the house. Grace would never be there. He would have to live with that for the rest of his life.

A splash of cold water removed the residue of sleep from Dakota's face. As he walked through the house, he sensed Grace's presence in every room. Everything he saw, everything he touched, rekindled memories of moments they shared together.

He was sitting at the kitchen table staring into his coffee when Lauryn and Heather came running in through the front door.

"Aunt Laurianne, we're home!" Lauryn called out. Her face shone with surprise when she entered the kitchen to find her father sitting there.

"Daddy!" she yelled and dropped her books. Heather was the first to offer a hug and Lauryn filled in around the side.

Dinner was pizza followed by video games at the local Chuck E. Cheese. When Heather started yawning, Dakota finally decided it was time to go home. It didn't matter whether they won or lost at the games; it only mattered that they were together. Lauryn clung so tightly to Dakota on their way to the car that he thought she was never going to let go.

Arriving home, Dakota called the command center for an update.

"Daddy, can we stay up late? There's no school tomorrow," Heather begged.

Dakota had to ease her away and stall his answer until he finished his call.

There had been two reported sightings of the Hellstrom woman in and around Phoenix. Neither had been confirmed, but the detectives manning the phones expected confirmation within twenty-four hours. Bronc had dispatched another team of detectives to Phoenix to assist local authorities. The local FBI office joined the forces on the streets to aid in the search. All together, forty-eight law enforcement professionals were scouring the streets of Phoenix in search of the Boulder Hill killer.

Bronc reported confidence was high that Hellstrom would be taken in Arizona and returned to New Mexico to stand trial. It was just a matter of time before the case was wrapped up and put away for good.

Dakota relished a tinge of elation as he hung up and went to the den to be with the girls.

It would seem that even in failure some good had become of Dakota's effort. No body had yet to turn up in Albuquerque—the third victim of the Boulder Hill Killer had been spared. They had forced Frankie Hellstrom to flee before she could claim her third victim. Now she would be forced to be on the run and keep out of sight. There was a good chance she'd never be able to kill again. A good chance she'd be arrested in Arizona and extradited back to New Mexico for the murders of five innocent people.

It was almost over. A killing spree that spanned six years was about to be ended.

Dakota awakened Saturday after a full night's uninterrupted sleep. He made no plans for the day other than to do whatever the girls wanted and to check in with the command center regularly for updates. By four that afternoon, the sightings in Phoenix had doubled, but they were still unconfirmed by authorities.

Still, time dragged on while Dakota waited. Waited for the call that would say the woman was in custody. The only way the Boulder Hill killer cases could be officially closed was with the arrest of Frances Hellstrom. Her written confession already confirmed they had the right person.

32

Dakota fell asleep Saturday night thinking about Grace. He knew what he must do. He knew why he must do it.

A sudden flash racing across his mind bolted Dakota awake and sent him out of his bed. Why hadn't he realized it before? He fumbled through the darkness in his search. Thirty minutes later, he returned to the warmth of his bed and found sleep anew.

In the morning, Lauryn and Heather lethargically pulled themselves out of bed and descended the stairs. Upon seeing them, Dakota quickly ended his telephone conversation and scooped them into his arms for a free ride to the kitchen table. Neither spoke while Dakota prepared a breakfast of watery scrambled eggs and limp toast.

"Can I have cereal instead?" Heather asked, picking through his eggs with her fork.

"As soon as you've finished, back to your rooms and get dressed for church," Dakota instructed, though neither of the girls wanted to hear that. They exchanged puzzled looks at his instructions.

"*You're* taking us to church?" Lauryn asked with extraordinary surprise in her voice.

"I didn't say that. No. I have somewhere to go. Aunt Laurianne and Uncle Cole are taking you to church this morning."

"Where are you going?"

"I'll be here when you get back."

Lauryn knew better than to ask further questions. She hurried Heather along and they dashed up the stairs to put on their fancy dresses. That was the only good part about going to church.

Cole and Laurianne arrived promptly at ten, asked no questions and waited while the girls rushed around to add those last minute feminine touches. It seemed even at their young ages, they had trouble being ready on time. Neither Cole nor Laurianne said anything, though they could sense that something was happening around them. At the door, Dakota checked over the girls before releasing them and giving them each a powerful hug.

"It's okay, right, Dad?" Lauryn asked.

Dakota's eyes had become soulful. What was he attempting to convey?

"It's okay, princess. I'll be here when you get back."

There was something in the way he said it that sparked concern in Lauryn's heart.

"We'll bring the girls back right after church. You're going to be here, right?" Cole said at the door.

Dakota reached out, took Cole's hand.

"I'm going to be here. You just have to trust me."

Dakota stared at Lauryn and Heather from the doorway until the car pulled out of the driveway. Lauryn waved an uncertain hand as they drove away. She kept her eyes on him until the car disappeared from sight.

Dakota locked the front door, climbed into his car and pulled out of the driveway two minutes after the girls had left—heading in the opposite direction.

33

Dakota arrived at the cemetery, where he parked a full fifty yards down from where he would normally park. Beneath a bright sun and cool morning air, he strolled amongst the head stones until he reached Grace's grave. An unadorned granite marker bore her name—a simple tribute to her. All that was once beautiful and alive was now reduced to this. Somehow, it seemed there should have been more.

Dakota could find no words; he just stared at the marker a long time before lowering himself to one knee.

"God, I'm going to miss you, Grace," he whispered in that same voice he used when she lay dying in the hospital bed.

A rippling breeze sucked a mound of dried leaves airborne; sweeping them along the ground until they became ensnared in the markers that populated the field.

Dakota bowed his head, clutching his hands together in prayer. It wasn't until he saw the long thin shadow that he realized someone had approached from behind him.

"Remember me, Clete?" the voice said, with an unctuous, effeminate wisp.

"I've been expecting you, Frances," Dakota responded, without looking back over his shoulder.

Dakota turned.

"It's your turn to die, Clete," Frances said as she thrust her blade into the flesh of Dakota's shoulder. He tumbled into a roll, knocking the arm away with one hand.

But Frances reacted by withdrawing a small revolver from her pocket. As Dakota came upright, she leveled the barrel at his forehead.

"You didn't think I was going to let you live, did you?" Frankie Hellstrom asked.

Crack!

The blast sent birds aloft, shattering the serenity of the cemetery. Frances Hellstrom toppled forward and away from a struggling Dakota.

Dakota scrambled for his gun, but as he did, a second hulking shadow appeared over the ground of Grace's grave.

"Don't even think about moving, bitch," Bronc said, kicking the gun away from Frankie's outstretched hand.

His bullet had ripped open her shoulder, but she would survive. Survive to be convicted of serial murder and executed for her crimes.

Bronc reached down, took Dakota's hand and aided him back to his feet. Then while Dakota clinched his jaw, Bronc removed the blade.

"Just a flesh wound. You were taking a big risk putting yourself out here for her. Why did you believe she'd use the knife instead of the gun?" Bronc asked.

"A killer of habit. She had to stick to her fantasy for it to be meaningful to her," Dakota said.

A pair of unmarked sedans rolled off the road onto the grass and four detectives dashed toward the scene.

"How'd you know, Dakota?"

"When no one could confirm the sightings in Arizona, I started thinking, where would she really go?

We knew her third victim had always been male, so she had to kill Clete Randall. And I was the one she was directing her confession to. As long as we thought she was in Arizona, she figured she'd be safe to come back here for me. And that might have been her plan all along. To make me her third victim."

"But why here?"

"I realized sometime in the middle of the night that she was very deeply involved in my life. So, I went to my den and rechecked the photos taken during Grace's funeral."

"And she was there?"

"Standing not ten feet from me. At the time, we weren't looking for a woman. I figured she'd feel safe coming here."

Two detectives yanked Frankie Hellstrom to her feet, ignoring her screams of pain. No one present cared if she screamed her head off when they locked the cuffs around her wrists. It was fitting that she hear her own screams instead of those she had killed.

"Let's get that shoulder looked at," Bronc said, stanching the bleeding with his handkerchief while helping Dakota back to his car. "You've got two little girls waiting for you."

It was truly over.

Epilogue

After dinner on the day following the Boulder HIll killer's arrest, a silent and somewhat mysterious Dakota rushed the girls into the car and set out for a secret destination. He worked with not so much a sense of urgency, but as if he sought to be some place at a particular time. Though Lauryn badgered, Dakota offered nothing in response to her questions as to where they might be going. She tried guessing, but quickly ran dry of ideas.

Even once they arrived, Lauryn remained at a loss as to the reason for the secrecy. A bandaged Dakota and the girls ascended the rocks with Heather in Dakota's good arm and Lauryn clutching his coat tail to stay upright. On a jutting rock plateau in Cachanga wash some twenty miles outside Albuquerque, they watched a reddish-orange sun set.

The girls said nothing, but sensed the aura present in this special place. Dakota felt Grace's presence here; as if she were beside them while the dying sun painted their faces a golden hue. It was here that Dakota would always hold Grace's memory the strongest. Here, among the strawberry cacti and distant rock cliffs, he could feel her—almost talk to her. Dakota thought he could see her face in the way the dying sun played off the jutting rock formations in the distance. She was smiling down upon them, telling him she was at peace now.

With the final fading rays of daylight in their faces, Dakota carried Heather down the precipice and through the sand while Lauryn picked her way carefully amongst the rocks.

Neither of the girls understood the true meaning of this place they had just visited. Perhaps when they were older, Dakota would tell them. Perhaps they, too, would be able to feel Grace's presence.

The End.

APPENDIX

Have they become a forgotten people? There are less than 2 million Native Americans left in the United States. The following organizations provide support to our nation's Native American population. To learn more about their missions and activities, visit their websites on the Internet. This listing is in no way meant to be exhaustive. Searching the World Wide Web will provide additional Native American related websites.

National Congress of American Indians
1301 Connecticut Ave. NW Suite 200
Washington DC 20036
202-466-7767   *www.ncai.org*

Native American Rights Fund
1506 Broadway
Boulder CO 80302
303-447-8760   *www.narf.org*

The Southwest Indian Foundation
PO Box 86
Gallup NM 873002

                              www.southwestindian.com

The Heritage Institute
5300 Denver Technological Ctr Pkwy
Suite 265
Englewood CO 80111
303-221-7410   *www.heritageinstitute.org*